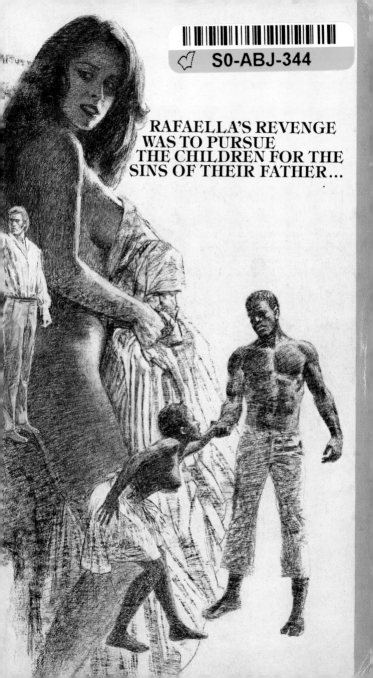

RAFAELLA'S REVENGE
WAS TO PURSUE
THE CHILDREN FOR THE
SINS OF THEIR FATHER...

PLEASURE
WAS THEIR GOD
AND LOVE THE ONLY SIN . . .

"What's wrong, Clayton? Don't you find me attractive?"

"You're a beautiful woman," he said, as her fingers stroked his ear, "but you're Gianna's mother, dammit."

"You can't have Gianna, Clayton," she said. "Never, ever. Besides, she's only a child. Why would you want her when you can have me?"

Before he could answer, she kissed him again . . . He twisted away from her lips and tore her hands from his body. "No, dammit! I've come to discuss Gianna. I love her! She loves me! We must be together . . ."

The countess ignored his protests; her eyes were wild. With a violent motion she unfastened her black dress. When she saw him looking at her, she smiled . . .

The Hellions

George McNeill

BANTAM BOOKS
TORONTO · NEW YORK · LONDON

THE HELLIONS
A Bantam Book / June 1979

ISBN 0–553–12549–4

Published simultaneously in the United States and Canada

Bantam Books are published by Bantam Books, Inc. Its trade-
mark, consisting of the words "Bantam Books" and the por-
trayal of a bantam, is Registered in U.S. Patent and Trademark
Office and in other countries. Marca Registrada. Bantam
Books, Inc., 666 Fifth Avenue, New York, New York 10019.

PRINTED IN THE UNITED STATES OF AMERICA

Prologue
Natchez, 1840

... At The Columns, Rafaella left the carriage on the house road. On foot, she crept up the big front lawn, shivering with the cold. She sensed that she was being followed, as she had been on the frantic ride out from town.

The big house was dark and quiet. She crossed the veranda and passed through the huge white columns. After one creaking step in the front hallway, she was able to move upstairs without making a sound. The nursery door stood partly open. A black woman was sleeping on a cot near the double crib. Rafaella slipped into the room. She snatched up a vase and smashed it against the woman's head.

Then she picked up a down pillow and moved toward the crib. The twins were fast asleep. ... Clayton and Cynthia, Storey had said they were called. They should have been named after her father and mother: Roger and Sarah.

As she lowered the pillow, she heard a voice.

"Raffles!"

The voice chilled her. She dropped the pillow and wheeled to face him.

Wyman Ridgeway stood in the doorway. His face was hideous, twisted, scarred. Part of his left ear was missing.

Rafaella shrank away from the sight of him. "Wyman? My God! What are you doing? Oh, Wyman!" Involuntarily, she stared at the ever-present sword in its scabbard at his side.

"*You were going to kill the children.*"

"*Yes, yes, so I was . . . But why should you care? A man like you?*"

"*I'm their father, Raffles! And I told you you'd pay with your life if you tried to harm them.*"

"*Their father! You . . . and Lucinda! Oh, God!*"

Ridgeway made a swift movement. His naked rapier suddenly glinted in the candlelight. "*I had hoped the last swordsman would kill me. But the scoundrel lacked the ability. How appropriate. Now we can die together . . . beloved husband and wife.*"

"*No!*" *Rafaella screamed.* "*No! I won't . . . I'll do anything. I didn't know. Oh, Wyman . . . They killed my father!*"

He moved toward her, his rapier high. She screamed again and threw a silver vase at his head. He ducked, laughing.

Rafaella ran into the hall, down the stairs, screaming incoherently. Ridgeway followed. She ran out the back door of the house, oblivious to the voices from the quarters, to the lights blinking on in the small cabins.

"*No, no!*" *she screeched as she reached the edge of the swamp.* "*No . . . Daddy . . . Save me, Daddy!*"

Rafaella turned to beg Ridgeway. He cut off her right thumb. The index finger dangled by a thread.

She lurched, screaming like a wounded animal, into the swamp. He followed . . .

1.

Natchez, January 1860

The twins stood in lantern shadow at the veranda's
edge and argued about kissing and responsibility. Chessie was upset because her brother was leaving the party
early for a rendezvous with some woman and Clayton
was annoyed because he had seen his sister being kissed
on this same veranda earlier.

As usual with the Deavors twins, discussion resolved
nothing, and five minutes later they returned to the
crowded parlor of the Clarence T. Pugh mansion,
where the raffle was about to begin.

The party was the first of many being given in honor
of the twins' mother, Lucinda, who was marrying Anthony Walker. Mrs. Pugh, a widow of uneasy social
standing who was scarcely tolerated by Natchez's most
prominent families, had set up an unusual entertainment—a raffle of expensive and unusual items, including a "surprise," to make her party different and to
lure Adams County aristocrats to her home.

Chessie glanced at the long table. Slaves were setting out items ranging from rococo silver sconces, a
crystal chandelier imported from Bohemia, and a bolt
of black Italian silk to a pair of chattering monkeys.
Chessie touched her own raffle ticket, safe in the pocket
of her blue silk dress, and wondered what she would
do if she won the monkeys.

The ten-piece orchestra stopped for a rest, and as
the Deavors twins crossed the parlor, the young people
who had been dancing gravitated toward them. A young

1

Natchez doctor and two Adams County planters looked eagerly toward Chessie but, as usual, since his return from school in the East a few months earlier, Clayton received more attention than Chessie from both men and women.

For Clayton was charming as well as handsome. As Chessie listened, he amused the group with a humorous story about a Yankee peddler being swindled by a Mississippi horse trader. Then he quickly drank two double whiskeys. Chessie dreaded her mother's reaction to Clayton's leaving early and hoped he would be discreet about it.

When the music began again Chessie danced first with the Natchez doctor and then with a handsome young planter named Dunbar Polk. Protesting weariness, she declined an invitation from the other planter and walked toward her mother, who was standing near open French doors at the far end of the room talking to several elegantly dressed ladies.

Lucinda Deavors smiled at her daughter and motioned for Chessie to stand at her side. The ladies' talk was light, mostly gossip, and Chessie tried to seem interested, but her mind drifted away. The wind was cool and brought the damp, sweet smell of japonicas from the garden. The smell was provoking, exciting . . . it stirred her senses, made her feel restless. She sighed. Then she realized that it was raining again. Had there ever before been so much rain in January?

Some of the ladies excused themselves and others joined the group and started another conversation, asking about the Grand Tour to the Continent planned for the twins right after their mother's wedding.

Yes, Chessie told the ladies, she and Clayton were very excited about going and had studied both Italian and French to prepare. Chessie was particularly looking forward to the chance to sketch the Roman ruins.

When the talk turned to the raffle and the surprise promised by Mrs. Pugh, Lucinda stepped closer to Chessie.

"I hope nothin's seriously wrong with your brother, Chessie," Lucinda whispered.

Chessie Deavors had been christened Cynthia Susannah, but called Chessie ever since a house slave named Cellus had declared she was too small a baby to carry such a big name.

"Wrong?" Chessie asked. "What do you mean, Mama?"

"Clayton told me he's not feelin' too well and that he plans to leave shortly."

"Oh, I . . . I think he's just . . . It's nothin', Mama. Just all this constant partyin' and all, so soon after the holidays."

"I hope he hasn't had too much to drink," Lucinda said. "Sometimes I think your brother became too fond of whiskey in that Eastern school, Chessie."

"Oh, Mama, don't worry. Clayton doesn't drink all that much." Chessie's was an automatic response, an unconscious defense of her twin brother although she increasingly resented having to lie for Clayton. It wasn't at all fair. The way Clayton took pleasure in confessing his affairs and all the while claiming that if she so much as let a boy kiss her that she was next thing to a fallen woman.

"Well, I hope you're right," Lucinda said. She shivered.

"Are you cold, Mama?" Chessie asked.

"A bit. There's nothin' colder than a damp cold," Lucinda said.

"I'll ask one of the slaves to close the windows," Chessie said.

"No, no, it'll be too stuffy in here," Lucinda said. "I'll send Myrtis out to the carriage for my shawl."

Lucinda turned and called to a young Negro girl who was standing in the shadows against the wall. Myrtis was fifteen. Her mother, who was Chessie's personal maid, was sick with diphtheria and this was the first party that Myrtis had attended.

Chessie had always been fond of Myrtis, even

thought of her as a little sister. Myrtis was slim and lovely and very shy around strangers.

"Myrtis, please fetch my shawl from the carriage," Lucinda said.

Myrtis glanced from Lucinda to Chessie. She licked her lips and glanced at the floor quickly, then back at Lucinda.

"Well, child, what's wrong?" Lucinda asked.

"Are you afraid to go out there to the stables alone, Myrtis?" Chessie asked.

"Yes'm, Miss Chessie," Myrtis whispered.

"Now, I'll hear none of that," Lucinda said. "You march yourself right out there, Myrtis. You hear me?"

"Yes'm, I'm goin', Miss 'Cinda," Myrtis said.

She walked away and Chessie turned back to her mother.

"You look lovely tonight, Mama," she said. "Ever since you brought that damask home from New Orleans I've been longin' to see it on you. It's perfect, Mama. It flatters your hair!"

"Why, thank you, dear," Lucinda said. "The dress has brought me any number of compliments. I only hope Anthony likes it. But . . . do you think the dressmaker made it too . . . ? Well, is it too young lookin' for somebody my age?"

"Oh, of course not, Mama," Chessie said. "It suits you and you look beautiful in it."

Her mother did look beautiful in the green damask gown but Chessie had private reservations. The gown was cut so low and fit so tightly that her mother's breasts were clearly defined. In truth, it was a dress more suitable for a woman younger than Lucinda's forty-two years.

Chessie could never say so—it would hurt her mother's feelings, but since she had met Anthony Walker, Lucinda had changed both her style of dressing and her behavior. Perhaps it was because Anthony was a bit younger—only thirty-five—but for whatever reason, it embarrassed Chessie to see her mother in provocative dresses, blushing and radiant like a young girl in love.

"I wonder what's keepin' Anthony," Lucinda said. "His note said he'd be here by ten and it's half past already."

"Well, didn't his note say that something had come up at the docks?" Chessie asked. "From what I understand, bein' a shipowner means one has to keep irregular hours."

"Oh, I know, Chessie," Lucinda said. "Anthony has great responsibilities. But it's just . . . I find myself missin' him, I reckon."

They talked to the other ladies about the trip to Europe, then Chessie danced with a lawyer from Natchez and a banker from New Orleans. She talked briefly to Clayton and his crowd of admirers, then returned to her mother.

"Just look how that woman is fillin' up the table for the raffle," Chessie said.

"Yes, she's got everything up there but Adam's off-ox," her mother said. "Lord, she must have spent a fortune on this raffle."

"I wonder what the surprise is," Chessie said.

"I don't have any idea, but leave it to Spoony to come up with something you wouldn't . . . Oh, there's Anthony!"

Chessie glanced toward the door and saw Anthony talking to Mrs. Pugh. She looked back at her mother and read in her expression the mixture of emotions: happiness, relief and anxiety. Lucinda looked so vulnerable Chessie was almost afraid for her. She put out a restraining hand. Was her mother actually capable of running across the room and flinging her arms around Anthony's neck?

As they watched, Anthony took his time chatting with their fat, fawning hostess.

2.

Myrtis walked slowly from the house. She paused at the back of the veranda and looked into the deep shadows in front of her.

She glanced over her shoulder and saw all the white people dancing and talking and she heard the music and laughter. Miss Chessie was dancing with Mist' Dunbar and she thought of sneaking back inside and begging Miss Chessie not to send her out to the stables alone. But she shook her head at the idea. If Miss 'Cinda found out, she would be furious.

And so would her own mother. Her mother was forever scolding her for being so afraid of the dark, for fearing every night sound. And she had the responsibility of taking her mother's place tonight. It was important. It was the first time she had ever attended a party, one of the few times, in fact, that she had left the security of The Columns.

Myrtis moved off the veranda with quick, uneasy steps, and half a minute later she left the halo of light from the brightly lit house and walked down a path through a rose garden, toward the stables.

She hummed a song she had heard from the driver of a New Orleans guest at The Columns. She thought of the shiny new shoes that Miss Chessie had bought her in Natchez. But her heart thumped and she glanced from side to side at the shadows, and even the familiar sounds of crickets seemed menacing.

The stables loomed in the distance but they looked so far away. Myrtis heard a fiddle from the quarters, heard laughter. The drivers would be dancing, she knew, gossiping, sneaking drinks of whiskey or beer. She hated it when slaves got drunk. Then, men she had known all her life seemed different, seemed to threaten

6

her as they looked up and down her body with strange expressions on their faces.

Finally, she neared the stables and the dozens of carriages parked around them. She glanced about, looking for the Deavors' carriage, but she was also looking for anyone who might be lurking in the shadows.

Two minutes later she located the carriage. She found the shawl and turned to run back to the house.

Myrtis stifled a scream. A huge black man loomed over her.

The man laughed and she smelled whiskey on his breath.

"You must remember old Scaggin, girl," he said. "I'm Miss Spoony's lead driver, met you out to The Columns at a party, few weeks ago. We had us a dance together."

"I've got to get back to the house," Myrtis said.

A chill raced down her back. She did remember Scaggin. He had been rough and had used bad language and other slaves said he was a man to avoid when he was drinking whiskey.

"Let the white folks wait," Scaggin said. "They not goin' to miss you for a while. Come on, let's have us some fun. I got me some whiskey good as the white folks drink. Come on, girl, dammit, don't shy away from me like that!"

"No, don't touch me!" Myrtis gasped. She bolted from his hand and ran among the carriages.

She glanced over her shoulder. She couldn't see him. But when she stopped a moment she heard the sound of his feet on the gravel as he moved toward her. She turned and started running again, clutching the shawl to her breasts as though it would protect her.

Finally, Anthony left Spoony Pugh and came over to Chessie and her mother. He kissed Lucinda's cheek and gave her a smile that always annoyed Chessie, a smile she considered patronizing. Anyone with eyes

could see how much her mother loved Anthony Walker
—she just hoped he was worthy of her.

"Darling, I'm sorry to be late," Anthony said. "But
the rain had damaged several crates of that last ship-
ment from Africa and I had to try and salvage what I
could. I've been so anxious to be with you. You look
ravishing in that shade of green!

"And you, Chessie," he added quickly. "I trust
you're well this evening. I like your blue frock. But not
nearly so much as your mother's gown."

"Thank you," Chessie said. "I'm fine."

"Darling, did you see Myrtis when you arrived?"
Lucinda asked. "I sent her out to fetch my shawl."

"No, I didn't see anything of her," Anthony said.
"I was much too eager to be with you."

Lucinda blushed as Anthony flattered her. Chessie
felt her embarrassment mount and she could have
kissed a Woodville planter for asking her to dance.

When the dance ended, Spoony Pugh announced that
it was time for the raffle and everyone crowded around
the long table. There was an empty space in the center
of the table between a pair of caged thoroughbred
hunting dogs and a set of jewel-studded silver goblets.
A strapping young black man, bare to the waist, ran
into the room and climbed onto the center of the raffle table.

The man wore skin-tight white satin pants that clung
to his genitals and muscular thighs. After a moment's
silence, there was a chorus of gasps and murmurs as
the guests realized that he was the grand prize, Spoony
Pugh's surprise.

"Well, I think it's shockin'," Dunbar Polk said. "I
mean the way that boy's dressed—with women present. And the idea. Rafflin' off a nigger just as though
we were at a slave auction when many of us disapprove
of slave tradin'."

"Yes, it is unusual . . . and rather despicable," Chessie said. Like Polk, the Deavorses were strongly opposed to slave-trading and they never sold their own
slaves.

Excitement mounted as the guests' numbers were called and they received their prizes—Chessie won an ivory brush and comb set—and soon only the slave was left on the table. Everyone glanced around the room, trying to remember whose number had not yet been called.

Then number twenty-seven was called.

Frannie Deavors rose from a chair at the side of the room and walked slowly through the crowd to claim her prize.

Chessie glanced at her mother and her mother shook her head. Frannie had married into the Deavors family many years earlier, had married some granduncle named Lavon no one ever had anything good to say about, and she was never so much as acknowledged by the family now. In addition to everything else, Frannie had the worst reputation in Natchez, as far as men were concerned, and it was said that the men weren't always white.

People whispered as the slave climbed down from the table and Frannie, a big-breasted woman in a tight lavender dress, left the room with him.

The orchestra played a waltz but no one moved to dance. Everyone talked, gossiped, compared their prizes and accepted fresh glasses of whiskey and cherry cobblers with straws.

Chessie began to feel melancholy and she took a glass of punch. As she put the cup to her lips she saw Clayton at the door. Their eyes met and he winked, then walked out.

By watching, Chessie seemed to condone Clayton's behavior, but she truly resented it. It was unbearable—outrageous—that he had the audacity to wink at her knowledge of his little rendezvous.

Chessie flushed with anger as she gulped down her punch and, for the first time in her life, she ordered a whiskey.

3.

Half an hour later Chessie was both angry at Myrtis and worried about her. She had sent her driver to the stables but he had not found the girl. Now Lucinda and Anthony had left the party, and Chessie felt that Myrtis was her responsibility, though she very much wanted to leave and Dunbar Polk had offered to escort her home.

"It happens all the time, honey," Spoony Pugh told Chessie between sips of whiskey. "Niggers, they reach that age, their juices get to flowin' like only nigger juices can flow, and they get so irresponsible they not hardly worth their keep."

"But Myrtis isn't like that," Chessie said. "She's just a girl. She's shy, responsible, hard-workin'. And she blushes and hides her head if a man so much as looks her way."

"Well, then she's the exception," Spoony Pugh said.

"Maybe I don't know her as well as I thought," Chessie said.

"She's all right," Polk said. "She's young. And you did say she never leaves the plantation. She probably met some young buck out there and forgot all about the time. She'll be back before we leave, I'm sure."

Chessie let herself be talked into another dance but despite the swirl around the room and her light talk with Polk she continued to worry about Myrtis. She considered asking Polk to search for the girl, considered sending her driver again, then decided that she would feel better if she simply went out to find Myrtis herself.

Chessie made an excuse to Polk and left the parlor. She hesitated on the veranda, listening to the fiddle music from the slave quarters. That's it, she told herself angrily. Myrtis was down in the quarters, dancing, having a good time. The girl had completely forgotten her duties. As Chessie walked down the veranda steps she vowed she would punish Myrtis.

The path was dark and shadowed from minute to minute by fast-moving clouds that slid across the full moon. Chessie hurried along the path through a rose garden. In her haste she walked too fast and stubbed her toe on a large stone and nearly fell. She caught her balance and started to move off again.

A sound from the darkness to her right stopped her. Something was thrashing on the ground. Chessie feared it was some preying night creature that was devouring its catch. She shivered.

The shivers became a shudder: Those were human sounds! Someone was moaning, whimpering. Another, deeper voice was cursing and there was erratic, labored breathing.

Chessie glanced around at the big house blazing with lights, back in the darkness. She was afraid to go toward the sounds but she sensed someone needed help. She was about to turn and run back and get Polk when the clouds cleared the moon.

Chessie gasped. There, on the ground in the moonlight, lay Myrtis, her face bruised and bleeding. A huge black man was ramming his body between her quivering thighs.

Chessie was immobilized and made speechless by the horror of the scene and for what seemed an eternity she could only make little mewling sounds as she watched the man's savage thrusts at Myrtis' body.

Myrtis' eyes met Chessie's a moment later and Myrtis' mouth opened. No words came out, only a barely human moan of agony that snapped Chessie from her trance.

"No, no!" Chessie cried. She ran, half stumbling, toward Myrtis and her attacker. "Myrtis! Oh, Myrtis . . ."

The man craned his head around. His face was distorted with passion and hatred. Chessie stopped. She screamed.

He staggered up, his penis still erect. He lurched toward Chessie, his enormous hands doubling into fists. She staggered backward and screamed hysterically.

There were shouts from the house and the quarters. But the man had nearly reached Chessie. He towered over her . . .

But he ran past her and disappeared into the darkness.

Chessie trembled with fear and relief. Her legs were rubbery. She felt faint.

A whimper reminded her of Myrtis. Chessie fell to the ground beside the girl. Tears swelled in Chessie's eyes. She hesitated, gathering her strength and courage, then touched Myrtis' cheek.

Myrtis tensed and cried out.

"It's me, Myrtis," Chessie said. "It's all right now . . . I'll take care of you, Myrtis . . ."

Chessie could barely bring herself to look at Myrtis. Her face was cut and bleeding and her left eye was swollen shut to a shadowy purple mass of pulp in the moonlight. Her dress was torn open, baring her small, dark-tipped breasts which were scratched and bruised. Below her waist, Myrtis' skirt had been ripped apart and a stream of blood trickled between her thighs.

Slowly, with obvious difficulty, the girl turned toward Chessie and opened her eyes. She swallowed hard and her body shook.

"Miss Chessie," she whispered. "Oh, Miss Chessie . . . He's done hurt me bad . . . He done ruined me . . . I want to die . . ."

Chessie took Myrtis in her arms and tried to soothe her, stroking her soft, thin shoulders.

There were shouts all around Chessie now and people ran up, both white people and slaves, and Dunbar Polk was the first to reach Chessie.

"My God!" he said. He sank to his knees. "Chessie, what in hell happened? Are you all right? The girl . . ."

"He raped her," Chessie mumbled. "And he hurt her so badly. Why did he have to hurt her this way, Dunbar?"

"Someone send for the doctor," Polk said as people crowded around.

A gray-haired slave woman knelt beside Myrtis and covered her body with a cloak.

"He'll hang for this!" a man in the crowd said.

"Yes, he will," Polk said. "Who did this?" He looked up at a male slave. "Dammit, boy, don't you think about not tellin' me or I'll have your hide from here to sundown!"

"Honest, I wasn't nowhere 'round when it happened," the slave said. "We was all in the quarters or in the house tendin' to the party."

"It was Scaggin," the gray-haired woman said. "I seen him runnin' away. And it ain't the first time he done somethin' like this to a girl."

"Whose nigger is Scaggin?" Polk asked.

"He belong to Miss Spoony," the woman said. "He her pride and joy, her lead driver, can't do no wrong in Miss Spoony's eyes."

"Where did he go? Is he still on the place?"

"No, I reckon he done runnin' far as he can get, seein' as how he done raped hisself a Deavors nigger."

"You, boy, ride into town and fetch the sheriff," Polk said.

"They dogs on the place here?" a man in the crowd asked. "Good trackin' dogs?"

"They no decent dogs to this place," the woman said. "Miss Spoony, she don't care nothin' 'bout no trackin' dogs."

"Who's got the best dogs, Dunbar?" the man asked.

"Crane Whindle?" another man suggested.

"No, Anse Felson's got the best dogs," Polk said. "And they're nigger dogs, too. Mean as a snake but best dogs in the county for trackin' down a nigger. You, boy, yes, you there, you go find Anse Felson and tell him to bring his nigger dogs."

The slaves left. Polk asked that everyone leave Chessie and Myrtis alone and the crowd began to drift away, whispering and glancing back as they disappeared.

Polk and the old woman stayed with Chessie and Myrtis. The woman mopped Myrtis' forehead with her kerchief. Chessie stroked the girl's hair and cried softly.

4.

A posse of forty men on horseback, with Anse Felson's dogs, set out at dawn the next day to track Scaggin, who had stolen a horse before he fled. Felson's six dogs were Conahoma hounds, huge dogs with large jaws that were specially bred to track down fugitive slaves.

The dogs led the posse into deep woods and the edge of a swamp but it seemed clear after an hour that Scaggin was trying to stay out of the swamp and make his way to the Mississippi River where he might escape on a boat. Word was sent to Natchez to warn all river captains and to have a boat patrol the banks for several miles.

The posse had ridden hard in the coolness of dawn but as the sun rose and the morning became warm the men discarded garments and slowed their pace. The posse was made up of wealthy planters, friends of the Deavors family, and poor farmers who owned no slaves or one or two at the most. There was a natural antagonism between these men and only on occasions such as this did they ride together.

By noon the men in the posse had drunk a good deal of whiskey. They were silent as they followed the dogs through thick underbrush near the river. Their faces and arms had been scratched by low-hanging limbs and thorn-vines and they were sore from so much riding. At mid-morning they had found the stolen horse, judged him lame, and shot him. Now they drank and cursed and marveled that "one weary nigger could cover so goddamn much ground so fast on foot."

"It's all that bastard John Brown's doin's," Anse Felson said. "They ought to hang one like him ever' day, string up one of them Yankee abolitionist bastards ever' mornin' when the sun comes up."

Three months earlier, Brown and a small group of men had attempted to seize the federal arsenal at Harper's Ferry in Virginia and arm slaves in the South for an uprising. Federal troops under Colonel Robert E. Lee had crushed Brown's effort quickly and Brown himself had been hanged.

Because of Brown's raid and the fear that the Yankee abolitionists wanted nothing less than a slave insurrection and the wholesale slaughter of whites in the South, a mood of anger, bitterness and resentment had permeated Natchez for weeks. As a result, many slaves had suffered unusually harsh punishments for minor offenses and several had been murdered by mobs or slave patrols.

"This is one nigger, though, that I'm takin' back to town for a trial," the sheriff said when they stopped at a clear stream to let the dogs and horses drink. "The law'll deal harshly enough with him for what he done to the Deavors nigger."

"There ain't but one law ought to apply to bad niggers," Anse Felson said. "And me and my dogs, we know how to dish out that law, don't we, Slade?"

Slade, the largest of the dogs, turned from the stream at the sound of his name. He trotted over to Felson, a large, black hound with a mangled ear and cuts along his snout, and as if in response to the grin on Felson's sharp, unshaven face, the dog bared its teeth.

Felson patted Slade's head. "Yessir, Slade, you and Fred and Courtney and the rest, you better than any nigger ever lived, and when you do your work with that Scaggin nigger you goin' to have a swell supper as a reward, no matter the cost, don't care if it harelips the governor."

Several of the men laughed and drank more whiskey. Dunbar Polk and his friends looked embarrassed.

The men led their horses when the posse set off

again and Felson held his dogs on long leashes. The posse splashed through bogs and slime-filled bayous and the men's bodies were lacerated by the razor-sharp edges of whipsaw cane.

Slowly, the weary planters began to leave the posse, including Polk, who had hurt his ankle when he slipped on a moss-slick log while fording a creek. At Hunker's Point, a hamlet on the river, there was word that the sheriff was needed back in Natchez, so he left also, after warning the remaining men that they were acting under the law and that they must return Scaggin to Natchez unharmed.

By mid-afternoon, there were only thirteen men left, and all of them except Felson were ready to abandon the chase.

But Felson was livid with anger at the suggestion that his dogs might not be able to track Scaggin. He bullied and threatened the other men to keep them going, and everyone drank more whiskey.

If the men were now in some state beyond anger, bitterness and exhaustion, the dogs seemed in a state beyond that. They drooled and slobbered. Their long tongues hung out as they loped, at times almost stumbled, through the sharp-edged cane. Their eyes were red-lined and malevolent.

But they kept going. They seemed more determined even than Felson, and when they would suddenly rush upon some small cane creature and rip it apart, not for food, nor for sport, but to vent their frustrated fury on something warm and bloody, they would willingly return to Scaggin's trail.

By late afternoon the skies had darkened drastically and lightning crackled low over the horizon. Large raindrops began to fall and the men muttered that it would be impossible to find Scaggin in a rainstorm. But the rain stopped after a few minutes and the dogs strained at their leashes and sniffed the damp air.

Slade lifted his huge head and bayed. He glanced around at the men, his red-tinted eyes gleaming in the dim gloom of the thick gray clouds. The other dogs bayed. Felson's hands trembled with excitement as he took the dogs from their leashes.

"They got the Scaggin nigger," Felson said and saliva dribbled from his lips as though he were trying to imitate his dogs. "They not the finest nigger dogs in the county for nothin'. And you men wanted to turn back!"

The dogs barked as they raced into a narrow stretch of swamp growth along the river. The men galloped behind them, eager and enthusiastic in the sudden realization that the long chase was over.

When they reached the dogs, who had cornered Scaggin against a gnarled oak tree, they dismounted clumsily and tried to reach the slave on drunken legs.

The dogs didn't wait.

They went for Scaggin with teeth bared, with hatred in their low, gutteral snarls. Slade reached Scaggin first.

Scaggin was in a crouch and Slade lunged for his throat. A knife flashed in Scaggin's hand. Slade's throat exploded with blood.

"He's killed Slade!" Felson screeched. "Slade, honey, don't die!"

Felson rushed to the blood-soaked dog, who was convulsing in his death agony. Felson hugged Slade once, then turned on Scaggin, his dog's blood dribbling from his chin and chest.

"Lucille, Courtney, Fred!" he screeched. "Eat him alive! Eat the nigger alive! Tear him limb from limb!"

"Kill the bastard!" a fat man shouted.

"The nigger ain't worth Slade!" another man screamed.

The dogs hardly needed the urging.

Scaggin managed to cut Courtney across her shoulder but Fred knocked him down and Lucille tore jagged pieces of flesh from his knife hand.

Scaggin kicked and flailed his arms. He tried to get up but he was helpless against the jaws that took out flesh and blood here, flesh and blood there, part of an arm, a bit of leg, a thumb, a patch of cheek, an eye, so

17

that in a few minutes Scaggin was reduced to a blood-drenched, quivering creature of inhuman sounds beyond pain.

As Felson buried Slade half an hour later, he muttered: "At least I won't have to spend money on that swell supper I promised 'em."

5.

The news that Myrtis had been raped roused anger and sadness among the Deavors' slave population, four hundred men, women, and children, who lived in rows of whitewashed shacks some two hundred yards from the big house, behind the barn, stables and vegetable gardens.

Only a few house slaves had actually seen Myrtis, whom Chessie had put to bed in the little room next to her own. But rumors circulated that Myrtis had been "ruined" and "beat up real awful," and this was taken as a bad omen, particularly with Lucinda's wedding less than three weeks away. The news that the posse had shot Scaggin when he resisted arrest had little effect on the slaves, since the ones who knew him detested him.

Even before the rape, there had been unrest and apprehension in the quarters. All the slaves knew that their mistress was getting married, and they viewed this event as they did others with great potential and immediate impact on their lives—with wonder mixed with dread. Of course, the wedding itself promised them some good times. They would have their own parties with fiddlers and dancing and rations of beer and whiskey. For the field hands, it meant time off from the winter tasks of fence-mending and ditch-digging.

For the house slaves, however, Miss 'Cinda's wedding meant an overload of work in cleaning and preparing the house for the ceremony and lavish reception. In addition, there was Miss 'Cinda's new trousseau and all the special clothes for every member of the family. There were already special cakes made and in storage, peaches and plums soaking in brandy, and there would be even more cooking and cleaning when out-of-town relatives and friends arrived. And, finally, there was all the sewing, mending and packing for Chessie and Clayton because the week after the wedding the twins were traveling to the Continent.

No matter what individual slaves thought about the extra work, there was a general apprehension about this Mist' Anthony that Miss 'Cinda was marrying. Miss 'Cinda had always been a kind and generous mistress and the young master, Mist' Clay, seemed the same way since he returned from his college a few months earlier.

But this new man, the slaves asked each other, sitting around their winter cook fires, what was he going to be like for the people in the quarters? The slaves knew little about Anthony Walker, but from what they knew, they feared him. When Miss 'Cinda was present he acted decent enough. But when she wasn't present, he was often short-tempered and sometimes harsh. And the house slaves suspected that Miss Chessie disapproved of Mist' Anthony.

So, as the wedding preparations continued, tensions mounted. There was more fighting than usual among the men, and more misbehaving among the children.

"These childs actin' like the devil chasin' 'em," an old woman said to her cronies on a night in early February.

The other slaves nodded and smoked their pipes and dipped snuff and drank coffee in the early dusk and told each other that things were different in the old days, when Mist' Lawton or his daddy was the master. Children knew how to behave then, they agreed.

That same evening the commotion caused by a group of noisy children became too much for Ed, a gray-haired, broad-shouldered man who had been the plantation's hostler for many years. Ed jumped up from his stool and separated two ten-year-olds who were fighting in the mud.

"You two, you keep this up, I'm goin' to turn you ever' way but loose!" he shouted. He glanced around to make sure no white people were within earshot, then lowered his voice. "You know what's goin' to happen you don't start behavin'? Miss Raffles, she gone come out of that swamp shakin' her bloody thumb and she . . . goin' to get you!"

Both boys shuddered and looked back at the darkening swamp.

"We'll be good," one of them mumbled.

Ed's threat had worked. The children walked away quietly, whispering. Ed returned to his stool and said, well, maybe he'd been too harsh, they'd probably have nightmares now.

But disciplining naughty children with stories of "Miss Raffles and that bloody night . . ." had been common practice in the quarters for many years, and it wasn't only the children who felt chills run up their spines when they glanced at that path into the swamp by the big, lightning-shattered cypress tree, a path that they would not go near for any reason.

The Deavors' slaves knew that Miss Raffles had been as evil a woman as ever became a haint and that she was responsible for the death of Mist' Lawton, the twins' father, twenty years earlier. And after Mist' Lawton died, Miss Raffles had come out to the plantation in the dead of night and was just about to smother the twins when her former husband, Mist' Wyman, had caught up with her and cut off her thumb and chased her into the swamp.

The screams they had heard that night still haunted the slaves, as did the memory of finding the tip of the thumb at the end of a trail of blood. Aunt Frony, the midwife and healer, had quickly buried the piece of flesh, then scrubbed the blood from her hands until her skin was raw. Leaving Aunt Frony, Ed and some other slaves had rushed to the big house where they found the twins crying hysterically, though unharmed.

Ed still talked about the wild, terrified look he'd seen in Miss Chessie's eyes.

Ed had stayed outside the twins' door that night, and in the quarters the slaves lit bonfires and huddled in their shacks, singing dirges and praying for dawn and hoping that evil, crazy white woman didn't suddenly appear at their door.

The next morning a posse with dogs had gone into the swamp. They searched for a week, but though they found bloodstains and bits of black hair, they never did find Miss Raffles nor Mist' Wyman. At the point where they found the macabre evidence, the swamp was known to be particularly treacherous, and the county coroner ruled that the two must have fallen into one of the deep quicksand bogs and died.

The white people believed this, as did Cellus, Ed and a few of the house slaves. But the rest of the people had always believed that Miss Raffles—Mist' Wyman was generally forgotten—still roamed the swamp and came out at night to do terrible things. Any odd or unexplained happening, a tragic accident, any stillborn baby, any unusual illness or unexpected death, was held to be Miss Raffles' work.

For the first few years, talk in the quarters was much more open. But one day when Miss Chessie was five she was wandering among the cabins and heard a slave woman telling her children how Miss Raffles had tried to smother the baby twins, how she had had her thumb cut off and still haunted the swamps and punished bad children. Miss Chessie had been terrified and became hysterical.

When Miss Chessie ran home and told her mother, Miss 'Cinda was so angry she threatened to have the woman whipped, though no Deavors slaves had ever been punished with the lash. Miss 'Cinda had relented when Miss Chessie calmed down, even though the house slaves reported that the child had nightmares for months.

Since then, the slaves were always careful not to be overheard when they threatened unruly children, as Ed had done, or when they blamed things on the haint in the swamp, but over the years they had come to accept the story as an old truth.

And now, with the excitement stirred by the wedding, the arrival of this new and unknown master and Myrtis' rape, Miss Raffles was inevitably recalled, and before the week's end one old slave woman swore she had seen a dark-haired wraith dressed in white, a beautiful woman with bloody hands, standing under the cypress tree on the very night Myrtis was raped.

6.

During the long journey from New York to New Orleans on a dreary, slow-moving coastal boat, Jolette Clauson had badgered her mother, Joleen, with endless questions about life at The Columns and in the South. Joleen was Lawton Deavors' sister and had grown up at The Columns, though she had not visited Natchez for many years.

"For heaven's sake, stop pesterin' me, Jolette," Joleen had snapped, losing patience before they had cleared the Outer Banks. "You'll see for yourself soon enough. I regret ever fillin' your head with all those stories about the days when I was growin' up in Mississippi."

Her mother's refusal to embroider any of the stories she had told Jolette when, as a child, she was bedridden with a lingering illness, and the plain, inexpensive passage they had taken to New Orleans had disappointed Jolette. By the time they reached New Orleans she was weary, bored and even a bit sorry that she had agreed to travel to Mississippi for her aunt's wedding.

But now, traveling up the Mississippi River toward Natchez on a huge gold-and-white paddlewheeler, Jolette's mood changed. She was increasingly excited and expectant, and relived her childhood fantasies of plantation life as she strolled the decks of the majestic *Bayou Princess* and sat in her elegant dining rooms and salons.

Jolette was pleased with her cabin, too. It was an enormous and well-appointed room with pale yellow wallpaper flecked with silver crests. The curtains were blue velvet and the soft carpet a varicolored Brussels woven in intricate geometrical designs. Handsome oil paintings of pastoral scenes hung about the room and the ornate crystal chandelier was reflected in tall baroque-framed silver mirrors.

The dining room of the *Bayou Princess* was so grand Jolette was at first too impressed to eat a thing. It was elegant as well as grand and service was lavish. Every meal consisted of eleven courses eaten on pink-and-white French china painted with a likeness of the steamboat moving past an island, and food was served from silver trays and dishes by thirty Negro stewards dressed in crisp white linen. At dinner, a ten-piece orchestra played.

Jolette thought she had never seen anything finer. It made the dinners she had occasionally eaten with her parents at Delmonico's in New York seem quite modest. She enjoyed all the meals, and between them she explored the steamboat's seemingly endless corridors, the salons, the bars, the crowded gambling rooms, and the cosy tearooms.

It had been a memorable voyage, and now she stood on the promenade deck and leaned out against the white filigree railing. Behind her, the steamboat's tall funnels sent up columns of white smoke. To her left, making the most pleasant and rhythmic sound, the two enormous wheels churned through the water.

Sighing with pleasure, Jolette turned her face into the wind and let her long, wheat-colored hair blow about her face. It was hard to remember, on this mild, damp February morning, that she had ever had any reservations at all about this trip.

Jolette had been opposed to slavery all her life. The Clausons were numbered among New York's leading abolitionists, and they and their friends had always told dreadful stories about the tragic injustices of life in the slave states. Yet, from the moment she had stepped aboard the *Bayou Princess* with its wealthy, sophisticated clientele, her life in New York seemed so distant and alien it might have been the life of some other girl. The easy grace, charm and manners of the Southern planters and their wives had overwhelmed her.

She recalled the witty, sophisticated, slightly provocative conversations at supper the night before and compared them with the abstract and self-righteous conversations of her parents and their abolitionist friends in New York. There was no fair comparison. And as for suffering slaves—all the slaves she had seen on the boat seemed quite content. They were nothing like the angry, outspoken Negroes she had seen at abolitionist gatherings.

Jolette saw her mother coming up the steps to the promenade deck. Joleen Clauson waved at her only child as she walked along the deck and Jolette waved back. Jolette felt guilty for her enthusiasm for the South, and a bit apprehensive. Would her mother, she wondered, cause unpleasant scenes with her strongly held beliefs about slavery? Perhaps not. Jolette had noticed that during every anti-abolitionist tirade they had heard since arriving in Louisiana, and there had been many, her mother had sat quietly and not said a word.

"Hello, Mother," Jolette said. "Isn't it lovely?"

"We ought to be gettin' ready," her mother said. "We'll be landin' at The Columns shortly."

"Oh, Mother, what else is there to do?"

"Well, are you all through with your packin'? Are you sure you packed everything?"

"I'm absolutely sure," Jolette said. "And I don't want to leave the deck for even a minute. I want to watch everything while we pull up and land at the plantation. Imagine! This huge boat making a special stop at a plantation, just to put us off! Why, people at the table last night were quite impressed when they heard. It seems everybody knows about The Columns and the Deavors."

"Stoppin' at a plantation landing isn't all that uncommon, Jolette."

Jolette looked at her mother but didn't speak. She was determined not to let anything spoil her good mood. Their eyes met: the same deep blue eyes, just as they had the same wheat-colored hair and the same tall, graceful and voluptuous bodies. People often remarked that they looked like sisters, and the comment never failed to distress Jolette. How, she asked herself, could people even think such a thing? After all, her mother was more than forty years old, an age Jolette could hardly imagine. She glanced quickly at her mother and noticed with relief that when Joleen squinted in the bright gray light the wrinkles at the corners of her eyes were clear. Joleen was no longer young and soon, her daughter hoped, she would never be compared to her again.

A steward came up and informed both ladies that the *Bayou Princess* would land at The Columns in five minutes. Jolette leaned over the rail and strained for her first glimpse of the plantation.

By the time the Clauson women and their baggage had been shepherded down the gangway Jolette was so thrilled and delighted she felt nearly faint. It was even more wonderful than she had hoped. On her right was what her mother called "the little summer house," a two-story building that was twice as large as Jolette's New York home. There were a dozen white people and twice that many slaves waiting at the landing below, and three black stewards from the boat had gone ashore to pass around silver trays of gin fizzes, mint juleps and orange sherbets, "with the Captain's compliments."

Eagerly, Jolette stepped off the gangway and met her Mississippi relatives for the first time. First she kissed Aunt Lucinda, who was small, auburn-haired, fine-boned, and had such friendly blue eyes. Then she met the twins. Chessie had her mother's fine features and large, wide-set blue eyes. Her hair was a fine-textured golden color. Chessie seemed shy, unlike Clayton. Clayton was tall and muscular, and showed two dimples when he smiled. Jolette exclaimed that Clayton and Chessie looked so much alike, despite the difference in their sizes, that she swore she would have known they were twins.

Next Jolette was introduced to some planter families who were old friends of her mother's. Then she met an elderly Negro man named Cellus, who was quite tall and stood very straight and who seemed taken aback —almost alarmed, when Joleen ran over and hugged him.

Jolette was becoming confused by the time she was introduced to Anthony Walker, the man Aunt Lucinda was to marry. In the crowd of Deavorses, Anthony Walker's dark good looks provided a powerful contrast. He was dark-eyed and dark-haired and his clear skin was deeply and evenly tanned. His eyebrows were thick and darker than his hair and set off his eyes, making the pupils look intensely black and compelling. Jolette found her attention caught and held by him, found him extremely attractive in a masculine way that seemed uncommonly forceful and authoritative. Then he smiled, showing even, white teeth, and she decided that he was the most handsome man she had ever seen.

After the Deavorses and their friends had hugged and embraced, the slaves loaded the trunks from New York into two wagons. Everyone climbed into a number of comfortable carriages and drove away from the river. Jolette tried to look everywhere at once. There was too much to see. Behind lay the wide, shimmering river. On the horizon were the swamps, which she had seen from the river, ominous and impenetrable beneath the darkening gray sky. There were acres and acres of green forests and some rolling meadows where horses grazed. And then, there were the cotton fields they drove through—at first disappointing for not being endless acres of bursting white cotton pods, but simply fields of red-brown earth.

But Jolette was impressed when they neared the plantation itself, passing the slave quarters where scores of black people stood in lines and bowed to welcome them. She felt her mother's emotion when several of the older slaves ran over to touch Joleen and speak to her. Why, Jolette told herself, these slaves showed no signs of ill treatment or unhappiness. Their neat little cabins were far better than the housing many emigrant workers had in New York. And with her own eyes she had seen Irishmen in New York whose clothes were not as good as the ones these slaves wore.

She was impressed, too, by the plantation's outbuildings. The barns, stables and sheds would have covered a New York city block. There were enormous vegetable gardens and corn fields. And there were actually flowers blooming! Bright, red flowers were blooming though it was still winter!

All of a sudden Jolette's heart sank. The carriages were slowing and approaching the main house from the rear.

"Oh, no! Please!" Jolette exclaimed. "I thought we'd . . . Couldn't we drive around so I can . . . approach the house from the front?"

"Oh, Jolette!" Joleen said. "Act your age!"

"It's no trouble at all," Clayton said. "Ansey, drive around the house and up the road a bit, then turn around and come in toward the front of the house."

So they went around the house and Jolette shut her eyes as they drove up the road. Her heart was thumping as Ansey turned the carriage around.

She opened her eyes and there it all was, just as her mother had described it so often: The long drive was lined with massive magnolia trees and the huge, graceful white house was fronted by twelve tall columns. Jolette gasped.

It was real and she was here and suddenly she knew she belonged here and she wanted to stay. She never, never wanted to leave The Columns!

7.

Chessie stood at a parlor window and stared through the rain-streaked pane at the storm that had kept everyone inside all day. She was restless, bored and tired of all the wedding fuss, the parties—and there was another one at the Mandells' this evening—of her mother's constant worry that it would rain on her wedding day, of the endless sewing and packing for the trip, of Clayton's usual inconsiderate behavior and her own helpless resentment. And she was more than a little weary of Jolette's unending enthusiasm about The Columns and plantation life.

But what troubled Chessie even more was the depressing situation with Myrtis. It was her constant concern, and she had kept Myrtis here in the house rather than send her back to her mother's cabin in the quarters. Myrtis was recovering from her physical injuries, and the doctor said that in time she would mend completely. But Chessie was worried about Myrtis' spirit.

Chessie had done all she could, but Myrtis was convinced she had been ruined for life, that the other slaves would never consider her normal again, that no man would ever want her.

Thinking of it, Chessie again felt cold anger at Scaggins and told herself she was glad that the posse had shot him. She remembered that night at Spoony Pugh's, remembered how she had cradled Myrtis and felt her terror and shame. She also recalled her own terror when Scaggin turned on her. Yet, Chessie was almost shocked to realize that the idea of rape had a strange fascination. It must have been a fascination, for she could not get it out of her mind, just as lately, she could not stop thinking about sex.

In past years Chessie had paid little attention to the whispers of her bolder and more curious girl friends. And her sexual experience had consisted of innocent kisses from boys she had known all her life.

But recently that had changed. Chessie now listened eagerly to tales of passion from her friends. Her kisses on verandas were becoming bolder. They would leave her breathless and aroused in strange new ways. And twice, she had let a young man caress her breasts through her gown.

Particularly, Chessie had become more aware—and more resentful—of the way Clayton attracted women, took what he wanted from them, then selfishly dropped them, though she had never approved of any woman he chose.

Chessie seethed with a constant, helpless anger because Clayton made certain she knew about each of these women, taunted her, winked at her, while demanding that she keep her distance from the most innocent kind of passion.

What particularly disturbed and confused Chessie was the fact that even as she resented Clayton's letting her know about his women she found herself wondering . . . the words had difficulty forming from her guilty, troubled thoughts . . . wondering just what Clayton actually did with those women, what it was like.

And once, recently, while kissing a boy she had found herself thinking of her brother.

Chessie's cheeks went warm. Her mouth flew open.

How could she let herself dwell on such matters? She must get hold of herself. She must stop thinking of sex and Clayton constantly.

Chessie looked at the rain, which was slackening into a mist, and tried to divert her thoughts to the trip to the Continent, to her mother's marriage. A minute later she was thinking of her own marriage.

Chessie had always assumed that she would fall in

love and marry. It was expected of her. She would have a steady beau, marry him, give up The Columns to Clayton—she resented this, but it was the family tradition—and go to live on some other man's plantation.

She would be his—some other man's—wife and she would . . . satisfy his physical needs. Who the man would be she had no idea. She had never thought much about it, but now, she wondered, what if she married a man who was as selfish and thoughtless as Clayton?

Or what if her husband was not . . . gentle? What if he took his pleasure roughly? Then, she thought, wouldn't her wedding night resemble Myrtis' rape?

To escape such thoughts, Chessie longed to get away. As much as she loved the plantation and her mother, she was ready to sail to the Continent. There she would relax, have time to sketch and postpone decision-making. She would feel free for a time, for a last time, because already people were saying she should think about marriage.

Still looking out the parlor window, thinking about all these things, Chessie saw a movement behind an oleander bush in the yard, and then saw Aunt Joleen walk around the house with a bunch of rain-soaked camellias in her hands. Aunt Joleen had gone out without an umbrella! Chessie smiled, remembering that up North this weather would probably be considered mild.

Chessie had decided that she really liked her aunt from New York City, especially as Joleen had avoided any talk about slavery or the abolitionist and underground-railroad work that had finally driven her and her husband, Aaron, out of Mississippi. Joleen was obviously delighted to be back home after so many years, and all the family's friends and neighbors seemed equally delighted to see her.

"Oh, here you are, Chessie!"

Chessie turned as Jolette came running into the room. Jolette looked radiant in a pink-and-white ribbon-striped dress over the largest steel hoop Chessie had ever seen—the latest style, she had been told, in New York.

"I was just tryin' to wish away the rain," Chessie said.

"Oh, I don't mind the rain," Jolette said. "I was out walking in it earlier. And I just love exploring your beautiful house. But, Chessie, I have an idea! Mother told me there may be some of her old clothes in the attic, and I wondered if you'd take me up there. I'd so enjoy seeing some things from the days when Mother was growing up here."

"All right, Jolette," Chessie said. "I'll go up there with you. Lord knows what we'll find, though. I haven't been up there in ever so long."

Chessie led Jolette up to the cobweb-filled attic and they searched among piles of papers and dilapidated furniture and old linen. But they found nothing that could have belonged to Joleen.

They had started for the door when Jolette stopped abruptly.

"Wait a minute," she said. "What's that over there under those gunnysacks?"

Together, they crept into a dark corner and pulled the sacks off a trunk they had not seen before. The trunk was copper-banded and, although old-fashioned, it was clearly expensive. It was monogrammed with the initial "B," and on a tag there seemed to be writing in Italian—Chessie had studied Italian for her trip —but the ink was too faded to be legible.

They tugged the trunk out of the shadows and lifted the lid. The trunk gave off a musty smell that made them frown, but opened to reveal dozens of old-fashioned women's dresses and petticoats and shawls, fine gloves and fancy bonnets.

"They're lovely," Chessie said, fingering a yellow silk.

"Oh, let's dress up!" Jolette said. "I've never seen clothes so grand! I'm sure they weren't Mother's. From what she told me she was never interested in such fancy clothes. But I am!"

"I'm not much interested myself . . . But, all right, let's do," Chessie said. "Wait. What's this?"

Chessie had found a small gold-rimmed brooch in a side pocket of the trunk. The brooch held a miniature portrait of a young woman with a pale, oval face and dark eyes framed by a cloud of dark hair.

The woman was exceptionally beautiful and she was no one Chessie had ever seen—in life or in a family portrait. The face in the portrait was innocent, vulnerable, yet as Chessie examined it she felt uneasy and when she opened her fingers and let the brooch fall back into the trunk, she was relieved.

"Isn't she pretty?" Jolette said. "I wonder who she is. Well, we'll ask somebody later. Come on. Let's try on some of these clothes, then go down and surprise everybody with our finery."

Their first audience, two maids in the downstairs hall, gasped and seemed so surprised that it set Jolette off in a fit of giggles. With high spirits, the cousins marched into the kitchen where they found their mothers supervising the cooking. Arm in arm, they smiled and pirouetted, showing off so boldly that both Lucinda and Joleen broke into smiles.

But when Chessie stopped whirling around and stopped in front of her mother, Lucinda's smile faded suddenly. Chessie was startled at the look that passed between her mother and Joleen.

"Stop! Take those clothes off, get rid of them at once," Lucinda said harshly. "And that brooch, too! Wherever did you find them?"

Chessie was shocked at the tone of her mother's voice.

"What's wrong, Mama?" she asked.

"Just do as I tell you!" Lucinda said. "Immediately! And answer my question. Where did you find them?"

"In a trunk in the attic," Jolette said. "But why are you . . . ?"

"Jolette, do as your aunt says," Joleen snapped.

Chessie seized her mother's wrist. "Mama, I'm not

movin' a step till you tell me what's wrong with puttin' on some old clothes we found in the attic."

There was a moment's silence as Lucinda and Joleen looked at each other, then back at Chessie, and Chessie realized they weren't staring at the dress, but at the brooch.

Chessie backed away and a shudder ran through her body, a shudder so strong that she began to tremble. She felt her knees buckle and she knew at once, although she still had difficulty speaking. "Mama, did they . . . ? Did it . . . belong to Rafaella Blaine? Am I wearing Raffles' clothes? Is this her portrait?"

Lucinda's lips quivered. "Yes, Chessie. And it gives me a fair turn to see you in Raffles' clothes . . ."

"Oh, no, please, no!" Chessie cried.

She felt weak and faint. It was as if she were being smothered. Why had she done it? She had felt frightened ever since she'd touched that brooch! Her eyes clouded and all the bad, old dreams came back to her in a rush . . . She was gasping for breath . . . A pillow was being pressed over her face . . . She was fighting for her life. . . .

"Mama!" Chessie screamed. The dress was too tight. The cord around her neck was choking her! A violent sob shook her body.

Hysterically, Chessie clawed at the dress with her fingernails as Lucinda and Joleen rushed to her side.

8.
Natchez, 1840

. . . *Rafaella turned to beg Ridgeway. He cut off her right thumb. The index finger dangled by a thread.*

She lurched, screaming like a wounded animal, into the swamp. He followed . . .

The pain was horrible. Blood spurted over her arm, up into her face. She gagged and vomited.

She fled deeper into the dark swamp, nearly fainting at the sensation of clasping her hand over the stub of thumb and the dangling flesh as blood gushed between her fingers. Tree limbs and thorny vines scratched her face and shoulders. As she ran she screamed and babbled and bile rose into her mouth.

A touch like a razor slashed at her back. New pain scalded her as she looked over her shoulder. Her blood dribbled from the edge of Ridgeway's rapier. He laughed and mocked her with the blade and drank from his flask.

Rafaella staggered against a tree. The force of the impact nearly knocked her unconscious. She vomited again as she stumbled on, her mind spinning and blanched with terror and pain.

And always behind her she heard Ridgeway coming, calling out her name in mocking tones, calling her his beloved wife, promising her a deadly honeymoon this night in the swamp.

Rafaella's face was lacerated from the vines and limbs and her body convulsed as she staggered on, losing strength quickly from loss of blood.

"Daddy . . . Daddy . . ." she babbled, saliva spilling over lips too numb with horror to control.

And then Ridgeway was in front of her. He loomed above her, his gray eyes narrowed, his distorted face set in a pale, hideous grin of death. He mocked her with the bloodstained rapier, parrying and thrusting as her weak body jerked this way and that, like a berserk puppet on half-severed strings.

She tried to beg but she could not. No words could part lips bitten shut, clenched against the pain and the constant flow of blood from the loathesome stump of her thumb. She moaned and her teeth sank deeper into her lips.

Then the rapier slashed out and cut her across her breasts. She threw back her head and screeched as she recoiled from the agony. Ridgeway laughed. He spat

34

brandy and walked backward, two feet in front of her, still mocking and cursing her.

Rafaella's knees buckled, she swayed to the right, to the left, her eyes were glazed, she could barely see the grinning apparition in front of her. The rapier slashed her breasts once more and dragged a wordless howl from her throat.

As she convulsed and swayed, a kind of pain she had never known gripped her body and she saw, hazed, half-dreamed, a vision of her entire body being dismembered in this way, being cut apart, bit by bit, but not dying, just bleeding, becoming a hideous, deformed cripple that would horrify the most loathesome swamp creature . . .

Some time passed, it could have been an eternity, before she heard another sound from Ridgeway, a different tone, one of supplication, of desperation. She shook her head, leaned forward, strained to see, but he wasn't there. He was gone. She saw his brandy flask on the ground and just beyond it his rapier. She squinted through blood.

Another foot further, and there was Ridgeway, helpless, struggling in a sucking, churning pool of quicksand, fighting to rise, to reach out and claw at the solid ground an inch beyond his grasp.

Rafaella howled with delight at the sight. Their eyes met, his fingers grasped at a sassafras root. With her last strength she kicked at his grasping, clawing fingers, smashing them from their only hope, and as she sank, fainting, to the ground, she saw Ridgeway's head and shoulders disappear into the quicksand.

As her laughter faded, there was another sound and she twisted around, all but blind now. A huge, dark shape loomed above her. With no voice left for another scream, she was far beyond terror. She lay on the ground, her eyes closed, her body convulsing, her lips quivering with the word that was her delirious prayer: "Daddy . . . Daddy . . ."

9.

At half past eleven on a cool, wet February night, some one hundred representatives of Mississippi's most prominent families drank champagne, ate oysters and gambled recklessly in the grand casino of the Mansion House hotel. Every family able to give a ball in Lucinda Deavors' honor had tried to outdo its neighbors, but most everyone agreed that this party, given by the Roccalini family, was the most fabulous yet.

Except for the actual wedding and wedding reception, invitations to this party had been the most eagerly sought, and Natchez women had saved their best and most expensive finery for the event.

Carlo Roccalini, the head of Natchez's oldest Italian clan, loved gambling, and weeks before this night, everyone had heard about the party he had planned. On arrival, each guest was given one hundred dollars in gambling chips. Any money a guest won at poker, blackjack, roulette, craps or baccarat was his to keep, but if a guest lost his hundred dollars he gambled on with his own money.

The party had started at nine and now, as slaves in red-and-gold livery served the guests more and more champagne from the silver trays, some people were winning heavily while others had already lost thousands of dollars. Yet even the losers had been caught up in the drunken excitement, and most of the guests were still gambling.

Carlo Roccalini was well loved by the Deavors family. The Roccalinis owned hundreds of acres of the best cotton land in Adams County and knew how to work it as well as they knew how to play. Carlo's uncle was a wealthy, powerful *don* in Sicily, and it was to the Italian island that the Deavors twins would be sailing the next week.

In Palermo, they would be Don Roccalini's guests before they continued their trip to Rome and Paris. And there a distant Roccalini cousin would become the twins' chaperone. Everyone agreed that the planned tour sounded very adventurous and exciting, and next to the wedding and the gambling, it was the main topic of conversation.

Chessie had quickly lost her chips and also her interest in gambling. She began to feel too warm in the crowded casino and went into the ladies room to sprinkle water on her flushed face. The room was also stuffy and she closed her eyes to steady herself, but in the blackness came unwelcome memories.

"Am I wearin' Raffles' clothes? Is this her portrait? . . ." she remembered saying, and with her shudder of memory at the words came a powerful memory of choking, of being smothered as she tore at the old white dress with her nails, screaming as her mother and aunt helped her take off the tattered silk.

After the incident, Chessie had calmed down soon enough, coddled by her mother with hot chamomile tea and a warm bath. She had been very ashamed of her behavior, and bewildered by it.

Why, she wondered, should she have so violent a reaction to thoughts of a woman who had been dead for twenty years, no matter what the woman had tried to do to her? She had thought about it that night and often since, fighting the impulse to call out to her mother or to a slave, frightened that if she fell asleep those dreams of being smothered would haunt her. And often, she hadn't been able to sleep until first dawn.

Chessie was determined not to give in to her haunting melancholy about the long-dead Rafaella. To prove her determination she had kept the gold-rimmed brooch and hidden it in her room. There it was still, though she had not yet had the courage to take it out of her jewel casket and look at it.

Chessie opened her eyes. She scolded herself for giving in to these fears. She washed her face and returned to the party where she sipped champagne, danced with all the young men and enjoyed seeing old friends. Rafaella and the brooch were soon forgotten.

The only flaw in her enjoyment of the party was her concern for Clayton.

Clayton looked marvelous. He was wearing a new gray suit with a blue striped silk tie and his white teeth flashed in a constant smile that showed his dimples, but it seemed to Chessie that he was drinking too much. She sensed, as she always could, that her twin was upset about something and it troubled her nearly as much as if it had been her own problem.

No one was enjoying the party more than Jolette. She felt she looked her prettiest in a new mauve silk dress with a huge hoop skirt that was the latest New York fashion and showed her figure to good advantage. She had never seen gambling before and she found it terribly exciting despite the fact that she had lost her chips.

In one spin of the wheel Jolette had seen people win or lose more money than anyone she knew in New York earned in a year. Some of the people cursed, some ground their hands into fists, some glistened with perspiration, but, win or lose, the mood of the party was still very high, and Jolette found it thrilling.

Earlier in the evening Anthony had been winning, but now his stake of chips was low. He had shrugged off a hint from Lucinda that he quit and she had left the table. Jolette crept closer and closer to him, admiring his coolness and confidence as he continued to bet. And each time, before he shoved his chips onto a number or a color, he turned to Jolette, as though to ask for her approval, and Jolette smiled and nodded encouragingly.

Oh, she prayed, let this losing streak be temporary. Standing close to Anthony, she felt a part of the play and a part of Anthony's every move.

"What do you think, Miss Clauson?" he asked her, breaking his concentrated silence.

Jolette stared into his dark eyes. "Are you asking me to . . . to make the choice this time?" she asked.

"Yes, I have a feeling that you'll bring me luck," he said.

Her heart began to thump. "Oh, I hope so!" she exclaimed. "Let's see . . . oh, put it all on the black!"

"All?" he asked. "Yes, all right, I will if you say so!"

Jolette had spoken impulsively and as Anthony pushed all his chips onto a black square her heart beat faster. Had she spoken too recklessly? Anthony glanced at her worried frown and smiled.

"It's only money, Miss Clauson," he said. "Nothing is more important than the moment, this moment of excitement . . . of win or lose all! There's always more money somewhere. You seem to be a woman who can appreciate the importance of the moment. And enjoy the risk!"

The risk, Jolette said to herself. The word thrilled her. Yes, she wanted to take risks, take any risks that could give pleasure. She smiled at Anthony and nodded bravely as the big wheel began to spin.

The idea of so much money riding on one chance made her dizzy. She thought of the frugal, self-sacrificing life her parents led, the life she had always known. The Clausons were not poor but they always spent their money carefully and wisely, on life's necessities. Their friends had been mostly intellectuals—preachers and teachers, and they had always supported half a dozen abolitionist movements with their generous donations.

I never realized how dull and poor our life was, Jolette thought as the wheel reached top speed and blurred past red-and-black sections. This was the life she wanted, this planter life with its lavish balls and beautiful homes with huge staffs of smiling, contented black people in attendance.

Oh, certainly slavery was wrong. She had always believed it wrong and could not easily desert the conviction, and she had been shocked by the incident with Myrtis and Scaggin, but of course incidents of rape and brutality occurred every day in New York City.

I won't think of all that tonight, Jolette vowed. She smiled quickly as she realized that Anthony was looking at her.

"We'll win," she whispered like a prayer, but she was apprehensive as she looked down at the spinning wheel. It was slowing . . . ever slower . . . and her nerves tingled when she glanced at Anthony's chips. He had put more than seven thousand dollars in chips on the black.

The wheel had nearly stopped now, and its pointer was clicking past a black! It was stopping on a red! Jolette wondered just how much money Anthony had. Had she impulsively cost him so much he might lose one of his ships? All her conservative upbringing rose in her and for one truly agonizing moment she went rigid with guilt and horror.

Then the pointer slid onto a black with a final click.

"Oh, we did win!" Jolette shouted in triumph and relief. "We won, we won!"

"Yes, you brought me good luck!" Anthony said.

He shoved his chair back and stood up. Smiling, he hugged Jolette, lifted her off her feet, and swung her around. Blood rushed to her head. She caught her breath and felt his own breath on her cheeks.

Then he released her and turned to collect his chips amidst a chorus of congratulations from others at the table.

"Let's give our luck a rest," he said. "I've yet to taste an oyster and I could drink a magnum of champagne."

"Oh, so could I!" Jolette said and glanced around the room, thankful not to see her mother. She wanted to feel alone and completely grown-up tonight. After all, she was eighteen years old. It was the most exciting night of her life and she felt that somehow, tonight, her new life was beginning.

Two hours later, neither Anthony nor Jolette had returned to the gambling tables. Jolette had encountered her mother and been duly scolded for drinking so much champagne, but finally Lucinda had complained of a headache and Joleen had left the party with her, accompanying her to the Roccalini home, where they were all staying. Anthony had sent them off with apologies, saying he must remain to settle a private matter, and Jolette had recklessly hidden in another room while the women were making their farewells.

Clayton had disappeared, too, leaving with that loathsome Frannie Deavors, whose presence no one could explain. Unfortunately, Chessie was still at the party and Jolette knew that eventually she would have to go home with her cousin, but Chessie was on the other side of the room, dancing with Dunbar Polk.

Jolette sipped champagne and savored the excitement of every moment with Anthony. They had joined several of his friends on a veranda overlooking the garden and the talk was witty, at times naughty, the kind of talk men indulge in with ladies present only when the hour is very late.

A Natchez banker had just told an amusing tale with more than subtle sexual undertones and everyone had laughed and, as expected, the ladies, including Jolette, had all blushed just the right amount. Jolette thought the banker witty, but it was Anthony who was the cleverest and most handsome and who told the most amusing stories. Everyone, she noticed, seemed to agree.

She was proud to be at his side, proud that he was on the verge of marrying into the Deavors family. In the very near future, she hoped she would meet someone who was as daring, charming and handsome as Anthony. In fact, Jolette admitted to herself, she rather envied her Aunt Lucinda, and didn't quite understand why Anthony had chosen to marry a woman several years older than he. Aunt Lucinda, though still attractive, was not strikingly beautiful, and was, well, Jolette stifled her guilt at the thought, rather small.

The lovely, dark-eyed daughter of a planter was trying, rather blatantly, to flirt with Anthony and Jolette felt a sudden stab of anger and jealousy. But Anthony politely extricated himself from the girl's attentions and turned back to Jolette.

"Shall we sample the refreshments?" he asked. "This time I'm determined to coax a raw oyster down your throat!"

"Oh, Mr. Walker, I don't know," Jolette said. "I'd love more champagne, but oysters . . . Eating live things . . . I never . . ."

He laughed and they walked over to a sideboard arranged with cakes and fruits and silver trays of raw oysters on beds of ice, as well as oysters cooked in a dozen different ways. Jolette would have done anything in her power to impress Anthony, but she felt a bit out of her element. At other parties and with other men, she had always felt relaxed and self-possessed, but Anthony was so confident and worldly wise that she was terrified he might find her unsophisticated or dull.

Jolette had already sampled the oyster stew, thick with heavy cream and egg yolks. She had loved the oysters Beinville, baked with heavy cream, scallions, mushrooms and shrimp, and the oysters casino with bacon, bread crumbs, red pepper and chives. And there were an oyster loaf and deep-fried oysters and oysters in a mignonette sauce of vinegar, scallions, peppercorns and tarragon. And a half dozen other kinds, all cooked. But raw?

Anxiously, Jolette watched Anthony slide a fat raw oyster past his lips and felt both a pleasant stirring and a queasiness in her stomach. She nibbled at a slice of oyster loaf and watched Anthony eat another raw oyster, this one topped with caviar and sour cream.

Meeting her eyes, he shook his head and laughed. "Oh, Jolette, it must have been a brave man who ate the first oyster, as someone once said. But I see that, despite the fact they've been proven harmless, you're unwilling to show the same spirit you showed at the roulette table. Perhaps I've misjudged you."

Jolette drained her glass of champagne. She stared up into his dark, teasing eyes and for one instant she nearly hated him. No man should make her feel foolish. Never!

"We shall see, sir," she said. "You, nigger, hand me that oyster, that small, plump one there . . ."

The slave placed the opened oyster on a tiny silver plate and passed it to Jolette. She swallowed quickly, shuddered, then popped the oyster into her mouth. For one terrible moment of near panic she didn't know what to do, to chew or swallow . . . And then the oyster was slithering down her throat, all cold and soft and sweet and unexpectedly sensuous.

Why, she loved it!

"A half dozen, boy," Jolette said to the slave. "And some with the caviar, too."

She looked at Anthony triumphantly and he smiled and nodded. She smiled in return and began to eat her raw oysters very, very slowly.

10.

As Clayton hurried away from the Roccalinis' party, riding down Natchez's dark, silent streets with Frannie Deavors, his sense of guilt was nearly strong enough to overcome the lust aroused by a friend's story of Frannie's "goddamn unbelievable ways of usin' her mouth on a man . . ."

But now, snuggled against Frannie's fleshy body, her plump, eager fingers moving tantalizingly between his thighs, he sighed with pleasure, enjoying her kisses on his mouth and anticipating them on other parts of his body.

Expertly, Frannie licked the roof of his mouth,

sucked his tongue, nibbled at his tongue tip, and in less than two minutes Clayton had a full erection.

"Umm, honey, you sure taste good," Frannie sighed. "But where are my manners? I haven't even offered you any brandy or nothin'."

Frannie climbed off the sofa and stood in front of Clayton, her smiling lips moist, her large breasts straining against the crumpled pink lace at her bosom.

"I don't know, I had so much champagne," he muttered. "Well, perhaps a little brandy . . ."

"Good, I'll have some with you," she said. "Just got me this here imported stuff from Paris, France, just come up the river, cost an arm and a leg, but hell, I say nothin' but the best for me and my friends."

She turned and swung her ample hips as she went over to a marble-topped sideboard. "Damn nigger!" she said. She shook her head and turned around. "I'll have his black hide for forgettin' to put out the quality stuff. Just wait, Clay, honey, I'll be back quick as a wink."

Frannie left the room and Clayton relaxed against the pink velvet sofa. His tongue still tingled from the work of Frannie's sharp teeth but his erection was beginning to soften.

He glanced around the small, overheated boudoir, over-decorated in various shades of pink. His curiosity was aroused. He had agreed to go with Frannie on a sheer sexual impulse. He had never had a woman so old—in her early forties—but Frannie was still an attractive woman. He smiled, remembering his friend's description of Frannie as "wild and willing."

Clayton found it ironic that Frannie was actually a Deavors. Many years ago, she had married his Uncle Lavon, a man with a terrible reputation who had tried to destroy his family and been killed in the process. His uncle, from what he had always heard, had married Frannie for her dowry.

Clayton also found it amusing that Frannie, who recently had come back to Natchez after many years, always seemed to show up at the best parties, though the hostesses swore they hadn't invited her. He'd heard a rumor about Frannie and Carlo Roccalini, and he guessed that it was the men who saw to Frannie's invitations in return for her favors.

Clayton stirred and inhaled the room's excessively sweet perfume. Would Frannie expect some invitation to The Columns in return for this evening? The thought made him uneasy. His mother had never invited Frannie to The Columns. By nature polite and mild, Lucinda had no use for Frannie and would not discuss why, but Clayton suspected it was more than the woman's bad reputation—or her marriage to Lavon Deavors. His mother had once said Frannie didn't have the wit to be any part of Levon's schemes.

Of course Clayton could not even consider issuing Frannie an invitation to his mother's wedding. Even if she asked him straight out, he must refuse.

Clayton stood up and began to pace the room. He was too warm. Sweat trickled down his back. The close, sweet air was smothering. He would have opened a window, but the entire room was hung with pink velvet draperies and he had no idea where the windows were.

His penis was still stiff from the memory of Frannie's touch and he thought with pleasure of what he could anticipate. Yet, as always in the past few months, with the anticipation of sexual pleasure came the inevitable guilt.

There was the immediate, specific guilt about being with Frannie, particularly if his mother learned from someone at the party that he had left with her. And there was the continuing, general guilt about indulging in whiskey and women and not settling down to full responsibility for The Columns, as he had vowed to do when he came home from college.

Clayton sighed and brushed sweat from his forehead with the back of his hand.

With a shudder, he forced himself to admit the source of his real guilt. It had little to do with Frannie or his mother or the plantation. It all went back, somehow, to Chessie, and tonight his guilt had been triggered when, leaving the party, he had looked around and seen Chessie staring at him with helpless, hurt eyes.

A flood of anger came with the guilt. Chessie always knew what he was thinking, anticipated his moods, could read his thoughts—and she always condemned his little pleasures with women and never understood that men could do things that were forbidden to women.

But Clayton could not sustain his anger at Chessie, nor could he deny responsibility for the dangerous situation that had developed between them lately. He didn't know what got into him at times, concerning his sister. For months he had given in to sudden impulses to taunt her about his women, to wink at her at indelicate times, to make certain she knew of each affair.

Clayton felt feverish. He crossed the room to the sideboard and poured half a glass of whiskey and gulped it down. He swallowed hard and began to pace the room. His relationship with Chessie had all the elements of the childhood rivalry that had always existed between them, a rivalry that he assumed was common to twins.

We're not children any longer, he reminded himself. The girl he often thought of when he made love to a woman was no longer a child, and, far worse, she was his sister!

Two more whiskeys numbed Clayton but did little to soothe him. He became horrified as he recalled what was said about sexual feelings, even of the most innocent nature, between brother and sister, recalled how contemptibly such feelings were damned and condemned.

"And rightly so!" he mumbled.

Clayton was sickened by a strange, searing guilt and he could not erase Chessie's face from his thoughts, a face that was the mirror-image of his face—except that Chessie's beautiful face showed love and innocence and he feared his own revealed the effects of dozens of sordid, loveless nights . . .

Clayton was struck by the sudden fear that just as their features were identical, just as so many of their moods and feelings were shared and the same, just as at times they could feel each other's pain, that by involving Chessie in his fantasies and by making her a part of each affair, he was corrupting her innocence in an odd, vicarious way . . .

"I'll stop it all!" he muttered. "I swear I will. I'll never think of Chessie like that again, never taunt her, never give her the slightest knowledge of my women . . ."

Clayton realized he was talking to himself. He sucked in the warm, perfumed air. The whiskey was sweet and sticky in his mouth.

Surely Chessie would soon fall in love and marry, he told himself desperately. He knew he must. He could no longer continue these ephemeral, unfeeling affairs. Recently he had had a vision of the girl he wanted to marry, dark-eyed, with long, black hair, a face of love and innocence, and if he ever found the girl, he would do all he could to marry her. And when he and Chessie were both married, they would be . . . less close to each other, there would be less intimacy and less rivalry than in the past.

Chessie might move far away. He might seldom see her.

The thought made him sad for a moment. He did love Chessie. He would miss her. He felt very protective toward her. He had never approved of any boy who kissed her or showed any interest in her. He had never found one worthy of Chessie.

No, no, he thought, it would be far better for them both if Chessie married soon and left The Columns.

Then Clayton remembered that he and Chessie would be spending many months together on the Continent.

He became uneasy at the thought, so uneasy that he felt the impulse to bolt out of the sweltering room.

11.

But he heard voices beyond the door. Frannie returned, and behind her was a short black man carrying a bottle of brandy on a tray.

"Lord, niggers just not what they used to be," Frannie said. "I told Elthorp here half a dozen times 'bout the brandy. Well, Elthorp, you pour us a couple of drinks now, and get on out of here. And tomorrow, I'm goin' to be on you tooth and toenail."

Elthorp muttered excuses, poured the brandy and left the room. Frannie handed Clayton a snifter.

"Ain't these pretty, honey?" she said. "I got 'em in New Orleans when I was livin' there. So many swell things to buy down there. You like New Orleans?"

"I was in school there for a while," Clayton said quickly. He was desperate to escape his misery in the pleasures of her body. "I liked it, yes, though I prefer Natchez." He tasted the brandy. It was good, rich and strong.

Frannie sipped the brandy eagerly and when she pulled the snifter away, her lips pouted with a sheen of liquor in the soft light.

"Well, I'm glad to be back here, too," she said. "Guess there's no place like where you was brought up. 'Course we got culture here, too, just like in New Orleans. Dancin'. Singin'. All that stuff . . . Oh, listen to me rattle on!"

Frannie drained her brandy and set the snifter on the sideboard. Clayton looked at her face. It was eager and sensual. The flickering light played on Frannie's large green eyes and long, silky brown hair. His eyes were drawn to her magnificent breasts.

"Here," Frannie said, reaching for his glass. She

stepped closer, but then her boldness stopped. Suddenly, she seemed confused, almost shy. She looked past Clayton, then at the floor, and her full breasts rose and fell.

Clayton inhaled deeply, sucking in the cloying smell of the room. He found it arousing now, part of the room's erotic quality.

Without speaking, he reached for Frannie, took her in his arms and kissed her. Her small, warm hands slid around his neck and while she sucked his lips in a wet kiss and touched his tongue with hers, her nails ran along his neck and tickled his ears.

Clayton closed his eyes and lay back on the velvet sofa. He sighed with pleasure. Ah, the woman was voracious, just as his friend had told him!

Moaning slightly, she opened his shirt and unfastened her bodice so that her breasts fell forward. Clayton felt their soft, warm weight on his bare chest. He took them in his hands.

They were so warm, so firm and resilient! He stroked them eagerly and she whimpered. The sound excited him, as did her tongue which licked him constantly, moving down his face, his neck and shoulders, his chest, bathing him with kisses.

Clayton took off his clothes as fast as he could. He opened his eyes. Frannie's hair was a tangle, her face hidden as she crawled over him, licking every inch of his body. He hoped—dare he hope?—yes, she was doing it—she took the tip of his hard penis in her mouth and sucked on it enthusiastically.

Clayton groaned. He dug his fingers into her hair and twisted. She knelt between his knees and bent over his penis, burying it in her wet mouth and sucking, sucking . . .

He had never experienced such a sensation. He closed his eyes and gave in to the unbelievable pleasure.

"Clay, honey, you're so hard and hot," Frannie mumbled, gasping for breath.

"Don't stop!" Clayton begged.

She opened her mouth wider and started sucking again, her sharp teeth hurting and arousing the tender flesh.

Clayton felt an enormous pressure building up in his loins. He was so hot. He was drenched with perspiration. Every nerve and muscle in his body was tense. He writhed, shook his hips and shoved himself deeper into Frannie's throat.

His fingers tightened in her hair and he moved her head up and down in a fierce rhythm that matched the pulsing of his blood . . .

His release came with a scalding explosion that brought a scream from his throat . . .

Later, Frannie banked the fire and brought more brandy to the bed where Clayton lay collapsed, staring at the shadows moving on the ceiling. He turned as Frannie settled on the edge of the bed. Sweat glistened on her shoulders and bathed her breasts and nipples. Over the strong scents of brandy and perfume he smelled the results of their lovemaking on her body. He took the snifter and slid up in the bed. He felt drained, trapped, and again as if he were being smothered. He had the urge to gulp down the brandy and leave at once.

"You're so . . . so good-lookin' and all, Clay, honey," Frannie said. "Been a long time since I've enjoyed bein' with a man much as I've enjoyed bein' with you."

"I enjoyed it, too, Frannie," he muttered.

"And it's different, sort of, Clay, you know . . . Keepin' this kind of fun in the family," she said. "If you know what I mean."

Family? Clayton shuddered. He was afraid he knew only too well what she meant. He gulped the brandy and slid up further.

"Uh huh," he mumbled and avoided her eyes. When she touched his shoulder, he tensed. Yet as her lips slid over his shoulder and grazed his nipple, his penis stirred.

Frannie pulled back and sipped her brandy, her

green eyes narrower, her lips parted, her breath ragged.

"Oh, I know what all your folks thought 'bout me all these years, Clay," she said. "But I wasn't no part of all those terrible doin's. I'd swear on a stack of Bibles I wasn't. I always liked your family a real lot, Clay. I'd have done anything for 'em, just like I'd do anything for you."

Clayton drained his brandy and set the snifter on the side table. Time to pay the piper, he warned himself, and he must leave before his treacherous penis betrayed him.

"Yes, I know, Frannie," he said. He inched away. "No one blames you. No one ever did. I know it was all my uncle's fault . . ."

"Oh, yes, that, too, Clay," she said. "Lord, I'd plumb forgotten 'bout Lavon. And he was bad enough, let me tell you. But Lavon wasn't nothin' compared to that stepdaughter of mine. Don't think I didn't suffer at her hands. Oh, nothin' like your folks, with her killin' Lawton and all. But she done cheated me out of my rightful property, then she run me out of the county!"

"Your stepdaughter?" Clayton asked. He turned back to Frannie. "What stepdaughter? Who do you mean?"

"Why, that Raffles Blaine!" Frannie said. "It was on 'count of her I had to leave Natchez and live all them years in New Orleans."

"Raffles?" Clayton asked. His stomach churned. He wiped the sweat from his forehead. "She was your stepdaughter?"

"Why, didn't you know?" Frannie asked. "When she and her daddy first come here from Italy, poor as Job's turkey, Lavon was dead and I married Roger Blaine, Raffles' daddy. I loved him. I know he loved me. And I had lots of money and slaves and cotton, and we'd have had a real fine marriage. But that Raffles, she hated me from the first minute, and she was determined to ruin ever'thing. Why, I believe she forced her daddy to kill hisself. And then she cheated me out of my property and forced me to leave and go live in New Orleans . . ."

"Christ, I had no idea!" Clayton said.

He shivered. It was all very long ago but the horror of it was still strong. All his life he had known vaguely about Rafaella Blaine, knew she had somehow caused the death of his father and scores of other people in a steamboat explosion. He'd been told that Rafaella had tried to kill him and Chessie, because she had gone mad after the death of a father she loved too much, a death her madness blamed on the Deavors.

But it had never affected him as it did now. He had never thought of it or had the nightmares Chessie often suffered. He had not understood his sister's hysterical reaction recently when she had accidentally put on one of Rafaella's old dresses, but this confrontation with Frannie brought it all to life.

He shuddered. To find himself in bed with Rafaella's stepmother, to have made love to her, to speak so easily of the girl who had killed his father . . .

Calm down, he told himself. He took a deep breath, but when Frannie touched his arm his flesh crawled. He pulled away, hesitated, then scrambled out of bed. It was nothing, he thought, only the slight melancholy that sometimes followed sex, the *petit mort,* little death, as the French called it. That and the brandy and whiskey, the heat and the cloying scent and the smell of sex on Frannie, and the stupid woman's talk of his family.

"Clay, what's wrong?" Frannie whined. "Oh, honey, I'm sorry I done said somethin' wrong. Please, don't run off this way in the middle of the night!"

"It's all right, Frannie," he mumbled as he started dressing. "It's a long ride out to the plantation and I have to be there at first light to supervise some ditch-drainin' . . ."

Frannie stood up. She took a step, then stood still. She shook her head. When she spoke, her voice was low, her words hesitant.

"That damn Raffles," she said. "Won't it ever end? Here she's costin' me your friendship, Clay. I should've known not to talk 'bout that little bitch. Lord, she's come out of the grave to haunt us all again. Well, now, no . . . I'm not superstitious enough to believe that. But, 'course, I never really believed she died in the swamp. Girl that mean, she wouldn't die easy. No, Raffles . . . I believe she's still alive to haunt us all."

Clayton buttoned his shirt and pulled on his boots. He didn't know what to say. Frannie seemed stupified. Her words made no sense. But they were frightening.

"Look, Frannie, everybody knows that Raffles died in the swamp," he said. "Except some of the slaves, I reckon. So don't you worry about her being alive."

"Well, maybe you're right," she said. "And then, maybe the niggers are. But, Clay, there's somethin' I've never told before. I was in New Orleans a few weeks after the steamboat blowed up and Raffles disappeared in the swamp. Well, one evenin' on Canal Street . . . I'd swear I seen Raffles there, her hand all bandaged up, walkin' 'long with some nigger woman . . ."

12.

It was two days before the wedding and the Deavors household was in an uproar. Seamstresses were still putting finishing touches on Lucinda's dress for the Sumralls' ball that night, and there seemed at least a week more of work to do for the wedding and reception and a month of sewing and packing for the trip to the Continent. Clayton had gone into Natchez on some business, Joleen was visiting family friends up in Rodney and Lucinda was in such a state of nervous exhaustion that she had retreated upstairs for a late afternoon nap.

As usual in such situations, Chessie quietly took charge of everything, despite her own weariness, and she was glad, in a way, for her apprehensions about her mother's marriage had been growing stronger and now she was far too busy to worry at all.

Chessie could not have defined her apprehension—she knew her mother wanted to marry Anthony Walker and that everyone considered the match a good one, but she could not bring herself to love or trust him. Some unbidden intuition cautioned her that he was not quite what he seemed, and despite her effort to put her fears aside, she could not.

A young slave interrupted Chessie's supervision of the sewing with word that she was urgently needed back in the kitchen. Chessie sighed and hurried down the hall.

The kitchen was a separate structure behind the house, connected to it with an open covered passageway, and as Chessie hurried along the passage she heard laughter from the yard beyond. It was Anthony and Jolette, she noticed, walking together around the house. When they saw Chessie, they waved and she stifled an annoyed thought that they might have helped, or at least have offered help, considering the situation and the pressure of last-minute arrangements.

Of course, they're both our guests, Chessie reminded herself as she waved back half-heartedly and entered the busy kitchen.

The head cook was in tears. Two of the special hazelnut fruitcakes concocted for the wedding reception had been burned and the cook's young assistant had cried so hard she'd set everybody off. Chessie soothed the girl and tried to mollify the head cook, praised the color of the cherries in compote, and had just begun to discuss the menu for dinner that night when she heard excited voices and the sound of horses outside.

She ran into the back yard. Four strange white men on horseback were reining up near the stables. They dismounted and pulled a black man off one of the horses.

Chessie recognized the black man. He was Bernard, one of their slaves. Bernard had been missing for three days, and everyone had been very upset about it, for it was the third time that he had run away. Bernard's face was swollen and bleeding and Chessie saw that his back and chest were crisscrossed with deep lash marks.

"We picked him up in the swamp, ma'am," a tall, red-faced man said proudly. "We're the slave patrol for this here part of the county, and we knowed you'd reported a nigger been missin'. Well, we seen this nigger lurkin' in and out the swamps, and we took off after him. He made a run for it into the swamp when he spotted us. Give us a good fight when we cornered him. But we know how to handle these niggers get themselves riled up—it's all 'cause of what Abe Lincoln and John Brown been preachin'."

Chessie was horrified at Bernard's condition and touched by the look of agony and terror in his eyes. Her hands trembled as she faced the four men. She knew that many of the patrol members were poor whites who owned no slaves and who hated Negroes. Often they felt no sense of responsibility for returning runaways to their owners unharmed.

"What'll we do with him?" the leader asked. "'Course, the best thing this nigger'll understand by way of bein' punished is a good whippin'!"

"No! We never whip our people here on The Columns," Chessie said. "I . . . There's a slave jail by the barn . . ."

"What's happening here?"

Chessie looked around to see Anthony and Jolette walking toward them. Jolette's face paled as she saw Bernard's condition but Anthony's expression seemed to Chessie hard and arrogant.

"We caught one of your runaway niggers, sir," the patrol leader said. "Caught him skulkin' 'round the edge of the swamp, near that old, lightnin'-struck cypress, and I was just suggestin' to the young lady here that this nigger ought to be whipped good . . ."

"I'm surprised that Bernard was in that part of the swamp," Chessie said. "Why, most of our people are scared to death to go in there . . ."

She stopped short, startled to see Anthony's eyes narrow, his mouth twist. His handsome face became ugly. He stepped closer to the patrol and the slave on the ground.

"This nigger was hidin' in that part of the swamp?" Anthony asked. His voice was odd, harsh. "How far in there . . . ?"

"Well, we don't rightly know," the leader said. "Guess we could get the nigger to tell us, though he don't seem to be one for talkin'. Want me to string 'em up and beat it out of him?"

"Yes, take him . . . Tie him up back there, around the back of the barn," Anthony said. "But then you can go. I'll see that he's adequately punished . . ."

"No!" Chessie said. "Absolutely not, Anthony! You must know that no slave has ever been whipped at The Columns."

"This is no matter for women," Anthony said. "You and Jolette go into the house, Chessie."

Two of the patrollers hoisted Bernard to his feet. He was sobbing.

"Wait, Miss Chessie, please," Bernard begged. "That swamp . . . I'll tell you 'bout it. Don't let 'em beat me no more . . ."

"They won't beat you," Chessie said. "Jolette, go and get my mother."

Jolette glanced at Anthony, then turned and ran to the house.

"And you, sir," Chessie said to Anthony. "You're not yet a member of the family, and you have no right to give orders on this plantation!"

"I'll tell you what you want to know," Bernard said. "I went in real deep to hide, 'cause I thought wouldn't be nobody else there, 'count of them stories 'bout the haint, but I . . ."

Anthony took a step forward. He slapped Bernard across his mouth. "Shut up, you black bastard!" he shouted. "All your whining and lying won't help you now. This is the third time you've run away."

"Anthony, stop! You're losin' your sense of reason," Chessie said. "Hittin' him when he's been hurt so badly. Just wait until . . ."

"And I've had enough of your precious Deavors nigger-lovin'!" Anthony said. "I'm within hours of being your stepfather. I'm the only white man on the plantation right now. I know what I have to do! And I won't be ordered around by a spoiled, arrogant girl! Now, stand aside, Chessie . . ."

"I'll talk! I'll tell you all 'bout the swamp and what I saw," Bernard said. "Miss Chessie, don't let him take me away. I'm scared! He'll kill me, for sure."

Anthony grabbed Chessie's arm and tossed her aside. Pain shot up her arm and through her shoulder. Her eyes stung with tears but she bit her lips against the pain and the impulse to cry aloud. Once more, she stepped between Anthony and Bernard although she was terrified by the wild look in Anthony's eyes. His hands curled into fists at his sides and as his right arm came up slowly, Chessie was sure he was going to hit her.

Then a huge black hand locked around Anthony's wrist like an iron cuff and easily spun him away. Cellus stood there, massive and powerful despite all his years, and Chessie did not doubt that he could snap Anthony's wrist.

Anthony gasped with surprise and pain. Cellus released his wrist. Anthony cradled it and cursed softly as saliva dribbled from the side of his mouth.

"I warn you, sir," Cellus said. "Never put your hands on Miss Chessie again."

"Nigger! Don't you dare to threaten me!" Anthony bellowed. "I'll see *you* hanged! I've got witnesses! You'll die for this . . ."

"We should kill the bastard here and now," the patrol leader said. "Hangin's too good. We ought to burn the black bastard alive!"

"Get off this place!" Chessie said. "You're trespassin'!"

"We're a duly sworn patrol doin' our legal duty," the leader said. "And it's a capital offense for a nigger to hurt a white man."

"Sir, you'll answer to my brother for this," Chessie

said, but her voice was weak and choked up and she asked herself bitterly where Clayton was when she needed him. Her legs trembled, ready to buckle. It took all her strength to stay on her feet.

"Anthony! Chessie! What's happening?" Lucinda called, leaning from an upstairs window. Her voice was frantic. "I'll be right down!"

Anthony's face and manner changed quickly. The color drained from his cheeks.

"All you men," he said to the patrol, "get out of here! Dammit, go!"

"But this here nigger hurt and threatened you! It's . . ."

"Dammit, it's a family matter! Now get the hell off this plantation!"

The men grumbled and the leader cursed but they climbed on their horses and rode way.

"Chessie," Anthony said. His voice was hoarse and pleading. "I . . ." He licked his lips. "I don't know what came over me. You know your mother's very anxious. Please, let's keep this unfortunate incident between us and avoid distressing her just before the wedding. I'm truly sorry for my behavior . . ."

"And Cellus?" Chessie asked.

"Cellus?" Anthony's lips trembled as he glanced at Cellus. "He . . . Cellus, you have my word that . . . that the matter won't be mentioned again . . ."

Lucinda ran up. Her face was flushed and she was gasping for breath. She stopped abruptly as she saw Bernard. "Oh, good Lord," she said. "What on earth . . . ?"

"Don't take on, my dear," Anthony said in a placating voice. "A slave patrol found him and he put up a fight." He reached out to steady Lucinda. "That's all, darling . . ."

Chessie glanced at Cellus and saw that he agreed that they should spare her mother any distress over what had really happened.

According to Lucinda's instructions, then, Bernard was sent off to be treated for his wounds, then to be locked up in the slave jail. On Anthony's advice, Lucinda returned to her bedroom, and he went into the parlor where, through an open door, Chessie saw him gulping a large glass of whiskey.

Chessie herself went back to the sewing room and tried to take an interest in the work, but it was impossible. After a few minutes she retreated to her own room and collapsed.

In solitude she swallowed back tears. She didn't trust Anthony Walker, not at all.

13.

"If we do secede, the Yankees won't fight us," Anthony said. "It's simply not in their nature."

Anthony, Clayton and a dozen of their friends were having drinks in the gazebo at The Columns on the day before the wedding.

"Not from what I know of them," Clayton said.

"No, they'll never fight," Carlo Roccalini said. "Why, they're cowards. Emigrants. Just off the boat, for the most part. Shopkeepers. Men in little stores and offices. And if they're foolish enough to fight us, then, boys, we'll turn 'em every way but loose!"

"Damn right, we will!" Theron Sumrall said. "Why, we Southerners, we all know how to ride, how to handle a gun, know how to live outside. Hell and damnation, a war'd only last a couple of months, at best."

The men went on to talk about the upcoming presidential election and the disaster that would surely follow if Abe Lincoln were nominated by the Republicans in May, and won the election.

There was some talk of economic differences between the North and the South, but as often happened in such conversations, the talk returned to slavery, and over more brandy the men vowed that they would fight and die rather than give in to the Yankee abolitionists. Slavery was essential to their way of life. Abolition would cause ruin in the South, and the damn Yankees wanted to subject the South to the bloody rule of free Negroes.

When their anger had been vented and the brandy had soothed them, the men went on to discuss the issue of reopening the slave trade with Africa. Since 1808 the U.S. Constitution had outlawed the importation of slaves from Africa and most Southerners had come to accept this law, particularly since there was no shortage of slaves, more in every generation, and they could still be sold and traded freely all across the South.

Recently, however, there had been increasingly strident minority demands to reopen the African slave trade.

The men in the gazebo, wealthy planters and brokers and lawyers and bankers, were strongly opposed to reopening the African trade. Most of them, in fact, were opposed to the domestic slave-trading. And even those who argued that such trade was necessary condemned the traders themselves.

"Trash, pure and simple," Clayton said. "We planters, we understand our people, we know them, we take care of them, from cradle to grave. But these traders, with them it's anything to make a dollar, no matter how much misery and death they cause!"

"Yes, just last week a trader came into Natchez with a dozen emaciated slaves," Theron Sumrall said. "He'd started out from Carolina with twenty and marched them unmercifully. Of those who made it here, two died before he could get them on the block. We all know that slavery is the natural condition of the nigger, but that sort of man is not fit to be a master, not that sort."

"Morality aside," a cotton broker said, "reopenin' the slave trade would give grist to the mills of those abolitionist bastards. And the British, they'd be likely to set their Navy to stoppin' the trade, like they've done in the past, and with the possibility of secession comin' up, we might well need the British as allies against the Yankees."

"I reckon a man who brings slaves over from Africa

is even lower than a slave-trader," Clayton said. "From what I've heard, niggers died like flies in squalid, miserable conditions on those slave ships."

"And how do you feel about the matter, as a ship-owner?" the broker asked Anthony, who had turned to look at the ladies in the parlor window.

"What?" Anthony asked. He turned back to the men. "I'm sorry, Bruton. Would you repeat your question?"

The broker smiled and glanced around the gazebo. "Our friend here has far more important matters on his mind than niggers and the African slave trade. Don't fret, Anthony, I'm sure Lucinda's as anxious for tomorrow night as you are."

The men laughed. Anthony picked up a brandy offered by a slave and gulped down half of it. His smile was quick, nervous.

"Oh, the African slave trade?" he said. "Well, naturally, I detest the practice as much as you gentlemen do. No, I'll stick to tradin' goods . . ."

"Gentlemen," Theron said, "isn't it time we decided exactly where we're goin' to take Anthony tonight for his bachelor party? And what kind of entertainment we're goin' to provide?"

"It is time," Clayton said. "But what does the bridegroom fancy? I fear we can offer him little that will amuse or interest him. See there? He's starin' at the parlor window again!"

"What can I say?" Anthony asked after the laughter had subsided. He drained his brandy. "It still seems an eternity until tomorrow. But I'm sure you gentlemen will see that the time passes both quickly and in an interesting manner."

Clayton called for more brandy and Carlo Roccalini began to tell a ribald story about a Sicilian bridegroom who got locked in a whorehouse the night before his wedding.

A dozen ladies from Natchez and neighboring plantations, wives and daughters of the men outside, sat in the parlor and sipped sherry.

The ladies had assembled for the wedding rehearsal tonight. They had lunched and discussed all the details of the ceremony and their matching gowns, admired Lucinda's ivory *peau de soie* wedding dress, and marveled at the presents already displayed in the gallery. Tonight a lavish rehearsal supper and dance would be held at the Sumralls' nearby plantation.

Jolette pretended to listen to the ladies' talk, but her mind had wandered far away. For a few minutes she had tried to let herself believe this would be her life forever—this world of elegant balls and parties, splendor and servants and handsome, witty and audacious men.

Then her thoughts became troubled, and the most troubled concerned her feelings for Anthony Walker.

Since that evening gambling at the Roccalinis' party, Jolette had managed to be alone with Anthony— briefly—half a dozen times. Each meeting had been more exciting and had left her feeling more confused.

In the shelter of the ladies' chatter, Jolette allowed herself to ponder her feelings. She admired Anthony very much, but he mystified her. She had no idea what he thought of her, and longed to know.

Once, when they had been riding together in the woods and had dismounted to rest, they had stared into each other's eyes and Jolette had suspected that he wanted to kiss her. She wasn't sure how she would have reacted, but the moment had passed.

Ever since then, she had longed for his kiss, just one, just to see what it was like, even though it could lead to nothing, for he would soon be her uncle. There would be no real harm in it, she told herself, none at all.

In the days that followed that ride Jolette found herself searching him out, both in family gatherings and when she was alone. She was not really flirting, she thought. It was just that he was so handsome and kind and she was a stranger here, too. She had done nothing provocative, and he had always been scrupulously polite. It was innocent.

Although Anthony had sought her out and had even paid her some charming compliments, he had never been more than avuncular with her and had never revealed his feelings for her.

Or any feelings at all. Until, that was, the incident yesterday with that poor slave. That incident had shown Jolette a new side of Anthony, and the revelation had troubled her and fascinated her more than she could easily admit. Every time she thought of him now, she felt a chill of fear and respect.

And a strong desire to see more of him, Jolette admitted to herself. But it was impossible. Tomorrow he would become her uncle. Soon she would return to New York and probably never see him again. There would be no more possibilities of kisses, no more little secret fantasies about living at The Columns or some place just like it, married to Anthony.

Jolette finished her sherry. Her attention wandered out the windows, toward the gazebo where the men had gathered to drink. She squinted, trying to see Anthony.

Unless she was mistaken, he seemed to be laughing. Suddenly she felt odd—excited and resentful, a little nauseous, almost like crying.

She swallowed and realized she was jealous. She honestly didn't want Anthony to marry Aunt Lucinda. It was preposterous, but true.

I wish I'd met him earlier, she thought. I know, I just know he could come to love me . . . terribly.

Jolette felt cheated and frustrated. Dammit, she hated them both! Lucinda was standing here so calm and confident, it made her feel lonely and sick. And as for him—she was suffering at the thought of never seeing him again, and he was standing out there drinking and laughing!

14.

That night Jolette moped through the wedding rehearsal, the ride over to the Sumrall plantation, and the elaborate rehearsal supper. She felt so sorry for herself she was physically ill and could only pick at her food. Even the imported champagne tasted sour, though she told herself miserably that she might as well drink a whole case by herself.

Jolette was miserable because Anthony had ignored her all evening. He didn't seem to notice her new blue lace dress, didn't compliment her, had barely spoken to her at all. She was hurt and bored. All the men were drinking heavily and she knew that soon they would go out for a bachelor party. I can't bear it, she thought as she endured the flattery of two admiring young men and sipped champagne. How could he ignore her on this last possible night they might . . . well, at least have a few private minutes together, might talk a bit, might even have one forbidden kiss?

Jolette knew that serious involvement with Anthony was impossible, but she longed for any contact at all. His appeal to her was strong, so strong that here, at the last moment, she was growing faint. Perhaps it was love. She had been in love once before, and she knew this feeling was nearly that strong. And yet she had no idea at all what he thought of her. It was insulting and painful. She had never been ignored like this, and she hated it.

Her misery turned to anger a few minutes later when she saw Anthony and Lucinda holding hands and smiling at each other. Jolette took a big gulp of champagne and began to flirt outrageously with her two admirers. She even let one of them escort her out to the veranda and kiss her cheek, but it became a kiss the man regretted when Jolette happened to see Anthony's arm around Lucinda. "You fool! You rogue!" Jolette said, tears in her eyes. "How dare you try to force yourself on me this way!"

Half an hour later Jolette huddled under a poinsettia tree in the shadows of the rear garden, shivering in the damp cold and telling herself that her whole life was hopeless. She hadn't even known, before visiting The Columns and meeting Anthony, how dull and hopeless it was. She hated the prospect of leaving here and going back to New York and her self-righteous parents and friends. She would never, never be happy. She would never marry, never again meet a man like Anthony, a man who so well fulfilled all her fantasies. It was miserable, unfair! She stifled a sob.

Someone touched her shoulder. She turned and gasped. Anthony stood there.

"Are you all right, Miss Clauson?" he asked.

"I'm . . ." Her throat felt thick. She swallowed. "Yes, why shouldn't I be all right?"

"Well, it seems to me that you've been acting strange, distant, all evening," he said. "I've been worried about you."

"Me? Distant, sir? Why, I'm surprised you noticed. No, no, I'm quite all right. I've managed to amuse myself."

"Yes, as usual you've been surrounded by admirers," he said. "And you even let one of them take you out onto the dark veranda."

"You saw that?" Jolette asked with surprise.

"Oh, I've seen everything you've done. I've watched you closely," he said. "And I've been almost . . . almost too obvious about it. Just this afternoon I was caught staring at you in the parlor window."

"Mr. Walker . . . Why are you telling me this now?" She was excited but confused. His implications thrilled her.

"Because I must," he said. "And I must call you Jolette. Please, call me Anthony, if you can. Tomorrow, I'll be married and soon you'll be gone. But I must tell you how very beautiful you are. You're the most beautiful woman I've ever seen. And at the risk of my pride and reputation, I must confess that you excite me . . . And I desire you more than any woman I've ever known."

"Anthony!" Jolette whispered, stunned but delighted. She inhaled his cologne and the night air. Her face was hot and she was glad that in the darkness he couldn't see that her cheeks were burning. Still, she was confused. "You are very flattering, sir. But your declaration is inappropriate, as you're marrying my aunt tomorrow!"

Jolette knew she must be cautious, must be modest and proper. Yet, she longed to throw away caution and propriety.

"We have time only for boldness, Jolette," Anthony said. "We must live for the moment, take the risk, as with gambling."

He stepped closer and the moon came through clouds as she looked up into his eyes. She stiffened when he put his hands on her waist, but she did not pull away.

"Anthony, taking risks with roulette is one thing. But if we . . . This risk is far greater. I fear it's too late for us. And . . ."

And what? she asked herself as she sucked in her breath. Words of caution, of scandal, of propriety, raced through her frantic mind but had faint strength against the power of Anthony's physical presence in this forbidden moment that was the fulfillment of all her fantasies. What if he told her that he wouldn't marry Lucinda tomorrow? Then, scandal be damned!

"I'm infatuated with you, Jolette," he said. "I confess it. I've thought of you constantly, longed for the sight of you. Dammit, why didn't we meet earlier?"

Anthony moved close to Jolette and kissed her lips. She resisted for only an instant, then opened her mouth and responded fully to the urgency of his kiss. A delicious chill ran up her spine as his tongue touched hers.

She pressed against his body and twined her fingers

in his dark hair. His lips sucked hers, his tongue touched the roof of her mouth. His hands slid down her back to her buttocks and cupped them.

Jolette trembled. She had never felt such desperate passion in a man. Nor had she felt such a strong sexual urge. As their kiss continued, her nipples began to grow hard. Without realizing what it was, she felt his penis stiff against her and was both electrified and frightened. Finally, she pulled away, gasping and flushed, but still holding his hands in hers.

"My God, you're beautiful, Jolette," he muttered. "I'm crazy with desire for you!"

"Desire?" she asked with an edge in her voice.

"Desire . . . and love," he gasped. "And you? May I hope you have . . . some similar feelings for me?"

"Similar feelings? Yes . . . yes, of course, Anthony, or I would never permit you to kiss me. No one has ever kissed me like that. With all my heart I want your . . . your love and your affection. But we must speak of tomorrow. And afterward . . ."

"Yes, we must," he said.

But he did not. He moved to her quickly, through her half-hearted protests and uplifted hands, and once more took her in his arms and kissed her. This kiss and the force of his body, of his strong hands on her buttocks, was too much for her and she surrendered to a depth of sensuality—the first passion she had ever known.

Instinctively, she kissed him deeply and sucked at his tongue. Her fingers touched his neck. She moved her hips against his loins and again experienced the excitement and shock of his firm penis.

In her innocence and excitement Jolette misinterpreted their embrace. He'll be mine now, she told herself. After this evening, he'll be bound to me forever! He must be!

Anthony's hands moved to her breasts. Deftly, he fondled them through her dress and she trembled with anticipation. When he freed her breasts she whimpered as the cool air caressed them.

His first touch was gentle. He stroked her small pink nipples and they ached with delicious pain. When his hands closed over her breasts she gasped and sucked at his lips.

Jolette was bathed in perspiration. She felt it running down her stomach, trickling between her warm thighs. She rubbed her thighs together.

Anthony stiffened, then began to thrust against her roughly. His breathing was irregular. He squeezed her buttocks as he continued to grind his penis between her thighs.

Then he grunted, went limp and his arms slackened.

"Anthony, what . . . ?"

Abruptly, he stepped back and freed himself. "A sound!" he whispered. "Down the path!" His face was flushed in the pale moonlight and he looked weary and drained.

"What sound?" she asked. "Anthony, darling, come back to me, please . . ."

"My God, Jolette, what are we doing?" he asked. He smoothed his hair. "Someone will discover us! We'll be ruined!"

"I didn't hear anything," she said. "We can . . . Let's go farther into the garden, Anthony."

He shook his head. "No, Jolette! No matter how much I want you, I . . . Listen, I heard it again! Quickly, get dressed!"

"It was nothing," she said. "Only the wind."

She stepped toward him but he backed away and glanced down the path.

"Dammit, pull up your dress," he said. "This is impossible! I must be drunk! I must have lost my reason!"

There was no tenderness in his voice now, nor passion. Jolette stood trembling, gasping for breath. Her bare nipples still throbbed and her aroused, betrayed body ached.

"Later?" she asked. "Can we meet later tonight?"

"No, not tonight," he said. "Jolette, I'm going to marry your aunt tomorrow. This is an impossible situation for us. If we had time, if there were any time at all before the wedding, I want you so much that . . . that I might change my . . . But not tonight, not just a few stolen minutes of passion in a garden. No, Jolette. We must . . . At least we must know more of our feelings for each other."

Jolette began to fasten her gown. Her excitement was banking, her passion cooling. With shock she realized that he was actually rejecting her and the realization brought intense humiliation and a surge of bitter anger.

"Sir, we'll never know more of each other," she said. "In a few weeks' time I won't even recall your name."

"Jolette, please! As soon as this wedding nonsense is over, I'll have much more time. I want to see you then—I must see you. Perhaps we could take a little trip, perhaps to New Orleans . . ."

"You're very sure of yourself!" she said. "Just because of a few kisses in a garden! Do you really think that I'll wait around for you or sneak off on a little trip? Do you think I'll spend my time pining for kisses stolen from a married man?"

"Stop! This is impossible!" Anthony said. "I beg you . . . Jolette, it's too late for me to . . . to cancel the wedding. Surely you can see that! But you mustn't doubt my deep feelings for you, my obsession with you? I don't want to insult you, darling. The marriage must take place, or we'll all be scandalized beyond repair. But marriages don't last forever, Jolette. No matter what vows one makes before the altar."

"A pretty speech, sir," she said.

"I love you, Jolette," he said, "in a way I've never loved another woman. Believe it or not, dammit, it's true! And believe this, also. I'll have you one day. I'll do what I must to have you, to show you my love . . . As God is my witness!"

"Oh, no, I . . . No, I don't want . . ."

His last kiss was sudden, rough and she fought against responding. But even as she cursed Anthony she parted her lips. The kiss was brief but so fierce it left her lips bruised.

Then Anthony pivoted and hurried back across the lawn to the house.

Jolette trembled. She brushed a finger across her aching lips and tried to steady herself, to collect her thoughts.

Anthony had said he loved her and wanted her—but he still intended to marry Lucinda. Jolette knew she wanted him—very much, but how far was she prepared to go to get what she wanted?

He's too sure of himself, she thought, but she was very afraid that he was rightly sure of her. Oh, no, she whispered, clasping her shaking hands. I must feel very angry and outraged.

But in truth she only felt confused and helpless.

15.

Rafaella was lost in a stupor of self-hatred at her deformity for several days after the fugitive slave woman found her. The woman, whose name was Flora, had been taught healing and she deftly stopped the bleeding and bandaged the finger and bathed the wounds to clean them.

The blank first days of weakness and half-consciousness were a blessing for Rafaella. Whenever she became conscious she howled at the horror of her mutilated body. She became hysterical and ripped the bandage and tried to bite off the hideous stub of her thumb. She tore her clothes and scratched along the jagged, red scars on her breasts until they once more became deep rivulets of rushing blood.

When she became hysterical, Flora forced a potion down her throat that sent her back into a trance-like state very near euphoria.

Helplessly, Rafaella resigned herself to the black

woman's control. She realized that the woman had moved her far back into the swamp, beyond reach of the sheriff's posse and dogs. Flora had been a fugitive in the swamp for many months, and she had come to know it well.

She was determined to make her way to freedom and, she told Rafaella, she had seen its possibility at once when she came on Rafaella and Ridgeway in their deadly duel. She had seen that the white man was dead and guessed that the white girl must have done something awful to be treated in such a way.

Once, after she could no longer hear the baying dogs in the distance, she had given Rafaella a particularly potent draught and had visited two other fugitives, slaves who had built a little cabin in another part of the swamp. From them, she had learned that a white girl from The Columns was being blamed for causing the steamboat explosion that had killed many people. And then she understood.

Rafaella lay in her drug-induced stupor for two weeks. Whenever she woke, the realization of what her life had become was as horrible as her repulsion at her body. She was a wanted criminal. She would surely be found guilty and executed if she were captured. She was totally dependent on this slave woman. Her home was a lean-to hovel deep in the swamp, her life a desperate existence of cringing from the centipedes, the snakes, the alligators, and eating herbs, roots, berries and an occasional fish or bird the woman caught.

After a few more days' time, Flora brought word that the sheriff had concluded that Rafaella had perished in the swamp. She had been declared legally dead.

Then Flora revealed her ambitions. She spoke of fleeing the swamp, of making their way downriver to New Orleans, where she could pass as Rafaella's slave and be safe, until they could escape on a ship to some place where there were no slaves. At first Rafaella refused to go, refused the chance to live again, but as she grew stronger, her emotions stirred and she swung between despair and rage.

71

One day she realized that despite her deformity, she did not want to die. She wanted to live. She would agree to Flora's plan for escape. She would travel to Italy, where she had been born, where she had lived so happily with her father until she came to this cursed America. She would somehow survive.

And then, when it was safe, she would avenge herself and her father on the Deavors! She would kill Lawton's twins—she didn't doubt that Ridgeway had lied, that the twins were Lawton's—in a way that would make them wish they had been smothered in their cribs!

At once, Rafaella became practical and cunning. She still had the rings and jewelry she had been wearing the night of the steamboat explosion, the night she had tried to smother the twins. Flora knew of a man on the Mississippi River south of Natchez who owned a small boat and who, for enough money, would take fugitive slaves to New Orleans.

Together, the two women made their way to the river and made arrangements with the captain. Rafaella darkened her face and hands with pitch and dirt. She wore a shawl over her head. They crept on board on a dark, rainy night. Rafaella paid the captain in jewelry, and after a rainy voyage, they reached New Orleans late one night and went ashore without trouble.

In New Orleans, they began at once to prepare for the ocean crossing. Rafaella went to a French-speaking doctor who bandaged her thumb and deformed finger. She bought a few decent clothes. She and Flora took a modest room and walked the streets as any white lady with her maid. Rafaella feared she might somehow be recognized, so she tinted her hair with henna and avoided the places the Deavors or their friends might visit. There was an anxious moment one night when Rafaella saw Frannie Deavors on Canal Street but the moment passed without incident.

With the money from selling her rings and the last of her jewelry to a pawnbroker in the French Quarter,

Rafaella bought passage for herself and Flora on a ship bound for Italy.

16.

The early morning was wet and cool and everyone at The Columns lost hope that the weather would improve in time for the mid-afternoon wedding. But the rain stopped at noon, the sun came out a quarter-hour later and by one o'clock the blue sky was cloudless and the temperature had climbed into the fifties.

"Deavors weather," one neighbor muttered, driving out to The Columns.

"Yes, even the heavens wouldn't cross a family like the Deavors," his wife added.

If the guests thought providence had arranged Lucinda's wedding, no one at the plantation thought so. Everyone gave thanks for the change in the weather, but both the family and the slaves knew that the decorations and details, the displays of fancy foods and liquors, the buffets and arrangements of flowers, were not miracles, but the result of many weeks of hard work.

And now the day had come. Only the last, finishing touches remained.

Lucinda retreated to her bedroom at noon to dress and compose herself, but before she could rest, she had decided she must have a talk with her daughter. She was distressed about Chessie's recent behavior toward Anthony. Chessie acted as if she didn't like Anthony at all. She was rude and unreasonable, silent and belligerent by turn, and it was enough to take the shine off Lucinda's wedding day.

Lucinda couldn't and didn't care to understand why Chessie disliked Anthony. Everyone else, she believed, found him charming and gracious.

It wasn't like Chessie, either. Perhaps Chessie was

being snobbish. Anthony, it was true, came from a poor family and had become wealthy and successful entirely by his own efforts. If it was snobbery, it did not reflect well on Chessie's own character, Lucinda felt. Or, perhaps, Chessie was jealous that her mother loves someone else as much as she loved her own family. But whatever the reason, it must stop.

I deserve this happiness, this marriage, Lucinda told herself as she paced her room. I've managed this vast plantation for almost twenty years, ever since Lawton's death. I've sacrificed myself to raise the twins, seen to their health and schooling and taken responsibility for the crops and for the hundreds of slaves. I've no regrets, but neither do I feel that I've failed Lawton or the Deavors family.

And now I'm forty-two, Lucinda thought, at the last edge of youth, and I'm desperately in love with a man who loves me. In this light, Chessie's feelings and behavior were selfish and unpardonable—and she would have no more of it! The matter would be settled this very day!

Lucinda's cheeks were pink with anger when Chessie entered the room, but the girl's head was lowered.

"Please, Mama, I know why you're upset," Chessie said at once.

"Chessie, it grieves me to scold you, but I am disappointed in you," Lucinda said.

"And I'm sorry. Please forgive me. I love you, Mama, and I promise that I'll try with all my heart to get along with Anthony," Chessie said.

The two women kissed each other, both of them so slim and well proportioned, so graceful and gentle, so like, and when Chessie left the sitting room Lucinda was satisfied. Her daughter could not have given her a better wedding present.

Clayton woke up at ten that morning, feeling like five miles of gravel road. He, Anthony and the others had continued their bachelor party until four the previous night in an elegant whore-barge on the Mississippi River. Clayton was now paying the price of mixing enormous quantities of brandy and champagne.

During the bachelor party Clayton had gained new respect for Anthony, when his future stepfather refused all the luscious mulatto whores the other men tried to entice him with, and insisted that he wanted no woman but Lucinda.

Clayton was so glad for his mother. For twenty years she had dedicated herself to her children and to running this vast plantation—not an easy task for a city girl—and now she deserved a life of her own. She and Anthony seemed ideal for each other.

Clayton soaked in a hot bath for half an hour, then had a breakfast of eggs, ham and grits sent up to his room. He managed to eat most of the grits but his stomach was too queasy for the ham and eggs.

As he dressed, he paused from time to time to pace the large room, or stare out at the slaves working behind the house. He told himself that despite all the excitement and adventure of going to the Continent, he would miss The Columns. And he vowed that when he returned, he would become the best master the plantation had ever had. He only hoped he would soon meet the beautiful girl with dark hair he had thought about so much lately.

As he sat down to pull on his boots, he glanced over at the large oak cabinet that held his collections of antique guns and toy soldiers.

The guns were his special pride. He had collected them for years, since the time when he was too small to pick up the heavier ones, ancient Moorish rifles inlaid with ivory and long-barreled Italian dueling pistols decorated with silver and gold. He had sought them out all over the East when he was in college, as well as in Mobile, Memphis and New Orleans. The dealers in these Southern cities knew him well, and always informed him when they received a gun they thought would interest him.

Clayton pulled on his boots and walked over to the cabinet. He looked forward to buying many more beautiful old guns on the Continent.

Though he had stopped buying soldiers some years back, he was still proud of this collection. He had played with cheaper soldiers when he was a child, had fought them in battles on dirt mounts in the back yard, for hours at a time. But these soldiers had never seen a speck of dirt. They had been purchased in expensive stores in the cities. They were handmade. Their arms and legs moved. Their faces were finished to perfection in detail.

There were troops of fierce Abyssinian warriors on horseback, disciplined Prussian soldiers, red-jacketed British dragoons, and, most interesting of all to Clayton, a company of ancient Roman infantry.

Clayton went to the mirror and brushed his hair. The dissipation that showed in his face worried him, almost disgusted him. He thought of the soldiers, the lives their real-life counterparts led. It was a life of discipline, of a kind of obedience and order he had never known, in addition to the danger and glory of battle.

He told himself he should have spent some time with a regiment, as wealthy young British men still did. He almost hoped war came, almost hoped the Southern states seceded from the Union.

He would be among the first to volunteer. He would raise a company of local men. He would have to wear a uniform then, to be not only brave, and a leader, but follow orders, submit himself to a discipline he felt would serve him well for the rest of his life.

Clayton finished brushing his hair. He decided he would order a lunch of cold chicken and whiskey, then go for a long ride and take a swim before the wedding.

Lucinda and Anthony were married at two o'clock in the front parlor, stripped of its usual furniture and decorated with masses of pink-and-white flowers and white candles. Only the family and a few of their closest neighbors attended the ceremony, although half the county had been invited for the buffet and reception to follow.

Chessie and Joleen stood up as bridesmaids for Lucinda, and Anthony, who had no kin nearby, had asked Carlo Roccalini to serve as his best man. The simple ceremony was performed by the Very Reverend John Kilbourne of the Benton Presbyterian Church and the Reverend's daughter Lucille played two hymns on the antique spinet that had been in the Deavors family for generations.

Lucinda had never looked lovelier or more serene. She wore a simple gown of ivory *peau de soie* satin in the latest style with a voluminous hoopskirt and lace sleeves. Chessie and Joleen, as well as Lucinda's friends who attended her, wore matching gowns—all styled with lace over silk in fragile pastels chosen to suit each lady's particular complexion.

Clayton gave his mother away.

After the ceremony the close friends who had witnessed it strolled in the gardens at The Columns as the carriages bearing the other guests began to roll up the house road. In all, nearly four hundred guests attended the reception, danced to the music of two Natchez orchestras and helped themselves from the long tables laden with meats and cakes and punches.

Waiters moved among the guests constantly, offering food on silver trays and refilling glasses with champagne or one of the potent whiskey punches. As darkness fell, slaves lit candles that had been set on poles around the edges of the garden and in lanterns hanging from the trees. By nine, the guests were intoxicated. The wooden dancing platforms in the front yard were crowded.

It was a wonderful party, everyone agreed, and it lasted until midnight, but long before that Lucinda and Anthony had slipped away upstairs.

Lucinda had given more thought and effort to the gown she would wear on her wedding night than she had to her wedding dress itself. More than ever before, she wanted to look young and seductive, beautiful and provocative, but now she fretted as she sat in her dressing room brushing her long auburn hair.

Lucinda had not made love to any man in twenty years and she felt an intense sexual excitement she could not deny. Anthony was so handsome, so young and confident, and she loved him desperately. But her fears were as strong as her excitement, the fear that she would disappoint her new husband, that she would not be young or beautiful enough, that she would not know how to please him.

Lucinda set down her brush and studied herself in the mirror. She saw her blue eyes, her shining auburn hair, but saw also the network of tiny wrinkles around her eyes, wrinkles that she had come to hate and fear in the past few months.

She heard Anthony stirring in the bedroom. She was taking too long, she must hurry. She stood up and nearly blushed as she stared at herself in her nightgown of pale green satin. The gown hugged her slim body so tightly that her nipples showed clearly—curved in at her waist, hung on the bias to outline her hips and thighs, and was short enough to show her ankles.

Perhaps it's too daring, she thought nervously. Perhaps she was immodest. Yet she was determined to let Anthony know that she was a sensual woman who enjoyed and expected physical pleasure.

Slowly, she walked into the bedroom. Anthony was sprawled on the bed in a maroon lounging robe. When she entered he rose and moved toward her, then paused. There was nothing subtle about the way he looked up and down her body. Her cheeks were hot. She knew she was blushing.

"Lucinda!" he whispered. He came to her quickly. "You're so beautiful . . . so beautiful. I've wanted you since the first moment I saw you, darling. And tonight you look so . . . so incredibly provocative! Where did you find that wicked nightgown?"

Anthony slid his hands down the fine satin to her waist. Lucinda trembled.

"My seamstress made it," she said. "Just for you, darling. I want so much to please you. I love you, Anthony."

"And I love you, Lucinda," he said.

He pressed his lips against her mouth and she moved her hungry body against his. They kissed passionately, then he picked her up and carried her to bed.

"I've waited so long," Anthony said.

He took a bottle from a silver bucket on the bedstand and poured champagne into two long-stemmed glasses. Playfully, they kissed and sipped champagne as, with one hand, Anthony caressed her breasts until her nipples became hard and her entire body glowed.

"You're so lovely," Anthony murmured. He buried his lips in Lucinda's soft hair and teased her ear with his tongue. He praised her breasts and thighs and vagina, while his hands stroked and explored. Lucinda moaned with pleasure and passion.

"Yes, darling . . ." she whispered.

Anthony poured more champagne. She drank a second glass, another, a fourth. The champagne and his voice and hands ignited her—she became bolder than she could imagine being and her love talk became as intimate as his, her tongue and hands as daring as she undressed him and kissed and stroked his body, touching his thighs and penis with shaking fingers.

Anthony was fully erect when he slipped off her nightgown.

"Oh, Anthony, please, darling, hurry," Lucinda begged.

17.

Chessie's whole frame trembled as she listened to her mother and Anthony through their bedroom door. She went hot, then cold, and her legs felt so weak she put her hand against the wall for support. Her mother's voice was low and guttural, and she moaned and cried out and said words Chessie had never before heard spoken aloud.

Chessie's heart fluttered and she glanced nervously down the dim corridor. No one was there. The blood throbbed at her temples and she felt sick with guilt, but she bent down and looked through the keyhole.

"Come inside me, Anthony!" her mother was begging. Chessie saw it all, saw her mother spread her thighs, saw Anthony take his stiff penis in his hand. He wasn't gentle. Lucinda whined and her hands flew out to her sides and her nails dug into the sheets as she locked her legs around Anthony's body and he thrust his penis into her vagina.

Chessie stumbled back from the door. Her stomach churned. She nearly vomited. Dizzy, she fought for balance, then turned and ran, trailing her hand along the wall to keep from falling.

Back in her own room, she collapsed on her bed, overwhelmed by guilt and horror at what she had done. She had heard Myrtis cry out and had gone to look in on the girl. On her way back, she had heard a far different sound from her mother's room and given in to a feverish and irresistible impulse to see what was happening.

Chessie rolled over and curled up against herself. Could she ever forget? Could she ever get the sight out of her mind? She shivered and sweat cascaded down her face.

Her mother had begged Anthony to invade her body with his swollen penis. It was too dreadful! She hated it all! She hated herself, her mother, Anthony!

And worst of all, she realized, she hated Clayton, who could do that . . . had done that . . . to any woman he chose.

Chessie staggered to her feet and splashed cold water on her face. Surely she was going mad! She was becoming obsessed with sex, anyone's sex.

What kind of a girl was she? To watch others making love—her own mother—to think of her brother at such a moment, and worse, to find her body responding. For respond it had, with her face flushed, her breathing labored, her nipples tender. It was a fascination mixed with repulsion and disgust.

Chessie forgot her mother and Anthony but she could not stop thinking of her brother.

Soon, however, her frightening new feelings began to drain her little remaining strength and she sank into bed. She lay on her back, staring up at the canopy without seeing it, and a total exhaustion numbed her body.

Chessie did not know how long she had been lying there when she heard someone moving in the hallway.

Fearfully, Chessie scrambled up and crept to her door. She listened. There was silence. Then she heard the sound again. Someone was walking down the hall and had trod on those old, creaky boards that never seemed to get fixed.

Chessie hesitated, then opened her door just a bit.

Anthony was creeping down the hall, leaving her mother's room. It was so late! Where was he going?

Chessie ran to the window. The sky was faintly light. In a moment she saw Anthony come out of the house. He cut around the barn and stables as though headed for the slave quarters.

Chessie was stunned and angry. Was it possible? After making love to her mother, was Anthony sneaking off to the quarters for a rendezvous with some black woman?

She was horrified and outraged. Her first impulse was to dress and follow him and confront them. She would see that the woman was severely punished, that Anthony's treachery was exposed!

But then she stopped. It would only hurt her mother. She must never tell her mother, it was too awful— he was awful. Choking back tears, Chessie went to bed to spend a sleepless night, shamed and filled with an impotent anger.

18.

Deep in the swamp, over the echoing calls of night birds and the cacophony of frogs and crickets, came the mournful sounds of two hundred black Africans crying, praying and vomiting into their blood-soaked gags. One of them tried to tear the gag from his mouth with feeble, fettered hands. Anthony lashed the man to the ground, then cursed and drank brandy from a flask. He glanced at the silhouette of the ship moored at the Deavors landing and at the last file of Africans who were being forced ashore down the gangway.

Anthony stepped over to a quivering, bleeding mass of black flesh lying in the mud.

"Dammit, Guese," he said to a swarthy, fat man. "I told you to subdue the wretched niggers, not beat them to death."

"They so wild, some of 'em, ain't nothin' to do but whip shit out of 'em," Guese said. "Hell, like always, you done lost half your niggers on the trip over from Africa. What's another dead one now?"

"Christ, he's a sizeable profit!" Anthony said.

And he's a man, even if he is a nigger, he thought, but did not say. Such sentiment would be lost on Guese, he knew, and he was as responsible as the rest of the poor bastards involved in this business, even if he was smarter than the rest of them. He was smart enough to be at the top, and honest enough to know that he, too, would beat one of the Negroes to death, if he had to. He poured down more brandy.

"Well, this here one'll never fetch a dollar on the block the shape he's in," Guese said. "Shall I drag him into the swamp and throw him into a bog?"

Anthony nodded. He drank more brandy and wiped his mouth with the back of his hand. "And make sure none of them gets their gags out."

There was a band of pale pink light in the eastern sky, toward the house and the quarters. Anthony cursed. What wretched luck—to have the goddamn ship arrive on his wedding night! He had thought he would never get away from Lucinda. Surely after all that champagne and sex, she would sleep soundly until he returned.

And he could only hope none of the Deavors slaves took it into his head to go prowling around tonight. As a precaution, Anthony had sent two men wearing blood-smeared masks to stand guard up near the edge of the quarters.

Anthony had been pleased to find out that the slaves had an ignorant superstition about the swamp—it played into his hands, but recently one of them, Bernard, had wandered into the forbidden part of the swamp and he had obviously seen something there. If Bernard had talked, that day with Chessie and the patrol, Anthony would have been ruined. But once the damn nigger was locked in the slave jail it had been easy enough to kill him and make it appear he had died from his wounds.

Easy enough, Anthony thought. He had done it himself, and it had been the first time. And here he was again tonight, supervising the beatings, seeing these men die right before his eyes. When they died on the ship from Africa, that was one thing. But it sickened him to see it here.

The sky was lighter now.

"Dammit, move those niggers into the swamp!" Anthony said.

He shivered. The morning was damp and cold. He drank more brandy and remembered the sight and feel of his new bride in bed. She had been passionate, surprisingly passionate, but he thought of the much younger, much sexier Jolette and felt a stirring in his loins. It had been years since he'd seen a more desirable woman than Jolette. Perhaps he was half obsessed with her. He wanted her badly, and he was determined to have her, but he cautioned himself. Haste and recklessness could cost him dearly.

Everything was going so well, going according to plan. He had fulfilled his ambition. He was married to one of the state's wealthiest, most influential women. She loved him and would do anything he asked. He would ask everything, in time. In time, he would take The Columns from Clayton.

His slave-smuggling business would prosper. He would no longer have to take dangerous risks to find a safe spot for the unloading. He would no longer have to pay ruinous bribes to landowners and corrupt officials. Now he had a hidden landing area no one could touch. He had the cover of The Columns and the Deavors name.

Despite his weariness, despite his distaste at the hideous process of unloading, Anthony's spirits improved. Anything was better than being poor. He would pay any price to have an enormous amount of money, enough money to be proud and live lavishly, enough money to be able to afford the most expensive doctors and surgeons and cures if he were ever afflicted with a crippling or debilitating illness.

Bitter and guilty memories nearly formed themselves among his thoughts but he cursed and refused to consider them. That was the past. It was far away. No one here in Mississippi would ever know.

"To hell with it!" he muttered.

And to hell with all those proud and blue-blooded planters who sat in gazebos and condemned slave-traders. Soon he would pay off the last of the high-interest loans that had bought his ships. He would be socially prominent. And very wealthy.

And that was all that mattered.

The last of the slaves had been moved off the ship and into the swamp. Anthony spoke to the ship's captain, making plans to meet him three days later in New Orleans. Then he called the two guards and followed them along a trail into the swamp.

The men held their lanterns carefully and moved slowly down the narrow, dark trail, feeling their way with anxious hands and suffering from thorn-vines and low-slung limbs that left them scratched and bleeding by the time they reached the camp that Guese had set up a mile inland from the river.

There, the Africans were collapsed in a muddy clearing that Anthony's men had hacked out two weeks earlier. It was work on this secret clearing that Anthony suspected Bernard had seen. A dozen white men with rifles and whips stood guard over the Negroes, ready to crush any signs of rebellion. But fear and pain had weakened them in body and spirit and the shackled slaves huddled together, heads bowed, shivering and crooning.

"I must return to my bride," Anthony told Guese. "Have this lot of niggers fed up and tamed enough to put on the block in two weeks. Then get them into town and sell them. And Guese, I don't want to lose any more because of your lash."

"You know my way with niggers," Guese said. "They'll be ready in two weeks. The whole lot. Like always. And I'll take them in there in small bunches so it won't raise too much suspicion."

"Be damned careful about runaways and any prowling niggers from The Columns," Anthony said. "Keep guards out all the time."

Anthony stalked out of the clearing. He cursed as he fought the vines and limbs that reached for him as he held up his lantern and followed an extension of the trail that came out nearer the plantation house.

A hundred yards farther he came on two of Guese's men and half a dozen Africans, some already dead from the lashings and rifle blows that had shattered their skulls and cracked their eyes open, others half alive and squirming in the mud as their shackles were hitched to a horse.

As Anthony watched, the men dragged the Africans into a bog, unhitched the horse and the Africans began to sink, weighted by their heavy chains.

Anthony shuddered. It was an obscene business. He hurried on, reminding himself of his profits.

19.

Chessie stood on the deck of the *Siracusa,* which had brought the twins on the long voyage from New Orleans. Palermo lay just ahead, bathed in pink-and-gold morning light. It was a fascinating and beautiful view. High mountains encircled the city in a natural amphitheater and the tallest and most dramatic of these was the bare crag of Mount Pellegrino. Chessie was thrilled. *"La Concha d'Oro,"* she whispered reverently. None of her books had done justice to the beauty of the panorama of sea, sky and sunlit city framed by the "golden shell" of mountains.

Along the marina Chessie could see small ships and fishing boats bobbing up and down against a backdrop of villas and churches and *palazzi,* all set among palm trees and drenched with red-and-purple bougainvillaea. Excitedly, she realized that she had truly arrived—she was truly in an exotic place.

The crossing had been interesting enough, despite some rough seas and the tiresome sameness of shipboard food, but when Chessie was helped down into the longboat that would take passengers ashore, she was thankful to be leaving the *Siracusa* and full of curiosity about this new city, and all the adventures that awaited.

"What shall we do first? What about customs? How shall we find Don Roccalini?" Chessie asked Clayton as they neared the shore in the longboat. She began to worry.

And when they disembarked Chessie's worries became fears as she and Clayton were surrounded by a swarm of dark-complexioned men and women offering them carriages, help with customs, and hawking leather goods and gold and silver items they half concealed under long coats.

One old man spat and touched Chessie's hair and showed his stumps of teeth in a hideous smile as he babbled, *"Bella, bellissima . . ."* Chessie shrieked as she lurched away and Clayton shoved the man back and stood ready to fight him.

Suddenly there was a stir in the crowd and people muttered as they cleared a path for an elegantly dressed old man with gleaming black eyes in a pinched face.

Don Mario Roccalini had come to meet them personally, accompanied by eight servants and three carriages. A customs official hovered behind the don, nodding at his every command and in less than five minutes Chessie and Clayton had climbed into an open carriage which bore two crossed lilies, the Roccalini coat of arms, on its side, and settled comfortably on the purple velvet cushions.

Chessie had wanted Torine, the slave girl who was accompanying them, to ride in her carriage, as she would have in Mississippi, but she saw Torine being ushered into one of the carriages that followed with their trunks.

"Normally we'd travel along the Via Toledo to my villa," Don Roccalini said. "But parts of the Toledo are being repaired so we must drive through a few wretched streets, I'm afraid. But, please, pay no attention to them. They've nothing to do with the Palermo you'll come to know."

The carriage turned away from the bay and rumbled

into a residential quarter. The streets were so narrow—
no more than four yards wide—that Chessie could look
into the dark houses they passed and feel as if she
could reach through the dim doorways and touch the
faces of the pale, wide-eyed children and solemn wom-
en in black who stared out.

The smell of waste was sickening and Chessie saw
beggars and cripples scavenging for garbage amid rats
and cadaverous dogs. Chessie was sickened by the
stench, then, gasping, her nostrils were assaulted by the
pungent smell of frying garlic and peppers. The streets
were airless and stuffy. No breeze from the harbor or
hills reached into the squalid streets, no breath of
hope, it seemed to Chessie.

But when she looked to Clayton for his reaction, she
saw that her brother was fascinated by the sights.

Don Roccalini inquired for the health of his American relatives and politely asked for details of the twins'
journey, but Chessie realized that he was somewhat distracted. He glanced constantly and apprehensively from
the carriage.

When Clayton asked him a question about farming
he replied, "Oh, yes, we have our plantations here, too,
and, for all practical purposes, our niggers, as I believe you call them. Our peasants, sir, are more trouble
than slaves, let me tell you . . ."

Chessie noticed a cluster of grim, shabbily dressed
men standing on a street corner. There was no mistaking the hostility with which they watched the carriage passing. A short, stocky man with huge black
eyes gave a sudden, sharp gesture with his fist and,
though Chessie didn't know exactly what it meant, she
knew it was obscene and insulting. From the next
corner a man shouted, *"Bastardi!"*

Don Roccalini muttered under his breath. He leaned
forward and spoke to his driver. Chessie saw that
both Don Roccalini and the driver carried pistols. She
glanced at Clayton who smiled as though to say, Don't
worry, everything will be all right.

During the sea voyage, Chessie had heard Clayton

and other men on the *Siracusa* discussing rumors of trouble in Sicily. They had heard that the island had been ruled for many years by a French-Italian aristocracy called the Bourbons and that most Sicilians disliked their foreign rulers and wanted to be free. She knew that the Roccalinis themselves were Bourbons and considered themselves to be more French than Italian. But Chessie had been assured that there was no real trouble, in fact.

Chessie had little interest in the politics of her own country, much less in the politics of Italy. She was interested in art, in doing a lot of sketching, and she liked history. She had enjoyed reading about ancient Sicily, when the island was ruled by the Phoenicians, the Greeks, the Mohammedans, the Spanish. From what she had heard and read, she had thought of Sicily as poor but quite pleasant, sunny and rather exotic, with enormous cathedrals and vast, romantic Greek ruins. She realized she knew nothing of present-day Sicily.

"Your distress is obvious, Miss Deavors," Don Roccalini said. "Please don't worry or be disturbed by this wretched quarter. You're quite safe with me. And in a moment we'll be out . . . Ah, here we are . . ."

They turned onto a broad boulevard fronted with large, rambling palaces and churches. The boulevard was lined with tall palm trees and the air was sweet with orange blossoms. Chessie's spirits rose at once. Women in elegant carriages and men on horseback waved and called out to Don Roccalini.

Chessie admired the wide, handsome boulevard and the lush, fragrant gardens they passed. And over all loomed the crown-shaped Heights of Mount Pellegrino, toward which they were heading.

Chessie had seen a troop of mounted soldiers in the last block and now they were passing a company of infantry. Farther along she saw a company of dragoons with drawn sabers. The dragoon captain, a broad-shouldered man with a huge, black mustache, bowed to Don Roccalini.

"Why are there so many soldiers?" Chessie asked. "Those terrible men we passed near the docks, now all these soldiers . . ."

Don Roccalini shook his head. "In Sicily, we, too, have our John Browns, as I was telling Clayton earlier. Self-serving brigands, men who would stir up our peasants . . . our niggers, if you will. The latest one is called Garibaldi. And like your soldiers under . . . What was his name? . . . Colonel Lee? Well, our troops will make short work of the brigands. Don't trouble yourself, please. If you're distressed I must consider my hospitality and my protection inadequate."

"Oh, I'm not distressed, sir," Chessie said quickly. "Merely curious . . . and so excited and pleased to be here!"

Chessie had told the truth. She was excited but she was also rather disturbed. The dirty, narrow streets had oppressed her, and she could not help but be alarmed by the presence of so many soldiers. Of course, it's all new and strange, she told herself, and she must try to understand it.

She felt better as the carriage passed through a park Don Roccalini called the English Gardens. It was laid out symmetrically with yuccas, palms and flowering tropical plants, and as Chessie was admiring them, a man on a brown mare rode up and trotted beside the carriage.

"Good morning, Don Roccalini," the rider said. "Sir . . . Miss . . ."

Chessie looked up at a man with eyes as blue as the sky and curly reddish-blond hair. He was strikingly unlike any of the dark-haired, dark-complexioned Sicilians she had seen, but though handsome, she sensed a not altogether attractive arrogance that hinted at mockery in his self-confident expression and easy smile.

"Good morning, Signore Settimo," Don Roccalini muttered.

The don looked away quickly, without making any introductions. Who is he? Chessie wondered.

Her question was answered when the man rode away.

"Carlo Settimo!" Don Roccalini said. He shook his head. "What a disappointment to his parents! The Settimos are one of our finest families, but Carlo went north, to Piedmont and to Paris, and he's come home with . . . I won't mince words! With treacherous thoughts and ideas! As for his morals . . . I can't mention them in front of a lady."

Exhausted by his tirade, the don sank back into his seat, his chest heaving with anger and his exertion. Neither of the twins spoke.

A few moments later, the carriage turned a corner. They were climbing now, rose-gray Mount Pellegrino looming closer. Chessie was enchanted by the lovely villas they passed, and tried to discern elements of Spanish, French and Arabic influence in their architecture. Squat domes of churches and towers rose between the villas, many of which had lovely walled gardens, vineyards, and groves of lemon and orange trees.

The carriage turned up a winding street, then onto a narrow avenue lined with royal palms and squat cactus plants. Behind them were trellises of red-purple bougainvillaea. In the distance was an enormous villa of faded pink brick with a red tile roof.

"This is my Palermo estate," the don said. *"Benvenuto* . . . Welcome to Villa Roccalini."

They approached the villa through a huge park with curved, pebbled drives among cactus, palmetto and rose gardens. The park was filled with gardeners, all of whom rose to their feet and bowed as the don's carriage approached.

"Please look behind you," the don said.

Chessie turned around. Behind them lay the stunning panorama of the *Concha d'Oro,* the quay and the blue Tyrrhenian Sea, the distant hills and, far behind them, to the east, the outline of a massive, snow-capped mountain.

"Mount Etna," the don said. "A hundred miles distant. Beautiful . . . and dangerous. From time to time, the volcano explodes. But don't worry. It hasn't erupted for many years."

The carriage passed through a high arched gateway and into a vast courtyard filled with tall marble columns and colonnades that seemed to stretch back to infinity. Beyond was another garden surrounded by the wings of the three-story villa.

A dozen men were working in the courtyard and inner garden. Several others, bowing, stood on the stone steps as the carriage pulled up.

Chessie was helped from the carriage and escorted inside, where still other servants were working, then up a huge staircase to her bedroom on the second floor, a magnificent room whose cedar-beamed ceiling had gold-flecked angels in the recesses.

As several maids bustled in with her luggage, Chessie wondered if the Roccalinis had as many servants as the Deavors had slaves.

20.

Chessie stood on the balcony outside her room and gripped the wrought-iron railing with tight fists as she succumbed to the terrible, guilty thoughts of Clayton that had finally overwhelmed her.

Clayton's behavior toward her had changed drastically on the *Siracusa*. Not only did he no longer flaunt his affairs in front of her, but he went to great lengths to hide them altogether. Chessie had been surprised, then grateful for this change.

Yet, to her further surprise, Chessie found that the change annoyed her. She became petulant when she could not know for certain which of the women passengers were Clayton's lovers.

Chessie had lain awake at night in her bed, listening to the waves lapping the sides of the ship, and imagined she could hear the sounds of passionate lovemaking from Clayton's bedroom, which was beyond a sitting room they shared.

One night, after an evening that included kisses from a handsome Englishman, kisses that had stirred her and sent exciting, unusual feelings throbbing through her body, Chessie had crept from her bed and crossed the sitting room to Clayton's door.

She had heard the same sounds she had heard behind her mother's door and quickly surrendered to the impulse to look through the keyhole. Kneeling, she had watched for long moments, paralyzed with guilt and jealousy, and she had seen everything: seen the red-headed woman's flushed, naked body, her large dark-pink nipples, seen her twin brother in full erection, then writhing between the woman's thighs.

And she had seen Clayton's handsome, scarlet face. He had been looking directly at the door . . . at her . . . And it was her own face she saw, distorted by passion . . . And for one terrifying moment, she was both of them, Clayton and the woman, and she felt their passion as if it were her own. Chessie had felt her head spin, felt her nipples harden and her thighs open and she knew that in some vicarious way she had been there with her twin, with each of his women, as though she and Clayton had been lovers . . .

Chessie opened her eyes. A convulsion shook her body. Her stomach tightened. She felt nauseous.

Her fingers curled around the wrought-iron rail. She bit her lips together. She found it almost impossible to continue with the memory, yet, now that it had surfaced, she was determined to deal with it.

Yes, she told herself, she had to confront all these awful memories . . . and then forget them forever. But the words she needed to describe what she was doing, what she had done, were so sinful, so disgusting, and so damning that she felt her brain would burst with the effort.

What she had done was unforgiveable! She longed to get inside her own pounding head and scratch away those memories, those sexual images and fantasies of Clayton! She choked back a sob. She clenched her teeth. She blinked . . . and the images were gone!

It was such a relief that she vowed never to let those images return, no matter what the effort cost her. She could not live with them. She would never, ever, be so bold and wicked again.

Even if she had to ignore Clayton, to jeopardize their strong, supportive love, to force a coolness into their relationship. She might never feel close to her brother again, but at least she wouldn't feel so damned!

"I swear to God I will!" she mumbled. "I'll stop . . . Or I'll run away from him, never see him again . . ."

Chessie heard noises outside. She turned her back to the door and brushed at her eyes as Torine bustled in, followed by the Roccalini maids.

"Time to get dressed for lunch, Miss Chessie," Torine said. "From what I can understand of this foreign chatterin', that don, he's not one to be kept waitin' for his food, not even by guests."

"All right, I'll get dressed," Chessie said wearily.

"I hope you don't intend to wear that same old thing you got laid out on the bed, Miss Chessie," Torine said. "Lord, they done worked their fingers to the bone back at The Columns makin' new clothes for you, and half of 'em you ain't even put on yet."

"Oh, Torine, I don't care what I wear!" Chessie said. "You know that. Now, please, I'm tired. Don't scold me about some dress."

She and Torine had carried on a running argument about her dresses and her lack of concern for her toilette all the way from New Orleans, but she was too upset and too exhausted to continue the argument now.

"Well, wear an old gunnysack then, for all I care," Torine said.

"I just might," Chessie mumbled as she headed for the bathroom where two maids were filling a tiny tub with hot water.

Don Roccalini presided over a seven-course lunch served by six maids. The meal was eaten in a long, bare dining room hung with enormous, fading paintings of hunting dogs attacking wild boars and deer, and of pheasant and quail, hare and rabbits, on wooden tables stained with their blood.

The don's wife and only son had died a year earlier, of cholera, and his remaining children, all daughters, were married and lived outside Palermo. To meet his American guests the don had invited a dozen relatives to lunch and, from the way they ate and drank the wine, Chessie wondered if they had eaten in a week.

Chessie almost wished that she had let Torine bully her into taking some trouble with her toilette, for all the ladies present were elaborately dressed and coiffed. One of them, a cousin named Maria Cristina, seemed to have been invited particularly to keep Chessie company, for the voluptuous, dark-haired young woman took her place by Chessie's side and chattered constantly as if they were already the best of friends.

"What a long voyage you've had!" Maria Cristina marveled, and Chessie felt adventurous. Maria Cristina had only traveled as far as Salerno, never even to Rome, and yet Chessie sensed that the vivacious young woman was more sophisticated and experienced than she, in most other aspects of life. Maria Cristina's laugh was silvery and she fanned herself gracefully with a painted ivory fan as she chatted and whispered to Chessie, explaining to her who all the cousins were and who was married to whom.

After eating a rich fish soup and mounds of glistening macaroni, the other guests were more inclined to conversation. They all seemed interested in life in Natchez and everyone inquired for the health of the Roccalini family members there. Spirits rose as they drank glass after glass of a heavy red wine and by the time the zabaglione, a sweet dessert of whipped egg whites and Marsala wine, was served, talk had become gay and animated and they forgot America and discussed affairs in Sicily.

A gray-haired aunt with more wrinkles than a prune chattered about the return of Carlo Settimo as she spooned in the zabaglione. "Oh, yes, I understand fathers for fifty miles around locked up their daughters when they heard he was returning from France," she said.

Chessie recalled the blue-eyed, arrogant young man on horseback. He is handsome, she thought.

"He's a devil!" Maria Cristina said with obvious delight.

Everyone agreed that young Settimo was surely headed for hell and damnation in the next life and arrest by the authorities in this one if he didn't reform his morals and his politics.

By the time a second helping of zabaglione was served, the American guests were all but ignored in a flurry of local gossip.

Chessie gathered that apart from Carlo Settimo, the Roccalini relatives were most interested in gossip about a certain Countess Corloni of Rome, who had visited Palermo the previous week. The countess was described as beautiful, ruthless and ambitious. Everyone knew of the woman's determination to marry her only child, a daughter named Gianna, to a prince.

"She married far above her station herself," the wrinkled aunt said. "Poor old Count Corloni lasted less than a year after that marriage, but I expect he lived long enough to regret his choice."

"Yes, the countess was a commoner," a plump, red-haired cousin said. "And not even Italian. English, I think. Though she may have been American . . ."

"Yes, American," Maria Cristina said. "Definitely a commoner . . ."

Chessie glanced at Clayton. She wondered if the Roccalinis had forgotten that their guests were American.

"An American? Well, then, perhaps that explains her curious and ill-mannered habit of never removing her gloves . . ."

"Enough of this gossip!" Don Roccalini said. He slammed his hand down on the table. Glasses tinkled and some wine spilled onto the linen. "We have guests present, may I remind you. It's time for coffee. And today, I think, a good bottle of an old Sauterne."

A half hour later Chessie, a bit dizzy with wine, went up to her room for the siesta that she was told was a never-varying afternoon ritual in Sicily.

To her great relief there were no disturbing images or memories of Clayton. As she drifted off to sleep, though, thoughts of Carlo Settimo filled her head.

21.

The following evening Don Roccalini held a ball to welcome his American guests and introduce them to Palermo society. Maria Cristina had offered Chessie her special hairdresser, but Chessie refused to go to such trouble and endured only a hurried brushing by Torine. Chessie also paid little attention to choosing her gown, despite Torine's scolding, and selected a modest blue silk with white ribbons. She wore no jewelry.

But as she and Maria Cristina descended the staircase together at half past ten, Chessie had to admit that the Sicilian girl looked beautiful, and she knew that the heads turning at their entrance were turned by her. Maria Cristina had twined her long, dark hair with pink-and-lavender ribbons that fell to her waist. She wore an elaborate gown of silver lace threaded with tiny flowers and more pink ribbons. Silver rings dangled from her ears, around her neck was a strand of huge baroque pearls, and she moved gracefully, confident of her beauty, expectant of the admiration she deserved.

The ball had been in progress for an hour but neither Don Roccalini nor the guests of honor were expected to descend to the main floor until it was well under way. Now the don and Clayton greeted Chessie and Maria Cristina at the bottom of the stairs and escorted them into the main salon where an orchestra was playing a polka. Chandeliers set with dozens of candles blazed from the ceiling and walls, illuminating the tapestries and fading frescoes of fauns and nymphs and satyrs.

As soon as they entered the ballroom the excitement began. Chessie was introduced to so many people that she stopped trying to remember names. Everyone was welcoming her and she received many invitations to dance polkas, waltzes and mazurkas on the patterned white-and-black marble floor. She smiled and danced and chatted, declined offers of whiskey, brandy, Marsala and champagne from liveried servants, and sipped an occasional glass of punch to satisfy her thirst.

The ball seemed grander and more formal than balls at home, Chessie observed. Partly it was the setting: so elegant and austere. Chessie had never seen such tapestries and frescoes and reckoned them to be hundreds of years old. She was impressed, too, by the abundance of gold—the chandeliers and mirror frames glinted with it and an immense golden punch bowl in the shape of a swan stood in the center of the gold-and-mahogany buffet table. The music was the same as at home, though, and Chessie felt familiar dancing.

When the orchestra paused to rest, some couples strolled in the cool gardens, some of the men retired to an anteroom to play whist, a card game that fascinated the Sicilians, and most of the women sank onto satin-covered sofas and chairs to eat ices and fruit tarts. The women's talk, Chessie noticed, was quite shocking and laced with the double-entendres the otherwise modest Sicilian women seemed to love. But just like Mississippi women, what they most loved was gossip, as Chessie had already observed.

They gossiped about the love affairs of high-born women, about proud but impoverished noblemen who tried to keep up their image by retrieving their finery from pawnbrokers before a grand ball. The most fascinating story, to Chessie, concerned an aging countess who believed that fresh ass' milk was essential in preventing wrinkles and who had a servant lead an ass behind her, no matter where she went.

There was also more talk of the Roman, Countess

Corloni. One tiny, elegant lady was particularly upset to report that the countess' personal maid was "far too haughty for a nigger . . ."

The music started again. Maria Cristina seemed inexhaustible, but Chessie declined an invitation to dance and took a few minutes to catch her breath as she joined a group of Bourbons around Don Roccalini.

Chessie learned that from time to time the Sicilians had tried to overthrow their foreign rulers to unite their country and govern themselves. They had never been successful, Chessie assumed from the talk, but in 1848 there had been an uprising during which the Sicilian insurgents held Palermo for a short time before being reconquered by Bourbon troops.

It was of this brief period that the Bourbons now talked, their faces growing redder, their voices angrier. Chessie listened avidly and shuddered at the tales of the insurgents' brutality, of the slaughter of nobles and government officials, of *palazzi* being burned by mobs of screaming peasants.

"And now this murderous rabble wants to rise up again!" a Palermo judge said. "While the brigand, Garibaldi, waits up north in Piedmont, ready to come down and invade Sicily, to arm the peasants and lead the slaughter."

The situation reminded Chessie of John Brown's raid and his plan to arm slaves and cause an uprising in the South. Through the comparison, she understood the anger and fear of these Bourbons, although she saw a difference: the Bourbons, though entrenched, were foreigners, unlike the people in Natchez. And as bad as Sicilian peasants might be, they were neither slaves nor Negroes.

"Of course, our troops would crush these invading dogs!" Don Roccalini said. "We could run our own affairs here so well if those outside agitators would leave us alone! We know how to handle our people. This talk of invasion and uprising is already causing serious discontent. Why, half my vineyards and sulphur mines lie untended because men have run off into the hills to play at brigand and soldier! They're loafers and rabble up there. Just look at their insolent bonfires!"

Chessie glanced over her shoulder. She was startled and frightened by the fires that cut the darkness of the hills. She could see at least a dozen fires and they seemed so close.

"Of course, Don Roccalini," a banker said, "our troops can crush this Garibaldi if he invades Sicily. But what if there's a general uprising of the people here? Tens of thousands of them? What if we look at the hills one night soon and see hundreds of bonfires? Not only will we be in danger, but the economy will be ruined."

"They will all be crushed!" Don Roccalini said. "No matter what the cost! The social order must be preserved at any cost. And the wretched peasants are one thing, sir, but what I most detest are those few Bourbons who seem willing to betray their own class!" The don paused and lowered his voice. "And to think, because of my affection for a family, I have to entertain one of them in my own home!"

"I assume you refer to Carlo Settimo," the judge said. "He's done nothing but spread seditious talk about Bourbon excesses and the rights of the peasants since he returned. Yet, I don't believe him. I suspect he's only mocking us and trying to seem audacious in front of the ladies. A man of such weak character and low morals is unlikely to care for anyone's welfare."

"Indeed!" the don said. "He speaks only to scandalize. But mark me, his words may soon land him in serious difficulty. Look how he preens and prances in his fine Paris clothes, while his cousins prepare to enlist in the king's service."

The don had gestured as he spoke. Chessie looked toward a group of women, including Maria Cristina, clustered around Carlo Settimo. As she watched, several young ladies were vying for his attention, but he seemed to be talking to Maria Cristina.

For a moment, Chessie fancied that Carlo was gazing past Maria Cristina, looking straight at her! Chessie blushed, then realized that Carlo was actually looking at a woman on her right, who waved at him with familiarity.

Chessie looked away. How silly I am, she thought. She resolutely endured more of the don's talk of peasants and uprisings, trying not to glance at the ominous bonfires on the mountain, until the dragoon captain with the mustache whom she had seen the day before asked her to dance.

22.

The men hovered around a bonfire on the windy crest of Mount Pellegrino and ate onion stew as they looked down at the blazing lights of the Roccalini villa. Behind them, other bonfires burned all up the slopes of the mountain.

The men had been slipping away from the sulphur mines and olive groves and vineyards, from the hovels and windblown houses, for the past week, driven by a murderous rage fired by hatred and despair. They were armed with old guns, antique swords, even scyths, and they had no certain plan. They only hoped Garibaldi would come soon. If he did not they would take matters into their own hands, as they had in 1848.

Many of the men around the fire were miners. All their lives, they had worked in the sulphur mines and lived in airless grottos at the mines. Miners and their families often went days without seeing the sun, and the constant exposure to the sulphur eroded and yellowed their skin.

The work was dangerous and most of them had lost some relative in the mines. Some had lost children, since child labor was cheap, cheaper than running machines or steam-operated carts and carriages to move the mined sulphur to the surface, and many of the mine shafts were too low for adults. Armies of boys and girls carried the sulphur up on their backs.

A recent reform law against employing children under the age of ten had aroused anger and bitterness on the part of the mine owners, and some owners simply ignored the law.

This night on the mountain was cold. Rain had fallen earlier and threatened to fall again. The damp cold cut through the men's thin garments and an emaciated man whose face was covered with yellow blotches and scabs hugged his whimpering son to his side.

A jug was passed frequently.

The men had been silent for a long while but now the wine began to stir them.

"How many is Don Roccalini entertaining this evening, Luigi?" a man with stumps of teeth asked as he took the jug from his mouth. "As many as last week's ball?"

"Two hundred or more, Bruno," Luigi said. He was a short, stocky man with huge black eyes. "I wonder what it cost the don, this evening's ball? A lot more than what it would have cost him to give us a living wage in his vineyards when we asked last month."

Other men mumbled curses and drank more wine. The yellow man's mouth fell open and his lips quivered, but he didn't speak.

Bruno spat and smiled and the firelight showed the ruins of his teeth stretched in a hideous grin. "Yes, scores of the damned Bourbons," he said, "and some fancy foreign guests. I saw the don meeting them on the dock yesterday. Twins, they were. Fair-haired. I touched the girl's fine hair and she nearly jumped in the water. I guess she's down there now, dancing and drinking champagne."

"Yes, and they passed my brother's house, while I was visiting him," Luigi said. "I gave them the fist and my brother shouted 'Bastardi.' The old don squirmed in his seat and the fair-haired girl trembled. She should pray to the saints that she quits Palermo before we drag the don's kind from their carriages and villas, just as we did twenty years ago."

"Ah, you were just a lad then, Luigi," Bruno said, "but I remember it well. It started off just like now. We were bolder at the beginning. We'd creep down at night, into isolated villas like Don Roccalini's, and do some good, quick work with our daggers."

"Perhaps a lad, Bruno," Luigi said, "but old enough to fight. Why, I was even in the don's villa one night. I remember well. We held it for several hours, and slit some throats, and I remember how I lay down in a fancy bedroom, on silk sheets, and looked up at the golden angels on the ceiling. I'd love to creep down there again some night soon."

The wine flask was passed around and the men sat silently once more and stared down at the villa's blazing lights.

The dragoon captain was named Pierre Sebastiano and Chessie found him pleasant enough. He evidently found Chessie more than pleasant, and claimed her for three successive mazurkas.

"Captain Sebastiano! I must rest!" Chessie protested, when the music had landed them at a far side of the huge ballroom.

Pierre Sebastiano frowned, and Chessie turned to see that Carlo Settimo stood just behind her. Reluctantly, with disapproval evident in his tone of voice, Sebastiano performed the introduction.

"Ah, the young Miss Deavors from Mississippi," Carlo said. "You're Clayton Deavors' sister, then . . ."

Chessie did not like being considered Clayton's sister and though earlier she had disliked the easy, flirtatious way she had overheard Carlo talking to other ladies, she was upset that he made no effort at all to flirt with her. Feeling rather ill at ease, she nodded severely.

Captain Sebastiano and Carlo Settimo exchanged only a few words before their conversation took on an edge of seriousness.

"Perhaps Don Roccalini is right, then," Pierre said, "when he describes as most detestable those Bourbons who would betray their own class!"

The antagonism between the two men upset Chessie, but Carlo only smiled.

"If the esteemed don meant me," he said, "then I'll have to admit that I'm less than loyal to the Bourbons. I don't want to see friends and relatives hurt, although I find many nearly insufferable. But, Captain, what else have we to amuse us on these dull spring evenings?"

"What if those brigands should pour out of the hills, sir?" the captain said. "Would that end your boredom? Would you find the courage to fight the insurgents?"

"An uprising?" Carlo asked. "In that case, Captain, I should hope to find the courage to . . . return to the safety of Paris." He turned to Maria Cristina, who had joined the group. "I ask you, Miss Roccalini, do I look like a soldier? Why, fighting in the spring mud would spoil my French tailoring."

Maria Cristina laughed, but the general tension was not lessened and the captain's face reddened with anger. No one spoke for a moment. Chessie understood the others' outrage at Carlo Settimo. Even Clayton, she thought, with his self-indulgent passions for women and whiskey, would be eager to fight in such a situation.

"Sir, one day you'll be called to account for your arrogance and treachery," the captain said.

"By you, Captain?" Carlo asked. "Do you long to spoil your handsome uniform in a fight? No, no, on closer observation, I see that it's a bit crushed and not so handsome as it seemed. Have you already been in a fight this evening?"

There was no smile this time. Chessie was afraid the captain would attack Carlo on the spot. Yet she thought Carlo outrageous and half wished the captain would fight with him. Her mixed feelings disturbed and confused her.

"Captain, may I trouble you to get me a glass of punch?" Chessie asked. "I'm feeling a bit warm and thirsty and my simple mind seeks rest from all this wit and bombast . . ."

She was startled at the audacity of her words. Carlo glanced at her. He frowned.

"Yes, Miss Deavors," the captain said. "At once. I, too, would like something to drink." He took Chessie's arm and guided her a step away before he looked back at Carlo. "I promise you, sir, we will continue this discussion, soon, when there are no ladies present to temper my actions."

As Chessie and the captain walked away she thought she heard Carlo saying something about her, but she would not let herself turn to look back at him.

23.

After a desolate, storm-tossed voyage the two women reached Italy and made their way to Rome, where Rafaella had lived as a child. In Rome, they were destitute. Rafaella had no more jewelry to sell. She dared not contact people she had known before. It was too possible that word of what had happened in Natchez might have reached Italy. She kept herself disguised, tinted her hair, wore a black shawl and deliberately drab costumes.

Without money, they could not last long. They had to move from a modest hotel to a small, mean room in a narrow street that stank of garbage and cooking peppers and garlic. Rafaella grew despondent and depressed. She sat for hours, huddled in bed. Flora shouted at her, abused her, tried to rouse her from her stupor.

Once a day, Rafaella would force herself to dress and she and Flora walked down the winding street to the small piazza that held the Trevi fountain. While wealthy tourists admired the glistening, rushing baroque fountain and tossed in coins to assure their return to Rome, Rafaella and Flora stood at a small booth decorated with decaying leaves and choked on the thick

*smoke from paraffin lamps as they dined on thin, greasy
cauliflower stew, bits of tripe or, when they could afford
a treat, a plate of fried squid.*

*Flora took in washing to earn a pitiful few coins
and finally found some work as a seamstress. Now their
little room stank of soap and lye.*

*One day, after a dream-wracked and sleepless night,
Rafaella pulled herself from her stupor. She had one
fine dress left and she ordered Flora to mend it and
sew on some ribbons. She took what coins they had
and went out recklessly. She did not care who saw
her.*

*She had had a long talk with her father during the
night and she was determined to live the life he wanted
for her. In a small shop on Via Cinque Lune, she
ripped the bandage from her thumb. She did not even
wince at the sight of the thumb-stub, as did the clerk
who sold her a pair of black silk gloves with one
cotton-stuffed thumb*

*Resolutely, she put on the gloves and went to the
fashionable Caffè Moro. Within fifteen minutes a gentleman in expensive clothes approached her. He apolo-
gized profusely for presuming to be so brash but said
he was overwhelmed by her beauty. Rafaella smiled
with just the right degree of reserve.*

*The gentleman introduced himself as the Count Cor-
loni.*

24.

Don Roccalini's ball launched a round of parties,
dinners, sightseeing excursions and other entertain-
ments. The Deavors twins found Palermo society exciting and exhausting. They also felt the growing climate
of danger and fear. Every week more Bourbon troops
arrived in Palermo and every day there were new rumors about Garibaldi's threatened invasion.

Chessie was often awakened from her siesta by distant gunfire as the troops tried to track down the brigands in the mountains. But the brigands merely fell back into the wild hills they knew so well. An earlier, night expedition had resulted in ambush and slaughter for the army so now, after dark, the troops dared not venture out of Palermo when the mountain bonfires garlanded the city.

The number of brigands in the hills was a subject of constant talk. It was said they might number in the thousands and that each night more men joined them. One of Don Roccalini's servants, a man named Crespino, had become a brigand.

With one breath, the Bourbons assured each other of their safety, but with the next they talked of ambush and massacre.

Don Roccalini had the army station a squad of dragoons at the foot of the mountain near his villa. He argued that his American guests were quite safe and insisted that he would be insulted if they did not enjoy themselves as if nothing were happening.

However, he also insisted that they confine their sightseeing to Palermo and its immediate environs, even in daytime, and neither Clayton nor Chessie ever left the villa at night without an armed servant as escort.

Chessie was quite disappointed by this stricture as she had particularly wanted to make some sketches at the famous Greek ruins still standing at Syracuse, Agrigento and Segesta. But Maria Cristina told Chessie she was fortunate not to be asked to travel over what she described as some of the worst roads in Europe.

Anyway, Chessie was kept busy with sightseeing near Palermo and the constant parties and other social gatherings. She was never alone with Clayton, he obviously went to great trouble to shield her from his romantic affairs and they seldom held a conversation of any length.

A cool, formal relationship had developed between them, a coolness and formality that she understood would be essential until they had each fallen in love and were married. She loved Clayton deeply and cared for him and she did not doubt his deep feelings for her but something in their natures, some aspect of being twins, something she dared not try to understand, made it necessary that they not show even the mildest affection, or even think about each other.

At least, since that awful time on the Roccalini's balcony the day she arrived, she had not thought of her brother even once in any . . . forbidden or sexual way.

One cool, rainy evening, with the air smelling of the sea, Chessie rode into Palermo with Don Roccalini and the others for a performance of *Il Trovatore*.

Squads of dragoons and infantry stood about the broad boulevards and the captains saluted with their sabers as the don's carriage passed. But the Via Toledo was still being repaired so the carriage had to detour through the narrow, serpentine streets of a poor quarter whose sullen residents stared out at the richly dressed party and made obscene comments and gestures.

Halfway down a narrow street lined with fruit and vegetable carts Chessie realized that a coach was gaining on the Roccalini carriage. She was glad that their driver and the two footmen were armed.

Don Roccalini shouted for his driver to move faster. The whip cracked. The carriage lurched about the ragged stone street.

At a corner the careening carriage swayed to the side of the street and a cart was knocked down and its owner smashed against a building. Another cart was upset and another by the frantic horses and soon the carriage's way was blocked by splintered carts. Their owners shook their fists and cursed as they gathered around the carriage that had caused their ruin. Other men came from their hovels and a mob began to form.

Chessie glanced around. She was frightened and

could see that Clayton was too. Only the don remained calm as he instructed his men to "Clear the rubbish from our way or we'll miss the overture . . ."

"Pull the bastards out of the carriage!" someone shouted.

The mob pressed closer. The don's men drew their pistols. Chessie backed up against the velvet cushions.

Then the coach clambered up behind them. Ten policemen poured out. With truncheons, they flew into the mob and the men screamed and fell back with bloody heads. The carts were shoved aside. The Roccalini carriage moved on, once more speeding recklessly along the narrow streets.

Chessie sat huddled in her corner, shaken by the experience. As they turned a sharp curve the mountain loomed up and she stared at the garland of bonfires. Dear lord, she thought, there must be hundreds of them.

In the shadows of the next block she saw a squad of soldiers watching as three policemen beat a man to the ground.

Chessie was nearly in tears by the time they reached the opera house, and for the first time since her arrival she thought of leaving Palermo much sooner than they had planned.

When Chessie wandered into the lobby of the opera house at intermission she was calmer. At once, however, she saw Carlo Settimo drinking brandy with a group of friends. Carlo was calling out toast after toast to Verdi, the opera's composer, in a loud, mocking voice.

"The scoundrel cares nothing for Verdi," Don Roccalini told Chessie. "The name is merely an acronym for *Viva el Re d'Italia!*—Long live the king of Italy! A toast to that wretched king of Piedmont who wants to ruin us and the Pope and unite Italy, the king who employs Garibaldi! One fine night young Settimo will make this loathesome toast in public and the police will seize him. Even his family won't be able to save him!"

Just before intermission was over, as Chessie talked to two British couples of her acquaintance, Carlo appeared at her side.

"Ah, the young Miss Deavors from Mississippi," he said, but his wide, handsome smile annoyed Chessie.

"The young Don Settimo from Paris," she replied. "And also from Palermo, or so I've heard . . ."

Carlo bowed. "Are you enjoying the performance?" he asked.

Chessie said she was, although, in truth, she had been rather bored.

"I must say I'm surprised to see you here, Signore Settimo," one of the men said.

"I haven't come for the music," Carlo said, "though I'm always prepared to toast Verdi. No, I'm here simply because I was caught in the downpour just at intermission. And the brandy here is as good as anywhere."

Chessie was glad when it was time to return to their box and leave Carlo behind. They're right to call him callous and arrogant, she told herself, yet she could think of nothing but Carlo for the rest of the evening and did not even realize the opera was over until the audience burst into applause.

Chessie did not see Carlo as her party left the opera house and on the drive back to the Roccalini villa fear of another incident in the poor quarter diverted her thoughts.

But they reached the park of the villa without incident.

The five brigands were making their way down the rugged rocks at the base of Mount Pellegrino toward Don Roccalini's villa about the time the opera was letting out.

The men were driven by a desperate frustration. For months, they had waited for Garibaldi's forces. Still, they felt isolated and hopeless. They approached Palermo without any clear military objective. Like other bonfire brigands they were driven to small, purely vindictive actions against available victims and the blazing lights of the don's villa had taunted them for too many cold, wet nights.

A sixth brigand, the yellow-scabbed man, had started from the bonfire with them. The man's son had died the day before. He blamed Don Roccalini and had sworn revenge against him. But the man's physical illness and grief had so debilitated him that a quarter of the way down the mountainside he had turned back.

At the bottom of the mountain the men were running through a patch of cactus when they heard a horse snort nearby. They fell to the ground and watched a troop of dragoons pass a few yards away, then disappear into the darkness.

By the time the brigands reached the villa's park they felt a blood madness. They whispered that in addition to slitting the old don's throat they would rape one of his fine young women.

They were crouching in the shadows, arguing about how best to invade the house, when the sharp sound of horses' hooves silenced them and they turned to see the don's carriage coming into the park. They smiled. Dragging the don and his women from the carriage would be even easier than invading the villa.

The carriage slowed as it turned a sharp curve and neared the villa's entranceway. In the glow of light from the villa the men saw Don Roccalini. Someone leaned forward into the carriage's window. It was the fair-haired girl. The men drew their pistols and smiled again.

They crouched and ran just behind the carriage, prepared to kill its armed footmen and take its occupants when it stopped.

Two elderly servants came out. The carriage door opened. A servant gave his arm to the fair-haired girl. Bruno was only a few feet from her. He remembered the touch of her silky hair, thought of ripping open her dress to bare her pale skin.

Bruno and the other brigands were suddenly aware of an approaching coach. They fell back into the darkness as the coach drew abreast of the carriage.

A police lieutenant got out and approached Don Roccalini.

"I want your men to stay the night," the don said. "One never knows what the rabble might try, after that incident before the opera."

The lieutenant saluted and began to deploy his men around the villa.

The brigands hurried away in the darkness before they were seen.

25.

A few days later Chessie went into Palermo for a shopping expedition with two middle-aged Roccalini cousins. After they had chosen some ribbons and a scarf Chessie caught sight of a brightly painted marionette theater on the bay.

"Oh, please, let's stay and watch the marionettes," Chessie said. She had once seen a Punch and Judy show and was delighted by the setting of this theater.

Grudgingly, the cousins agreed to let Chessie stay but said they would wait for her in an outdoor café.

As Chessie sat in the little theater she soon realized that American Punch and Judy shows were quite unlike the *Orlando Furioso* epic as played by Sicilian marionettes. The marionettes were elaborately carved and more than three feet tall. As a small boy turned the crank of a barrel organ, oddly realistic knights pranced and rode about the stage and drew their swords to decapitate Moors and dragons.

Chessie let herself be caught up in the magic of the performance. By the intermission, she had forgotten where she was, and when she looked around her she was surprised to see Carlo Settimo near her in the audience, eating a lemon ice and laughing with everyone else. Knowing he was there somehow inhibited her pleasure, and after the performance she tried to escape without speaking to him. It proved to be impossible.

"You've caught me indulging one of my secret vices, Miss Deavors," he said, intercepting her at the door. "I hope you'll keep my secret."

"You wouldn't want it known that you enjoy marionette shows?" Chessie asked. "Of course. At Don Roccalini's, I believe you made light of such heroics."

"Perhaps it's only that I think heroics should remain in the theater, where they belong," Carlo said. "It wouldn't amuse me to see living men have their heads cut off. Though, of course, your gallant dragoon captain would disagree. I daresay he would take heart to learn that I enjoy *Orlando Furioso*."

"Your secret is safe with me, Signore Settimo," she said. She turned to go. She was uncomfortably aware that they were now alone in the theater.

"So you're trustworthy," he said. "An amusing trait. Useful, I suppose . . . Now, now, please don't get angry. I apologize. Before you go . . . do you know the history of these marionettes? It's curious about the Palmeritans' passion for them. When the Normans invaded Sicily in the eleventh century they brought along their traditions of knights in armor, of brave deeds and chivalry. We had no such legends of our own. So we Sicilians still worship these alien traits and cheer for heroes with blond hair . . ."

"But, sir, your hair is fair," Chessie said. "And why do you refer to . . . we Sicilians? Why, you've insisted that you Bourbons should be driven out of Sicily."

"You're very clever," Carlo said. "You remember precisely what I say. How unusual. I'm surprised how much I've enjoyed our little talk, and I appreciate your promise of silence. But perhaps people should know of my weakness for theater. I owe them that, after their indulgence of my other weaknesses." He laughed.

"Good day," Chessie said.

She started out and expected him to follow, but he did not.

"I saw you with those two old cows earlier," he called.

"I won't compromise your reputation by going out with you, Miss Deavors."

"Thank you," Chessie said.

She wanted to say something more. The conversation had stimulated her, though she was confused as to her real feelings, so she said nothing, and joined the two women, who were waiting patiently in the café.

Chessie continued to see Carlo, always by chance. Sometimes they met at a ball or saw each other during the late afternoon *passeggiata* when the Palmeritans turned out in their finest clothes to stroll along the quay and through the parks and piazzas.

Chessie tried to remain indifferent to these encounters but failed. Carlo confused her. Why, she wondered, didn't he flirt with her as he did with other women, particularly Maria Cristina? Since she condemned flirtation, she had no reason to complain about his courteous, circumspect behavior toward her, but she felt odd about it. She didn't think she wanted to see more of him, but his coolness provoked her and despite her efforts, she thought of him constantly.

At the end of April Chessie saw Carlo at a ball. Although she was constantly aware of him, he ignored her. Finally, at the end of the evening he invited her to dance a mazurka.

As they danced, Carlo smiled and Chessie smiled back, without thinking, then looked away in confusion, avoiding his disturbing blue eyes.

The dance music became faster and faster as they whirled around and around. Chessie was acutely conscious of Carlo's hands on her shoulder and waist. Had he tightened his grip? Was he holding her over-boldly? She blushed. She felt so warm . . . too warm.

And then the music ended. They had not spoken, though Chessie felt strangely closer to him. Carlo thanked Chessie and left. Soon she was dancing with a Palermo lawyer and Carlo, she noticed, was dancing with Maria Cristina.

Then, in a tall mirror at the end of the room, Chessie caught a glimpse of her own reflection. She saw a slim girl in a simple pale-green dress, saw reddish-blond hair in an artless, natural style. She glanced at her reflection again.

Suddenly, she felt despair. She looked awful in green, and the dress really did not fit at all! Her eyes glazed with tears and she remembered that Maria Cristina had spent two hours choosing her gown, had had her hair brushed for half an hour, had taken forty-five minutes to have it plaited with tiny red ribbons that trailed to her waist, and had deliberated over a perfume nearly that long.

Chessie became so self-conscious that she wanted to run from the room and hide in the shadows of the garden.

26.

The night after the ball, Chessie lay awake until dawn thinking of Carlo Settimo and trying to sort out her feelings for him. She realized that, despite all his annoying ways, she found him attractive and that she wanted him to like her. She pondered the meaning of his behavior toward her, for he definitely treated her differently than he treated other women.

Perhaps, she thought, she was becoming infatuated with him. The idea both excited and frightened her, particularly when she lay half asleep and imagined kissing him, remembered his arms around her as they had danced. These thoughts made sleep impossible, made her excited and warm, and she realized that her hands were caressing her own body.

The next morning Chessie felt too fatigued to leave her room. She read for a while, then restlessly searched through a trunk of extra clothing that she had never unpacked. Amid some silk petticoats she came across the gold-rimmed brooch and looked again at the portrait of Rafaella Blaine. At once she was flooded with memories of finding the brooch and the whole experience at The Columns, although she had not thought of it nor of Rafaella for many weeks. Why, I wonder, was I so panic-stricken that day? Chessie asked herself. She examined the face of the beautiful young woman and began to feel uneasy once again. The black eyes attracted her, held her, like the seductive but dangerous eyes of a bird of prey.

I really know very little about her . . . or that terrible time, Chessie realized. As a child, she had overheard the stories . . . How Rafaella had plotted Lawton's murder, how she had tried to smother Chessie and Clayton because she had gone mad, how her husband had arrived just in time to murder her in such a gruesome way. But she had never really asked why, or discussed these old family stories with anyone. She really knew very little about it, and she felt distinctly curious and uneasy. Chessie shivered as she held the cameo and looked into the woman's haunting eyes. Then, resolving to forget it for now, she tucked it back into the trunk.

That day passed and another and a third. Oddly, Chessie did not see Carlo at any of the social functions she attended. She thought of him often and could not deny that she was looking for him and listening for any word of his activities or whereabouts. As the days passed, she gave in more and more often to vague erotic thoughts of him, and when she imagined his lips on hers or his hands on her body, her own hands began to wander over her body and she savored the strange, exciting new feelings that they aroused.

By the fourth day, Chessie had begun to worry that something had happened to Carlo. Anxiously, she began to pay attention to the talk of politics and possible invasion, denunciations, and the arrests of anti-Bourbon suspects. That night bonfires on the mountain reminded her that the brigands now crept into Palermo at night to rob and pillage and murder. If something had happened to Carlo, she worried, surely she would have heard.

In circumspect ways, she introduced Carlo's name to callers at the villa, but she learned nothing. Finally, she asked Don Roccalini, but Carlo's name launched a tirade of furious denunciations. She resolved not to ask Don Roccalini any more questions, ever again.

On the first day of May, a hot day with no wind and the sound of intermittent gunfire in the hills, Chessie returned to the villa from a morning sketching expedition.

When her carriage paused before the villa she encountered Don Roccalini, who invited her to walk with him in the park. Chessie agreed, though she was weary of the don's temper and would have preferred to be alone in her room.

The late spring sunlight was brilliant and Chessie realized with sudden shock and sympathy that the constant tension and fear of an uprising had taken its toll on the old don. His skin looked dry as parchment and his face had taken on an odd ivory color. His dark eyes were watery and distant. At times his voice trembled and he had to work his lips two or three times before any words came out.

As usual, the don launched a gasping monologue about the sanctity of institutions and classes as he led Chessie through a grove of lemon trees. Chessie listened patiently and tried to enjoy the sunshine.

Suddenly, an apparition appeared from behind a tree that made the don's worn face seem childlike and serene by comparison.

Chessie gasped and shrank from the sight of the emaciated man whose face was covered with horrible yellow blotches and scabs.

The don also stepped back.

"Who are you?" he stammered. "What do you want? Get away from us! Are you mad to invade my estate this way?"

"Aiee, mad!" the yellow man babbled. "Mad as a man can be whose family perished in your sulphur mines! Mad enough to hide here all night so I can kill you!"

The man pulled a dagger from a rope at his waist.

Chessie screamed. The man lunged at Don Roccalini. The don tried to avoid the thrust but the blade sliced into his arm.

The don grabbed the arm. Blood flowed between his fingers. Chessie was too frightened to run or even cry out again. She stood there, trembling, as the don stumbled backwards and his assailant advanced again, taunting him with the bloody knife.

"Your death will be too easy," the man babbled. "Unlike my poor Giuseppe, who died slowly on the cold mountain because he worked in your mines." He glanced at Chessie. "And you, *bella,* my friends around the fires have plans for you! We have plans for all of you, and you're first, Don Roccalini!"

The don screamed for help. The man parried his knife, feinted a thrust with trembling hands, while his yellow-streaked eyes mocked the frantic don.

He raised his knife for another thrust. Two gardeners ran up. The man glanced around wildly, giving Don Roccalini time to stumble away. The man attacked a gardener, but the gardener held a hoe and easily parried the thrust.

The second gardener swung his hoe and hit the man across the head. The blow lifted him off the ground, and he fell back, clutching a gaping wound in his scalp.

Still, Chessie lacked the strength to move. Other people ran up. One of them was Clayton. He glanced at the don, whose arm was being bandaged with a torn shirt, at the man on the ground, then put his arm around Chessie and led her into the villa.

Chessie was given a sleeping draught and slept until late afternoon. When she awoke she learned that Don Roccalini's wound wasn't serious, but that his assailant was badly wounded. He had been arrested, given a hasty trial and sentenced to be shot. The sentence would be carried out, within the hour, as soon as the firing squad returned from its siesta.

Chessie was still stunned by the affair and refused to join the others for dinner. Why would the man do it? she asked herself. Why would he take such a desperate chance? And why was he so hideously yellow? Was he really mad?

These questions seemed so important to Chessie that she voiced them to the first person she saw, one of the don's servants, a man named Peppino, who brought her a tray of food during the evening.

"They don't fear danger, for their life is living death," Peppino told her. "They're yellow from working in the sulphur mines."

Tears filled Chessie's eyes. From her own observations of the suffering and squalor in Palermo's poor neighborhoods she could believe that Peppino was right. In a drained and melancholy state, she remembered the yellow man's threats that his friends had special plans for her.

She stood on her balcony and stared at the growing cobweb of fires that seemed ready to burst down on Palermo and became frightened. Why would she be singled out by people who did not even know her? Surely the yellow man was mistaken, or only trying to torment the don.

Later, she took a solitary walk in the interior garden, and tried to clear her thoughts. But though she knew she was safe inside the villa's walls, every shadow was menacing, every night sound made her tense, and after ten minutes she returned to her room.

That night Chessie suggested to Clayton that they leave Sicily at once. They had been waiting for their chaperone, a Roccalini cousin, to travel to Palermo from her home in the island's interior. First illness, then the brigands had prevented her reaching Palermo.

Clayton said that people back in Natchez might be scandalized that they would travel without a chaperone, but he agreed that the danger in Palermo was too great to allow them to worry about the niceties of social behavior. He said that the next day he would arrange passage to a seaport near Rome.

The twins had expected an indignant protest from Don Roccalini but the attack by the yellow man had had its effect on the old man. He merely muttered that if they felt they must leave, he understood.

The earliest ship on which Clayton could book passage was leaving in a week. Chessie realized that she was glad they would be in Palermo a little longer. In a week, if Carlo had any interest in her, he would surely seek her out and . . .

And *what?* she asked herself as she stood on her balcony and stared out at the bonfires that lit Mount Pellegrino like daylight.

What would happen? What did she want to happen? In truth, she did not know, except . . . she longed to see Carlo again.

Luigi and Bruno stood in the shadows of the inner garden and watched Chessie on her balcony. With them was a man named Crespino, who had worked for Don Roccalini until he ran away to the mountain a few weeks earlier. Though the don now had more armed servants and half a dozen policemen guarding his villa, Crespino, who had been in the don's service for over twenty years, knew of a gate far back in the garden, hidden by thick vines, that allowed entry inside the walls.

"We should have taken her when we had the chance," Bruno whispered. "We may never have a better one."

"But that policeman was over there," Luigi said.

"One man . . . We could easily have slit his throat!"

"Well, it's too late now, for tonight," Crespino said.

He lead the other two men back to the vine-covered gate.

27.

Jolette excused herself from the small party of friends gathered in the front parlor at The Columns and slipped out alone into the hot, humid twilight. Outside, she kicked off her satin slippers and left them near one of the massive white columns that gave the plantation its name, the same twelve columns, alternating Doric and Corinthian, that Jolette's great-great-grandfather had brought downriver when he built the house.

Jolette sighed. She had heard the story of the building of the big house and many other stories about old times and early days at The Columns, but she could not think of them now. Tonight, she had problems of her own to deal with, emotions and feelings to sort out, feelings so strong and conflicting that she had been unable to bear the atmosphere of polite chatter in the parlor.

Weeks had passed since the twins had left for the Continent, since Anthony and Lucinda's wedding, and Jolette still lingered at The Columns. Last week Joleen had returned to New York, but Jolette's own plans were very indefinite.

At first, Jolette admitted to herself, she had wanted to stay on the plantation to be near Anthony Walker. She had never met a man who attracted her more, and he felt the same way, she knew—after all, he had confessed to her, on the eve of his wedding, that he loved and desired her.

But now, Jolette was upset. She had thought it over and decided that it was wrong. Anthony had gone ahead and married Lucinda. He'd said that otherwise they'd be scandalized beyond repair, and Jolette had agreed . . . in a way.

She had agreed, but her feelings for Anthony had

not changed, only strengthened, and she had stayed, half hoping that Anthony would realize how much he loved her and break off his marriage at once. Instead, he had left The Columns on some business trip, and Lucinda had fallen ill, and with Chessie and Clayton both gone, her mother had decided that Jolette should stay here a while, to look after Lucinda.

So she had stayed, and fallen more in love with Mississippi and The Columns. More than ever she had come to think that this was the life she wanted— forever—this life of huge, airy houses and parties and visiting back and forth all over the county, this graceful life with its slow, easy pace. More than ever she wanted to be mistress of a big plantation herself, and married to Anthony Walker.

Anthony was back from his trip, now. He had returned three days ago, and during those three days Jolette had taken great pains to avoid being left alone with him or even meeting his eyes in company.

Damn it, Jolette thought, walking barefoot across the lawn toward the formal flower garden, damn it and damn him. I don't know what to do! I can't stay here —not with Anthony married to her! She stepped around a hedge of sweet-smelling yellow roses and walked along a path bordered with honeysuckle and scuppernong vines.

I can't bear it . . . I can't, she thought. Just tonight, at dinner and afterwards in the parlor, Anthony had watched her with mocking eyes and had tried to involve her in the conversation. But his mere presence excited her, even his slightest flirtatious gesture was torment for her, and it all made her feel terribly guilty. I could never do anything to hurt Aunt Lucinda, Jolette thought. The better she came to know Lucinda the surer she was of that, for Lucinda was sweet and generous and good. She and Jolette had spent hours together since her illness, talking softly and confidentially, and Jolette admired her aunt—her character, her courage and her nature.

It's not my fault, Jolette thought. If she's too good for him, it's not my fault . . . And yet, I resolve to have nothing to do with him while she is married to him. If I stay here, something will surely happen between me and Anthony . . . So I must go. As soon as Aunt Lucinda is a bit better, I will go.

Having made a decision, Jolette felt sad, but a bit less unsettled. She picked a dew-soaked rose and then turned to retrace her steps back into the house. As soon as she turned she saw that she was no longer alone.

"Anthony!" she gasped.

Without speaking he caught Jolette in his arms and swept her into a passionate embrace. Holding her inches from the ground, he kissed her boldly and greedily.

"I missed you so! Why have you been avoiding me?" he asked.

"I . . . I . . . No!" Jolette said. She squirmed but could not get away from him.

"My God, you excite me!" Anthony said. "I thought I'd go mad tonight, watching you across the room. I swear, I've never felt this way."

"Please! Don't swear anything to me, Anthony. I've thought about it . . . and decided it can't be. We mustn't see each other, mustn't go on with this. I've decided to go home, to New York, as soon as I . . ."

"Don't say that, Jolette!" Anthony's hands boldly caressed her breasts, holding them in his hands as he backed her up against the vine-covered trellis. "You can't deny that you desire me." He bent his head and sucked one of her breasts into his mouth. Jolette stifled a moan. She felt passion, unbidden, unwelcome and devastating, stir deep in her body.

"No!" Jolette said. "Anthony, we can't! It's not right!"

Boldly, insistently, Anthony kissed her, opening her mouth with the pressure of his lips, twisting his tongue in past her teeth. Her head spun as she found herself kissing him back. After the weeks of wanting and deliberation, the weeks of doing without any affection at all, Jolette was stunned by his passion, and swept away by her own response to it.

"Jolette, I want you. I want you more than I have ever wanted a woman!"

"Oh, no!" she murmured. "What are you doing? You mustn't! The others . . ."

"Lucinda has gone to bed and the guests are driving home," he said. "We're alone."

Jolette could hear that he was right. She heard the creaking of carriages and the soft, muffled sound of horses' hoofs on the house road.

Smothering her protests with another deep kiss, Anthony slid one hand up along Jolette's thigh, under her skirt and petticoats, and reached through the leg of her full, lacy pantaloons. Jolette gasped. She was too shocked to move. His hand probed, played with her, found its target, and he thrust his middle finger deep between her legs, into her, and held her pelvis with his strong hand, the finger still extended as he rocked her toward him.

"See?" he whispered, breaking their kiss. "Do you see now that I really want you, Jolette, and that you want me, too? Do you doubt that I'll have you?"

"Oh . . ." she moaned, writhing.

She had never experienced, never imagined such a feeling, and now couldn't imagine resisting it. She could not. He controlled her, absolutely, with the finger he had thrust into her. In an instant, her whole body had gone hot, her skin tingled and her heart beat throughout her frame, pulsing insistently.

"You want it," Anthony said. "You want me. I can feel how much you do. And I'm crazy for you."

Jolette closed her eyes. Perspiration bathed her face, her body. She was sick with guilt, but swallowed it and reached out for him as he twisted his hand away from her and seized her by her shoulders.

"Listen to me, Jolette, and understand me well," he said. "I admit that I love you. I said it before and it's true. But you're very young and a woman, and you must do as I say. You must never speak of our affair..."

"What affair, sir?" Jolette gasped with her last effort of will, "I'm not your slave. I'm a free woman and I will not..."

"Will not what?"

"Will not . . . allow you . . . until we are married . . ." she mumbled.

Anthony drew her close to him, holding her so that she could feel the muscular power of his body, feel his heart beating in time with hers, feel the long hardness of his penis pressed against her belly. Now his touch was more gentle, seductive. He stroked her shoulders and arms and kissed her searchingly.

"Darling, you know what the situation is and that I'll change it as soon as I'm able," he said. "I won't lie to you about my feelings, nor deny them. If you refuse me, you're a liar and a fool, but I must accept that."

He kissed her again, with soft, expert, teasing lips and when he pulled away Jolette felt as if she'd been robbed, felt tears spring to her eyes, and knew that she would do anything to have his lovemaking continue.

"I . . . I don't know . . ." she breathed.

Abruptly, Anthony brushed away her arms and stood away from her. She swayed, leaned toward him, feeling the loss, feeling helpless and bereft.

"Oh . . . please . . ." she whispered, "I do love you, I do . . ."

He frowned, and Jolette felt the chill of his displeasure like the first warning of a storm. I can't resist him, she thought. Only this once I must take him to me, take his love. I can't think, tonight, of any consequences.

"Please," she said softly, stepping toward him.

Cruelly, he turned away. "I guess I'll go down to the quarters," he said. "You've roused me to a fine passion."

"No! Oh, please don't go. Stay! Please, Anthony . . ."

He stopped and Jolette threw herself toward him, wrapped her arms around his body and clung to him. "I do love you . . ." she repeated.

"Beg me to make love to you," he said. "Beg!"

Jolette turned her face up to his and her lips parted as she pronounced the words. "Please . . . I want you to make love to me."

"Take off your clothes," he said, stepping out of her embrace and dropping his jacket onto the soft grass as a blanket. "I want to see you naked by moonlight. Take them all off."

"Yes," Jolette said.

As she did his bidding she was dizzy with an excitement that made her body tremble and made her heart beat so fast she put one hand over it. She looked away as Anthony took off his trousers, then shut her eyes as he came toward her quickly and set her on her back on the ground as easily as if she were a baby.

"You are beautiful by moonlight," he said. "Gold and silver and pink and white. And do you want me?"

"Yes," she said, moaning as his strong hands stroked her, set her on fire.

His penis was large and pointed toward her and her eyes were still shut as he thrust it into her, into the soft wetness he had readied with his finger. She moaned again, louder, and then she whimpered and kissed his face as he made love to her.

Don't stop, don't ever stop, she thought, and as she felt for the first time the blinding ecstasy of orgasm, she knew without thinking that she must have this feeling again and again, no matter who was betrayed or hurt.

28.

Several days passed during which Chessie looked in vain for Carlo. Finally, she learned that he had traveled to Marsala on family business but had been back in Palermo for three days. This information did nothing to improve her spirits.

Surely he could have tried to contact me, she thought. He could have attended one of the balls or concerts where he knew I'd be. But what depressed Chessie was that her long-awaited news of Carlo came from Maria Cristina. Chessie did not ask Maria Cristina how she happened to know about Carlo's activities, but she felt a sharp resentment toward her Sicilian friend and determined to put dreams of Carlo Settimo out of her mind.

Chessie began to spend more time alone. Frequently in the evening she took solitary walks in the inner garden, despite the vague but nagging sense of apprehension she felt there. She told herself that it was only that she could see all the bonfires so clearly from the garden. There was absolutely no reason to be afraid here in the villa's garden.

One night, however, she imagined she heard men walking in the shadows near the back wall, and she realized how tense she was. She forced herself not to run away, though when she saw a policeman on the other side of the garden she felt great relief.

Her longing to see Carlo once more before she left Palermo became desperate. There seemed to be one more good chance, for the Roccalinis had planned a ball the next evening, in honor of General Landi, the commander of the Bourbon army, and Chessie thought it likely that Carlo would attend.

Seeing him again will satisfy me, she rationalized, even if he dances all night with Maria Cristina.

The thought was painful, but Chessie knew she must not dwell on the idea of her beautiful, voluptuous friend as a rival. Maria Cristina was sweet and generous and she had made Chessie's stay in Palermo far less lonely, especially since Chessie and Clayton still behaved as strangers to each other.

In fairness, Chessie couldn't dislike Maria Cristina, or blame Carlo for enjoying her lively company. She

vowed not to think of it, or of anything else trouble-
some, until the ball.

By midnight that night, Chessie was both happy and
miserable. She was happy because, whatever might
happen, Carlo Settimo had appeared at the ball for
General Landi. On the other hand she was miserable,
for he had danced repeatedly with Maria Cristina. It's
my own fault, she mourned, as she waltzed past them.
As usual, I'm not dressed as well as Maria Cristina. This
yellow gown looks childish and homemade and my
hair probably looks disheveled.

Earlier in the evening, Chessie's heart had flooded
with excitement and hope. Carlo had invited her to
dance and she had been totally elated. The touch of
his hands, his conversation, his smile, had delighted
her, although, as usual, she had been confused by his
coolness.

Their conversation during the dance had been subdued. Chessie felt shy, felt she sounded stupid. Her
eagerness to please made her tongue-tied, and she
waited with declining hope for some sign of real romantic interest from Carlo.

But he had said nothing, and they had parted after
two dances. Now, Chessie watched Carlo leaning close
to Maria Cristina, watched him whisper in Maria Cristina's ear, and hated the happy smile that crossed
Maria Cristina's face. I mustn't watch them, Chessie
vowed. If I do, I'll surely burst into tears.

"What did you say, Miss Deavors?" Pierre Sebastiano asked. The captain was Chessie's most regular
dance partner, although she was tiring of his conversation and suspected he had drunk too much brandy.

"Nothing," Chessie said. "Oh, there's General Landi.
I must make his acquaintance."

Proudly, Pierre presented Chessie both to General
Landi, who commanded the garrison in Sicily, the
guest of honor, and to the Prince of Castelicala, who
was the governor of Sicily. Both men looked old and

tired and frail, and both seemed to Chessie to be extremely apprehensive.

After the introductions, Pierre and Chessie lingered near the men and listened to their bitter, angry talk. Chessie studied their anxious faces, reddened by too much whiskey and punch and had the odd sensation that these Bourbons were crumbling right before her eyes.

Finally, Chessie could endure no more.

She excused herself and walked away. She had taken only a few steps when she heard Carlo saying, ". . . can't believe the motley state and outrageous demands of that peasant rabble on the city's outskirts . . ." She turned in disbelief.

Their eyes met for a moment. Carlo smiled, then looked away as Chessie fled, overwhelmed with anger and disappointment. Although she danced and smiled, she could think only about what she had heard. She had often heard Carlo mock the Bourbons. Tonight he criticized their adversaries. Was there no end to his cynicism? Was he totally false? If he was a spoiled, vain, shallow man without feeling or conviction, she would be foolish to give him another thought.

I'm so glad, she told herself, that I'll soon leave this wretched city behind!

And until then she was better off with men like her partner, a handsome, attentive young American naval lieutenant from Mobile whose talk of the South made her homesick.

When the musicians stopped to rest, she made a sudden decision. She excused herself from the American lieutenant and dashed upstairs.

29.

An hour later Chessie returned to the ball. She walked back down the staircase with her silken skirts rustling, wearing the most expensive and elaborate gown she owned, one she had never worn before. It was a Prussian blue silk with embroidered ribbons, ruffles, and Alençon lace, it fit tightly and was cut very low over her breasts. She had let Torine brush her hair for half an hour and arrange it in a sleek cluster laced with matching blue ribbons.

Chessie smoothed her hair and skirt self-consciously as she reached the bottom of the stairs. She was excited but apprehensive. If no one noticed the change in her appearance she would be desolate, yet she dreaded seeming vain or pretentious for having changed her clothes.

The party was at its height. The American lieutenant appeared at once at Chessie's elbow, and two other men called out compliments for her dress. Chessie smiled and nodded but her eyes searched the dance floor.

Her spirits fell suddenly. She could not see Carlo, and where was Maria Cristina? Had they gone off together? The thought made her feel very lonely and depressed. What was she doing here in this crowd of drunken, jaded people, so very far from home? She looked for Clayton, but she couldn't see him either, and began to feel sorry that she had ever left The Columns. Nostalgically, she thought of her mother and wondered what she was doing this evening. It would be deep spring in Mississippi. The cotton would already be in the ground. The weather would be very hot and the flower gardens in full bloom.

Chessie felt increasingly melancholy. Had the lights been turned down while she was upstairs or was it her imagination? The faces around her seemed changed, dimmer, somehow shadowed so that both men and women seemed to frown, almost to glower. Everywhere she looked she saw leering smiles and drunken eyes, heard people chattering loudly with angry, twisted mouths.

Chessie wandered across the marble floor as if sleep-walking, speaking to people automatically, but feeling totally alienated. Why was no one dancing? she wondered, then realized that there was no music.

She paused, almost ready to run back upstairs, when Pierre Sebastiano appeared at her side.

"Miss Deavors," he asked, "will you walk with me in the garden?" Through the open French doors, Chessie saw that a number of people had gone into the garden, and she gladly accepted the invitation.

After the fetid closeness of the crowded ballroom the night air was fresh and mild and carried the scent of night-blooming stock.

The garden, as usual, was lovely and almost restored Chessie's spirits. It was wilder than an American garden. Vines hung over wooden trellises among tall, well-pruned rose bushes. She heard a bird singing. Hanging lanterns with brightly colored shades lit the garden walks, and as Chessie and the captain passed a moss-covered marble fountain she heard the talk and light laughter of other people who had strayed from the dance floor.

How pleasant, she told herself, and such a change from the grim political conversations inside.

Then, just beyond the fountain she saw a cluster of people—obviously excited about something. In the lantern-light she saw that their faces were animated. They seemed to be gathered around something on the ground.

Chessie followed Pierre to the edge of the crowd. Expectantly, she leaned over to see what was going on, and then gasped in horror and disbelief. Everyone was looking into a pit dug in a low bed of purple flowers. Three dwarfs were climbing into the pit. The dwarfs were stripped to the waist, and their bodies glistened with sweat. Their faces were grim, their eyes narrowed with fear and hatred, and one of them, a tiny man with no neck and shaggy, unkempt red hair, was baring his teeth, to the delight of the crowd which had begun to call out wagers.

Chessie was utterly horror-struck. It was obvious that these dwarfs were being set to fight in some horrible way.

As everyone watched, some of the Roccalini servants approached with wire cages. The crowd parted. The servants opened the cages into the pit and released a dozen huge squealing rats. Chessie gasped. The rats had evil, red eyes and large, yellow teeth. At once, the rats lunged at each other and the dwarfs, squealing and attacking, all of them crazed with hunger. One dwarf tore a gnawing rat from his leg, took its head into his mouth and bit it off. The crowd cheered.

Chessie stepped back. She could not believe her eyes. Bile rose into her throat. She felt she might faint. Her legs were weak.

Pierre Sebastiano glanced back at her and smiled. "Ah, Miss Deavors," he said, "don't tell me you're so squeamish! It's all in fun! Come and help me decide which of these freaks to wager on . . ."

When Chessie made no move, the captain shook his head and turned back to the pit. Chessie heard a hideous sound, a scream of pain she knew no rat had made.

Desperately, she stumbled backwards, looking for something to lean on. Her head was spinning. Her legs began to buckle. Just in time someone appeared behind her and a hand gripped her arm. She staggered a few feet to a trellis and leaned against it.

"Miss Deavors, are you all right?"

The voice sent a shiver up her spine. She opened her eyes. Carlo stood in front of her.

"Yes, I'm . . . Oh, it's horrible! I've never seen anything so awful . . . Please, I must leave . . ."

"Who brought you out here?" Carlo asked. "You should not see this! It's inexcusable! Who was your escort?"

"The . . . the captain, but please don't . . ."

Carlo stalked back toward the pit. "Captain Sebastiano!" he called.

The captain glanced over his shoulder, then made

a caustic remark about Carlo to his companions. They laughed.

Carlo muttered an oath, then suggested that a man so ill-mannered as to expose a lady to this brutal contest should be down in the pit with the dwarfs and the rats.

The captain's nostrils flared. His eyes narrowed and the veins stood out on his neck. He stepped toward Carlo. They exchanged another remark which Chessie could not hear clearly.

Then Carlo reached out and slapped Captain Sebastiano. Another man stepped forward. More heated words were exchanged, and Chessie realized that a duel was being arranged.

"No," she whispered. "You mustn't!" she said to Carlo when he returned to her side. Tears filled her eyes.

"Yes, I will fight the insolent bastard!" Carlo said. "At dawn. He insulted you, Miss Deavors. Here, let me escort you inside at once. You must be spared any more of this wretched scene."

Chessie let herself be led back through the garden. Now the lanterns cast an eerie light and the night air seemed oppressive. They walked very slowly, Chessie clinging to Carlo's arm. At the edge of the garden she stopped.

"You mustn't fight!" she exclaimed. What if he were killed? Looking into his blue eyes disturbed her so that she had to look away as she pleaded with him. "You mustn't do it for me. The man is a soldier, sir. How can you hope to match his skills?"

"The matter has already been arranged," Carlo said. "Your honor must be upheld, Miss Deavors, the insult avenged. I can take care of myself."

"Signore Settimo, discourteous as the captain was to take me out there, it isn't sufficient reason for a duel," Chessie said. "I insist that you . . ."

"The duel will take place!" Carlo said vehemently. "The captain insulted you. It's important to me that your honor . . ."

"My honor, indeed!" she said. "I hardly know you!

I suspect, sir, that you're settling a personal matter with the captain, and using my honor as a pretense."

"The captain and I despise each other, Miss Deavors," Carlo said, "but I'm fighting this duel for you ... Because of my special feeling for you."

"Special feeling?" Chessie asked. "You've revealed no special feelings for me. I fear you'll be killed! I can't allow you to do it! I don't trust your motive, sir. You're a cynical man, without convictions. To fight for me, for my honor, is to mock me!"

"I'm sorry you find me so wanting in qualities you admire, Miss Deavors," Carlo said. "I believe you to possess qualities I value highly. But it's of no concern what either of us thinks. The duel will be fought at dawn. Good night, Miss Deavors."

Chessie gave in to her tears as she watched him walk away. She felt abandoned as well as bewildered. She didn't trust him. When people learned he was fighting for her she would be ridiculed. Don Roccalini and Clayton would be furious. She couldn't trust Carlo. How could she when he had shown himself to be totally cynical?

And yet ... No man had ever affected her as he did, no man had stirred her so profoundly. Why, she could not even bear to look into his eyes, and he had spoken of "special feelings."

Chessie dragged herself toward the villa in despair and confusion, willing the strength to reach her room.

30.

The quiet hours between dawn and full light were the longest Chessie had ever endured, seeming longer even than the night before. Finally, she rose, but could not face the others. Claiming fatigue, she stayed in her room to await news of the duel's outcome.

Her anger and confusion had lessened during the

night. She felt only fear for Carlo's life and a helpless infatuation for him that overwhelmed any sense of reason. She still disliked his cynicism and she was sure he didn't care for her at all. But she convinced herself that it was because of some feeling for her that he was risking his life. She had been far too hasty with her anger and suspicion last night, and she regretted it now.

The morning hours passed, but there was no word about the duel. Chessie became frantic. She longed to dress and run out of the house, but she had no idea where to go to find out what had happened. Surely, if Carlo were alive, she told herself, he would contact her. But it was nearly noon now and there had been no word.

That same morning, however, word did arrive that Garibaldi and a thousand soldiers had landed at Marsala.

It seemed inevitable that General Landi, with his 25,000 professional soldiers, would crush so small a force, in any open battle. But the night before, Mount Pellegrino seemed inundated with a mass of fire that, at any slight spark, would explode down into Palermo like lava from Mount Etna, and the sheer numbers, the tens of thousands of men, might suddenly overrun the city's garrison.

Already the brigands had become bolder and more audacious. The past few nights they had crept into Palermo to murder and plunder and burn. One group had seized a church, used it as an arsenal, and rung the bells wildly to rouse the city to rebellion. Bourbon soldiers had quickly and ruthlessly crushed the group and prevented the uprising.

The Bourbons babbled that, surely, the troops could protect them. But no one felt safe, and everyone dreaded another long, tense night of the taunting fires.

Clayton willingly paid a high premium for passage on a ship out of Palermo the next day. He was adamant that they leave at once.

Chessie protested but Clayton would not listen to

protests, so, in misery and desperation, she confessed to him that she did not want to leave until she knew how the duel had ended.

"You're a romantic little fool, Chessie," Clayton said angrily. "Everyone talked of the duel last night, and there was no mention of you. That scoundrel Settimo fought the captain for his own reason—an attempt to prove in some pitiful way that he isn't a coward. It has nothing to do with you. I won't allow you to compromise yourself with such romantic notions!"

Chessie was furious but Clayton refused to argue and left the villa to make final arrangements for the trip.

Desperately, Chessie fled into the garden and hid there, sitting alone, fighting back tears and trying to think of some way to get word of Carlo. It came in an unexpected way. The servant Peppino approached her.

Peppino whispered that he was sympathetic to Signore Settimo and had a message for her from him. He told Chessie that the captain had been wounded in the shoulder and that Carlo was unharmed. Then he handed Chessie an envelope.

As Peppino left the garden, Chessie opened the envelope with shaking fingers. The message read:

> Miss Deavors—My engagement ended successfully. May I ask to meet you secretly and in private this evening? I must see you before you leave Palermo, and I fear to be seen in public. Please meet me at nine in the little park behind the villa.
> Your faithful servant, Carlo Settimo.

Chessie read the letter twice and she was flooded with happiness. Without the slightest hesitation she would meet Carlo, and she cared nothing for the impropriety of meeting at night.

She smiled with hope and relief as she walked back to the villa. She felt wonderful—utterly changed and fully a woman. It was true! Carlo had chosen *her*— over Maria Cristina and all the other women who had pursued him. This moment, she felt, was really the beginning of her life. Never again would she be that shy, unhappy girl who once lived at The Columns.

A much subdued Chessie emerged from a small back door of the Roccalini villa that night at nine. Waiting for this moment had drained her. Now the sight of the hundreds of bonfires from her balcony weakened her resolve.

Every sound frightened her as she crept down a narrow, twisting path lined with thick-leafed bushes whose limbs were laced with bougainvillaea. She hadn't dared bring a lantern, for fear of being seen from the villa, and as she inched along the dark path the bonfires reminded her of the stories of brigands creeping into the city at night. She remembered the yellow man and his threat to her.

She nearly shook with fear and apprehension, yet nothing would have stopped her from meeting Carlo.

Finally the path opened into the park. The moon was obscured by clouds and Chessie stood at the path's end, straining to see ahead in the darkness. There was no sign of Carlo, no light, only the night sounds and her own frightened breathing.

She waited a minute, then another, glancing around constantly. She was sure she heard someone approaching in the darkness, and not just one person, but several. What if a band of brigands had invaded the park?

Suddenly Chessie remembered Myrtis.

She pivoted and ran squarely into someone. She gave a small scream but a hand over her mouth smothered it.

Then she realized it was Carlo. He released her mouth and steadied her.

"We must speak quietly," Carlo said.

"Are we safe?" she asked.

"You are perfectly safe, Miss Deavors," he said, "but there's an order out for my arrest."

"Then you've taken a risk coming here," she said.

"But how can they arrest you merely for saying some impertinent things?"

"Ah, Miss Deavors, how little you know," he said. "The police spies are everywhere and they've learned that I once joined a secret group called the *carbonari,* a group which opposes all forms of tyranny. I was very young and haven't been a faithful member, but this makes no difference to the police."

"Then you were insincere when you joined them?" Chessie asked.

"No, no, I was sincere enough," he said. "You've seen the injustice here. But it was all talk, vague talk in those days. None of us believed it would come to invasion."

Chessie realized that Carlo was frightened and unsure of himself. He seemed very different from the arrogant, confident and infuriating young man she knew from parties and balls. His fear and vulnerability endeared him to her even further.

"What will you do now?" she asked, adding "my darling" in her mind but afraid to voice it.

"I'm not so indecisive as I might seem, Miss Deavors," he said. "I do believe in Garibaldi's cause. I think I may join him. I have friends who are officers in his army."

"But you're no soldier," she said. "You can't fight . . ."

"I've fought already today!" Carlo exclaimed. "I'm no coward, Miss Deavors!"

"The duel, oh yes," Chessie said. "You were wonderful to do it! I never thought you a coward. I've worried so for your safety."

"For that I'm sorry," he said. "I was fortunate that the captain's over-confidence led to his undoing. But I have something more important to speak of."

Chessie waited, but Carlo did not speak. For the first time she realized that they were alone in the darkness. She felt his physical presence, his nearness, like a powerful, attractive force. She caught her breath, waiting . . .

His kiss was sudden and her body stiffened at the first touch of his lips on hers. She resisted a moment, then relaxed. It was a kiss like no other. Strange feelings stirred her whole body. His hands flowed to her waist, slid around to draw her close to him.

"No," she mumbled as she tore her lips from his mouth and wriggled away. "No, please, we mustn't continue, Carlo!"

"Ah, Chessie," he said. "It's the first time you've spoken my name. How I've longed to hear you say it. You're so beautiful! If you hadn't come tonight I'd have suffered terribly."

Chessie's head swam. He had called her beautiful and spoke of suffering without her! His words, like his kiss, were far too bold, she knew. But she longed for such words and such a kiss, and she could not quell the excitement she felt.

Carlo took her hands in his. "You're so unlike other girls I've known," he said. "I adore you, Chessie! Yet I know nothing of your feelings for me."

"Carlo, I adore you, too," she said. "I confess I do. Otherwise, I would never have come here tonight."

"Come, sit on this bench," he said. He guided her to the bench and they sat down, still holding hands.

They stared into each other's eyes, but Chessie stiffened.

"Is that . . . Did you hear something over there by the path?" she asked. "I'm sure I did!"

Carlo glanced around, then looked back into Chessie's blue eyes. "It's nothing," he said. "It's only the wind, or some night creature. We're safe here in the park. And I'm armed."

"I do feel safe with you," she whispered. She repeated it to herself. She did feel safe. Yet she could not escape the sense of sounds in the darkness, the feeling that they were being watched.

It's nothing . . . Only my guilt at being here, she thought, as she gazed into Carlo's eyes, felt the pressure of his hands on hers. She vowed that she would suffer no more guilt about such a depth of feeling as this.

Carlo kissed her lips again, a softer, shorter kiss than she would have liked, but she did not feel bold enough to prolong the kiss. She did touch his cheek with her open hand a moment.

They began to talk softly, hesitatingly, then beginning with a rush of words, clumsily interrupting each other. Each was anxious to learn everything about the other. Chessie told Carlo of her life at The Columns, of her feelings about travel, her interest in sketching. Her words came faster and faster. She could ask him a thousand questions!

Carlo put his arm around Chessie's shoulder as he answered her questions.

"My parents fled Palermo some weeks ago," he began. "My father is old and rather feeble. They closed our villa here and went up to Naples. I never stay in the villa any longer, Chessie, but I visited it just yesterday, before the duel. I wandered about the grounds, in the musty rooms, accompanied by an old servant, and I was surprised at the . . . the sadness, the nostalgia I felt. I remember so many times when I was younger, when I was a child, and played there . . . And now, well, one way or another, I feel quite strongly that I'll never live there again. Probably, I'll never even set foot in the place again."

Chessie thought of her love for The Columns. She felt a stab of sympathy at the thought Carlo might never live in his childhood home again.

Chessie asked him about brothers and sisters.

"I'm an only child," he said. "Because the birth was difficult, my mother wasn't able to bear other children. At times in the last two or three years, I fear she's been sorry she bore me."

Without being asked, Carlo went on to tell Chessie of his childhood in Palermo. He spoke with little emotion, with no self-pity.

"That's simply how it was," he said. "The usual childhood for the only son of a wealthy, aristocratic family. Sicilians are notorious for pampering sons. I am, I suppose, still quite spoiled."

Then, Carlo told Chessie of going away to school in Paris, where he neglected his studies to drink and pursue ladies, and spent night-long sessions with other young aristocrats who fancied themselves liberals, drinking brandy and talking, in the most idealistic and vague terms, of righting terrible wrongs in Italy, and complaining, as the sun rose, that their allowances from their families were late again.

"Not a pretty portrait, I'm afraid," he muttered finally, and withdrew his arm from Chessie's shoulders. "I've never told this story to anyone. You have the . . . the oddest effect on me, Chessie. It's both exhilarating and frightening."

Chessie was startled to learn that she could frighten anyone, particularly a man such as Carlo. But his confidences gave him more depth of character, and she was flattered that he had chosen her to confide in. She searched his handsome, troubled face, and wished she could find the courage to kiss him passionately and to express feelings that were far deeper than mere infatuation.

Carlo put his arm around her shoulders again and she snuggled against him. She met his kiss with open lips. His tongue touched hers and she ran her fingers against his neck. They continued to kiss, with eager soft kisses on the eyes and cheeks, then deep, passionate kisses that left Chessie trembling with desire.

Carlo began to caress Chessie's body. She tensed at the first touches of his fingers along her breasts, over her stomach, then the tension became an extension of her sexual excitement.

"Oh, Christ, you're beautiful," Carlo muttered.

He buried his face in her lap, kneeling before her as he slipped his hands up under her silken skirts to stroke her soft skin.

"Carlo, Carlo, darling," she gasped. She opened her thighs to his eager hands.

Her thighs quivered as his fingers skated higher over

the warm, tender flesh. She felt a pulsing deep inside her keeping time with her heartbeat.

Chessie was lost in passion now, beyond thought. Carlo's hands found her buttocks and he stood up, lifting her a little, then lying her down gently on the bench. She trembled and succumbed to his hands which were pulling up her petticoats, parting her thighs, while his lips kissed her breasts.

Suddenly, he stiffened. He pulled from her body and sat up.

"Chessie, no, we mustn't," he mumbled. "We must not, despite my intense desire for you! You're too important to me. It must be done in a proper manner, Chessie. You inflamed me!"

Chessie caught her breath and her sense of propriety returned.

"Oh, Carlo, I, too, became inflamed," she said.

She smoothed her rumpled dress and petticoats. Her breathing was ragged. She felt hot and weak. Her body was completely aroused, yet she, too, wanted to stop, and she respected Carlo's gentleness and restraint.

"Thank you for being so strong . . ." Chessie said. She kissed his lips gently. "I'll always remember this and be the fonder of you, Carlo."

"Must you leave tomorrow, Chessie?" he asked. "Yes, you must! It won't be safe much longer in Palermo, and I won't be here to protect you."

"What do you mean?" she asked. She became alarmed. "You're not going to join Garibaldi? No! Come to Rome with me, Carlo."

"I must join Garibaldi," Carlo said. "For myself, for the rightness of his cause . . . and for what you may think of me. I do believe in Garibaldi's cause, and now my love for you emboldens me, Chessie. I can't live without convictions. You'd soon begin to despise me. As soon as I can, I'll join you in Rome."

Chessie could not persuade Carlo to change his mind and though she hated the thought that they would be separated, hated the risk he was taking, she knew he was right.

Clayton had handled all the arrangements of their journey and lodgings and Chessie did not know where she would be staying in Rome. Carlo said that he would arrange for Peppino to get the address from her and bring it to him. They would meet in Rome, and he promised that it wouldn't be long.

They kissed and each shyly admitted that love, not infatuation, was what they felt for each other.

"We must go now," Carlo said finally. "Very soon, I'll come to you in Rome. Never doubt my love, Chessie, '. . . For this love I bear you is deeper far than oceans, and more constant than the tides.' "

"I'll remember that . . . and wait for you," Chessie said. "Come quickly, Carlo. Just be safe and come to me."

31.

Chessie's face was wet with tears as they parted. She hurried down the dark path without looking back, bold and confident now, glowing with her new love.

Her boldness began to fade into anxiety as she walked toward the villa. She was certain she heard footsteps in the darkness of the bushes and vines, and she knew they weren't Carlo's.

Chessie started running. She heard the crunch of gravel nearby. She stumbled, nearly fell. A shadow cut the path behind her, another shadow loomed in front.

Chessie stopped. The villa was far away, too far for anyone to hear her cries. The shadows smothered in on her as she stood trembling, shadows made long and menacing by the bright fires on the mountain.

"Carlo!" she screamed. "Carlo, help me!"

A third shadow crashed through the bushes. She lurched away and the man's hand grazed her arm. She screamed again.

"Quick, grab her, shut her up, Bruno!" someone cried.

"No, please," Chessie begged.

Her legs began to lose their strength. The three men closed in on her. An old man grinned. His mouth opened. She saw the hideous stubs of his teeth.

"Please don't hurt me," she whimpered.

A filthy hand closed over her mouth. Her arms were pinned behind her back. She kicked, feeble kicks that were useless. A hand squeezed her breast so hard it hurt.

"Ah, she'll warm us well till the old don pays for her release," the man said as he pinched her nipple.

"Idiot," a fat man said. "Stop fondling her and tie her hands!"

Sharp rope bit into Chessie's wrists. She couldn't breathe. She had never known such terror.

Another shadow moved. The men cursed, pulled pistols.

"Release the girl!" Chessie shuddered with relief at the sound of Carlo's voice. But alone, he would have little chance against three armed men.

"Cattiva!" the stump-toothed man said. "We should have taken them as they kissed."

"We'll kill you," another man said, leveling his pistol at Carlo, who was also holding a pistol.

"Don't be a fool," Carlo said, walking slowly toward Chessie. "I'm not your enemy, and shots will only bring the police and soldiers . . ."

"The young don's right," the fat man said. "And I know him. He favors Garibaldi!"

"Crespino?" Carlo asked.

"Yes, Don Carlo," Crespino said. He released Chessie's wrists. "Come . . . Dammit, we must escape."

The other two men mumbled curses, but they put their pistols into their belts and followed him down the path.

Carlo hugged Chessie, kissed her softly on the lips and, vowing his love, he begged her to hurry inside.

She kissed his cheek, then turned and ran toward the villa.

For a second night Chessie could not sleep. All night she lay awake and relived her meeting with Carlo. She was sad to have been parted from him, but sustained by strong memories—of his voice saying, ". . . This love I bear you is deeper far than oceans . . .", of his kisses and his bold hands exciting and awakening her body. And toward dawn Chessie's own hands became bold, too, exploring her body as Carlo had done. Darling Carlo, she whispered again and again, remembering that he loved her, loved her so that he had put aside his own passion, that he had decided to fight with Garibaldi . . .

The thought terrified her. Please God, let him be safe, she prayed. Of course she wished he would not go, but she knew Carlo was right about himself. He must act on his convictions and beliefs, and she was the cause of his strengthened convictions. He won't be away for long, she thought, and found comfort in a fantasy of their reunion in Rome, their happy days together there, and afterwards, perhaps . . . surely, at The Columns. We will be married at The Columns, Chessie planned, and then blushed at the idea of such perfect happiness.

The next morning the Roccalini house was abuzz with rumors about Garibaldi's landing in Marsala. Apparently General Landi was marching overland to intercept Garibaldi. They must make haste, Clayton said. Maids dragged out their trunks and the hallways were full of trunks and stacks of clothing to be packed.

Chessie paid little attention to the activity. She was in a world of her own. For almost an hour she stood staring from the window, strangely calm and radiant. Seeing her, Clayton commented on how happy she looked. Torine kissed her and said this surely wasn't the same girl who had sailed from New Orleans.

"You're lookin' much more like a grown-up lady now," the maid said. "You look prettier, you act prettier. If I was the pryin' kind, I'd ask which young man has taken your fancy, Miss Chessie."

Twice, when she was alone, Chessie took out Carlo's note and looked at it. Just seeing it made her blood pound. She kissed her index finger and rubbed it over his handwriting. I never knew I could feel so much . . . be so alive, she marveled.

Carefully she wrote a note for Peppino, telling Carlo where she could be reached in Rome and adding a few lines sending him her love. Peppino had been out all morning but was expected back before they had to leave for the docks.

Then, just before noon, while Chessie stood at the window again, Maria Cristina came in and confided to Chessie that she had a wonderful secret.

"I simply must tell someone or I'll burst," she said. "But please, Chessie, don't tell anyone else. The truth is . . . I . . . I'm deeply in love with someone and have been for weeks!"

Chessie was used to Maria Christina's impulsive infatuations—it seemed that she fell in love once a week, but she felt a new sympathy now. "Maria Cristina, do tell me who it is," Chessie said impatiently. "I swear to keep your secret."

"Chessie, I met a man—alone—in . . . private circumstances," Maria Cristina said. "I'm in love with him. Really in love! Oh, he spoke such fine words of love and passion and said he had suffered for me! What he really wanted was to seduce me, Chessie! Oh, dear, I took such a chance. He pretended to be boyish and fearful of fighting with Garibaldi, as he was declaring his love to me. He'd have done anything to make me surrender. He even quoted some love poetry . . . 'This love I bear you is deeper far than oceans, and more constant than the tides' . . . Well, he did get a few kisses, I'll confess, and . . . Why, Chessie, dear, whatever has come over you?"

Tears burst from Chessie's eyes. Her mouth fell open and she gasped for air. She felt she might vomit. A wave of nausea tightened her stomach and she bent over in pain.

Maria Cristina reached for Chessie's arm, but Chessie shoved her hand away and stumbled out of the room.

32.

Clayton and Chessie arrived in Rome on a fine day in May. Although Chessie was quite exhausted from the last leg of their journey north along rough and dangerous roads, she insisted that they both drive around the city in a hired carriage, "Just to see the principal sights."

Clayton was glad enough to see Chessie showing some spirit, although he would willingly have postponed a glimpse of the ruined Colosseum, the Forum, and the Capitoline Hill until a later day. Chessie had been pale and despondent nearly all the way up from Sicily, and he had no idea why. Woman troubles, he surmised.

He had nearly forgotten her declarations of love for Carlo Settimo and supposed that she had forgotten them, also. At any rate, he did not associate them with her recent languor. And now she seemed better, seemed delighted with Rome, for all it was crowded and dusty, and he left her at their hotel, the Minerva, and went to look for the *portiere,* who had promised that when they had returned from their ride, there would be mail.

He found the *portiere* asleep behind a gigantic potted palm in the Minerva's mosaic-tiled conservatory and was at first astonished and then amused when the man explained that the postman was indeed in the quarter and could be found in a certain tavern from which he always distributed the mail.

"Si, signore, it's the custom," the *portiere* said. "You can't expect a man to carry all those heavy letters around on his back . . ."

Clayton went out to find the postman in a small tavern off Via del Corso, one of Rome's main streets. Letters were spread out on a rough wooden table near a flask of wine and several cups.

"Pay me a *baiocco,* one copper coin, and take whatever you see that's yours," the postman said.

"But what if someone else has taken my letters?" Clayton asked.

The postman shrugged and poured wine into his cup. "Ah, well, that would be too bad. Usually, people want only their own mail. In any case, I can't read, so how can I tell?"

Clayton found two fat letters from his mother. He picked up the letters and left two copper coins on the table.

In an elegant tavern on Via del Corso Clayton drank a brandy and read the letters from Lucinda. Her news of crops and planting made him nostalgic for Mississippi and some of her light gossip amused him, but news of the presidential election and the growing mood of resentment in the South angered him.

It all seemed so far away, yet it, not Roman customs, would shape the rest of his life. Not for the first time, Clayton questioned the purpose of this European tour. There was nothing in Rome for him—he knew not a soul here, although he had a case of introductory letters, and he had heard that a gentleman could amuse himself here. Oh, well . . . He sighed.

The brandy had stimulated Clayton for a few minutes but now he felt weary. The carriage ride had been both boring and exhausting. He walked back toward his hotel and decided he would take a nap before lunch.

A block from the Minerva Clayton was stopped by the sight of a huge funeral procession coming through the wrought-iron gates of a small *palazzo.* He stopped to watch the carriages and horses and began discussing it with a French officer he had seen in the tavern. It was a curious sight. The corpse, openly displayed in its bier, was dressed in rich and elaborate ceremonial vestments and followed by a parade of servants, empty horse-drawn carriages, and a multitude of monks in the robes of many orders, chanting prayers as they walked.

"The dogs of the deceased should be in the procession but the weather is too hot for them," the officer commented. He explained to Clayton that none of the man's family or friends were taking part in the services.

"I went in to have a look at the old fellow," the officer said. "To satisfy my curiosity. Many people do, you know, just to see the furnishings of the house, the paintings, and of course, the corpse. He was surrounded by masses of candles. But his family, ah, they would have fled at the first indication that death was near. Many Romans believe that the dying are cursed with the evil. No, this old fellow's relatives are likely out in their country place, and they've left the monks, the paid mourners, the servants and the horses to bury him. Look, here comes one of his more faithful dogs now . . ."

But Clayton was no longer listening to the soldier. He was staring at a girl, modestly but elegantly dressed in blue silk, who stood across the street.

Clayton was arrested by the sight. He caught his breath. She was the loveliest girl he had ever seen. Her oval face was pale, her large black eyes wide-set and heavy-lashed, and a cloud of black hair framed her face. Her eyes seemed sad, so sad that Clayton was touched with compassion as they fixed on him. She was Clayton's vision of the girl he would love forever, the girl he would marry.

As Clayton stared, an old woman in black, with a black shawl over her head, leaned forward and spoke to the girl. Clayton realized with surprise that the old woman was as dark-skinned as a Negro but he could not see her face. The girl shook her head, as if to say no. The woman turned to a man in black livery. The man glanced at Clayton, then said something to the girl.

The funeral procession passed in front of Clayton. For a moment he could not see across the street. "Who is that girl? Do you know?" he asked the officer eagerly, but the officer said no.

Slowly, with rising chants and the mournful beating of a drum, the procession crossed Clayton's view and when the last mourners had passed, the girl had disappeared.

Clayton ran across the street. He fought through the crowd, rushed up a flight of steps. From the top step he saw her being helped into a huge carriage by a church in a nearby piazza.

Clayton rushed down the stairs and into the piazza, but her carriage was pulling away as he reached it. The driver whipped the black horses. The carriage quickly gained too much speed for Clayton to follow, and he stopped, disappointed, and wiped his forehead with the back of his hand.

But from the window of the big carriage, the girl's pale face looked out at him with an expression that seemed both longing and wistful. Clayton was struck by its beauty even more forcefully than before. If he never saw her again, he knew he would always remember that pure, pale, lovely face, and the crest on the side of the carriage, two black eagles in a field of white.

Clayton was still catching his breath and wondering what he would have said had he caught the carriage when an old woman in rags hobbled up to him.

"Ah, I see the gentleman has lost his race," she said.

Clayton's first impulse was to pull away. The woman's pock-marked face repelled him, but he sensed that she had not come up without a purpose.

"Yes, I have," he said. "Do you know whose carriage that was?"

Her laugh was shrill. "Perhaps I do, sir," she said. "I've seen other gentlemen lose that race. But some, to their regret, have outrun the horses."

The hag's as crazy as she is ugly, Clayton thought. And probably diseased. He stepped away and turned to leave.

"Oh, I could tell you whose carriage it is," she said.

Clayton turned back to the woman. "Without speaking in circles?" he asked.

"Ah, *bello,* I can speak straight as any," she said. "But I best find my tongue at the touch of a coin in my palm."

"Yes, I should've realized," Clayton said. He took a copper coin from his pocket, then hesitated. "How do I know your information is accurate?"

"Why should I lie?" she asked. "If I do, you can find me near the church every day, selling my pictures of the saints and martyrs to the devout and other pictures to those with more worldly interests. Ask anyone about me. They all know Zia Tania."

"All right, all right," Clayton said. He dropped the coin into her outstretched palm, careful not to touch her withered skin.

"The carriage belongs to the Countess Corloni," the woman said. "The girl who caught your eye is her daughter, Gianna. A devout girl, I hear. Raised by the nuns, I've heard tell."

"And is she still in a convent?" Clayton asked. "What was she doing here just now? Why was she watching the funeral procession?"

"Ah, beauty, the Corlonis don't confide in me," the woman said. "I don't know if the girl is still with the nuns. As for the procession . . . It's strange to see a member of the family so near the evil eye. The Corlonis were related to Count Ettore, who just died. All those noble families are related. They all marry each other, to keep us poor folks out. I've seen the girl visiting his *palazzo* before."

Clayton was lost in thought. He was sure he had heard of the Countess Corloni, but he couldn't remember where, or what had been said about her.

"Where does the countess live?" Clayton asked.

"Where does she live?" The woman broke into a hacking laugh. "Where does the Countess Corloni live? Ah, beauty, when she's in Rome, where would she live but in the Villa Corloni? And she's an exception to what I just said about the nobility marrying each other. She was just a commoner when she married old

Count Corloni. The *pasquini* say she was so poor she wore rags before her marriage, she and that nigger who's always been with her."

"What are the *pasquini*?" Clayton asked impatiently. He was tired of talking to the woman. He didn't care about the countess. He only wanted to find the girl. "No more stories . . . Just tell me how to find the Villa Corloni."

"But, beauty," she crooned, "no one in Rome can forget the *pasquini*. Those who try make a mistake . . . The *pasquini* are Rome's talking statues . . . statues that tell the truth about what goes on with our betters, our holy rulers and the nobility."

"To hell with it," Clayton said, sure he could learn the location of the Villa Corloni from a more pleasant source. He muttered thanks to the woman and walked away.

"You'll find the Villa Corloni easily enough!" the woman shouted after him. "Oh, it's easily found, but take care, *bello,* for some have found it to their sorrow . . ."

33.

The Countess Corloni pulled on a pair of black silk gloves, then she entered the small, private chapel at her villa on the edge of Rome and lit a taper beneath the portrait of her late father.

She sank to her knees and as she prayed she glanced from a gilded statue of the madonna to her father's portrait. As always, when she prayed, she felt that her father's spirit was very near. Finally she crossed herself and left the chapel.

She went to her bedroom where a servant told her that Gianna had not yet returned.

"Inform me at once when she comes in," the countess said.

Impatiently, she stepped onto a rose-filled balcony that overlooked some of the villa's parks and gardens. The Villa Corloni was a four-story baroque manor house built in the last century when the first Count Corloni had received his title and land from a grateful pope to whom he loaned several million lira in a time of crisis.

The gardens had been laid out in high baroque style —a horticultural fantasy of curved paths and *escaliers,* little low fences and pools, carvings and arabesques, grottoes and waterfalls.

The countess saw a group of visitors coming into the villa's lower park. How tiresome, she thought. How had it ever become customary for the nobility to open their parks to the wretched public one day a week?

The countess turned away from the visitors, who were coming nearer the villa. She hated to be stared at by common people. She felt sure they despised the nobility. Some were the very ones, she was sure, who crept out at night to tack malicious drawings and cartoons on their *pasquini.*

The countess smiled at a bitter and refreshing memory. Her late husband had known how to deal with such arrogance and for many years she had been spared such attacks. Now that she was determined that Gianna marry Prince Vittori she wondered if the drawings and cartoons would attack her again.

Her thumb began to itch. She scratched it with quick, delicate strokes.

No gossip or graffiti could stop her now, the countess thought with satisfaction. No one on earth could prevent Gianna's marriage. Not the reluctant old prince, who had long hesitated to marry beneath royalty, despite his obvious infatuation with Gianna and his desperate need for her dowry.

"Not even Gianna herself," the countess muttered aloud.

Gianna might protest, but she would not defy her mother's wishes.

No, Gianna would obey, so the countess had only

one fear: that Gianna might accidentally become infatuated with some young suitor. So far, she had been home from the convent only a few weeks and the countess had used her influence and wealth—and some hired thugs—effectively to discourage the men who tried to call on Gianna.

The countess wished she could forbid her daughter to go out at all. But she supposed that if the girl were well chaperoned and went out only briefly to shop for ribbons, as today, or to visit family friends, such as Count Croce, no harm could be done.

The countess walked into her drawing room. She scratched her thumb but the itching did not stop. She grimaced when she saw her distorted face in a mirror. She rearranged her face quickly and deliberately. She was satisfied. Her face was still beautiful, she thought. Her face, at least, bore no marks . . .

The countess shuddered at her thoughts. She turned so abruptly that she nearly knocked a chair over.

She ran into the hall and summoned a servant.

"Hasn't my daughter returned?" she demanded. "She's long overdue! Where can . . . ?"

But the countess broke off her sentence. She heard Gianna's voice downstairs. The countess sighed. Gianna, her baby, her daughter, her only loved one, was safe. She longed to run to her, but she caught herself and descended the stairs very slowly and with deliberate dignity.

"Hello, Mama," Gianna said, averting her eyes from her mother.

"And just where have you been, Gianna?" the countess asked. "You promised that you'd only visit that ribbon shop off the Corso, then come right back home."

"I'm sorry, Countess," the maid said. "There was nothing we could do. Once there, she insisted that she watch Count Ettore's funeral procession."

"But that's dreadful!" the countess said. "Gianna, how could you be so reckless? You didn't go close to the body? You know the evil eye has infected the poor man . . ." She crossed herself.

"Oh, Mama," Gianna said. "There's no evil eye! Besides, I was across the street. Ettore was my favorite cousin. I think it's barbaric, his entire family running away . . ."

"Do not dare speak of Romans as barbarians!" the countess said. "Just what did those Florentine nuns put into your head? Gianna, I want to be able to allow you to go out. But I won't have you disobey me!"

"I'm sorry, Mama," she said. "I'm sorry I worried you. May I be excused now? I'm exhausted and rather melancholy, and I'd like my siesta."

"Yes, go have your siesta, dear," the countess said.

Gianna kissed her mother's cheek, then went up the stairs. The countess was filled with an aching and desperate love as she watched her go. She would do anything for Gianna, and marrying her to a prince was, she felt certain, the best thing she could possibly do.

"I trust that Gianna spoke to no one," the countess said to the maid.

"No one, Countess," the maid said. "One young man stared at her from the opposite side of the street and as we were driving off, he ran after us. But we lost him quickly. Some tourist, most likely. No harm was done."

"I suppose not."

"You're tired, Countess," Flora said. "You should have a siesta yourself."

"No, no, I've too much to do," the countess said.

She hesitated a moment, then walked up the stairs and returned to the chapel, afraid that sleep would bring the nightmares that had returned after so many years.

34.

Chessie and Signora Nantes decided to walk home and sent their easels back in their carriage. Signora Nantes was an artistic young widow who gave painting lessons to foreign ladies. Chessie was fond of the vivacious, dark-eyed signora who today had taken her to sketch in the Borghese gardens.

Chessie had loved the view over the red-and-buff tile roofs, the green terraces and the domes of the churches, with the great cupola of St. Peter's in the background, all flanked by the gray-hazed Alban Hills.

As they strolled down from the gardens, Chessie was in high spirits and delighted to be in Rome on this warm afternoon in late June. She loved sketching in Rome's parks and piazzas and in the gardens of the private *palazzi* that the nobles opened to the public once a week. She felt quite comfortably settled, now that she and Clayton had moved into an apartment on Via Frattina, between Via del Corso and Piazza di Spagna.

As Chessie and Signora Nantes entered the Piazza di Spagna they were approached by a man Chessie had met at a party the previous evening, Count Paola Croce.

Bowing courteously, Count Croce paid his compliments to the two ladies. He asked about their health and commented on the weather. But his eyes held Chessie's for long moments and Chessie sensed that he was more than casually interested in her.

A bit shyly, she studied him. He was a stocky, muscular dark-haired man with a handsome, square-shaped face and dark, penetrating eyes. Everything about him suggested wealth and an easy acceptance of power—his rich, elegant suit and immaculate white shirt, his half-arrogant smile, and the casual grace with which he twirled a braided leather riding crop. Chessie watched him with growing interest as he chatted with her companion and then turned away in confusion when their eyes met again. His gaze is too insistent, too probing, she thought. Why, it was as if he were looking straight through her, and could guess all her secret thoughts.

When the count left, the signora said, "Count Croce seems to have taken a fancy to you, Chessie. One could hardly mistake the way he looked at you. Do you know him well?"

"Hardly at all, signora," Chessie said. "I only met him last evening. Do you know him?"

"Only slightly," she said. "But he's one of Rome's most influential men. He knows everything that happens here, and has a hand in much of it. I've heard he can be ruthless. He is quite handsome and charming."

"Yes, he seems most charming," Chessie said. She hoped she would see him again.

At Signora Nantes' suggestion, they stopped at the Caffé Moro for a pineapple sherbet.

As they ate their sherbet, Signora Nantes was approached from time to time by a French officer. She was the widow of a French captain. Some of the officers' talk concerned the fighting in the South between the Bourbons and Garibaldi's forces.

The news caused Chessie to worry about Carlo, despite all her efforts to resist.

The first few weeks after she sailed from Palermo, she had been heartbroken, even physically ill over Carlo's betrayal, and these twilight hours had been the most miserable of her day. At first she thought she would never recover and had no desire to do so.

For as much as Chessie had been hurt, she had been humiliated. Carlo had courted her and lied to her and she felt that everyone must be aware of it, felt she must show her humiliation on her face like a stigmata.

Yet, through all of this, she had worried about Carlo's safety. She could not wish him ill, no matter how she had suffered, but she was determined to forget him, and, in time, the pain lessened and she seldom thought of him.

She sighed now, and forced thoughts of Carlo out of her mind. She was glad when they finished the sherbet and left the café.

Rome's principal streets and piazzas were jammed with elegantly dressed people taking part in the evening ritual of the *passeggiata*. Signora Nantes suggested that they abandon fashion for a more leisurely walk. Chessie agreed.

The sky was a dark purple and the narrow streets they walked were dim and shadowed. There were no street lamps, only small candles beneath little shrines to the madonna and saints embedded in the walls. A few years earlier, gas lamps had been installed on a few main streets, but this had met with much protest, since the Romans felt that the light from religious candles was quite sufficient and anything brighter was sacrilege.

Their walk took them to a small, irregularly shaped piazza where Chessie became interested in an ancient, legless torso on a pedestal.

"If you find him so interesting, perhaps he'll talk to you, Chessie," Signora Nantes said.

"Talk to me? What do you mean? I'd be frightened to death!"

"Oh, no, dear, not like that," the signora said. "Not with spoken words. This statue speaks with cartoons and graffiti. He's very witty and knows the latest gossip about counts and cardinals and the rest. Haven't you heard of Rome's *pasquini,* our talking statues? The only way people can express opinions about the church or the high-born is to post satirical pieces on these statues."

"How very curious," Chessie said.

"Let me tell you about a most interesting graffito once left on this statue, Chessie," the signora said.

Some twenty years earlier, the signora began, the Count Corloni married a woman who had been so poor she took in washing. On the day of their wedding, the *pasquino* woke up wearing a dirty shirt. A lampoon attached during the night asked why. A second lampoon answered: "Since my washerwoman is becoming a countess, she has better uses for her time than to take care of my linen."

The joke circulated widely and was vastly appreciated. The count announced that both he and his new wife admired the author's cleverness. The count wanted to reward such wit, he said, but first he had to know who its author was. He promised that if the man came forward, he would, on his oath, give him a handsome reward.

"What happened?" Chessie asked.

"The author made himself known," the signora said, "and the count kept his promise. He gave the man a sack of gold coins. But he also had the man's right hand cut off."

"How dreadful!" Chessie said. "How deceitful!"

"The count argued that he had kept his oath to reward the man," Signora Nantes said. "He said he had never promised he wouldn't punish him, as well. The word was that it was the count's bride who was behind the deceit."

"Well, it's quite gruesome," Chessie said. "Corloni? I believe I heard people talk of her in Palermo. And aren't we supposed to visit the Villa Corloni soon, to see the park and sketch? I'm not sure I want to go."

The signora laughed. "Unless you've done something to offend the countess, you'll be quite safe," she said. "Besides, at present her only concern is marrying her daughter to old Prince Vittori."

"You can be sure I'll go out of my way not to offend Countess Corloni," Chessie said. "Now, please, may we hire a carriage? I don't feel like walking any more."

They secured a carriage and as they drove away, Chessie glanced back at the *pasquino* and shuddered.

35.

Fired by a zeal no better reasoned than his original decision to join the *carbonari* and impassioned by memories of Chessie's innocent love, Carlo joined Garibaldi's army outside Marsala.

At first sight, the army looked more like brigands than well-drilled soldiers. Most of the men were bearded, long-haired and ill-kempt. They carried outdated weapons and wore unmatched uniforms, many of them in scarlet tunics intended for use in slaughter-houses and so colored to camouflage the blood of animals. There were seasoned soldiers among The Thousand, as they were called, but there were also others, like Carlo Settimo, who had never seen battle before, and even a contingent of teenaged boys from an orphanage—some of them no taller than their rifles.

At the point when Carlo joined The Thousand, they were on a forced march through the hills behind Marsala, a long, ragged column of men moving toward Palermo even as General Landi with his Bourbon troops prepared an advance to seal off the mountain passes and trap Garibaldi's troops.

Before he had marched more than a few hours, Carlo had reason to respect his fellow soldiers, however irregular their appearance. The pace of the march left him gasping for breath. His legs and back ached, his feet blistered. It was swelteringly hot. Sweat soaked his fine clothes and the glaring light made his eyes sting and his head ache.

I've been idle and dissolute too long, Carlo admitted to himself, and my life of drinking and late nights has weakened me.

Almost at once, he regretted his decision to join Garibaldi, but he knew he could not give up. He saw at once that he lacked the firm ardor of the others—his decision had been, in truth, casual and selfish, but it was also for selfish reasons that he knew he could not desert the march.

I must do this, Carlo thought wearily. I can't turn back and retain my pride. My life has come to a point where I must stand by my resolution—I must prove myself.

Carlo knew he had been cynical, had lacked strong convictions, had slipped into a life of degenerate passions, but he was disturbed, in particular, by the deceitful and cruel way he had treated Chessie Deavors just before leaving Palermo. Despite his physical exhaustion and mounting fear of the battles that must lie ahead, his mind returned to the memory of his last meeting with Chessie and he was bitterly ashamed.

I'm afraid I've lost her forever, Carlo thought. I was false to her, I'm afraid I hurt her deeply and that she'll never forgive me.

When he thought back to their last meeting Carlo realized how blind, how stupid he had been.

In truth, Carlo had agreed to the duel with Pierre Sebastiano more for his honor than for Chessie's, but when he had asked her to meet him in the park it had been because he wanted desperately to see her. There was something quite different about the quiet American girl. In part it was the beauty and spirit of her face and in her utterly innocent blue eyes, a beauty and spirit yet unexpressed. Carlo had been surprised, even a bit frightened to realize how much Chessie appealed to him.

And he had intended to behave honestly with her. For a time, he had done well. He had guarded himself, refused to flirt with her and tease her as he did all other women. But when he realized that, for the first time in his life, he was confronting his feelings and weaknesses, he had been afraid.

Despite himself, at their last meeting, he had lapsed into his standard seduction speech and quoted the same love poetry. Carlo knew he could have seduced Chessie. That did not surprise him, but he had been surprised at the depths of feeling her innocent openness had stirred, surprised by the force of his honest love for her, despite his clumsiness in expressing it.

Chessie had left the park believing him, trusting him, loving him. He had felt new hope, real hope that with this woman's love he could change. She had inspired him to join Garibaldi—her love had convinced him that he could leave his old life behind, fight bravely for a real cause, and then join her in Rome.

But just before joining Garibaldi, Carlo had met with his man, Peppino, and Peppino had described Chessie's disappointed, angry mood when he had approached her to ask for her address in Rome. Carlo knew at once what that meant. Chessie must have learned from Maria Cristina that Carlo had tried to seduce her too and in the same way.

Carlo writhed with despair, imagining her shock, the pained confusion in Chessie's blue eyes.

How he despised himself for hurting her. She was rightly angry, and he feared that she would never forgive him or even see him again. Now she must think that all his declarations to her had been false!

And so, as Carlo marched on along the rocky mountain trail, his feet raw with blisters, every muscle aching as he moved toward a battle he feared he lacked the courage to endure, his mood was one of bleak despair.

Heading due east from Marsala, the *Garibaldini* marched through wild and desolate countryside in a parching heat, through dry, savage ravines and fields of huge, fallen boulders. Carlo heard constant talk of fighting and dying, of wounds and killing, and his fear of battle, his pain and weariness, distracted him from thoughts of Chessie.

Yet, she haunted his sleep.

On the second day, the land was less desolate. They passed groves of lemon trees and prickly-pear cactus.

And along the way the country people greeted Garibaldi with enthusiasm. There were celebrations of welcome in every hamlet they passed. Church bells rang. Village priests and Franciscan monks ran from monasteries and cheered wildly.

Even more encouraging, the exhausted marchers were joined by bands of volunteers, peasants and farmers armed with scythes and hunting knives, mattocks and pruning hooks.

The Thousand, swollen to about 2,500, marched on toward Palermo. They passed through groves of ancient olive trees on a high plain and camped at Salemi, a hill town above the groves.

Over a dinner of stew and onions, Carlo talked to some of his fellow soldiers, including a number of lawyers—he had heard that of the thousand who sailed from Genoa some 150 were lawyers—and some boys no more than fourteen or fifteen, who seemed like children in their baggy, oversized gray trousers and red tunics. One little boy fell asleep sitting before the fire, as innocently as a baby.

The sight of these child-soldiers with their antiquated weapons disturbed Carlo. He remembered the multitudes of well-dressed, disciplined soldiers with the fine, modern guns that he had seen in Palermo. Landi's troops were said to number at least 16,000.

Carlo thought of the battle the next day and his fear returned. How could this motley volunteer army stand up to Landi's seasoned soldiers? How could he himself find the courage?

He heard a *carbonari* friend laughing about their unofficial uniform of red shirts. "Of course, we wear them by chance—like so many butchers," the man said, "but the color does make conspicuous those who try to sneak away from the battle. Not that any of us would be so cowardly, of course."

"Of course not," Carlo said.

His fear was so intense as he spoke that he feared the others could read it in his face.

36.

That night, Carlo tried without success to sleep. As he lay awake he listened to rain falling on the roof of his tent with a desolate sound.

By dawn the rain had stopped. It was a cool, clear day. Buglers blew reveille and Garibaldi's small army began once more to march toward Palermo. Past Salemi the road was lined with poplars and cypress trees, prickly-pears and thick-leaved aloes. Lemon groves covered the hills in the distance. The morning grew warmer. Carlo was hot and thirsty by the time the column reached the haunting ruins of Segesta, near the small town of Calatafimi, and his head pounded with exhaustion and fear.

Garibaldi and a few officers had gone on ahead. Carlo tensed as he heard rifle fire in the distance. Soon word came down the column that a large detachment of Bourbon troops had been sighted. The *Garibaldini* climbed a tall, rocky hill and there, across a valley, Carlo saw the long lines of a light infantry battalion, thousands of disciplined, professional soldiers with the most modern weapons.

Carlo feared that The Thousand were already lost, and most of the Sicilians seemed to agree, as they crept into the cover of huge gray rocks.

Carlo's hands trembled as he fixed his bayonet to his ancient rifle. He swallowed hard and clenched his jaw. He heard a trumpet blow the call to charge from the opposite hill.

The Bourbon lines began to move in slow, steady, disciplined columns. Shells exploded all around. One of the orphan boys screamed in shocked agony. A shell had blown him apart so near Carlo that the boy's blood splattered Carlo's face.

The Bourbon troops were firing steadily as they advanced. Shots rang off boulders near Carlo. More artillery shells burst, sending up great mounds of dirt and inflicting terrible wounds.

Carlo fought a powerful impulse to bolt and run. He gripped his rifle with sweat-slick hands and put it to his shoulder. Sweat and blood stung his eyes. At first he fired without aiming, then he reloaded and more calmly took aim. His stomach was knotted.

The Bourbons came on steadily, firing in steady bursts. Carlo glanced down the line of his fellow soldiers—civilian volunteers, teenage boys, and lawyers in top hats, all wearing motley red tunics, firing old weapons. Some of the Bourbons fell back but their lines continued to advance.

Carlo realized that they would soon close in on the *Garibaldini* and there would be hand-to-hand fighting with bayonets. He glanced over his shoulder. Some ten yards back was a dense patch of prickly-pear cactus. He had a clear path to the cactus, he could use it as cover and run for his life. He had withstood the fire, he told himself. Surely, Garibaldi's cause was hopeless. He didn't want to die for nothing. He couldn't face those grim, professional soldiers with a bayonet ...

Carlo felt panic swell like poison at the base of his throat. When a shell exploded at his feet he screamed out in terror. A bullet splintered a rock five feet from his head. A shell slammed dirt into his face. The Bourbons were only a few yards away. Carlo began to cry and whimper. He was too frightened to fire his rifle.

Carlo rose to one knee and glanced around at the cactus. He prepared to flee ...

And then, without orders, on an odd, but disciplined impulse, the *Garibaldini* rushed the Bourbon troops. Carlo was swept along with the charge. To his surprise, the Bourbons began to retreat back across the valley. He aimed and killed a soldier. Bullets flew past his head. Men all around him were hit and he stepped over crumpled bodies.

The Bourbons were retreating up the opposite hill. Carlo looked up and his heart sank: how could they charge up the steep, rocky hill, exposed to the fire of entrenched troops? It was still hopeless. They would be slaughtered.

But, as he was swept along, Carlo realized that the peasant farmers had built terraces on the steep slope. The *Garibaldini* took shelter under the stone walls of the terraces. Carlo forced himself to fire two rounds and run to the next terrace, where he took cover and tried to catch his breath in the shade of a fig tree. His mouth was filled with dust. He had never known such thirst. The sun was relentless. There was no wind. All around him men and boys were wounded. One skinny teenage soldier held a shattered arm and cried aloud for his mother.

Carlo saw men creep away. Once more, he thought of fleeing. The charge had been brave beyond belief and he had done his part in it, but surely everything was lost now. Any moment the Bourbons would charge down and annihilate the ragged, wounded volunteers.

Then he saw Garibaldi, sword in hand, approaching the battle line, oblivious to the bullets and shells. Garibaldi came to within a few feet of Carlo. He heard one of the officers suggest that they retreat.

Garibaldi's eyes flashed dark with anger. "No!" he shouted. *"Coraggio!* Here we shall make Italy . . . or die!"

Garibaldi moved to the first terrace, calling out encouragement to troops on the verge of panic. Carlo was near hysteria as he cringed beneath his fig tree. Yet he did not bolt and run. He surprised himself by moving up, just behind Garibaldi. Suddenly, a rock hit the general in the shoulder.

"They've run out of ammunition!" Garibaldi shouted. "Come on! They're throwing stones. Charge!"

He waved his sword and charged up the steep hill. Without hesitation, Carlo went after him, straight into a volley of heavy fire. The Bourbons had not run out of shells. Many *Garibaldini* were hit, but they were again on the offensive.

The Bourbons fought with ferocious courage. When their ammunition did run out they threw more stones. A stone struck Carlo in the shoulder and pain tore down his arm. But he swung his rifle and sunk his bayonet into the side of a Bourbon soldier, sickened at the crunch of bone and rush of blood.

He staggered on. The Bourbons fought as though crazed. Carlo killed another man with a savage thrust of his bayonet. A moment later a bayonet grazed his thigh from the side. He pulled out his pistol and shot his attacker through the head.

Carlo stumbled over bodies. He fought blindly. Acrid shell smoke blinded him and singed his nostrils. He thought each step would be his last. His heart thumped, he gasped for air. Once in the confusion and panic he nearly bayoneted one of his own men. Finally, he could go no further. He collapsed to his knees.

Then he realized that he could hear no more firing. The Bourbons were retreating. The *Garibaldini* were standing firm. Carlo panted in the dry heat. He tried to spit the dust from his mouth, but choked, gasping until an aide gave him a drink from a canteen.

They had lost thirty men and five times that number had been wounded. But the victory was theirs. As Carlo watched, the most badly wounded were piled onto the gaily painted, two-wheeled Sicilian carts. Dead men lay all around, hosts to a million buzzing flies.

And through all this, after having his thigh wound treated, Carlo lay in the dust, exhausted and shocked, unable to move until the next morning.

A little more than a week later, Garibaldi's forces reached the outskirts of Palermo. Carlo was among them. Despite his wounded thigh, marching over hilly, rocky terrain no longer exhausted him. He was a battle-seasoned soldier now. For the first time in his life he felt himself part of something in which he could believe, though he would never forget the horror of seeing fellow soldiers die, seeing the slaughter of children and the acts of cruelty on both sides.

Garibaldi's forces entered Palermo by the Porta di Termini at the south end of the Maqueda. As they marched through the city gates, an enthusiastic crowd was already occupying the marina and waving the tricolors of the *Garibaldini*.

Some of the red-shirts were wounded when they drove the Bourbons from the high barricades, but the greatest threat now came from Bourbon ships in the harbor, which began a fierce and indiscriminate bombardment of the city. Many buildings went up in flames. Others were reduced to rubble by the big guns. Panicked civilians clogged Palermo's narrow streets and church bells tolled constantly, as though their sound could end the bombardment.

Carlo sought cover at the center of the city near the Spanish fountains called Quattro Canti, where he had played as a child. He found shelter in the crevice of a brick wall while the guns thundered and the earth shook with the force of the explosions. He was badly frightened. The bombardment was so heavy and random that neither bravery nor fighting skill was of any use.

Carlo thanked God his family had left Palermo and feared for the safety of some of their servants who had remained loyal to the Bourbon cause. One of them, an old man named Cecci, had been like an uncle when Carlo was young, and he knew that Cecci had become a Bourbon police spy.

Carlo tensed as a shell burst near the fountains. Dirt and mortar stung his cheeks and eyes. The wall behind him shook. It might collapse at any moment, but there was even greater danger in rushing into the open.

Carlo wiped his face with the back of his hand. Even more than on the battlefield at Calatafimi he was stunned with the fear that he was about to be killed. Unimportant things faded from his consciousness, but the image of Chessie Deavors remained. More than ever he wanted to live. Dear God, he vowed, if I survive this bombardment, I'll go at once to Rome and see her again. Dear God, I want her and . . . I love her.

The next instant a shell exploded just behind him and a wall of bricks began to crumble. The first bricks struck his shoulders and neck. Instinctively, he ducked and started to run.

Then the Quattro Canti exploded in the air.

37.

In Rome, Clayton had learned, spies were as common as wine and spaghetti, and his growing determination to meet Gianna Corloni took him to such a spy one evening in the middle of July.

Clayton hurried down a narrow street paved with black, stained cobblestones, through a shabby neighborhood of ancient, crumbling buildings. He shuddered at the poverty and filth but, as so often in Rome, through the curved carriageways of magnificent *palazzi* now half in ruin, he glimpsed spacious courtyards set with marble fountains and statues. Some of the courtyards were overgrown with weeds, and in one he saw goats drinking from a fountain and women hanging laundry on the statues.

At the end of the street he entered a tavern dimly lit by paraffin lamps and met his spy, a man named Rossi. They drank raw white wine from cracked cups and Clayton handed Rossi five coins. Rossi reported that Gianna Corloni would be attending a party the next evening at Count Croce's estate in Frascati.

Clayton was elated when he left the tavern. Count Croce had been paying attention to Chessie lately and had invited her to the same party. Clayton was certain he could arrange to escort his sister.

After three hours at Count Croce's party the next evening, Clayton's high spirits had begun to fade. Gianna Corloni had not arrived. He drank champagne recklessly, darted about the count's vast parks that looked down the hills to the lights of Rome, went into the villa, became so desperate that he very nearly bribed the servants for information.

Clayton had never been so infatuated with a woman. In the time that had passed since he had first glimpsed her and learned her name, his infatuation had not weakened but had grown stronger. From his spies he had learned when she went to church or shopped on the Corso. For weeks, he had watched her, always from a discreet distance. She was never alone—always escorted by the dark woman or another chaperone and the brute of a footman. Clayton knew it would be a mistake to force himself on her in the street. This party was the ideal place to meet her in a natural way.

And now it looked as if she would not attend. Clayton took another glass of champagne and gulped it in frustration. He cursed Rossi. And then he turned around and saw her—Gianna Corloni herself—not twenty yards from him!

A woman hovered behind Gianna, but it wasn't the old Negro, who was her usual chaperone.

Clayton walked closer. His heartbeat accelerated.

Gianna Corloni was the loveliest girl he had ever seen. Her black eyes, pale, oval face, her long black hair, were all even more exquisite than he remembered.

Clayton handed his glass to a servant. He declined more champagne. A group of people were clustered around Gianna but Clayton pushed eagerly through them. He was only a few feet from Gianna now. He inhaled her perfume. It was more intoxicating than the champagne. Her black eyes were innocent, yet provocative, shy yet bold. And, as Clayton had noticed when he first saw her, her eyes seemed strangely sad for one so young.

After what seemed eternity, Clayton stood near her and was introduced by a fat duchess to whom New Orleans friends of his family had written a letter of introduction.

"Ah . . . Mr. Deavors, may I present the Donessa Corloni?" the duchess said. "Donessa, this is Mr. Clayton Deavors, a visitor from America." As usual in Italy, the duchess mispronounced "Deavors." "Mr. Deavors was recently a guest of Don Roccalini in Palermo and he's been telling me how he and his party barely escaped Sicily before the *Garibaldini* invaded the island."

"I'm honored to meet you, Donessa," Clayton said.

Gianna extended her hand. Clayton took it. He hesitated, instantly inflamed by the feel of her soft, warm skin. Then, nearly trembling, he pressed his lips against her fingers.

"I'm pleased to meet you, Mr. Deavors," she said as she withdrew her hand. Her voice was soft, hesitant, and carried a hint of the sadness he saw in her eyes.

Clayton never felt awkward with women, was never at a loss for what to say. But now he felt tongue-tied.

"I'm so glad you escaped Sicily safely," Gianna said. "And do you like Rome?"

"Yes . . . Yes, I do like Rome," he said. "Especially now . . ."

Gianna's dark eyes widened, then she smiled. "Really, Mr. Deavors?"

"Truly, Donessa," Clayton gulped. His mind was racing. This was his chance, perhaps his only chance, and she was so beautiful that he found it hard to speak.

"Where in America do you come from?" Gianna asked.

"The Southern part," Clayton said. He had learned that Italians could not understand the word Mississippi and most of them had never heard of it.

"I've never been to America," Gianna said, "though my mother once lived there. Your George Washington and Thomas Jefferson, weren't they also Southerners?"

"Yes, yes, they were," Clayton said. He was aware that he had talked with Gianna longer than anyone else who had been introduced. A tall, haughty-looking man was practically breathing down his neck. "But how do you happen to know about them?"

There was an undercurrent of comment at this and Clayton realized his question might be considered brash.

"Donessa Corloni," the duchess said, "may I introduce Signore . . . ?"

"Please, I haven't answered the gentleman's question," Gianna said sharply. The man drew back, as did the duchess. Gianna's voice softened as she turned to Clayton again.

"How do I happen to know about them?" she asked. "I studied in a convent in Florence. One could hardly study the history of recent times without knowing of them, I would think. Or do you, as so many others seem to, think that young women should learn only music and needlework?"

"No, no, I believe that . . . that young women should be taught everything they wish to learn," Clayton said. "I'm sure, Donessa, that you're a far better student than I ever was."

Gianna's chaperone stepped closer. She whispered to Gianna but the girl shook her head.

"Perhaps," Gianna said, "though I suspect you're being modest, sir. For one thing, your Italian is good. You must have studied very hard. Perhaps you're a scholar . . ."

"I'm hardly a scholar," Clayton said. "I did study Italian diligently. I seem to have some flair for languages."

"Yes, diligently," Gianna said. There was a slight edge to her voice now. "I would imagine you are a man of considerable diligence, a persistent man, a man who could be . . . reckless if he were determined to do something."

Gianna's eyes had hardened. She no longer smiled. Clayton could not doubt what her words meant. She had seen him following her in Rome and she was letting him know she considered him too bold.

He started to speak but she stopped him with a gesture of her hand.

"I've enjoyed our talk, sir," Gianna said. "I hope you continue to find Rome interesting." She turned to the duchess and allowed herself to be introduced to the tall man.

Clayton stepped back awkwardly, nearly stumbling. He was shocked. He had never been dismissed so abruptly. He gulped champagne and hovered just outside the group around Gianna. His eyes caught those of the old chaperone. She frowned.

Clayton turned to leave. He glanced back at Gianna. To his surprise, she smiled at him. Then she turned to the tall man once more.

He was elated. Gianna in person was more than he could have hoped for. She was truly the girl he had always wanted.

He drank more champagne and made an effort at polite conversation with the duchess who had introduced him to Gianna. Count Croce and Chessie joined them, and the count offered to show Clayton some rare, antique rifles. They left the party for a few minutes.

When they returned, Gianna was gone.

38.

Anthony became bored one morning in July as he drank whiskey alone in the parlor at The Columns. Lucinda had gone to visit a doctor in New Orleans and Jolette had accompanied her. At first Anthony had welcomed the solitude and peace.

But now Anthony wanted them back. At least, he very much wanted Jolette. He drained his glass and told himself he would grieve very little if Lucinda never returned. He found it more and more difficult to pretend he loved Lucinda. He no longer enjoyed sex with her, particularly now that she was ill so often.

Anthony realized that the whiskey was not helping to improve his spirits. He decided to go hunting. Yes, he told himself as he walked down the gallery, a long trek in the woods was just what he needed.

A fat slave named Sawyer was ambling across the back yard. Sawyer was notorious for his laziness. The idea of an indolent slave angered Anthony. He summoned Sawyer and ordered the slave to fetch three rifles, ammunition and a jug of water.

The morning was hot and humid and an hour from the plantation Anthony began to regret his decision. The weather and the long walk through thick forest growth had put Anthony into an even worse temper. He moved with long, impatient strides and Sawyer, weighed down by the rifles, ammunition and water jug, had difficulty keeping pace.

Anthony came out of the thicket of small white oaks. He wiped perspiration from his forehead with the back of his hand and wished he had brought something stronger than water.

He stopped abruptly at the edge of a clearing. A magnificent young buck stood across the clearing. An-

173

thony was upwind and the deer had not yet seen him. He had a clear shot, and it was less than twenty yards. Excitedly, he turned to Sawyer for a gun.

But Sawyer was several yards back. Anthony gestured for Sawyer to bring up a rifle quickly. Sawyer started running. He stepped on twigs. The buck raised its head, glanced around at Anthony, then burst out of the clearing.

"You stupid bastard!" Anthony shouted. "I ought to take out a piece of your hide for being so slow and costing me a deer!"

"I'm terrible sorry, Mist' Anthony," Sawyer said. "Hard for me to make tracks in this heat, carryin' all this . . ."

"Are you complaining about your work, nigger?" Anthony demanded.

"No, sir, not complainin', Mist' Anthony," Sawyer said. "But even unloaded, I ain't the fastest thing on The Columns . . ."

"Well, you better get faster this morning, boy!" Anthony said. "You hear me? The next time I reach around for my rifle, you better be there!"

"Yessir, Mist' Anthony," Sawyer said.

They set off again, across the clearing and into thick woods canopied by the leafy limbs of oaks and sycamores and stringy gray moss. Smaller, lower limbs and tangles of vines impeded their progress and left them scratched and bruised.

Anthony saw another buck but it quickly bolted away. He came on a flock of partridges. They flew off before he could get his rifle up. Sawyer tripped over a log half submerged in a slime bog and lost most of the ammunition.

Anthony cursed and shoved his way through thick scuppernong grape vines hanging from a cypress tree. Despite the heat and his weariness he was determined to get off at least one shot.

Sawyer fell behind, was cursed, threatened, caught up with Anthony, began to fall behind once more.

Ten minutes later Anthony had about decided he would return to The Columns. He realized he was randy—Jolette had been away four days. That's the trouble, he told himself. And he wasn't certain when Jolette would return. He considered going into Natchez, to one of the elegant mulatto whore-barges on the Mississippi River.

Christ, he muttered. He hoped that goddamn New Orleans specialist could cure Lucinda. Nothing frightened and angered him more than lingering, debilitating illness. He had been forced to live with it, helplessly, for most of his life. The memory brought bitter guilt but, as usual, Anthony was able to dismiss it.

At least Lucinda's illness had its uses, he told himself. Jolette had been insisting that he divorce Lucinda and marry her. But last week Jolette had agreed with his argument that while she was ill Lucinda could not be subjected to the cruelty of a divorce.

Anthony stopped and wiped perspiration from his face. Sawyer was nowhere in sight. Damn lazy nigger, he muttered. Probably lost in the bargain. Let him stay lost for all I care, Anthony told himself. I'm going back to The Columns.

As Anthony turned he stumbled over a decaying log. The same instant he heard the warning rattle.

The rattlesnake that slithered from the log was the largest Anthony had ever seen. In an instant it coiled up to strike, its long strand of rattles rustling like a berserk metronome, its forked tongue darting out, its eyes tiny and malevolent.

Anthony choked back a scream. He tried to steel his body. The slightest movement and the snake would bury its fangs into his body.

From the corner of his eye he tried to see Sawyer. But the slave was nowhere in sight. Anthony cursed Sawyer bitterly.

Don't move, he told himself. He must not move. But the deadly rattling, the darting tongue, the hideous eyes, were driving him to a frenzy of fear and desperation. If bitten, he would die here. Or worse, somehow survive the venom but be crippled from it.

Anthony whimpered. Something slithered near the

log. Anthony saw the shadowed body of another huge snake. He whimpered again. A nauseous convulsion shook his body.

He screamed as the rattler in front of him struck . . .

But the rattler was attacked by the other snake in the air. The two snakes fell to the ground, their bodies coiled and thrashing.

Anthony staggered back. He nearly vomited. His stomach was churning.

He saw that the rattler had been attacked by an enormous kingsnake. The rattler struck at the kingsnake again and again, digging its fangs into the snake's soft black body, emptying the venom pits behind its head.

But the kingsnake was immune to the venom. Before Anthony's terrified eyes the kingsnake began to chew the rattler to death in great, gory bites, then its hinged mouth fell open wide and it devoured the rattler before it was dead.

Anthony gagged. He began to tremble uncontrollably as he turned and lurched away.

Anthony hurried into the parlor and gulped down a glass of water, then drank a double whiskey. He was appalled to see that his hands were still shaking.

Then, outside, he heard a voice and laugh that flashed cold anger through his body: It was Sawyer.

Anthony rushed to the window. There was a grinning Sawyer, riding on top of the wagon that was bringing supplies from Natchez.

"Lord, I had me some day," Sawyer was telling the slave driver. "Don't reckon Mist' Anthony ever goin' to take old Sawyer huntin' 'gain . . ."

The wagon disappeared around the house. Anthony stood at the window, trembling with rage.

Another double whiskey only fueled Anthony's anger. He ran out of the parlor, down the gallery, his hands in tight fists.

At the back steps he nearly knocked down a young slave girl. Slaves in the back yard stopped their work and stared as Anthony ran past them.

The wagon had disappeared into the barn and Anthony ran inside. The wagon was being unloaded and Sawyer was still grinning as he leisurely lowered his enormous bulk to the ground. He brushed himself off, then looked around as Anthony approached.

"Oh, Mist' Anthony," he said. "We got ourselves separated somehow. Glad to see you got yourself home all right . . ."

Anthony slapped Sawyer and the slave reeled back from the blow. Blood spurted from his mouth and nose. A look of shock and pain covered his face.

"You stupid black bastard!" Anthony shouted. "I almost died out there!"

He hit Sawyer with the back of his hand. Sawyer whimpered. His bloody lips quivered.

"And then you come riding up here on a goddamn wagon, laughing and making a joke of the whole goddamn incident!"

"Mist' Anthony, please don't . . ." Sawyer mumbled.

Anthony could not control his anger. In his mind he saw the snake's eyes, its tongue, its fangs. He cursed and grabbed a whip from the wagon seat. Sawyer gasped and tried to scramble away.

"No, please, Mist' Anthony!" he cried. "I'm sorry . . . I didn't . . ."

Anthony lashed Sawyer across the shoulders. Sawyer screamed. He turned and tried to run but he fell over a crate and crashed to the ground. Anthony lashed Sawyer across the shoulders again, then across the back. Thin lines of blood leaped from his body and he writhed and squirmed and screeched in agony.

"Mist' Anthony!" a voice called.

Anthony, his whip hand raised, glanced over his shoulder as Ed ran into the barn. A dozen slaves were watching from the door.

"Mist' Anthony, Deavors' people don't never get whipped!" Ed said.

"He gone kill me, Ed!" Sawyer screamed. "Make him stop!"

177

"Make me stop?" Anthony shouted as he turned back to Sawyer. "No nigger can make me do anything! And you'll find that out, boy!"

"Get Cellus," someone said behind Anthony and the mention of Cellus' name infuriated Anthony still further.

He lashed Sawyer's back, his shoulders, his chest. Sawyer screeched and babbled. His body jerked in spasms of pain. Blood poured from the deep cuts.

Anthony raised the whip again, then lowered his arm. He was drained of strength, of anger. He blinked and shook his head, as though coming from a trance. He shuddered as he glanced at the lacerated, bleeding man at his feet. He dropped the whip.

Anthony dragged his feet as he walked away. He passed the circle of slaves and avoided their eyes. Ed ran past him, to Sawyer, and several other slaves followed.

"Go get Aunt Froney!" Ed called.

In the yard, Anthony passed Cellus, and he avoided his eyes also. He stumbled into the parlor, poured a double whiskey and gulped it down.

39.

When the majordomo announced that the prince's carriage had entered the grounds, Countess Corloni left her private chapel in the middle of a prayer. She hurried to the main drawing room to receive the prince. The countess had chosen the setting carefully.

This room was famed throughout Italy for its splendid portraits by Renaissance masters, a fortune in art that could surely impress the prince, as would the massive, hand-cut crystal chandeliers, the French furniture and, through the tall French doors, the view down through the vast acres of flowering parks and gardens.

Still, the countess was apprehensive as she stood in a

French door and waited for the prince. The sight of a group of visitors in the lower park did nothing to improve her temper. One of them had even set up an easel and was painting.

The countess looked beyond the park and its visitors to the green-gray haze on the Alban hills. Weeks of maneuvering and manipulations had led to this mid-August afternoon. If everything went well today, the marriage contract could soon be signed. And the countess was determined that everything would go well, no matter what was required of her or of anyone else. With some annoyance she thought of her sullen, rebellious daughter, now sulking in her room upstairs.

What wretched bad fortune, the countess thought. To have Gianna take a fancy to some young man she had met at Count Croce's party! She had not been the same since that night. The regrettable, unfortunate encounter had stirred Gianna's willfulness—she had become moody and emotional and had foolishly, childishly, began to protest her mother's plans for her marriage.

Under ordinary circumstances, the countess would have taken simple and drastic steps to eliminate this young man by whatever means necessary, this young American man with the odd name. But she had encountered more ill fortune. Count Croce had taken an interest in the American's sister and the count had made it known that while he was involved with the girl he would hold her brother under his protection.

Countess Corloni and Count Croce had been intimate friends for years. They had once been lovers. They knew each other's secrets. Normally, he would do anything for the countess, as long as it didn't compromise the security of the church's rule.

But he had his sense of honor, and he would not be crossed when it came to that honor. The American could not be harmed for the time being, no matter how much the count wished to please the countess. Countess Corloni had been furious at this reminder of the limits of her power, but a chance turn of events had cheered her.

On a riding trip into the Abruzzi hills, the American

had been thrown and injured, her spies told her, and for several weeks he had not left his apartment. She was sure he had not contacted Gianna and hoped her daughter had forgotten him.

When the prince was shown into the drawing room the countess was seated on a blue velvet sofa beside the French doors. She rose slowly.

She had heard that when young the prince was a handsome man. But there was nothing attractive about this old man who was toddling over to her. His face was round and his flesh puffy, and red-and-purple veins stood among the ruins of his wrinkles across his cheeks. His lips were heavy and slightly moist. Only his black eyes indicated what the face might once have been. The eyes were bright and burning, with a disturbing, almost malevolent quality about them.

The countess bowed slightly.

"Welcome to Villa Corloni, Prince Vittori," she said. "Here, sit by the open windows. The wind is mild, for August. And it brings the smell of flowers from the gardens."

"Thank you, Countess," he said. He lowered himself onto a couch and she sat opposite him. "I love the scent of blossoms on a summer day. Have you. . . ? Of course, you've visited my gardens and greenhouses and know my passion for flowers, for orchids, particularly . . ."

"Yes, Your Grace was kind enough to give me a rare golden orchid," she said. "I wore it when I was presented to King Ferdinand in Naples. He commented on its beauty and I told him you were its creator."

"Ah, yes, poor Ferdinand," the prince said. "All that trouble down there, his armies in disarray. What is to become of us all, my dear countess? What if the ruffians sweep on up north, to Rome?"

"I don't think we need worry about that," she said. "The *Garibaldini* may defeat the Bourbon army but they would have no chance against the excellent troops the French emperor has provided for the protection of the Holy Father and his lands."

"Yes, yes, I'm sure you're right," Prince Vittori said. "I'm glad that you share my sentiments about such matters, Countess."

"How could I not, Your Grace?" she said. "Nothing is more important than protecting the established institutions, the wealth and legitimate rights of the nobility, the lands of the Holy Father. So I said just last night to your brother, Cardinal Apollini, and his secretary."

"My brother mentioned the discussion this morning," the prince said. "He always speaks highly of you, as does Don Santini."

"I'm flattered to be held in esteem by such men," the countess said. She had been Don Santini's lover for the past three months. The don had considerable influence over the senile cardinal, and for sex and money he would perform almost any tasks.

"My brother and Don Santini have been instrumental in bringing me to this . . . to our talks of marriage, Countess," he said.

"Then I'm in their debt," she said. "And I assure you that you won't regret your choice . . . should you decide to honor my family by marrying Gianna. My daughter lives only to become your wife. She dotes on every mention of your name."

"Gianna is beyond doubt the most beautiful and desirable girl in Rome," the prince said. "In all Italy, I'm sure. What grace, what beauty! And she's so very fresh, so innocent in her appearance that I . . ."

The prince was interrupted. A servant had entered with a tray and was standing by the door. The countess motioned him to come forward.

"Is that a bottle of . . . ? Why, my dear countess, that is indeed a Lafite forty-four. There are few still in existence. I haven't tasted the wine in years! How did you come by it?"

The countess gestured for the servant to pour the wine.

"I had heard that you were fond of old Bordeaux," the countess said. "Of course, your exquisite taste in all fine wines and foods is well known and respected. So I instructed my wine broker to secure some for you."

The prince tasted the wine. "Superb!" he said. He took another sip.

"Fill the prince's glass, then leave us," the countess said. The servant obeyed. He set the bottle on a table and left the room.

The prince sipped his wine. He was lost in the rare wine, the countess realized. She was pleased. The prince's taste for expensive wine and food was indeed well known. So was his taste for reckless gambling and, fortunately for her, he often lost. Despite his family's centuries-old heritage and his vast land holdings, the prince was very nearly penniless.

In Italy, a commoner might marry into the nobility, as the countess had done. But it was rare for a man of royal blood to take a wife who was not herself of royalty. Because of this, Prince Vittori had been reluctant, for many months, to sign a marriage contract. But he had lost heavily at the gambling tables in the last weeks, losses which the countess had arranged through Don Santini. Now, the prince was desperately in need of Gianna's lavish dowry.

And, the countess half admitted, no doubt for Gianna herself. She had long heard unsavory rumors about Prince Vittori's sexual tastes, his penchant for deflowering and abusing very young girls, but she could not allow herself to believe he would be crass enough to abuse his wife. No doubt Prince Vittori confined his appetites to maidservants—what else were servants for? —and besides it was as likely as not that the rumors were untrue.

Who knew better than she how vicious and uncontrolled were the gossips of Rome—she who had been their victim for many years? In any event, what mattered was that Gianna became the Princess Vittori, to link the prestige and influence of the Vittoris with the influence and wealth of the Corlonis. Gianna must learn, as the countess had learned in America, that what mattered in this world was influence and wealth.

Without money and power, life had no value. At any

awful moment one could become a chattel, a virtual slave, as had she and her father in Mississippi, because of the arrogance and deceit of Lawton Deavors and his accursed family . . .

- The prince had come out of his reverie and interrupted the countess' own. "Um, yes, yes, an exceptional wine," he said. "Now what were we discussing? Ah, the marriage. But before we resume our discussion, there is one item I must mention, concerning Gianna's behavior."

"Gianna's behavior, Your Grace?" The countess stiffened. "She was raised by the nuns, sir!"

"We all know of Gianna's chastity and piety. But I'm disturbed to learn that she has been seen in public frequently."

"Yes, she's been out a few times since she returned from Florence," the countess said. "She is young . . . It's customary. Always well chaperoned, of course. In any case, once our arrangements are secure, her little excursions will, of course, cease."

"Excellent, Countess," he said. "We of royalty have our own rather strict and old-fashioned ways. It would please me to have my little Gianna cloistered until our marriage. Now, let us conclude the arrangements so that I may visit with the delightful girl."

They discussed Gianna's dowry. The prince was obviously pleased that much of the large dowry would be in cash. He quickly agreed to the terms. Countess Corloni's spirits rose. She felt happier than she had in years, but just then a maid came into the drawing room and interrupted them. The countess was furious.

"How dare you come in here at such a time?" she demanded, but she saw the fear in the woman's face.

"I'm sorry, Countess," the maid said. "Pardon me, Your Grace. Countess, there's been an accident, I fear. In the . . . the kitchen. One of the kitchen girls has been badly burned . . ."

"Really?" the countess said. "Oh, very well! Prince Vittori, please excuse me for a moment. Here." She filled his glass. "I'll be right back."

The countess followed the maid from the room and closed the door. The servant who had served the wine stood in the hall.

"Uncork another bottle of Lafite and see that the prince's glass does not become empty," she said.

She walked down the hall a few yards and stopped.

"And now!" she said to the maid. "What could be so important that you disturb me with the prince? A girl in the kitchen, indeed!"

"Countess . . . I . . . It's Gianna . . . She . . . She . . ."

"Gianna!" A cold fury swept the countess. "Damn you, what's happened to Gianna!"

"She's . . . She's run out of the villa, Countess. No one could stop her."

"Where did she go?" the countess asked.

"She went out to the park," the maid said. "She's talking with the visitors in the park . . ."

"*Cattiva!*" the countess said. "Why, the prince has only to look from the window and see her mingling with that rabble!"

"Perhaps his eyes are weak from age . . ."

"No, the one faculty the old fool retains is perfect eyesight. And he expects to see Gianna shortly."

The countess was desperate. If she went out to the park and Gianna caused a scene, the prince might witness it from the drawing room. Then a far worse fear materialized. What if the American was up from his sickbed and was among the visitors in the park?

"Perhaps you can say Gianna is ill . . ."

"No, no, that's too lame," the countess said. "I've made no mention of illness. There must be . . . Is Stefania in the kitchen?"

"Stefania? Yes, I think so."

"Bring her to me. At once."

The maid hurried off. The countess considered a plan. Stefania was a pretty fifteen-year-old girl. Yesterday she had been caught with a silver goblet in her pocket as she was leaving the villa. The countess had deferred the girl's punishment. Stefania was terrified.

She had been caught stealing before and had been threatened with prison the next time. Yesterday, she had sworn that she would do anything to avoid being sent to prison.

Stefania came down the hall slowly. Her cheeks were red. Her lips quivered. She stopped in front of the countess. The countess realized that with her dark hair and eyes the girl even resembled Gianna.

"Yesterday you vowed you'd do anything to avoid prison for your thievery," the countess said.

"Oh, yes, I'll do anything. I couldn't stand being in that awful place. My father would disown me . . ."

"Hush your sniveling. Are you a virgin?"

"A virgin . . . ? Oh, yes'm! I'm a good girl. I've never gone near a man . . ."

"That will be your salvation, then," the countess said. "Do you know the Prince Vittori?"

"Oh, no, not a girl like me," Stefania said.

"The prince is in the drawing room now," the countess said. "You are to go there . . . Find some excuse . . . Take him some cakes. Tell the servant to leave you alone with the prince. You are to pour him glass after glass of wine, encourage him to drink. And you are to make it perfectly clear to him that . . . that you find him attractive and that you . . . you are available. Then go into that large pantry in the drawing room and leave the door open and wait for him . . ."

"But . . . but I'm terribly frightened . . ."

"Do as I say, or you'll spend this night and many another in prison!"

"But, madame, what . . . ? What will he do to me?"

"He's royalty, you little thief! He'll do precisely what he wants! And if you're not completely agreeable to his whims, then you are lost, Stefania!"

The girl made a final, feeble protest but she agreed to go to the prince and satisfy him.

The countess went into the salon and drank a glass of Madeira. She would give the girl time to absorb all the prince's attention. Her plan had a good chance of succeeding. The prince, when drunk, was an obsessive old fool who took what he wanted because he knew his rank would protect him from the consequences.

The countess finished her wine, then hurried out to the park.

40.

Stefania had followed the countess' instructions to ply Prince Vittori with wine. She was frightened, and her fingers trembled as she refilled his glass. Nervously, she studied the notorious prince, and what she saw puzzled her. He was old, yes, he would never see sixty again, but he was well formed and elegantly dressed. His dark hair was streaked with silver, he had the large, prominent nose of all the Vittoris, but it was his eyes that caught her attention.

They were black, so black that the pupils blended with the irises and made them look huge, and they were preternaturally alert. Like an eagle's eyes, they seemed quick and bright enough to see great distances, and when they focused on Stefania, they took on an expression of predatory delight.

"What's your name, girl?" he asked, pinching Stefania's plump round arm just above the elbow.

"Bella," Stefania lied. She longed to run. What had she heard about Prince Vittori? There were always stories being told in the kitchen; likely half of them were lies, but she wasn't sure. She sensed the prince's eagerness, his greedy lust, and although she could not admit it, she sensed his cruelty.

If only I hadn't been caught with that goblet, she thought. Now she had no choice. She had to endure the prince, or the countess would put her in prison—she knew her mistress too well to doubt it. How can it be so terrible?, she asked herself. He is only a man . . .

"Bella! Ha! So you are," he snickered. *"Bella* and

dolce!" His face was flushed from the first bottle of
Bordeaux and he had accepted a glass from the second
bottle. The wine brightened his eyes until they glinted.
Stefania lowered her eyes from his gaze.

"How old are you, Bella?"

"Fifteen, sir."

He laughed. "Excellent." With quick, strong fingers
he reached out for Stefania and pinched one of her
round, full breasts. She cried out in alarm and pain. His
fingers had twisted her flesh. "And as plump and juicy
as a pigeon," he said and laughed harder.

Stefania folded her arms over her breasts and backed
away. Tears had gathered in her eyes but she struggled
to hide them. I will not cry, she vowed. He cannot
make me cry. But her lower lip trembled.

"Come here," he said.

She hesitated at the doorway of the little pantry off
the drawing room.

"Come here, you little fool!"

"What . . . ? What will you do to me, sir?"

He took several quick steps toward her and seized
her arm, twisting it. With his other hand he dug into her
gown and pulled out one of her breasts. He bent to
take it in his teeth and bit hard. Stefania shrieked. She
was amazed at his strength.

Her shriek delighted him. He watched her sharply as
she wriggled and struggled to free herself, watched her
skin flush and admired her youthful plumpness. Excited, he spat at the floor, gulped and bit at her shoulder.

"Stop! What are you doing?" she cried.

Slapping and pinching her, the prince backed her into
the pantry. He closed the door and sat down in the single chair, gasping for breath.

Stefania ran to look out the window. It was high
and too narrow for escape. Her heart pounded with
panic.

"Kneel down before me, you whore!" the prince
grunted.

"I'm not! I'm a good girl!"

He laughed again. "Show me."

"I don't know what to do," she said, her eyes sliding toward the door. If only the cook would come in, or the butler with more wine, she thought. But no one would come. The countess had sent her here to please the prince. The countess would see that they were left alone.

Stefania dropped to her knees in front of the prince.

"Take off your gown," the prince rasped. He slumped in the chair as she slowly shrugged her crumpled gown off her shoulders. Her fingers shook.

"Hurry!"

Her gown fell in voluminous folds, baring a simple white linen shift.

"Off! Off!"

Head bowed, her long dark hair falling forward over her neck, Stefania slipped off the shift. She shivered and tried to cover herself from his eyes.

"Very young," he said. "Even younger than my fiancée . . . Where is my wine? Bring it to me."

Stefania reached for her shift as she stood up, but the prince jerked it from her hand and reached between her thighs. She started forward to escape his touch.

"Mmmm . . . Soft and wet! You are a naughty girl!"

"No! I'm not!"

He slapped her buttocks. "Go and hurry back."

Naked, Stefania ran back into the drawing room to get the bottle and his glass. She was lost, and too frightened to anger him by disobedience. She returned to the pantry.

"Lafite forty-four," Prince Vittori said reverently as he poured himself a glass. Only when he had drunk did he look at Stefania. "Why are you standing there? Part your legs! Pose for me! Dance! I want you to arouse me, you whore!"

"Yes, sir," Stefania whispered. She closed her eyes as she turned around in an awkward dance. Perhaps he would let her go, after this. What further humiliation could there be?

"Come here," the prince said, watching her breasts

bob, her pale body vibrate in her unwilling dance. She stopped, obeyed.

"I want to see you." Abruptly, he pulled Stefania across his lap, grunting at her weight. Roughly, he parted the cheeks of her buttocks with his fingers.

"Oh!" she gasped, horrified. She felt his finger, exploring, probing between the loose lips of her vagina, thrusting at her. She struggled free and landed on her hands and knees, panting.

"That's what you are—an animal!" he shouted. "Now I shall treat you like an animal!" He unbuttoned his trousers and showed her a small, shriveled penis, dark red with blood.

Stefania shuddered. What could he do to her with that thing? She was confused and frightened. He seemed to be angry. She knew she had to please him, to save herself. He looked anything but pleased.

Desperately, Stefania crawled to him. "What . . . what can I do?"

"Suck me," he ordered.

Closing her eyes, she leaned forward to do his bidding. As she took his penis in her mouth, he leaned back and groaned. Her nostrils flared and her face paled as she sucked. He seized her breasts in his hands and squeezed them roughly, scratching at the soft, tender skin with his nails, leaving dark tracks on the translucent flesh.

"Baby, just a baby," he murmured, "big-teated baby, sucking like a baby . . ."

Stefania gasped and choked. She was sucking as hard as she could, but his penis did not stiffen or rise. It was wet but still limp.

"I can't . . . I can't . . ." she moaned, looking up at his face. Her eyes were dimmed with tears. She was breathless and her dark hair was a wild, tangled mane.

Like a madman, the prince launched himself at her, stimulated beyond control by her helplessness. His chair crashed to the floor. Still half dressed, he sprawled over Stefania's naked body, his arms waving, and bit her again and again, on her arms, on her legs, on her breasts and stomach and thighs and buttocks and back as she writhed and struggled and rolled back and forth under him, trying to escape him, her tender body growing red.

Despite herself, Stefania was excited, partly by fear. Her eyes cleared, opened in horror and arousal. One savage bite at her breast drew blood. A few drops of blood ran between her breasts, down her stomach. Her legs parted involuntarily, as he attacked her lower belly.

Seeing them part, he bent his head between her legs, snapping and nipping. She yelped. He suddenly reached for the wine bottle and forced her thighs wider open . . .

41.

Despite her apprehension, Chessie found the parks and gardens of the Villa Corloni more beautiful than any she had seen in Rome. When the other visitors left, she and Clayton remained, and she set up her easel in the shade of a tall umbrella pine, in a spot looking across an upper garden to the villa.

Clayton, however, was impatient and restless, and Chessie wondered why he had decided to come today, when he had begged off visiting all of the other villas where she had gone to sketch. He had been in an odd state for the past few weeks, actually, and she wondered if he had gotten up from his sickbed too soon.

Clayton wandered away and Chessie lost sight of him. After a few moments' thought, she decided to paint the amber-colored villa itself.

Half an hour later she paused. She stared into a waterfall and immediately forgot her sketching. As sometimes happened in the late afternoon, she thought of Carlo, but she made an effort to dismiss the thought and turned her mind to Paolo Croce.

The count was a fascinating and attentive suitor, and

the gossip about his widespread influence and ruthlessness only made him more interesting. Chessie thought him very handsome and she could not deny the physical attraction he exerted. He was mature and demanding, she knew, and she both expected and looked forward to his kisses, possibly that very evening.

Chessie turned back to her easel. She was staring at her sketch, trying to decide if the proportions were right, when she realized someone was watching her.

Chessie turned slightly and saw a girl of perhaps nineteen, dressed in an elaborate blue silk gown.

The girl came forward. "I'm sorry to have disturbed you," she said, "but I couldn't resist seeing your sketch."

"Oh, I don't mind," Chessie said.

Chessie stared at the girl. She was quite lovely, but there was a melancholy quality about her eyes that disturbed Chessie. The eyes were red and Chessie wondered if the girl had been crying. Then Chessie had the odd feeling she had seen the girl somewhere before.

"Your sketch is really good," the girl said.

"Thank you," Chessie said, "but I'm afraid it's a bit out of proportion." She wondered where the girl had come from. "Were you in our group?" she asked. "I must confess I don't remember you."

"Your group?" The girl shook her head. The hint of a smile, then an expression of such sadness crossed her face that Chessie was touched. "No, I wasn't a member of your group. And pardon my staring. I've forgotten my manners this afternoon. It's just that you . . . you remind me very much of someone I met only briefly."

"I see," Chessie mumbled. Out of the corner of her eye she noticed that several people were hurrying toward them, from the villa.

"I have to go now," the girl said. "I've enjoyed talking to you. May I be quite forward and ask you a personal question? Is it possible that you have a brother who bears a striking resemblance to you?"

"My brother and I are twins."

"Ah, I see. I believe I met your brother briefly at a party," the girl said. "Well, then, good day."

Chessie said good day. She watched the girl walk very slowly toward the people who had entered the gardens from the villa.

Then, as Chessie watched, the girl met a woman in the shadows of an umbrella pine. Their angry voices indicated that they were arguing. The woman glanced around at Chessie and though the shadows hid her features Chessie could almost imagine that her face filled with anger and hatred.

A chill raced down Chessie's spine. Of course, the woman was the notorious Countess Corloni! Chessie shuddered, remembering Signora Nantes' story of the *pasquino* and the man's hand being cut off. She had been talking with the countess' daughter!

Several men had left the two women and scattered about the park. One of them came up and rather rudely escorted Chessie out of the park. Clayton and their guide were waiting by the gate. They all climbed into the carriage and it jostled away over the rough cobblestones.

After complaining that Chessie's sketching had cost him his siesta, the guide said that he knew one of the men who had forced them out of the villa.

"The talk from the house was that Prince Vittori arrived to discuss his marriage with Gianna," the guide said. "But Gianna was in a rebellious mood and wandered into the park. The countess was livid with anger."

"You mean Gianna Corloni was in the park just now?" Clayton asked.

"Yes, and it's just as well you didn't see her," the guide said. "There are strange tales of what happens to young men who try to meet Gianna Corloni."

The guide tried to stifle a yawn with the back of his hand. His eyes closed slowly. Chessie and Clayton sat silently, looking out the windows.

"Clayton?" Chessie whispered.

Clayton turned. Chessie glanced at the guide, who was snoring, then leaned toward her brother.

"Clayton, I met her . . . Gianna Corloni."

Chessie paused, sensitive to the look of anguish on Clayton's face. She suspected, now, why Clayton had wanted to come out to this particular villa.

"You did!" Clayton said. "Of all the goddamn bad luck! To be so close, and then . . . then have it be you, goddamn it!"

"Oh, Clay, don't swear. I didn't know . . ."

"I should have told you," he said. "I'm desperately in love, though I only met her briefly. What was she like, Chessie? Did she say anything about me?"

"Well, she was very pretty," Chessie said. "And polite. And rather sad, in a way. I felt she'd been crying. As for you, Clay, well, she only asked if I had a brother who looked like me, and mentioned that she'd met you briefly."

"I wonder if she was looking for me in the park," Clayton said. "She might have seen me from the villa. And she'd been crying. Then she doesn't want to marry that old prince! I'm sure there's still hope for me, if only I can meet her again."

"Oh, Clay, be reasonable," Chessie said. "How can you be desperately in love with a girl you've met only briefly? Every month you're infatuated with a new woman. You mustn't be reckless, Clay. This girl is about to marry a prince and her mother has a reputation for cruelty . . ."

"Dammit, don't tell me what to feel!" Clayton said. "It's not merely infatuation! I'm in love with Gianna! And you're hardly the one to talk about being reckless, after your flirtation with Carlo Settimo."

"And just what is that supposed to mean?" Chessie asked angrily. "I won't be judged by you!"

Clayton's face was red. "You've never understood these things, never understood that men and women . . . that men can do things that are improper for women . . . And besides, I think you're jealous!"

"Just who are you calling improper, Clay Deavors?" Chessie demanded. "And jealous . . ." Chessie knew this argument was both inane and dangerous, a subject she

193

had vowed to avoid with her brother, and she fought to bank down her anger. "Very well, Clay. You go and be foolish and impetuous. Try to court the little countess. But I won't help you if you get in trouble. I wash my hands of the whole damned matter!"

"Chessie, you shouldn't use such language . . ."

"Damn you, Clay, I'll use whatever language I want!"

Their outburst had wakened the guide. Chessie glanced at the man, who was rubbing his eyes, then turned from her brother and looked out of the window, seething with her emotions.

42.

The principal social functions in Rome were the evening *conversazioni,* which began two hours after the Ave Maria and continued late into the night, often until dawn, and were held in the great *palazzi.* Because she was being courted by Count Croce, Chessie was regularly invited to these affairs.

On a rainy evening in early September Chessie attended the *conversazioni* of the Countess Benedetti, in her *palazzo* in the Piazza di Spagna, near Chessie's apartment.

Count Croce had not yet arrived and Chessie wandered from salon to salon, talking idly and without much interest to the elegantly dressed guests.

In one salon five *castrati* sang arias to an enraptured audience. The plump, round-hipped and high-voiced singers had been castrated when they were seven and performed all female parts in operas, since it was considered immoral for women to participate in theater.

In another salon Chessie watched the crowded gambling tables, an inevitable entertainment for any level of society in Rome, whether the meanest tavern or the finest *palazzo.*

The Benedetti *palazzo* was furnished in the usual

Roman manner. Its vast salons held little furniture except for numerous small marbletop tables filled with crystal vases and china figurines of dogs and cats. There were a few stiff, tall-backed chairs covered with maroon silk but these were reserved for the elderly, titled ladies, ambassadors and cardinals. The walls were crowded with huge, dark portraits that Chessie found oppressive.

The Romans had a phobia about the night air, since malaria had ravaged the city since antiquity and it was believed the disease came on the night wind. So, as usual, every window in the *palazzo* was closed tight, despite the warm, muggy weather, and Chessie was soon uncomfortably hot.

Chessie nibbled at a lemon ice and listened to the *castrati,* watched the high-stakes gambling and talked with a woman she met at a *conversazione* the night before. Enviously, her eyes wandered to the dancers, but no one asked her to dance. No one had asked Chessie to dance in weeks and she knew it was because of Count Croce. Chessie had learned that the count was a possessive and demanding suitor. Though nothing had been said, it was understood that while he was courting her she would not be involved with another man, not even for a casual dance. No one in Rome was willing to displease the count.

At first, Chessie had been flattered by this arrangement, and even pleased by the gossiping by jealous Roman ladies who resented the count's ignoring them to pay attention to a girl from Mississippi.

Now she was less certain she liked the arrangement. In fact, though she still enjoyed the count's company, she was at times a bit frightened by his intensity. Lately, his kisses were becoming too passionate, his hands too eager to caress her breasts. At times as they kissed and he embraced her she sensed that his strong, impatient hands could very quickly become ruthless.

Chessie wondered if she wasn't becoming bored with Rome. Perhaps she had exhausted herself with sightseeing, with excursions, with sketching, with parties.

She began to look forward to traveling north, to visiting Paris, and she was glad that they would be leaving in a few weeks.

Chessie took a glass of Frascati and returned to the main salon, where she discovered that Count Croce had just arrived.

The count flattered Chessie's blue silk gown and the arrangement of her hair in long ribbons. They danced a waltz and two mazurkas. When she pleaded exhaustion the count found her a chair.

An hour later Chessie let Count Croce escort her along a hallway lined with family portraits while they talked of a museum Chessie wanted to visit. The museum was closed for repairs. The count said he would arrange that she be allowed to visit the museum the next day.

Without realizing where they were going, Chessie found herself alone with the count in a small, airless anteroom. Under his dark, disturbing gaze, Chessie felt naive and vulnerable. The count's mood both awed and disturbed her and she felt his physical presence to be hypnotic, nearly overwhelming.

She expected the count's next words to be intimate, and she would not have been surprised had he taken her in his arms.

"Miss Deavors, are you and your brother close?" Count Croce asked abruptly.

"Are we close, sir?" she asked. "Why, what do you mean?"

"I know that twins are often extremely close," he said. "Yet, at times, in trying not to be mirror-images of each other, they may grow apart and fail to confide in each other. I don't mean to intrude on your privacy. But I wonder if you're aware of your brother's activities?"

"What an odd question, sir," Chessie replied, although she suspected that the count was referring to Clayton's interest in Gianna Corloni.

"I assure you, Miss Deavors, it's not an idle question," he said. "It's of the gravest importance."

"I don't know if Clay and I are closer than other brothers and sisters," she said. "In truth, we've quarreled in Rome and as a result we haven't confided in each other lately."

"Word has reached me that your brother persists in his unwelcome efforts to court the daughter of an old friend of mine, and that he's using a varitable army of spies to discover her every move," the count said. "My friend has arranged an excellent marriage for her daughter and she considers no other suitors worthy of the girl."

"I won't stand here and have Clay called unworthy!" Chessie said. "He's good enough to court any girl he wants, sir, certainly the daughter of some social-climbing countess . . ."

"Miss Deavors, I did not say she was a countess," Count Croce said. "So you do know of your brother's reckless persistence."

"I know very little," she said. "And in any case it's no concern of mine. He handles his own affairs and so do I. In fact, sir, I resent this . . . Your inquisition, your charges . . ."

"Chessie, it's only because of my special friendship with you that I'm concerning myself with your brother's fate," the count said. Chessie was touched by his use of her first name. He had seldom used it—only when he had taken her in his arms, and she realized that his face and voice had softened.

"I appreciate your concern," Chessie mumbled. "Clay can be reckless and stubborn, I'll grant you. But his little flirtations seldom last long. And he's always involved with more than one woman."

"As far as I know, and I might add that little happens in Rome of which I'm not informed, your brother hasn't shown interest in any other woman in weeks," the count said. "As I mentioned, he's hired spies and he's haunted the Corloni villa—of course, you do know the girl is

Gianna Corloni—and when the countess took her daughter to their country villa, he tried to follow."

Chessie had suspected that Clayton was still infatuated with Gianna, but since their argument in the carriage they had hardly spoken and she had not realized the extent of his recklessness.

"I can try to talk with Clay, but he has a mind of his own about these things. And I don't see why his infatuation is so terrible."

"Chessie, you and your brother are strangers in Rome," the count said. "Clayton is a charming young man, and I'm sure in America he can court whomever he pleases, with your family's influence to protect him. But your family can't protect him here, and, if he continues to plague the Countess Corloni, neither can I."

"I still don't understand," Chessie said. "You're trying to frighten me!"

"It's an affair of mortal seriousness," Count Croce said. "The countess is an old and valued friend, but she becomes both obsessive and destructive when she desires something. May the saints protect anyone who stands in her way! She's determined to marry her daughter to Prince Vittori. Your brother, my dear Chessie, has already been given a sound beating by the countess' thugs. I intervened to save his life. But if he persists to threaten the marriage, not even I can save him. She will destroy him, no matter what the cost."

Chessie was stunned. Clayton had come home one night with a cut arm and bloody head, but he had said he'd been involved in a tavern brawl.

She looked into the count's eyes. She believed his warning. If she could not get Clayton to end this courtship, he would be hurt, perhaps seriously.

"I'll convince Clay of the danger," she said softly. "And . . . thank you. I'm in your debt for the warning, your concern and protection . . ."

"I hope to prove a satisfactory creditor," Count Croce said. "And that you'll find the payment of the debt to be pleasant."

"I . . ." She did not know what to say. She was so

warm, the air in the small room so stale and heavy that she felt almost faint. She was frightened.

He loomed over her, so powerful, so strong, his eyes holding her. She expected his hands to possess her at any moment, expected the crushing urgency of his lips on hers.

"You must visit me in Frascati soon," he said. "Alone. Now, we should join the others."

Chessie stiffened when he leaned forward and kissed her cheek. Her legs were weak as he escorted her from the anteroom, and when they entered the gambling salon, she vowed that if she could prevent it, she'd never again be alone with Count Croce.

43.

Chessie's discussion with Clayton, after Count Croce's warning, did not go well. Clayton became furious when Chessie tried to warn him.

"Let him threaten me face to face," Clayton said. "This is man's business, Chessie, and I'll thank you not to insult me by acting as the count's errand girl in the future."

"And just how well did you protect yourself the night Countess Corloni's thugs beat you up?" Chessie asked.

"Next time, I'll be ready for them," Clayton said in a low, frightening voice.

Then Clayton attacked Chessie for spending so much time "with that notorious count, who's well known for his sordid affairs . . ."

Chessie attempted a reasoned argument about Clayton and Gianna Corloni. But she ended by angrily defending her relationship with the count and, as usual, the twins' argument degenerated into an impassioned, emotional quarrel.

As she had so often in the past, Chessie resented having to play big sister to her twin. She also knew she would regret turning to the count for help.

Chessie had not admitted it to her brother but she was no longer happy about her relationship with the count. She had found one excuse after another for not visiting him alone in Frascati and she was reluctant to kiss him or let him take her in his arms.

The count was still charming and attentive but now she also saw him as overbearing and impatient. He was too insistent and she had little doubt about his idea of how she should repay the debt she had incurred for his help with Clayton.

And no matter how helpful or handsome the count might be, Chessie was determined not to surrender her body to him. She knew, though, that ending the relationship would not be easy and she feared his reaction.

So she continued to see him and looked forward to the time when she could leave Rome. She stopped sketching. She became lethargic. Her siestas became longer and longer. Her principal entertainment was to spend long hours drinking tea and listening to Signora Nantes' tales of Rome.

Chessie did not see Count Croce for nearly a week, though he did send her flowers and a book of etchings of ancient Rome. In a note that accompanied six dozen yellow roses he explained that he was caught up in politics—matters concerning the *Garibaldini*. When the count did appear one evening at a *conversazione* held by the Egyptian ambassador, his face showed his exhaustion and he cursed the *Garibaldini*.

He hovered over Chessie, undressing her with demanding eyes and repeatedly insisting that she visit Frascati. Chessie was disturbed by his appearance and behavior and made a vague promise that she had no intention of keeping.

Surprisingly, the count said that he understood Clayton had suddenly ended his pursuit of Gianna Corloni. Chessie did not know this. She and Clayton had not really talked since their quarrel. She was relieved to hear of Clayton's apparent change of heart, although upset by this further indication that the count knew everything happening in Rome.

After dancing a polka and a waltz, Chessie and the count strolled into the şalon set aside for gambling and Chessie saw Prince Vittori for the first time.

The prince was playing *farone,* a card game that resembled baccarat. Chessie felt immediate revulsion at the thought that Gianna Corloni would have to marry this old man. Her revulsion increased when she overheard whispered rumors that the prince took his sexual pleasure by cruelly using teenage girls and had, in fact, recently ruined a young maid employed by Countess Corloni.

Also at the *farone* table was Cardinal Apolloni's secretary, Don Santini, who was encouraging the prince to increase his bets. The Prince was losing heavily.

Finally, wiping his wrinkled, sweating face and mumbling to himself, the prince stood up and went to the banker.

As was the custom he told the banker how much he had lost. No one would have considered challenging his total, just as no one would have considered cheating on his own wins or losses. These gambling debts between ladies and gentlemen in the great houses of Rome were never settled the night of the game, but at the first convenient opportunity, which was usually at the next meeting.

When Prince Vittori left it was whispered that he would find it impossible to raise such a sum in a short time and that, though he had again delayed his marriage to Gianna Corloni, he would have no choice now but to sign the marriage contract.

"And perhaps the countess will provide another little girl for his pleasure," a man said.

The room fell silent as Count Croce turned on the man and called him down for his insulting suggestion about the countess. The man was pale and trembling when Count Croce finished with him and led Chessie out of the salon.

Chessie feared the count's mood, feared he would turn his anger on her, and she was even more alarmed to see him drinking far more than usual. If only I could escape, she thought, but it seemed impossible until one of the count's officers hurried in and told him that an agent of Garibaldi had been spotted in the city.

"How fortunate," the count said with a malicious smile that sent a chill down Chessie's spine. "I've been waiting for the opportunity to escort such a gentleman to the special facilities at the Castle of San Angelo."

Abruptly, the count bade Chessie good night, apparently forgetting about seeing her home. When he had gone she sipped another glass of champagne, then decided that since this *palazzo* was near her apartment she would defy convention and walk home alone.

44.

When she was only a few steps from the *palazzo* Chessie began to regret her decision. The gas lamps were turned off and only occasional candles beneath religious shrines lit the deserted streets. All shutters were drawn, all doors shut. It was ominously silent and Chessie saw no one ahead. She scurried along, glancing anxiously back over her shoulder.

In only a few minutes she realized someone was following her. Her first thought was that Count Croce had set one of his spies on her, but half a block later she felt less sure. Somehow she knew that the man following her was not one of Croce's men. She walked faster. So did he. She paused. So did he, careful to stay out of sight in the shadows. Still, she saw no one. She walked faster and faster, nearly slipping on the rough cobblestones. If she fell down he would catch her at once.

When she turned a corner she realized the man was gaining on her. She did not have far to go. Her apartment was in the next block. She broke into a run, stumbled, but caught her balance. Her heart was thumping and she gasped for breath, her breathing so ragged she no longer heard her pursuer's footsteps . . .

Suddenly a hand closed over her mouth and a man pulled her into a dark courtyard, smothering her scream. He was so strong she was helpless and she thought of Myrtis. It had been like this for her. She saw herself being raped, saw herself ruined, bloody . . .

Fiercely, Chessie kicked and scratched until she broke free and fell against a wall. The breath was knocked out of her. Weak, gurgling sounds escaped from her throat. Then the man advanced on her again. A sharp pain stabbed her stomach and loins.

Don't rape me! she wanted to beg. I'll do anything, give anything, but don't hurt me, please. But his hand was so firmly clamped over her mouth that she could not speak.

Suddenly a band of moonlight crossed the man's face and Chessie gasped.

The man was Carlo!

"Don't scream," he said in a low voice. "I didn't mean to frighten you. You're all right now . . ."

He took his hand from her mouth. Her stomach was tight. She was shaken and nearly nauseous, but stronger than her fright was all the pain of humiliation she had suffered in Palermo.

Shaking with outrage, Chessie raised her hand and slapped Carlo's face. He winced. She slapped him again.

Carlo grabbed her wrists. "Chessie, please . . ."

"Let me go!" she said. "Damn you, let me go! I don't want to talk to you. I don't ever want to see you again. I hate you!"

"You have every right, Chessie," he said. "But please listen to me." He released her wrists and tried to stroke them. "Give me a chance to explain my feelings for you . . ."

"No!" she said. "I won't hear ány more of your lies! You're hurting my wrists. Why did you follow me? You scared me half to death. Go! And don't follow me again!"

"Wait, just a minute!" he said. "I followed you to protect you, to make certain no one else was following you . . . Someone has been . . . I've watched you for two days and you've been followed constantly. I'm in danger, myself. If I'm found in Rome, it will mean certain arrest."

"Then why did you come?" she asked. "Don't think your lies will win you sympathy from me. Get arrested for all I . . . oh, Carlo! Your head, your shoulder . . . What happened?"

In the faint light Chessie had just seen that Carlo's head was partly bandaged and one of his arms was in a sling.

"The Bourbon bombardment of Palermo," he said. "Don't concern yourself with my wounds, Chessie. Listen to me. I've come to Rome . . . put myself in grave danger . . . only to see you, to tell you how much I . . ."

"To see me, indeed!" she said. "And the Lord only knows how many other women! Nothing you can say will change my mind! Save your pretty words and your poetry. And if you try to see me again . . . I swear, I'll turn you over to . . . to the police. Or to my special friend, Count Croce."

"Croce?" he asked. "You know that bastard? He's head of the political police in Rome, Chessie. He's a master of deceit, of torture . . ."

"You're a fine one to speak of deceit, Carlo," she said. "Now, unless you intend to hold me here by force, get out of my way. If you touch me again, I'll scream."

"Chessie, just a minute more. Please! Listen to me . . ."

But Chessie ran past him. She ran all the way to her apartment building before she stopped and looked over her shoulder. Carlo had disappeared.

The porter was clearly startled to see her without an escort, but she rushed past him and hurried up the stairs, brushing at the tears that wet her cheeks.

45.

Lucinda was incredulous and angry as she left Sawyer's cabin. She had never seen such savage lash-marks. To think they had been inflicted by Anthony because of some incident while he was hunting.

The people in the quarters were quiet and sullen and as she walked back to the house she felt a strange kind of guilt, a vicarious guilt, because her own husband was responsible.

Was the man she had loved so deeply capable of such cruelty?

She surprised herself by thinking of her love for Anthony in the past tense. It wasn't past, she assured herself. She still loved Anthony . . . but not as deeply, as blindly, as when she married him.

She didn't exactly know why, or even how, but Anthony had changed. She feared his love for her had cooled.

She supposed that his coolness showed most clearly in their lovemaking, or lack of it. His passion never matched hers and he often found excuses for not making love. She suspected that part of it had to do with her illness. Anthony was disturbed by illness of any kind.

Lucinda hoped it was only the illness. Though she had been sicker than she had let anyone know—and she had been careful not to spoil the twins' trip by making sure they were told nothing at all of the illness—the specialist in New Orleans had assured her that with the new treatment and medication he had prescribed she would begin to recover in a short while.

Then, if only the illness had cooled Anthony's love, they would soon resume their lovemaking with the kind of passion that existed when they were first married.

Her worst fear, and one she seldom let herself dwell

on, was that Anthony had found some other woman, that he had taken a lover.

Lucinda had nothing specific with which to accuse him, no evidence other than the cooling of his passion. She longed to discuss it with some other woman. She had considered Anna Roccalini. Or Jolette. But her pride would not let her, so she had kept her concern to herself.

And now there was this additional problem concerning Anthony. It upset her that he had not mentioned what happened when he met her pad'wheeler in Natchez this morning. He had only mentioned, in an offhand way, that there was a matter they must discuss but that it would have to wait because of a serious business problem that had just come up.

He had sent her and Jolette out to The Columns and promised to return home as soon as possible.

Lucinda dreaded the confrontation. But she had no choice. Such a brutal incident must never happen again and Anthony must be made to understand that.

Lucinda went into the parlor. She sat down and sent a maid to fetch a pitcher of lemonade and wished that she had Jolette to keep her company. But Jolette had gone over to the Sumralls' to deliver some gifts.

Lucinda was standing at the window when Anthony rode up to the house half an hour later. Her heart pounding, she stepped toward the door, then hesitated.

Anthony entered the parlor a minute later. He spoke while she was still trying to choose her words.

"I can tell by the look on your face that you've heard about Sawyer," he said. "I'm sorry it had to happen, Lucinda, but it was necessary. I should have told you in Natchez, but I was rushed . . . and didn't know how to go about it."

"No, Anthony, it wasn't necessary at all," Lucinda said. "It was cruel, and unprecedented at The Columns."

"Are you simply going to accept the nigger's version of what happened?" Anthony asked. "You might at least have waited to hear my side, before condemning me."

"You just admitted that you beat him, Anthony," she said. "What possible defense can you make? You know perfectly well slaves are never whipped at The Columns, not even for the worst possible offenses. And you whipped poor Sawyer because of some hunting incident . . ."

"Dammit, hear me out!" Anthony said. Lucinda was startled by the harsh tone of his voice and the anger in his eyes. "To begin with, that goddamn Sawyer is the laziest, most worthless nigger in Adams County. He was carrying my guns while I was hunting, and because he's fat and lazy he couldn't keep up with me and I came on a rattlesnake . . . Except for dumb good luck, I'd be dead now, Lucinda! And then the black bastard had the audacity to arrive back here on a wagon, after I had to walk, to arrive laughing, making a joke of the matter!"

"Yes, Anthony," Lucinda said wearily. "I know Sawyer's laziness and incompetence are frustrating, even unforgiveable. I'm . . . Oh, I'm so glad you escaped from that horrible snake . . . But that's still no excuse for whippin' Sawyer. Putting up with this kind of nigger is a price any decent slave owner has to pay . . ."

"Damn it, it's not a price I'm willing to pay," Anthony said. "I won't be made to feel guilty because of some goddamn incident with a nigger! It's not like Sawyer is a white man!"

Lucinda was stunned by this diatribe against Negroes. She had never heard such hateful talk from Anthony. She wondered if he had been drinking.

Half a minute had passed and Lucinda became aware of the silence. She supposed he was waiting for her to speak but she had nothing to say. Her illness had debilitated her and she had been warned against fatigue and stress. She knew she must end the argument quickly and sit down.

Anthony seemed to realize this. His face softened. His lips trembled slightly.

"My God, what's happening to me, darling?" he asked. "I can't believe I'm capable of such an outburst. It's just that . . . well, there have been some serious problems with one of my ships and I'm afraid I've let myself take out my frustrations on the niggers . . . And, my God, I've stormed in here and shouted at you . . ."

"It's all right, Anthony," Lucinda said. "I'm sorry about your business problems. I wish you had discussed them with me. Don't apologize for our argument. Just . . . Please, darling, just promise me you'll never abuse our slaves again."

"No, I won't," he said. "I promise you, on my oath . . ."

But as Anthony spoke, his eyes avoided hers and for some reason—the averted eyes, his insincere tone, the sudden reversal of his mood from angry defiance to almost obsequious apology—she did not really believe him.

In any case, she was too exhausted to continue the matter.

"Fine, Anthony," she said. "Then the matter's settled."

"Are you sure?" he asked. "Yes, it must be. You shouldn't be subjected to this kind of anxiety. You need a rest. Why don't we go upstairs and take a siesta together? I've missed you terribly."

"Yes, I've missed you, too, darling," Lucinda said. Despite her disappointment in Anthony, she did love him still, and they had not made love in nearly a month. Lucinda had been looking down and now she moved her face up toward his, to gaze into the dark eyes that always excited her . . .

But her own eyes paused at the lapel of his jacket. There she saw several long strands of silky black hair. She stifled a gasp.

"We'll go up and . . ." he was saying.

"No," Lucinda said sharply. "No, Anthony, not now. This talk has been too exhausting. I just . . . Leave me alone, please. I want to sit down and be alone."

"Lucinda, it would be better if you went up to bed . . ."

"No!" she said. "I'll rest here! Alone!" She felt she would scream if he didn't leave immediately.

He sighed. "All right, Lucinda," he said. "I'll be in our bedroom if you change your mind."

He left the parlor. Lucinda collapsed into a chair by the window. Her breast heaved with sobs but no tears came to her eyes. She shuddered and drew her arms tight against the chill that wracked her frail body.

46.

The maidservant Stefania paused outside Countess Corloni's private chapel and listened to her mistress praying aloud. She hated the countess so much that only lack of courage kept her from acting on her desire to drive a knife into the kneeling woman's back.

Stefania hurried away from the chapel and down the kitchen stairs. She took her blue cloak from a pantry and left the villa, walking as fast as she could, still stiff-legged and sore from her encounter with Prince Vittori. Choking back tears, she forced her body to endure the pain, a constant reminder of her humiliation and her hatred for both the prince and the countess. When her determination weakened the pain goaded her on.

Stefania was in search of the young American that Gianna was interested in. She was desperate to find him, for she had a plan for revenge that involved him, a revenge on the prince and the countess that would also be her salvation.

In sacrificing Stefania to Prince Vittori's sexual whims, Countess Corloni had not reckoned on the maidservant's independence and fortitude. Stefania saw her own plight very clearly. Because of the prince, she was ruined and humiliated. Not even her own family considered her fit for marriage—she was marked for life. Her family could not avenge her against royalty. She lacked the strength for suicide, and yet—how was her life worth living?

Stefania had thought of running away. But in an uncharacteristic gesture, motivated by guilt, the countess had promoted her from kitchen maid to upstairs chambermaid and Stefania had glimpsed a possibility of salvation.

Upstairs, she had become friendly with Gianna. Gianna was desperate for a confidante, and Stefania was glad to play the role. Gianna had told her everything, had revealed her hesitation about the marriage planned for her and confessed her infatuation with an American whom she had met just once, but longed to see again.

Stefania had little real sympathy for Gianna's plight, but she welcomed the chance to deprive the countess of success and extract money from the American. She would take his money and flee the Corlonis, flee her shame and humiliation and begin life again with a substantial dowry in some other city, perhaps Viterbo, where she had cousins.

Pray God I have the courage to do it all, she thought. If the countess caught her, the retribution would be terrible. But could it be more terrible than what she had endured or the life of misery she faced? Shaking her head, Stefania hurried on.

Despite her boldness, Stefania was apprehensive by the time she reached the Via del Corso. She had never visited this elegant quarter and she felt out of place, but she kept to the shadows and searched for the street where the American lived. She had overheard a conversation between some of the countess' agents and they had mentioned a building on Via Frattina.

When Stefania found the building, she hovered in a doorway across the street. Her thighs and buttocks ached terribly. She nibbled her lip and waited.

Clayton left a tavern in the early evening, despondent and consumed with an impotent anger. Lately, he had pretended to lose all interest in Gianna, and he had succeeded in fooling the countess' thugs who had followed him. Fear had forced him to do so, but he regretted it, for he had lost track of Gianna's movements.

Tonight, he had heard, to his misery, that her engagement had been announced and banns posted. In a few months Gianna Corloni would become the Princess Vittori. The thought filled him with despair.

Clayton visited a small shop that sold antique guns and he found an old Austrian dueling pistol with an inlaid ivory handle that he liked. But he lacked the enthusiasm to buy it.

He drank several brandies in a tavern, then stumbled along a crowded street paved with rough cobblestones and slippery with mud, garbage and excrement. He was intoxicated and lost and didn't care where he was going.

Clayton was weary of Rome, of the whole damn Continent. Lincoln had been nominated by the Republicans and was likely to be elected president. Several Southern states, including Mississippi, were planning to hold conventions to determine if they would secede from the Union. There might well be war, and Clayton longed for the chance to fight, both for the Southern cause, and to give his life some discipline, some meaning.

More than anything, he just wanted to return to Natchez. They would be harvesting the cotton at The Columns now, just as they were harvesting the grapes in Italy. But his only interest in grapes was their fermented juices. He longed to smell the rich soil of his plantation and see the bursting white cotton pods stretching to the horizon.

Absentmindedly, he stopped to watch some workmen building a tall wooden platform and realized it was a scaffold. Notices on the walls of nearby churches asked people to pray for the condemned man's soul.

If I were at home, Clayton mused, I'd go for a long, hard ride. Idly, he stopped for a glass of wine in another tavern, then wandered outside the city's walls.

There he came on a group of drunken revelers who appeared to be returning from a rural Bacchanalia where they had danced and celebrated the grape harvest.

Clayton resisted an invitation to join the revelers. He wanted to be alone in his unhappiness. He wanted to think, wanted the cool evening air to clear his head, for his thoughts were confused and jumbled.

I don't doubt my love for Gianna, he thought, but there's no way I can reach her. And how do I know that she cares for me at all?

Now that Clayton was beginning to accept the hopelessness of his love, he had to admit that he had been foolhardy and reckless. He had been frightened of the men who had followed him constantly. He had been brutally beaten by the same men. They might have killed him, he realized.

Even now, when he walked the streets, he found himself glancing around to make sure he wasn't being followed. He woke with nightmares of the countess' thugs dragging him from his bed.

The countess had had others killed, he had heard. Her ruthlessness was legendary. She would stop at nothing to have her way.

As Clayton walked, the sun had set, and the evening was growing dark. A rising wind brought a sharp, strange smell to his nostrils. He looked around and realized that he had wandered far beyond the city gates and had not seen anyone in some time.

In the last lingering light he saw a huge open pit just ahead. Curiosity drew him to the pit's edge. Beyond it stretched other pits of the same size, rows of pits as far as the eye could see.

The hairs at the back of Clayton's neck prickled as he saw a coffin beside the nearest pit. His nostrils were assaulted by the pungent smell of lime and another, more sickening stench that he knew without doubt to be that of death.

Behind him, he heard a rhythmic, morbid chanting. He looked around to see, on the horizon, a band of hooded men, carrying a coffin on their shoulders. One man held a tall cross, another a smoking torch.

In his intoxicated and badly frightened state Clayton had the sudden fear that they carried his coffin: The Countess Corloni's men had tracked him here and now they would kill him in some horrible way!

He stumbled backward and nearly fell into an open pit. He lurched one way, another, then stopped, his strength all but gone, as he watched the hooded procession approach.

"I don't want to die," he muttered. He stepped backward, his frantic eyes darted about. There was no weapon around. He knew his legs could never outrun the relentless procession. He dared not run recklessly, for fear of plunging into one of the lime-filled pits.

The hooded men were nearing him now, their chant lower and more bizarre. Their blue hoods were tall, with black skeletons on the top. The slits in the hoods showed dark, death-filled eyes.

Clayton stumbled backward a step, nearly plunged into a pit, lurched to the side toward the pit with the coffin. With a sudden movement that, in the dark, at first seemed a corpse rising from the coffin, a fat, hook-nosed man in black appeared.

"My God, sir. You gave me a start!" the man said.

" 'Tis you who have startled me," Clayton gasped. "What is this place?"

The hooded men had stopped on the other side of the pit and lowered the coffin. They turned away from Clayton, much to his relief, and began to perform some religious function over the coffin.

"Why, these are the burying pits," the man said. "If you don't know them, what brings you here? No one comes here to see the sights."

Clayton glanced at the hooded men again. He began to regain control of himself, though he was still badly shaken.

"I'm a visitor in Rome," Clayton said. "I lost my way. Burying pits? Who's buried here?"

"Everyone, sir. Except for some of the noble families who bury their own in the country. Everyone comes here eventually, though hardly ever in such good health as yourself, sir."

"I've never seen anything like this," Clayton said. "How many pits are there? It's barbaric! And that coffin at your feet? It's so fragile it could fall apart at one touch. How can it withstand the weight of the earth?"

The man laughed. "Ah, foreigners do have strange notions about the dead. There's a pit for every day of the year! We're burying the dead in this one today. As for the coffin, why, a coffin at all is unusual, sir. Usually, the corpses just arrive in a cart, and we dump them all in the pit and shovel over the lime . . ."

Clayton shuddered. "That's abominable . . ."

"Sir, they're dead, aren't they? Only corpses, aren't they?"

Clayton was appalled. His nostrils constricted at the pungent, sickening smell of death and lime. He shivered, and remembered the hooded men.

"Who are those men?" Clayton asked.

"The *Confernita,* sir," the man said. "The dead man's family would never go near the corpse. The evil eye, you know. The family flees the house at the first indication of death. These men perform this task as penance for their sins. It particularly pleases the Madonna. Blue is her favorite color."

"My Lord! In all my life, I've never . . . Who is the deceased, to rate both a coffin and these mourners?"

"Why, Don Santini, the cardinal's secretary," the man said. "Taken from life in the midst of health, they say. Either that, or . . . Well, there's no danger in gossip with a foreigner, I suppose. Others say that the don was in the pay of the Countess Corloni, that he was paid to make certain the old prince ruined himself at the *farone* tables. But when, they say, the don became too ambitious and threatened to ruin the countess' plans . . . He died of poison. Ah, sir, poisoning flourished here when I was a child. It's a dying art now, but if anyone tries to maintain the old values it's the Countess Corloni . . ."

Clayton turned and ran. He lurched past the ghostly blue-hooded men, barely keeping his balance, running and gasping for breath, until he was inside the city walls.

An hour later, after three brandies, Clayton walked down Via Frattina toward his apartment. He was still shaken by his visit to the death pits and well warned by the death of Don Santini. This town is godforsaken, in truth, he thought. He felt as if the stench of death and lime still clung to his clothes. No matter what Chessie said or wanted, he was determined now to return to Natchez as soon as passage could be arranged. His decision cheered him.

But as he approached his building a hand beckoned from the shadows across the street. Clayton halted, wary. He stared into the shadows. Had some blue-robed fiend followed him from the pits? Had Countess Corloni set another spy on him? His nerves jangled.

As Clayton hesitated, the figure moved cautiously into the light. He jumped, startled, then delighted. It was a woman! Was it Gianna?

He ran over to her. He stopped. It wasn't Gianna, it was a young woman of the servant class, although she had dark hair like Gianna's and was of similar height.

Clayton saw that she had been crying. Her eyes were red and her cheeks pale. She glanced nervously along the street, then stepped back into the shadows. Clayton followed.

"Sir, are you . . . ? Are you the American named Divorsi who . . . knows . . . Gianna Corloni?" the young woman asked in a timid voice.

"Yes, yes," Clayton said. "I am! Has Gianna sent you?"

"I've come to help you," Stefania said.

Stefania explained that the gates of the Villa Corloni were always kept securely locked and that vicious mantraps had been set out about the grounds. But she had stolen a map of the mantraps and a key to a back gate, which she had duplicated before returning it. Her plan was simple: She would sell this duplicate key and the map to Clayton and convey messages between him and Gianna.

Clayton listened to her proposal with elation and mounting hope. His prayers had been answered. He would see Gianna again!

But Stefania demanded a large sum of money. He did not have that much cash on hand. It might take him weeks to have the funds transferred from the Deavors' banker in Paris.

Clayton tried to plead for credit, but Stefania was adamant. She was not touched by his pleas. No, she said flatly, she would do nothing further until she was paid in cash.

His fears and his plan to leave Rome forgotten, Clayton turned into a tavern for another brandy. Rome suddenly looked beautiful to him, and he was impatient that he could not contact his banker's agent until the following morning.

47.

Chessie steeled herself to endure Count Croce's smothering kisses and probing, insistent hands a moment longer, then wriggled free and stepped back. She straightened the ribbons at her bodice and smoothed down her dress.

It was so dark beneath the umbrella pines that Chessie could not see the count's face clearly, but his breathing was ragged and she sensed his physical tension. This is wrong, all wrong, Chessie thought. She should never have agreed to walk alone with him in the garden. Count Croce had become too demanding, far too demanding, and now he was becoming angry.

". . . Please, sir, may we return to the other guests?"

Chessie said. "There's a wind, and I feel a chill. I'd like my wrap."

"Of course, my dear," the count said. "You're not accustomed to our chilly Roman nights." There was no mistaking the sarcasm in his voice.

Awkwardly, they walked back toward the count's Frascati villa where his two hundred guests danced and gambled and drank champagne.

"I'm sorry, sir," Chessie said, dreading his anger but determined not to be intimidated, "but your kisses and caresses are too intimate for . . . for the feelings I have for you. I'm indeed fond of you, sir, but in the future I'd prefer that we remain friends, and nothing more . . ." There! She had spoken plainly, and she dared him to mention the debt she owed him for helping Clayton.

"I've always valued friendship, Miss Deavors," he said. His voice was still sarcastic and Chessie realized that he was no longer using her first name. "Though each person, I would think, interprets friendship in his own way. Perhaps, here in Rome, we put a different meaning on friendship. And on what is expected of friends."

"I don't know much about your Roman customs," Chessie said. "And, since we will be in Rome only a few more weeks, I fear I shall have little opportunity to learn them."

"Ah, Miss Deavors, your education in Roman customs is far from over, I can assure you," he said. "You will certainly experience some new and unexpected things before you leave."

I must not let him frighten me Chessie vowed. "I've learned quite enough for this day, sir," she said.

"For this day, yes, Miss Deavors," he said. "We've both learned quite enough. It's unfortunate, however, that you didn't learn what I told you some time ago, about the danger of consorting with *Garibaldini* . . ."

Chessie stopped. She glanced up. The count's face was a mask of menace in the shadows. Looming over her, he seemed a giant and the implication of his words was clear and frightening: how could he know that Carlo was in Rome, that Carlo had tried to talk to her on three occasions? Once more, she refused to be intimidated.

"How dare you, sir!" she said. "You've had me followed!"

"Miss Deavors, in Rome I dare anything. Remember that," he said. "I do as I wish, so long as it doesn't offend the French or the Holy Father. In this instance, I acted in their behalf . . ."

"And in your own!" she said.

"Yes, certainly, in my own," he said. "How you glare at me with those beautiful, innocent, American eyes, Miss Deavors. Just like an outraged citizen! But, my dear, you're far from your serene little democracy now. I don't wish you as an enemy. I'd do almost anything to avoid it. Yet, few women in Rome would be so carelessly disinterested in my attentions as you obviously are. I'm quite capable of acting for my own benefit politically as well as personally. I'd do anything to crush the peasant rebellion in the South!"

"Count Croce, I've refused to see Carlo Settimo," Chessie said excitedly. "I can't prevent his being in Rome, but I have no interest in the man, and I'll thank you to . . ."

He interrupted her. "So it is Settimo! My agents were not yet certain. Thank you for your confirmation, Miss Deavors."

"I . . . I . . ." Chessie could not speak. Had she betrayed Carlo? How could she have been so stupid as to blurt out his name? "I'm not lying, Count Croce," she said.

"Perhaps," he said. "Perhaps not. I choose to believe you, Miss Deavors. Although it hardly matters. Settimo has eluded my agents so far, but if he's still in the city, we'll take him. And despite my . . . disappointment in you, Miss Deavors, I'm still fond enough of you to give you this last warning. Do not see

the man, not even once. I advise you out of affection.
Politically, I should hope that you lure Settimo out
into the open so that we may arrest him."

"I appreciate your advice . . . and affection," Chessie
said. "But I want no more favors from you, sir. Your
kindness so far has added to my enjoyment of Rome.
I want to remember you fondly, and I want to remain
your friend. But I won't . . . Oh, what's the use of talking? Please, may we go in now?"

"Yes, of course, your chill," he said.

They were silent as he escorted her back to the party
and left her with a group that included Clayton. A
maid handed Chessie a glass of champagne but she set
it down on a marble sideboard after two unenthusiastic
sips. Suppose she had endangered Carlo by mentioning
his name!

Chessie's head pounded anxiously and she could not
enjoy herself. Despite the music, the gay atmosphere
and the excitement of gambling, the party seemed dull
and she longed to go home, though it was not yet midnight. She was relieved when Clayton suggested they
leave.

Count Croce was coldly polite when the twins bade
him good night.

Two weeks after the party at Count Croce's villa,
Chessie returned to the Via Frattina apartment after an
excursion with Signora Nantes to the catacombs outside Rome. She knocked on the apartment door and
waited. She knocked again. Where was Torine?, she
wondered.

Finally she heard the maid's footsteps, then a pause.
The moment Torine opened the door Chessie knew
something had happened. Torine looked nervous. She
closed and bolted the door, then turned to Chessie and
smiled oddly.

With a sinking feeling, Chessie realized that she had
been naive to think that Count Croce would give up
so easily. Something had happened. Someone had come

to the apartment—the count?—his agents? Something was wrong! She could tell by the look on Torine's face. A chill raced up her spine.

"Torine . . ." she whispered. "Torine, what is it? Who . . . ?"

Torine looked toward the parlor door and Chessie ran into the parlor. Chessie had braced herself for trouble, but she was not prepared for the shock of seeing Carlo Settimo standing there.

48.

Carlo, his hand on his pistol, stood at a window shielded from the street by the draperies. He turned quickly as Chessie and Torine entered, lowered the pistol and stepped away from the window.

Chessie turned on Torine. "You let him in!" she said. "How could you, Torine? Why did you? You know how I feel . . ."

"Yes'm, Miss Chessie," Torine said. "I think I know exactly how you feel, despite all you say. I know better'n you do, sometimes. I knows you since you was born, Miss Chessie, and I wasn't never wrong yet."

"Hush, Torine!" Chessie said. "You're wrong this time. You've disobeyed me! You'll regret this, I promise you."

"Chessie," Carlo said. "It's my fault. I insisted. Don't blame her . . ."

"I blame you, sir!" Chessie said. "And I want you to leave at once! You can't seem to understand that I have no intention of seeing you. I have no interest in you. And you've endangered us all by coming here!"

"Well, I'll leave you two to argue this all out, Miss Chessie," Torine said. "I'll just go down the hall and keep a watch by the door . . ."

"No, you wait," Chessie said. "I want you to show Signore Settimo out, just as you showed him in . . ."

"Chessie, I won't leave until I speak to you," Carlo said. "And my coming here was less reckless than you think. I found a way to enter your building from the back, unseen, and the police would never think to look for me here in your apartment."

"He's right, Miss Chessie," Torine said. "They wouldn't never think to . . ."

"What are you still here for?" Chessie shouted. "Get out!" She was furious at Torine, at Carlo, and at herself for losing control this way.

"Yes'm, I'm on my way," Torine said. She left the room.

Chessie stared at Carlo. She tried to catch her breath, tried to steady herself. He hadn't run away, after all, despite the danger. He had stayed in Rome. She swallowed hard. The swallow lessened her anger and much of her strength.

She struggled to harden herself. She couldn't give in to him, despite the look of longing and need in his eyes, despite the disturbing nearness of the face she remembered so well. She tried to summon up other memories—memories of how he had lied to her and hurt her.

"I love you, Chessie," Carlo said before she could speak. "I love you deeply and truly. I've come here to tell you that—I've come a long way, and I'm determined to convince you . . ."

"I was fooled by your pretty words once before," Chessie said. Her hands were trembling. She clenched them together, looking down, trying not to look at him.

"And I let myself hope, Chessie, that despite my unpardonable behavior in Palermo, you still have some . . . some deep feelings for me . . ."

"Palermo seems a lifetime ago," Chessie said. "I've tried to forget what happened there . . . Perhaps I have. You shouldn't have come here to torment me again!"

Carlo stepped forward to Chessie and took her hands. "Darling! I can't bear to hear the sadness in your voice. I could never torment you. You must believe me, you must! I was childish and weak, but I've changed, I swear it!"

"Perhaps you have," Chessie said wearily. "How can I believe you? But I'm too exhausted to argue. And it's too late. You're in grave danger. The count's agents could take you at any moment. You must leave Rome immediately. If you know some secret way out of this building, then take it and go at once."

"No, dammit!" he said. He paced the room. "No, Chessie, I won't leave you like this, not until you believe me."

Chessie backed toward the door. She glanced over her shoulder. The door was open. She could run down the hallway and lock herself in her bedroom.

But as she moved toward the door Carlo seized her arm and stopped her. He slammed the door and stood with his back to it.

"You can't keep me here by force," Chessie said. "I'll scream. I have nothin' but contempt . . . I have nothin' . . ."

But as she looked up, Chessie was lost. Carlo's pleading eyes met hers and she forgot to breathe. She saw the new scar along his left temple and cheek, and shuddered to think of the pain and suffering that he must have felt.

For the first time, she realized that since Palermo, Carlo had become a soldier. He had faced fire, risked his life, been wounded. The change in him was obvious. Carlo was no longer the arrogant dandy who had trifled with her in Palermo. But who was he? Chessie was confused and unsettled. Her anger had deserted her. She was still wary, but . . .

"Darling?" Carlo asked.

"Carlo, it's so dangerous!" she said. "What if someone comes? Clayton may come back."

"Likely not for hours," Carlo said. "No one will come. And, if so, Torine will give us sufficient warning."

"Yes, I suppose so," Chessie said.

She raised her hand, hesitated a moment, then reached out to him and ran a finger along the scar on his face. She shivered at the touch of the rough skin. When she looked into his eyes she knew she could not hate him any longer. She still loved him.

With all her heart she loved him. He was the only man she had ever loved, or ever would love . . . And when she thought of Clayton at that same moment it was without feelings. She felt no guilt, only relief that her special love for her brother was now definitely over—a thing of the past, part of her childhood. She was a grown woman and she wanted this man who was caressing her fingers to be her husband.

Gently, Carlo took Chessie's fingers in his hand and kissed them one by one. She moved a half step closer. Carlo embraced her. She rose on her toes to meet his kiss. His lips were gentle on hers, on her cheeks, her eyes. Hesitantly, she put her fingers in his hair and kissed his cheek, kissed along his scar. A jolt of compassion and excitement coursed through her body. They kissed again, a more urgent kiss, but Carlo drew away just as Chessie began to nibble his tongue and press her body against his.

"Beautiful Chessie," he whispered and held her hands. "How I love you! I couldn't have lived much longer without you. Only thoughts of you sustained me these months. And now let me explain my conduct in Palermo . . ."

She silenced him with a finger on his lips. "Shhh," she said. "I do believe in your love, Carlo. I don't want to speak of Palermo ever again."

"You're right. Palermo is the past. We have the present now, Chessie, and the future . . ."

"Yes, Carlo, the future. But what of now? You're in terrible danger in Rome. I can't bear to think how much! . . . Count Croce is determined to catch you! You must get out of Rome!"

Torine ran into the room. "Two strange, vigus-lookin' men comin' down the hall," she said.

"Oh, no!" Chessie gasped.

Carlo took out his pistol.

"I'll go out the back, Chessie," he said. "Dear Chessie . . . Don't worry . . . I'll be quite safe, I promise you . . ."

"Carlo, take care! When will I see you again?"

"In a week, two at the most," he said. "I must return to Sicily, resign my commission, tell my family about you. I'll return as soon as I can, and when I return, we'll never be separated again."

There was a loud pounding on the door. Chessie gasped. Carlo bent and kissed her on the lips, a quick, strong kiss. Then he turned and ran.

Chessie touched the lips he had kissed. She straightened her dress and smoothed her hair. She was trembling. The knock grew louder.

"Open the door," she said to Torine, "but stall them."

Chessie stepped to the window. She saw three men down in the street. Any of them could be the count's men. There might be other men waiting at the back for Carlo.

She heard voices at the door. They sounded angry. Had they come to arrest her? What could she do? Had Carlo succeeded in getting away?

Torine entered the room, followed by two men in black cloaks. One man wore a patch over his left eye. His right eye stared as if to penetrate Chessie's very skull.

Then she saw the huge white lilies he held out.

"Compliments of Count Croce, signorina," the man said in a surprisingly gentle voice. He handed her the flowers.

The other man stepped back outside and dragged in an enormous cask of wine. "From the count's vineyards," he said. Chessie nearly cried with relief as she thanked the men and showed them out.

The Reillons

Carlo took out his pistol.

49.

The Countess Corloni examined the brooches and lockets displayed on a velvet cushion in her salon by Signor Destini and finally chose a large silver locket carved with roses and set with tiny diamonds. She dismissed the fawning silver merchant, waited impatiently for him to leave, then fastened the locket around her neck and admired it in the mirror. Her father would be pleased. She had done it for him—chosen this beautiful locket as the final resting place for his worldly remains. Now she would have his body exhumed from its far-off pauper's grave and returned to Rome for cremation. Then she would fill the locket with the ashes.

Until then, the countess decided, she would wear the locket as a pledge. She nodded, pleased with the plan. She rang for a servant and ordered a bottle of Marsala wine, then walked out onto her balcony to drink it.

The night was crisp and stars glittered through the thin, fast-moving clouds. The countess sipped her wine and watched the torches of a religious procession moving beyond the villa's walls. She herself had lit many tapers today. She had much for which to be thankful. Gianna was now engaged to Prince Vittori. The wedding banns had been posted. In a few weeks, the ceremony would take place and Gianna would become a princess. Lately, Gianna had seemed resigned to her destiny and never left the villa.

The countess drank more wine and savored the success of her plans. She had acted boldly to insure that success. She had not hesitated to have that fool Santini poisoned when he tried to blackmail her and threatened to expose her manipulation of the prince's finances. And despite her friendship with Count Croce and her appreciation of his enormous power, she would not have hesitated to cross him to get rid of Gianna's suitor—had it been necessary.

But fortunately, Gianna had come to her senses and had not spoken of the American in some time, and the American no longer pursued Gianna. And, at the opera last night, Count Croce had said that the American was no longer under his protection.

Count Croce had seemed weary. His face was drawn with fatigue and frustration.

"The American girl speaks to me of friendship!" he said. "And as she becomes more elusive my infatuation is heightened. The devil take her and her brother!"

"Paolo, dear, it's so unlike you!" the countess said. "Why don't you simply take your pleasure with her?"

"Of course, I'll have my way in the end," the count said. "But she is a very special sort of woman, my dear. I much prefer that she surrender. Strangely, it would be more meaningful. But I assure you, eventually, I shall have her, one way or another!"

"You seem so oddly agitated this evening, Paolo," the countess said. "Has this simple American girl really captivated and upset you?"

"Ah, my dear countess," he said. "I confess that she has. She had an annoying flirtation with a *Garibaldino* in Sicily and now my agents tell me that he has turned up in Rome and has been trying to see her again. I've warned her of the consequences of consorting with *Garibaldini* but I fear she hasn't heeded my warning. Chessie is so innocent that she's stupid! The fellow was an aide to Garibaldi. I planned to take him, but a few days ago he disappeared."

"Chessie," the countess said. "What an odd name. I've never heard it before."

"She was named by a servant, I believe," the count said. "She was born in the south of America, a region where they often give their children peculiar names, I've been told. Ah, she vexes me! But how are the wedding plans progressing, my dear?"

Splendidly, the countess said. Neither of them mentioned Don Santini's death. The countess knew that

Count Croce had loathed the cardinal's secretary and had often wished him dead. She knew he was pleased and that she was further endeared to him now.

The countess poured another glass of wine. She smiled.

Yes, everything is going splendidly, she thought. She raised her glass to toast her triumphs, the planned marriage, and Gianna's glorious future as the wife of the prince.

How well I've done, she mused, remembering her bitter past of poverty, dependency and humiliation.

Remembering wrinkled up her face and she squeezed the stem of the fragile wine glass. How well she remembered . . .

Tears fell from the countess' cheeks. Pain pounded in her head. She trembled, shutting her eyes. Her fingers clenched on the wine glass until the stem broke. A shard of crystal pierced her skin and she bled into her black glove.

She felt nothing, oblivious to the pain and blood, as she struggled to return to the present. She was wealthy now, wealthy and very powerful.

It was never too late for revenge. When Gianna was safely married, she would use her wealth and power to destroy the children of those she so hated.

Her trembling became convulsive and spread throughout her body. She lifted her wine glass. Her eyes opened and she stared with horror at the blood running down her wrist.

50.

Hidden in shadows, Clayton stood across the road from the Villa Corloni and watched the procession of pilgrims with torches pass by. In his hand he held the key he had bought from Stefania. Wind tossed the torch flames wildly and showed the faces of the pilgrims in an ugly, distorted light. Their low chanting was dirge-like, ominous.

Clayton waited five minutes, then five minutes more in the chill shadows. It was the first day of 1862. Clayton sighed. He was tired and dissipated from a New Year's Eve celebration and this final delay seemed as long as the weeks he'd waited for his money to arrive from Paris. However, Stefania had relented enough to convey messages between Clayton and Gianna, for a few coins each day, and he had felt close to Gianna during the wait.

The last pilgrim passed. Clayton waited another minute. He glanced up and down the road, then crossed to the wall. It was fourteen feet high and topped with pieces of jagged glass. The heavy iron gate was securely locked.

Clayton fumbled with the key. It did not fit! He cursed. Stefania had tricked him!

A moment later, the key slid into the lock and clicked so loudly he feared it would rouse a guard. Slowly, wary of the creaking hinges, Clayton opened the gate. He hesitated, then locked the gate and stood inside with his back to it.

Dogs barked in the distance. Stefania had warned him that the countess had set out mantraps with steel jaws poised on hairsprings powerful enough to snap an ankle.

Clayton inched away into the darkness, picking his way slowly and deliberately, following Stefania's map. The moonlight advanced and retreated behind fast-moving clouds. When Clayton saw the glint of metal in the grass he stopped abruptly. Another few inches and he could have stepped into a mantrap.

Then the moon came out from behind the clouds and he saw a woman in a light-colored gown standing on a balcony. Was it Gianna? . . . Or her mother?

He could not see the woman's face at this distance but decided that the body silhouetted was not Gianna's. So it was the countess. What kind of woman is she?, he wondered. What woman would poison a man, set mantraps, scheme to marry her daughter to a monster like Prince Vittori?

Stefania had only hinted at her reasons for despising the countess but Clayton suspected that she had suffered some sort of abuse at the prince's hands. Yet, as Stefania had warned him, Gianna loved her mother blindly. "She won't hear the truth about the countess," Stefania had said.

Clayton walked slowly, cautiously, deeper into the garden. He saw and avoided two more mantraps. Warily, he followed Stefania's map and arrived at the grotto waterfall where he was to meet Gianna.

He waited for a quarter hour. The dogs howled. They seemed nearer. Clayton concealed himself in the bushes. He started at the slightest sound. Gianna was late. Perhaps she had lost courage or had been discovered. Perhaps she was being held prisoner while her mother's men and dogs hunted him in the park.

Then he heard soft footsteps and a slight rustling in the darkness. It was Gianna, at last!

He jumped up to meet her. In the moonlight Gianna was more beautiful than he remembered. He was stunned by her beauty, made speechless by her actual physical presence.

Suddenly, they were holding hands. Gianna's hands were soft, delicate, warm. Clayton squeezed them and felt her fluttering pulse.

"Are you cold?" he asked. "Here, take my cloak . . ."

"No, no, it's nothing," she said. "It's only that I was so frightened, coming out here to meet you."

"There's no reason to be frightened now," Clayton said. "Gianna, lovely Gianna. After all our notes, to be alone with you . . ."

They stared at each other and did not speak for a time. There was little need to say much. In his second note Clayton had told Gianna that he loved her. And slowly, her own notes had become bolder. They had courted through their pens, and the unusual, distant yet intimate nature of this courtship had allowed Gianna to become bolder far sooner than she would have in a score of illicit, nighttime meetings such as this.

In her last note, Gianna had confessed that she loved him, also.

Clayton heard the dogs in the distance. He glanced around at the darkness.

"Are we safe here?" he asked. "Should we go outside the walls?"

"No," she said. "I can only stay a short time. Perhaps we'll never be able to go beyond these walls . . ."

"Of course we will," he said. "You can't marry that old prince. You can't let your mother ruin your life!"

"Clayton, I've always dreamed of meeting someone like you," Gianna said. "But my sense of obligation and duty to my mother is the strongest of my feelings. My marrying royalty is all she lives for."

"Dammit, you must have your own life!" Clayton said. "We could be so happy on my plantation, as I wrote you last week. You'll love The Columns . . ."

"Hush!" she whispered. "You frighten me with that kind of talk. It's too soon. I've confessed my feelings for you, Clayton, and against all propriety I've met you tonight. But I've made no promises, and I can make none . . ."

"All right," he said. "I know I'm being too impatient, for our first time alone."

"Yes, I must get to know you better," she said. "I must have time to . . . to think, to decide what to do . . . Oh, I do love you, Clayton. Now I must return to the villa, before I'm missed."

"Not yet!" Clayton said. "When will I see you again?"

"Come back here in a week . . . No, no, don't argue . . . A week, Clayton. I must be alone until then."

"I'll be wretched for a week without you, Gianna," he said.

"I'll be lonely also," she said. "Particularly now that Stefania has run away and can't exchange our . . ."

Clayton smothered her words with a kiss. Gianna's body stiffened but she did not pull from his lips. Slowly, her body softened. Her lips parted. Clayton longed to kiss her passionately, to crush her in his arms, but he sensed her fear and hesitation and he ended the kiss.

"I've never kissed a man before," she whispered. "I'll light a candle to the saints that it was you, Clayton."

Gianna leaned up and kissed his cheek. Then she turned and ran into the darkness.

When she was gone, Clayton touched his lips, his cheek. He stood a moment, his heart pounding, then made his way back to the gate and let himself out.

51.

The twins stood in lantern shadow and talked about kissing and love. Each had finally confessed his great, sub-rosa love to the other and for the first time in their lives there was no jealousy between them, or guilt, and they did not argue or condemn. Both Chessie and Clayton felt relief and poignant nostalgia that an intense, potentially dangerous kind of love between them had ended. They knew each other so intimately that in mood as well as words they understood each other's deep love and happiness. They held hands and spoke of a double wedding at The Columns.

"I judged Carlo harshly and wrongly," Clayton said. "When we're all safely out of Rome I look forward to makin' amends, Chessie, and gettin' to know him as you do."

"You will, Clay, you will, oh, you'll love him," Chessie said. "As for me . . . I was already taken with Gianna when we met in the garden. Please give her my love, tell her how happy I am for you. But Clay, please be careful."

The twins stared at each other with the same eyes. Their identical features were arranged in identical expressions of love and concern, and they felt their mutual fears without speaking them.

Since that first night, Clayton had managed other secret rendezvous with Gianna, first in the Corloni park, then across the road in the grounds of a deserted villa. Clayton assured Chessie that he took every precaution and that they had never been seen. But Chessie had a powerful, persistent fear of Countess Corloni and still worried about her brother.

"Nothin's goin' to happen to me or Gianna," Clayton said. "It's Carlo I'm worried about. Count Croce has spies everywhere, and he has more than one reason to want Carlo. When will he be well enough to travel?"

Escaping from a police patrol on his return from Sicily Carlo had reopened his head wound and he had been bedridden for several weeks, hidden and under the care of a sympathetic physician.

"Soon, Clay, real soon," Chessie said. "He's so much better now. Don't you worry. And I haven't heard from the count in weeks. I imagine he's quite forgotten me."

The twins' eyes met. Each knew the other was lying about the danger, and each knew it was impossible to avoid. Bravely, they talked in lighter terms about their weddings-to-be at The Columns.

"Chessie, why don't you and Carlo plan to live with Gianna and me on the plantation?" Clayton asked. "Wouldn't that be perfect!"

"Clay, I don't know," Chessie said. "We'll see. I don't know what Carlo'll have to say about it. But, Clay, I'll always love you for askin' me."

"I love you, Chess," Clay said. "No matter what happened between us in the past. I only want you to be safe and in love and happy."

"Maybe we loved each other too much while we were growin' up," Chessie said. "But that's over now, Clay. Now we have to get ourselves out of Rome and get married and . . . Clay, it'll all work out, I know it! I can't wait to have Mama meet Gianna and Carlo. You know, Clay, I miss her and the plantation and Natchez so much I can hardly bear it!"

"So do I," Clayton said. "I want to get back home. I've enjoyed seein' Italy, but we've been away too long. And now that several Southern states are holdin' conventions to vote on secedin' from the Union, I'm also anxious to get back in case there's a war."

"Oh, I don't believe there'll be a war!" Chessie said. "I hate war. Clay, we'll all go to France just as soon as possible. We'll see Paris and then go right home. I just hope Gianna can find the courage soon, Clay."

"I'm sure she will," Clayton said. "It's not easy for her. She's agonized terribly over what she's doin'. But I know she loves me and she's got a lot of spirit, a lot of courage."

"Kiss her for me this evenin'," Chessie said. "And Clay, be careful, you hear me?"

"I will," Clayton said. "You and Carlo be careful, too. Well, I guess I'd better be on my way. It's gettin' late."

The lantern flame leaped in a sudden breeze and they were startled to see each other's faces. It was like looking into a mirror. Chessie and Clayton smiled simultaneously and moved instinctively toward the kiss they had avoided for so long. For a breathless moment their lips met . . .

They drew apart quickly, without speaking again.

During the anxious walk from her apartment to Carlo's hiding place, on a cold January evening, Chessie took pains to avoid being followed. As usual, she browsed and shopped, stopped for tea in a Piazza di Spagna tearoom, and took enough random, circuitous detours to confuse anybody. And as usual, during this walk, she was tense with fear.

But now, an hour later, she was nestled in Carlo's arms and her fear was gone. As the coals burned low, they talked softly and touched each other frequently and interrupted their talk with kisses.

Chessie felt she had loved Carlo forever. Each moment with him, each kiss, seemed better than the last. She had come to trust him, trust his love for her and to know the depth of her own love.

Now, when he stroked her hair and quoted poetry they were able to laugh about his deceitful quotation in Palermo. Chessie took delight in his rich, deep voice and fussed over the scar that both marred and improved his handsome face.

Carlo was always gentle with Chessie because of what had happened in Palermo. With some effort, he held his passion in check as he very slowly, very gradually led her toward full sexual expression. Chessie was more willing than her lover guessed, for she was deeply in love, but she was still shy, and sometimes trembled uncontrollably when she tried to imagine the day when they would really make love for the first time.

"Chessie, Chessie, you're so lovely," Carlo whispered, studying her glowing, eager face in the soft light. Chessie had rested her hand on his lap and the feel of his stiff penis sent tremors of excitement throughout her body. Suddenly, Carlo became bolder in an unexpected way.

Gently, he embraced Chessie, then bent down and lifting her skirt caressed Chessie's thighs with his lips and tongue. Surprised and pleased, Chessie sucked in her breath. She spread her thighs and twisted her fingers in his hair as he licked the tender flesh. She was aroused, curious, hesitant. Her nipples grew hard. She lay back, her mouth open, and surrendered to feeling.

Carlo's lips skated farther up her thighs, thighs damp with sweat and covered with goosebumps. Chessie's stomach tightened as his lips hovered above her vagina.

"Oh, darling Carlo!" she gasped.

His fingers caressed her thighs as his tongue slid into her vagina. Chessie felt a profound shock jolt through her body. Her knees doubled up and she moaned with pleasure and excitement so powerful that blackness nibbled at the edges of her consciousness.

Carlo's lips were gentle and maddening. Chessie trembled with ecstasy and, her thighs locked around his face, her hands in his hair, she rocked back and forth

and crooned out her climax in abandon to his probing, knowing tongue.

Yet, in the midst of pleasure, an image of Myrtis
on the ground floated into Chessie's mind. She whimpered, opened her eyes. She stiffened. Her thighs parted.
She tensed and struggled.

"No, no, don't . . ." she gasped.

"Darling!" Carlo exclaimed. He took Chessie gently
into his arms. When she could speak, she told him about
Myrtis. "She haunts me," Chessie confessed.

"Then I must be even more gentle," Carlo said. He
kissed her tear-stained cheeks. "We'll go more slowly.
We'll wait until you're not afraid. We have time, Chessie, all the time you need."

"Carlo, I know it will pass," she promised. "I know
my fears will soon fade. I love it when you touch me.
I want you to kiss me all over like that, I want to make
love to you. And I will, darling, soon, quite soon, I
promise."

They held each other a few minutes more, then they
fastened their clothes and Chessie ate a light supper of
fish and wine. After supper she stood at the window in
his arms and watched a sudden rain turn the cobblestones black.

"The surgeon came this afternoon," Carlo said. Carlo was still under the care of an old friend who sym-
pathized with Garibaldi.

Chessie stiffened and looked up at Carlo. "What
did he say? Why did he come today? He wasn't due until tomorrow. What's wrong?"

"He must be out of town tomorrow," Carlo said.
"Please, don't worry. I sense the fear in your voice. I
should have told you when you first came in. In truth,
the news is encouraging, Chessie. He says my wound
is healing well. I should be able to travel within a
month."

"Oh, Carlo!" she said. She hugged him so hard he
grimaced. "Oh, darling, the wound! I'm so sorry . . ."

"It's all right, Chessie," he said. "It's nearly healed.
And just think! We'll go away together soon. So soon

. . . Florence . . . Paris . . . How I long to show you Paris, Chessie."

"And then will you come to America with me?"

"Yes, of course I will!" he said. "Haven't I promised? I want nothing more. I've had my fill of patriotism and soldiering. Sicily is an old, tired place, its people are exhausted. I want a new land. I want to marry you, work a plantation. America! A fresh, new country! And you! Ah, I'm the most fortunate man in Italy."

"And I'm the most fortunate lady, Carlo, darlin'," she said.

They talked and kissed a few minutes more. As Chessie left the apartment she dreamed of how wonderful their life would be together in Mississippi, but alone in the rain-swept, dimly lit streets she began to fear again. How she wished that she and Carlo could leave Rome at once.

52.

The Countess Corloni leaned out from her carriage window. "Faster!" she shouted. When the driver, cracking his whip over the horses, called back that more speed was dangerous on the twisting hill road, the countess threatened him with a beating. She sat back in the carriage, tousled and disheveled, but oblivious to her appearance. The driver's whip cracked again and again. The carriage lurched from side to side.

The countess was uncontrollably angry. She had just learned that Gianna had been secretly meeting the young American in the deserted villa near her home. It was outrageous, unbearable.

And how had she found out? Through those wretched *pasquini!* Through them, everyone knew, all the ignorant, malicious gossips in Rome! Flora had spotted the ill-spelled graffiti hung around the neck of the miserable talking statues. "The prince's bride-to-be has taken a lover of her own . . ." one graffito had read, and another, "Why does the Donessa Corloni creep into the dark gardens with the young American?"

Flora had come to the countess at once, seeking her out at Count Croce's Frascati villa, and now the countess was speeding into Rome to put a stop to this—once and for all.

The countess tugged at each finger of her black silk glove. She had never suspected Gianna capable of such deceit. How could she have been so easily fooled? She should never have trusted Gianna's apparent change of heart about the prince. Lately, Gianna had seemed docile, agreeable, even radiant. She curtsied and smiled and talked eagerly whenever her fiancé visited—and then at night she crept out to meet the wretched American!

The countess ground her teeth. What might have happened had she not found out through the *pasquini?* She shuddered, imagining the collapse of her plans, now so close to success.

She was glad that she was visiting Count Croce when Flora brought her the news. Only minutes earlier the count had admitted that he was furious with the American's twin sister, too angry to protect her—or her brother—any longer. So he told the countess to do whatever she wanted with the boy.

The count said that his agents had discovered that Chessie had been seeing the *Garibaldino* she had been warned about, and this very day she had visited him in his quarters.

The count vowed that he would arrest the *Garibaldino* at any moment he chose, and extract what information about Garibaldi the Sicilian might have, in the Castle of San Angelo.

"As for the girl," he said, "she, too, will be taken to the castle, and given one final chance to surrender herself to me. If not, then I'll take her by force!"

I should have contrived to meet these twins, the countess thought. They must be quite extraordinary to have captivated both Gianna and Paolo. Odd, too, that both her nemesis in America and Paolo's here should be twins!

The countess crossed herself, superstitious enough to be disturbed by the coincidence. Tonight, she decided, she would say a novena for good fortune, just as soon as she had eliminated Gianna's suitor.

"Darling Gianna," Clayton whispered. He kissed her gently. Her lips were so soft. He kissed her again.

Her kissing and petting had become increasingly bold. She stroked his hair and neck and tantalized his ears. Her body pressed against his as they kissed, and the touch of her firm, young breasts, the pressure of her hips against his erection maddened him.

Sighing, Clayton forced himself to pull away from Gianna, afraid he could no longer control his passion.

"Is something wrong, Clay?" she asked.

"No, Gianna, no, everything is fine." Her beautiful, innocent face had a sheen of sensuality that was highlighted by the alternating shadows and moonlight.

"Why did you pull away from me, darling?" she asked.

"I thought I heard someone . . ." he lied. She must never know how desperately he longed to possess her, not until she was ready.

Gianna shook her head. Her smile was sweet and sad. "No, Clay, you heard no one. You're holding back. You're treating me like a frightened child. You think your kisses are too bold. Well, you're quite wrong. I love your bold kisses!"

Laughing, they joined hands and sat down on a bed of pine needles, to kiss some more.

Clayton had lied about hearing someone, but in the next few minutes he was more alert and he did hear a disturbing sound. He listened with mounting alarm.

Perhaps it was only a rabbit stirring the leaves. He strained to hear. He became frightened.

But he didn't hear the sound again. He tried to relax, to hide his fear from Gianna.

"Darling, what's wrong?" Gianna asked. "You seem distracted . . ."

Clayton forced himself to smile and kissed her cheek. "I was just thinking of the future," he said. "When I bring up the matter, you always seem distracted yourself."

"Yes, that's been true in the past," she said. "Nothing more has been certain than our next meeting. Talk of the future has been impossible for me. I've spent many sleepless nights thinking of it."

Clayton was almost afraid to ask the question. "And? What have you decided, Gianna?"

"You've talked of America . . . your plantation, of our living there," she said. "At first it seemed impossible. I honestly thought I'd just meet with you a few times, then marry the prince. But now I know I could never marry anyone but you. I long to live with you on your plantation. But I'm still not sure it can be done. I love my mother, Clay, but she's very strong, and I know she can be ruthless."

Clayton was elated but he immediately became practical.

"Yes, I grant you she can be quite ruthless, and if she knew of our love she'd try to stop us. But our great advantage is that she doesn't know. So we must act now! I'll arrange passage to New Orleans on the first available ship."

"Yes, before my mother discovers us," Gianna said. "Oh, I tremble to think what she might do to you."

The Countess Corloni watched Gianna kiss the American. She held her breath and clenched her fists in anger. Four of her most trusted men were nearby, surrounding the couple. With one gesture she could signal for them to seize the American and force Gianna back to the villa.

But the countess hesitated. She had not yet decided whether to have the American killed here or outside the city, and she was horrified to see the two of them, horrified and maddened.

The young fools! How dare they think they could do this to her? She struggled to refrain from leaping out at them. She glanced to her right where the leader of her men was poised, dagger in hand. Enough!

She turned to signal the men . . .

And then paused. She sucked in her breath. She forced herself to wait and reason.

Would she ruin everything if she gave in to her anger? If she had the American killed or even abducted in Gianna's sight, Gianna would suffer. She would be greatly upset, would not easily forgive her, and might even refuse to marry the prince.

Perhaps I should wait, the countess thought. The American would surely leave soon. He could do no more damage tonight. It would be wiser to let Gianna return to the villa undisturbed, thinking all was well.

Then, when she had gone, her men would take the American. Gianna would never know where. She would let Gianna think that he had deserted her and returned to America.

Yes, that was by far the best plan. But something else troubled the countess. It was the recurring thought of another curious, ominous coincidence: not only did this wretched American have a twin sister, but apparently he lived near New Orleans . . .

Oh, it was no time to dwell on the matter! The countess shrugged it off. She had decided. She would let the American escape now and let her men take him on his way home.

She made a gesture to the men in the shadows, then crept away from the couple sharing an embrace.

53.

All that night, the countess' thumb itched terribly. On an impulse, she had instructed her men to follow the American, but not to harm him yet, and after seeing that Gianna was safely in her room, she went to bed. But not to sleep. Restlessly, she cursed and tossed, as the coincidence of the American twins haunted her.

The next morning, haggard and ravaged by a growing suspicion, she sent out her spies to learn more of the American twins.

At noon, in the villa's main drawing room overlooking the parks and gardens, she received an obsequious old man named Vespiri. She was nearly trembling with a mixture of rage and hope as the spy made his report.

". . . Their names are Chessie and Clayton Deavors, Countess," the white-haired man began. "Chessie is a nickname for Cynthia Susannah. Their home is on a plantation . . ."

"On a plantation called The Columns, outside the city of Natchez, in Mississippi," the countess said in a rising and high-pitched voice. "They are the children of Lucinda Deavors and the late Lawton Deavors . . ."

Vespiri's eyes widened.

"Yes, Countess, but if you already knew all this, why did you hire me?"

"Because, you old fool, I didn't know, I only suspected! I know more of the Deavors family than these twins do! Far more! I am . . . I was a Deavors. My poor father married a Deavors. They caused his death and tried to ruin me . . ."

"Countess, are you ill?" Signor Vespiri asked. "Shall I call for a doctor?"

"Ill?" she asked. "What do you mean?"

"Countess, you're trembling and your face has gone pale as death . . ."

"Don't speak to me of death!" she shouted. "Or you'll be speaking of your own!" She lowered her voice. "I'm not ill and I'll thank you to go at once! I need no more of your services. See my majordomo. He'll give you your fee. Good day, sir."

Signor Vespiri bowed and left the room.

As the door closed the countess gave in to her emotions. She trembled with outraged memory. Tears exploded from her eyes. She wrapped her arms around her body and in her mind she relived her horrible life in Mississippi . . .

As a girl of seventeen, she and her father had traveled from Italy to Mississippi to claim an estate inherited from her mother, Sarah Deavors Blaine, whose family had been from Mississippi. She and her father had arrived without funds and had unfortunately become dependent on the family of Lawton Deavors, the executor of the inheritance.

"Lawton Deavors . . . Lawton . . ."

As she spoke the name aloud her voice trembled. Except for her father, she had never loved anyone the way she had come to love Lawton. And, despite his marriage to a vapid woman named Lucinda, she knew that Lawton had truly loved her. But because Lawton was a Deavors, proud and greedy and arrogant, he had cheated her and her father out of their plantation, had spread rumors about her father that were so vicious her father had killed himself, had forced her into a desperate, disastrous marriage.

And then, because Lawton came to believe the rumors might be true, she had lived each day in Mississippi at Lawton's mercy, lived in fear that she would be ruined, humiliated, sold into slavery.

She had never understood how Lawton could have believed her father had once been a Mamaluke slave in Egypt and that she had tainted slave blood in her veins. But Lawton *had* believed it. He had scorned her love. He had made her suffer terribly until his own love overcame him and he became obsessed with her beauty.

Even then, Lawton had not left Lucinda to marry her. He would not do that.

And so from the beginning, although she loved Lawton, she had also hated him. She had vowed, finally, that she would destroy all his family and force Lawton to marry her. And although she loved him she would make him pay dearly, pay for the death of her father and for making her suffer the fear of being named a slave in that slave society he ruled.

She had hired an agent to blow up the steamboat and the Deavors family . . . except for Lawton. She had expected Lawton to remain ashore, but at the last minute he had gone aboard the wretched boat and he died while the other Deavorses lived.

She had been ruined by that. She had been labeled a criminal, hunted, but she had still been determined to have revenge. Desperately, she had gone to The Columns, and she had tried to kill Lawton's twin babies. But once again her luck had failed. Her despised husband had suddenly appeared, attacked her and maimed her, and she had fled into the swamp . . .

The countess became hysterical. She had lived with hysteria, never really conquering it, from the moment Lawton had told her that her father was dead, all those years ago in Natchez.

"So long ago, so long ago," the countess babbled, but in her mind it was as vivid and painful as her memories of seeing Gianna and that accursed boy last night.

The past was not dead, clearly. It had all come alive again, and at the worst time, just when she had arranged Gianna's marriage to combine the Corloni fortune and the Vittori prestige. She had arranged it so that she and Gianna and Gianna's children would never be helpless and pitiful, and now the accursed Deavors twins had crossed the ocean to ruin and humiliate her again, twins she knew with mortal certainty were Lawton's children, no matter what Ridgeway had said.

"But they won't succeed!" she muttered. "They won't! This time I'm too powerful for the Deavorses."

She laughed, a high, choking laugh.

It will be my victory after all, she thought. My prayers have been answered. My faith has been repaid. Oh, Daddy in heaven, you've sent me the Deavors twins! I swear I'll take our final revenge on them and . . . Then I'll have your ashes sent from Natchez and wear them around my neck forever.

The countess took out her handkerchief and wiped her eyes. She poured a glass of Marsala and forced herself to drink it. She made a great effort to control her fury. Finally, she no longer trembled. Resolve had calmed her. She had work to do. And, oh, how she would savor this work.

She crossed to the French doors and looked past the parks to the Alban hills. She would kill the Deavors twins and their deaths would be slow. They would know why they died and they would come to curse the Deavors name.

All afternoon she paced and plotted. Should they be tortured together. They could be forced to watch each other die. They could be forced to curse their family, each other. They could be forced to perform unspeakable sexual acts on each other.

The countess smiled. The idea excited her. Anything was possible, all was within her power, but she warned herself not to act impulsively. It must all be planned carefully.

She thought of young Clayton Deavors. She had not yet seen him clearly. His face had been shadowed in the park. Perhaps he resembled Lawton! The possibility excited her further and fired her passion.

She would kill him, surely, but first, she would summon him to her, talk to him, and possibly, before his long agony began, she would allow him to be her lover and her slave, as Lawton had been.

54.

On the day before Lent began, the streets of Rome were choked with revelers celebrating the carnival. Clayton, in no mood for celebration, fought his way through the crowds. In one pocket he carried his pistol, in another the curious summons he had received from the Countess Corloni. The countess' note read:

"My dear Signore Deavors: Please come to me this afternoon at my villa to discuss a grave problem of mutual interest."

Clayton was stunned and frightened to know that Gianna's mother knew of their affair and he was anxious to see Gianna. He had wanted to discuss the note with Chessie but she was out. He had waited until he dared wait no longer. As it was he would be fortunate to reach the Corloni villa by vespers.

The streets near the Via del Corso were so crowded that he decided walking would be faster than a carriage. Even so, he made slow progress.

Every taverna, every street and alleyway was mobbed with Romans and country people, men and women and children all dressed in costume—every bizarre costume imaginable. On one corner a large-bellied man in a ludicrous gown of purple velvet and an ill-fitting blond wig pushed against Clayton. At the next he was forced up against a doorway by a gang of obese Roman gladiators and tunic-clad Greeks. He saw Egyptian Mamalukes, lurching bears, dancing Chinamen, squat Punches and Judys, and then he was teased and delayed by a group of masked girls in antique dresses with tight stomachers that pushed their young breasts nearly out of their low-cut dresses. The girls pranced and giggled as Clayton fought to escape them, searching vainly for a recognizable face behind their wire-frame masks.

For everyone was masked, save Clayton, and embolded by anonymity and alcohol, the revelers' gaiety was almost oppressively wild. Clayton felt alone and alienated, felt he alone was on an important, perhaps dangerous mission in a town gone mad with merrymaking. Thankfully, he felt the weight of his pistol as he shoved his way through the throngs.

Clayton struggled across the teeming Via del Corso, where the carnival parade was assembling, and hurried along a serpentine street crammed with costumed and masked revelers. A group of gaudily costumed gypsies, red Indians with motley feathers and black-grease-smeared Negroes had stopped to read a huge black-and-white notice pasted to the wall of a church.

Caught in the crowd, Clayton saw that the notice implored the devout to earn indulgence by praying for the soul of a criminal who was to be executed that afternoon. Another notice instructed all cardinals to remain in their quarters, for the custom was that if a criminal met a cardinal on his way to the scaffold the cardinal could not refuse him a pardon.

Clayton had heard of the condemned man, Guido Lana. Officially, he had been convicted of raping and murdering a French duchess on a walking pilgrimage from Florence to Rome. But the tavern gossip and the *pasquini* said that Lana had been framed by an influential duke who wanted his daughter to marry a nobleman.

The parallel with his own situation seemed to Clayton the worst possible omen. Again, he realized how precarious was his status as a foreigner in Rome. In America he could always depend on the influence of his family, but here he was helpless. Here he had only his wits to save him.

And Roman justice was swift.

At the next corner Clayton came upon four policemen strapping a sobbing young woman face down onto a *cavalletto,* a sort of rack which consisted of two humped wooden boards on four legs sloping from back to front. The police kept *cavalletti* everywhere crowds gathered and used them on the spot to punish lawbreakers.

The woman was, he learned from the crowd, a courtesan. An invariable rule of the carnival forbade courtesans to wear masks, but she had been caught wearing a panther's face—the beastly mask now lay in the mud beside her.

One of the policemen ripped the courtesan's yellow silk gown off her back as another policeman took up a short whip and announced that she would receive ten lashes. Clayton was swept by pity for the young woman but the crowd howled. She was surprisingly young and lovely, with long, dark curls and a full, sensuous mouth. She struggled feebly as the crowd jeered, then gasped at the first cut of the lash.

The second blow brought a scream from deep in her throat. Clayton writhed in sympathy. He longed to intervene but dared not. Another blow left the woman sobbing and screeching. A rivulet of blood trickled down her back and into the crease of her heaving buttocks.

As the policeman raised his whip for a fourth lash the crowd parted as a fat old cardinal, waddling home quickly before the execution, passed the *cavalletto* and, waving a hand heavy with rings, stopped the beating.

The woman collapsed as she was freed from the *cavalletto*. Clayton pushed his way onward and two blocks further, found that the crowds had thinned out. He hailed a carriage and climbed in, his pistol heavy in his pocket, the memory of the courtesan's screams disturbing his thoughts.

Clayton tensed as the massive doors of the Villa Corloni slammed shut behind him. He stood in a cavernous, dimly lit entrance foyer with six doors and walls covered with grim-looking portraits.

"The countess will receive you in her upstairs drawing room," said the majordomo who had admitted him, a tall, severe man in a black frock coat.

Obediently, Clayton followed the majordomo across the slick, marble floor toward a curved staircase.

"And Donessa Gianna?" Clayton asked impulsively. "Will she also be receiving me this afternoon?"

"The Donessa has gone . . . out of the city, I believe," the man replied.

Clayton was shaken by this news. What did it mean? Where had she been sent? His legs trembled slightly as he climbed the stairs and his apprehension increased with his curiosity. He was actually inside the Villa Corloni and about to meet Gianna's mother, the notorious Countess Corloni.

On the second floor he passed a small chapel and

paused to look at the portrait of a handsome dark-haired man of about forty-five. Something about the portrait stopped him. The hairs on the back of his neck tingled.

"A compelling man, wouldn't you say, Signore Deavors?" a woman's voice asked.

Clayton turned to face the countess. He gasped in surprise. She was an undeniably beautiful woman in a tight-fitting, high-necked black silk dress, and her face . . . her face was so very like Gianna's face that seeing it sent shivers through his body.

"Yes, very . . ." Clayton mumbled.

"My late father," the countess said.

"Oh . . ." Clayton said, too disturbed by the likeness between Gianna and her mother to pay more attention to the portrait. So this . . . this was the infamous Countess Corloni.

Flustered, the majordomo stepped between Clayton and his hostess. "Countess Corloni," he said in a rush of words, "may I present Signore Clayton Deavors? . . ."

"Yes, thank you, Aldo," the countess said. "Though in this case introductions aren't necessary. I believe I'd have recognized Signore Deavors anywhere. Please leave us now, Aldo, and make certain we're not disturbed. Under any circumstances. Signore Deavors, please follow me."

Clayton followed her down the hall. Why, he wondered, did the countess insist she could have recognized him? Of course, her spies might have described him, but something in her tone made him uneasy.

Without looking back, the countess led Clayton into a drawing room that was at the same time over-furnished and cheerless. The room was crowded with massive pieces of furniture heavily gilded and, to Clayton's eye, French in style. Huge bouquets of funereal lilies gave the air an over-sweet, almost rotten odor and scarcely a ray of sunshine penetrated the curtains, which were of a dark green velvet and drawn nearly shut, despite the softness of the late afternoon. Clayton blinked at the dimness and had the unpleasant feeling that he had been led into a trap.

55.

As Clayton waited, fighting the sensation of being smothered, the countess closed the door and turned a key in the lock.

She offered Clayton a glass of brandy and he accepted. Without removing her gloves, the countess poured brandy from a cut-glass decanter and handed Clayton the snifter. He stiffened as her fingers touched his hand. How odd, he thought, that she wears gloves inside her home.

Clayton's eyes roamed the drawing room and settled, finally, on the countess in her old-fashioned black silk dress.

"This is a replica of the dress I wore at my father's funeral," she said as she poured herself some wine. "Of course, I didn't have time to pack the original."

"I see," Clayton said. He was puzzled by her comment.

She sipped her wine and smiled, a deeper smile that lessened her resemblance to Gianna, for it was a smile without innocence or sincerity. She's no longer really beautiful, Clayton thought, but she is handsome. And very strong-looking.

Clayton put the snifter to his lips, then remembered how Don Santini had died. His throat tightened. The smell of the brandy sickened him.

"May I have wine instead of brandy, Countess?" he asked.

She poured his wine and handed him the glass. He sipped it tentatively, even though she was drinking from the same bottle.

"Come, let's sit down," she said.

They sat on a maroon silk-upholstered couch. When the countess leaned toward Clayton, her knee brushed his and he barely controlled a shudder. His glance met her mocking black eyes and he remembered the courtesan's panther mask. All his instincts warned him to caution.

"And how is the cotton this year in Mississippi, Signore Deavors?" the countess asked.

"Countess Corloni, may we simply discuss the business for which you summoned me?" Clayton asked. "I want to speak of Gianna, of our plans . . ."

She cut him off. "What right have you to speak of my daughter, Signore Deavors? My daughter, sir, is engaged to Prince Vittori."

"I know that!" Clayton said impatiently. "But she . . . Where is Gianna, Countess?"

"Signore Deavors, I believe your impertinence shows a lack of breeding," the countess said. "In Italy, a well-bred young man would never inquire about the private affairs and whereabouts of a girl who's betrothed to another man."

"Then why have you summoned me?" he asked.

"To talk about you," she said. "You and your sister, Chessie. And your family in Mississippi. And rather intimate matters, past and present . . ."

"Countess, you try my patience!" Clayton said. He stood up.

"I'm only trying to be your friend. And stop you before you become too arrogant and reckless. You are in need of my friendship, Signore Deavors."

"Countess Corloni, I would welcome your friendship . . ." Clayton began. But he did not finish the sentence. He realized it was not true.

"Then come and sit down beside me again," the countess said, patting the sofa. "But first, my glass is empty. And the light . . . It's too strong. Please lower that lamp."

Clayton did as she asked, then sat beside her once more. The room was deeply shadowed and the heavy sweetness of the lilies was oppressive. Again he felt

250

nearly smothered. There was silence as they both sipped wine.

Finally, an enigmatic smile crossed the countess' face, then a frown. Clayton felt her tension and watched her toying with her gloved thumb. He was worried about Gianna but felt helpless to deal with the countess. He would endure her game for now—he had little other choice.

"Why do you draw away from me?" she asked. "Please move closer, so we can speak more personally."

Clayton moved nearer the countess. He inhaled the scent of her musky, disturbing perfume and the scent of the lilies. He drank two deep swallows of wine and felt her staring at him.

Suddenly, the countess leaned forward and took Clayton's hands in hers. He tensed.

"We have so much to talk about," she said. "We have so very much in common, Clayton, dear. Oh, I hope you don't mind my using your first name. I know Americans are much less formal than we are. And I once lived in America."

"Did you?" Clayton asked. The countess was squeezing his fingers. Her gloved hands were dry and he stiffened at their touch. There was something odd and disturbing about her right hand.

"Oh, yes," she said. "And, like you, I lived on a plantation. For a while, I thought I would always live there. But then my father died."

She pulled her hands away. Her dark eyes clouded, and she bit her lips together with a gesture that re-arranged her face so totally that Clayton was reminded of the grotesque carnival masks he had seen in the streets. For a moment the countess was truly ugly. Then her face settled into composure and regained its beauty.

"I'm sorry to hear that you lost your father," Clayton said. "My own father died when I was quite young . . ."

"Before you were a year old, Clayton," she said.

He looked at her with surprise. How could her spies

251

have discovered that kind of information? Her eyes caught his and held him. They were so like Gianna's eyes. He looked away.

"Please pour us more wine, Clayton," she said. "And bring the bottle over here."

Clayton poured the wine and returned to the couch. He was thankful for the wine's stimulus and drank down half a glass quickly.

"It's an excellent wine," he said.

"Yes, it is, isn't it?" she said. "It comes from my Marsala estate. No! Please, Clayton, don't look away. Don't be shy. That's right, dear. I want to see your face clearly. You're very handsome, you know."

Clayton was embarrassed. How oddly the countess was behaving—not at all as he had expected. "You're very kind, Countess," he said awkwardly. He finished his wine and poured another glass.

"Your eyes," she said. "I would have known them anywhere. And the lips, yes, definitely the lips. Now I'm curious about your sister. Does she also bear a strong resemblance to your father?"

"My father?" Clayton drank more wine. Everyone had always said that both he and Chessie resembled their mother. "I . . . I don't know. I mean, we're twins. But my father? Why do you speak of our looking like him?"

In response, the countess took Clayton's free hand and moved closer. He started as her body brushed his. Her musky perfume was both smothering and arousing.

"I'm sorry for you, Clayton," she said. "Despite your behavior, I find that I rather like you, dear." She lifted a lock of his blond hair from his forehead. "Now that we've become friends, now, as I look into your eyes and more pleasant memories come back, I'm inclined to be merciful to you for a time."

Clayton swallowed hard. He drained his glass and put it down. He was becoming frightened and confused.

"Yes, of course we're friends," he said. "And now

that it's so, Countess Corloni, I'd like to speak about Gianna . . ."

But the countess leaned forward and stopped Clayton's words with a kiss.

"Countess!" he gasped.

For a moment Clayton was too surprised to react at all. Then she kissed him again, and he pulled away, sitting rigidly while she sucked at his lips and ran her fingers through his hair. To his astonishment her probing tongue was somewhat arousing, but the thought of kissing her was not.

"No!" Clayton said. He drew back. "No, please, I don't . . ."

"What's wrong, Clayton?" she said. "Don't you find me attractive?"

"You're a beautiful woman," he said as her fingers stroked his ear. He was appalled to feel his penis respond. "But you're Gianna's mother, dammit!"

"You can't have Gianna, Clayton," she said. "Never, ever. Besides, she's only a child. Why would you want her when you can have me?"

Before he could answer she kissed him again. Her tongue teased his, touched the roof of his mouth. Her fingers slid beneath his shirt. She caressed his nipples.

Clayton had not made love to a woman in many weeks and his body began to betray his horrified mind. He shuddered but his penis began to harden.

"No!" he muttered. He twisted away from her lips and tore her hands from his body. "No, dammit! I've come to discuss Gianna. I love her! She loves me! We must be together, one way or another. Either we discuss Gianna, or I'm leaving!"

The countess ignored his protests. "Poor dear," she crooned. She sipped at her wine. Her eyes were wild, her breathing ragged. Clayton's eyes were drawn to her large breasts heaving with her heavy breathing. When she saw him looking at her breasts she smiled, a hideous smile that twisted Gianna from her face.

"Do we discuss Gianna or not, Countess?" Clayton asked.

"Poor dear, you can't keep your eyes off my breasts, can you?" she said. "They were beautiful once, Clayton. Long ago, when I was young, as young as Gianna. Ah, yes, once my breasts were beautiful . . ."

As she spoke her eyes closed and she seemed dazed. Clayton felt helpless. When she opened her eyes they were wet with tears and held a far-off expression.

"I must be going . . ." Clayton said.

"You couldn't resist me when my breasts were beautiful . . . when I was young . . ."

"Who . . . ? What do you mean?"

With a violent gesture the countess unfastened her black dress and sat naked to the waist. Clayton sat back in horror. There were dark, hideous scars across her pale breasts.

"Oh, my God!" he gasped.

The countess trailed a finger along the deep scars, again and again, as she stared into Clayton's eyes.

"Many men still find my breasts attractive," she said. Her voice was husky. "All my lovers have stroked my scars as they kissed my breasts, and then kissed the scars, caressed the scars with their tongues . . . That is, those who expected to have a tongue the next day . . ."

Clayton swallowed hard and started to stand up but she grabbed his hand and held him on the couch.

"No, come here, darling," she crooned. "Don't you want to have a tongue in the morning? And I have other uses for your tongue, Clayton, just as I had for Lawton's . . ."

"What . . . ? Why did you use my father's name?" Clayton's head was spinning. Blood pounded at his temples.

With surprising strength the countess suddenly forced Clayton's hand against a scar. He gasped at the touch of the rough, ruined flesh and tried to draw his hand away. But she held him for another moment, then brushed his hand over her nipples. They were hard.

He tore his hand from her grasp and bolted up from the couch.

"You'll soon get used to the touch of my scars," she said. "You'll come to howl and beg for them, you'll make my nipples grow hard with your fingers while you suck my scars . . . Oh, it all started so long ago, and the scars are your fault, Lawton, so you must love them, become obsessed with them, or you'll suffer . . ."

Clayton had backed up once, twice, but he couldn't take his eyes off the blood-dark scars, the pale breasts, the swollen nipples, couldn't look from the creature there so lovely, so ugly, flesh so exquisite, flesh so deformed . . .

"Yes, you will love me again, won't you, Lawton?" she crooned. "When you kiss my scars, I'll let you do what you really want . . . And the rest of me is still beautiful, Lawton."

She lifted her black skirt and petticoat and pulled them off. Naked, she spread her thighs wide.

"Come here, darling," she whispered. "Kneel down between my thighs, like you used to do. Admit that you love me! Tell me that you'll divorce Lucinda and marry me. Beg me, Lawton, worship my body, Lawton, kiss me here, Lawton, and tell me you don't think I'm a slave's daughter, with slave's blood, be my slave, Lawton, and then I'll cut scars on your own breasts, just as my husband cut on mine . . ."

As she raved, the countess' voice rose and fell and she writhed on the silken couch and stroked her thighs with gloved fingers. Through narrowed eyes she looked straight at Clayton.

Clayton was more than horrified. He was hypnotized by her mad eyes and her insane litany. He could not move or speak, but bit by bit his disbelieving mind began to make sense of all the madness.

The countess pulled off her right glove and slid the stub of her thumb along her thigh. She paused an instant, then stroked her vagina.

Bile rose in Clayton's throat when he saw the mutilated thumb. A convulsion swept his body. He gagged.

"Oh, no! Oh, Christ," he mumbled. "It can't be . . ."

The countess stopped abruptly. She blinked, as though waking from sleep. The faraway look of sensuous abandonment faded and her lips twisted into a frown. She stood up awkwardly, swayed a moment.

"By God, I hate you!" she said. "You'll wish you'd been smothered in the cradle. You've seen me naked and rejected me! You're as big a fool as your father, and you'll pay the same price. But slowly, my dear, unlike him—very slowly. It will take hours, days, weeks for you to die . . . you and Chessie . . . while I watch and remember the Deavorses and my father's death and my humiliation . . ."

"Rafaella!" Clayton gasped. "But you died . . . in the swamp . . ."

"Only part of me died there," she whispered. "And I have never forgotten or forgiven. I would have come for you and Chessie. But God has brought you to me. I offered you salvation through my flesh, as I did your father, but you refused. Now nothing can save you or your sister, nothing!"

"Rafaella . . ." Clayton repeated.

He lurched toward the door but the countess stepped in front of him, shouting for her servants. He pulled out his pistol. Still naked, she threw herself toward him to block his escape, but he knocked her aside, and she fell to the floor, her scarred breasts hanging free, her dark hair tousled.

"You'll never escape!" she screamed, as Clayton ran to the window and onto the balcony. With only a quick look backward he mounted the railing and jumped.

56.

Chessie was so preoccupied with her worries that she turned the corner into the Via del Corso and bumped into a fat cardinal. Embarrassed, she mumbled an apology and picked her way carefully through the masked and costumed carnival crowd.

The streets were choked with people, raucous with laughter and music and hung with banners and garlands of flowers. At the next corner she came upon a dreadful *cavalletto,* just in time to see a young woman, her back bloody and striped by lash marks, helped off the contraption. Chessie shivered.

The carnival mood oppressed her, and the mobs of drunken revelers in grotesque masks and costumes heightened her fear and anxiety. She wished she could have talked to Clayton. She was desperately worried about him—he had told Torine that he and Gianna planned to escape on an American ship that was anchored at Anzio instead of going to Paris. And Torine said he had received a mysterious note that had upset him. Why hadn't he waited to tell her?

How would it all work out? Carlo was determined to visit Paris, in order to secure some funds on deposit at a bank there. Chessie would have been happy to sail immediately to America, but she would not abandon Carlo, so she hoped that her brother would travel north with her. If not, Signora Nantes had promised to make the journey.

Carlo was now well enough to travel but he refused to leave Rome with Chessie, no matter how much she begged. He argued that until he was safely out of the Vatican States he was in too much danger of capture.

Carlo planned to leave this very evening. He would take advantage of the carnival and make his escape in costume, just one more masked man among thousands. But Chessie had been forced to promise that she would stay in Rome at least two more days. Even two more days seemed forever. She was frightened of this city, these people.

She thought of the bloodstained *cavalletto.* If Carlo were captured he would be tortured like that, then beheaded.

Gladiators and bears, Mamalukes and human marionettes, demons and hideous men in gowns and wigs, all swirled about Chessie. She sensed that more than merrymaking and the parade down Via del Corso affected the crowd. The carnival was an outlet for tension and anger made all the more grotesque and frightening by its disguise in gay costumes.

Carlo embraced Chessie, then pulled away and looked at her beautiful, familiar face.

"Did you speak with Clayton?" he asked.

"No, I missed him at the apartment," she said. "I haven't seen him all day, Carlo. Torine says he talked of boarding an American ship here, instead of traveling north."

"You wouldn't sail back with him, would you?"

"Of course not," Chessie said. "I'll talk sense to Clayton and meet you in Paris, as I promised. He won't abandon me. He's just worried about Gianna. In any case, as you know, Signora Nantes has promised to help me."

Carlo dreaded their parting. He had come to depend on Chessie. At times he thought she was the stronger of them, and her courage and strength made him love her even more.

There were anxious kisses then, and gentle caresses, and finally they sat with their arms around each other, savoring these last few minutes together.

Carlo stroked Chessie's hair and thought about his decision to go to America with her. He was not a farmer, and he was opposed to the institution of slavery.

But he had become disillusioned with what was happening in Sicily. Despite Garibaldi's victories there was still corruption and inequality and he could see that his homeland would be in turmoil for many years, that there would be a kind of anarchy and so much danger he dare not take Chessie to live there.

His conscience was clear—he had fought for Sicily's freedom. What mattered now was his love for Chessie and her love for him. She was desperately homesick. So he had decided their future was in America.

As for slavery, it was obviously a delicate subject for Chessie, and he had resolved that he would reserve judgment and keep his feelings to himself until they reached Mississippi and he saw the conditions first-hand.

The clock struck the hour. They lingered a minute more, then stood up. They kissed and vowed their love. Carlo arranged Chessie's light cloak over her shoulders as they reached the door.

He opened the door. Chessie paused, turned quickly and kissed his lips, then ran down the stairs.

57.

Within a half hour Carlo left the apartment costumed as a Turkish harem guard with bloused trousers and a curved sword. In his pockets he carried two pistols.

When he stepped into the street he was engulfed immediately by all the madness of the carnival. Torches flickered in the dimness. The music of flutes and horns and trumpets came from the Corso, and everywhere gaily dressed revelers lurched about, laughing, singing, drinking from flasks. At once, Carlo realized that the crowd's erratic movements made detection of spies impossible. He had trained himself to avoid capture by noticing the slightest extraordinary detail, but on this carnival evening, every detail was out of the ordinary.

Nervously, Carlo cursed under his breath, then plunged into the crowd.

"Have a drink!" a toothless man dressed as a red Indian said to Carlo, thrusting a cup of wine into his face. Carlo ducked, dodged a young woman and her chaperone, and turned the corner into the Vicolo dei Fiori. He faced four tall men dressed as gladiators, shoulder to shoulder, and at once he knew that something was wrong.

"Stop there!" one of the men growled. Carlo felt pistols jabbed into his ribs from both directions as a third man took away his pistols and sword and a fourth forced his hands behind his back.

"Don't cry out," said the man tying together his hands. "You're under arrest for sedition."

A black carriage with covered windows appeared at the end of the narrow street. Carlo was forced into the carriage and a gag was shoved into his mouth.

Numb with shock, Carlo nearly lost consciousness as the carriage lumbered over the ragged cobblestones. When he tried to speak one of the men gave him a cruel blow across his neck, and his wrists ached in the tight cords. Thank God, he thought, thank God that Chessie was safely gone before he was captured.

Carlo was driven across the Tiber to the massive fortress of the Castle of San Angelo and led along the circular ramp first built to entomb the Emperor Hadrian. He shuddered, remembering all he had heard about the terrible dungeons and torture chambers in the Castelo, chambers that had housed prisoners since the times of Benvenuto Cellini.

The castle's stone corridors were dank and gloomy, but when Carlo reached the upper level of the fortress, he was ushered into a large room warmed by an enormous fireplace. In the center of the room stood a massive walnut dining table with sixteen high-backed chairs, and at the far end sat a broad-shouldered man in a blue silk lounging gown, eating a supper of roast quail and white wine.

"At your service, Count Croce," one of Carlo's captors said. "We've brought him."

"Ah, Signore Settimo," the count said. "Be seated and pardon me while I finish my supper."

Carlo sat down. He was tense with apprehension. The count dismissed his men with a gesture. He did not speak as he finished his meal at a leisurely pace and drained a glass of wine, then took a stance with his back to the roaring fire.

"Your arrest has made my men quite happy this evening, Signore Settimo," the count said. "It has taken so much of their time, watching you and following you. They're quite tired of you . . . and I confess I am, too."

Carlo winced. His blindfold had been removed but his hands were still bound. He was powerless, whatever Croce had in store for him. The contrast of his situation to Count Croce's, dressed in a finely cut lounging gown, the remains of his supper still on the table, drinking wine as he contemplated his prisoner, did not cheer him. Carlo said nothing, but his eyes followed Count Croce warily as the count strolled about the room.

"Why are you so silent?" Count Croce asked.

"I have nothing to say, sir," Carlo answered. "What can I say?"

"I always imagined that you were a man of charm, a golden-tongued seducer of innocent young women," the count said.

Dear God, I must not allow him to speak of Chessie, Carlo thought. I must not. Anything that is said may endanger her.

"I'm surprised, sir," Carlo said, "that you brought me here to flatter me."

Count Croce smiled slightly. "In fact, I didn't. You're a fool, Settimo, a romantic fool, first to follow that upstart Garibaldi, and then to become involved with an unlucky American girl . . ."

"Unlucky? Why do you call her unlucky . . . That is, if I know of whom you speak."

"You know very well, Settimo. And as for her ill luck, I have a feeling that her luck has recently . . . changed."

"What do you mean?" Carlo demanded, struggling to his feet.

He had tried to prepare himself for the rack or the whip, but for threats and allegations about Chessie he was not prepared. He could not bear to think that her association with him had endangered her, could not bear to think that this man, known to be ruthless and cruel, was still interested in Chessie. He felt his heartbeat accelerate and his stomach knotted with tension.

In answer, Count Croce smiled.

"What do you mean?" Carlo demanded. "What do you know of Chessie Deavors? What have you to do with her?"

"Nothing . . . And everything I choose."

Carlo struggled against the bonds that held him. "Goddamn it! Where is she?"

"You're here to answer my questions, Settimo, not I yours," Count Croce said.

"I won't talk, sir," Carlo said. "And what if I did? You can't defeat right—or Garibaldi! There are *Garibaldini* all over Rome and soon his liberating army will march north and seize the city . . ."

Count Croce laughed. "My Lord, man, how passionate you are—for an aristocrat—and how patriotic! I am amused. If we had time we could speak of liberty, of rights and wrongs and the good of the common man. But you wouldn't care for my politics, I daresay."

"I'd rather endure your coercion than your despicable political beliefs!" Carlo said.

"I'm afraid, sir, that you will have to endure both," the count said. He took out a tiny silver box and packed snuff into his nostrils. "That is, unless you have wings to fly away. You'll endure exactly what I arrange for you. Settimo, you have annoyed me . . . and angered me . . . But despite your misdirected enthusiasms, which have been a source of inconvenience to me, I'm willing to treat you as a fellow aristocrat. Therefore, I'll speak bluntly. You will tell me everything you know about Garibaldi's military plans in the south . . ."

"Damnit, I won't!"

"Oh, you will. But I shall not myself force you to confide them. Two of my . . . men will persuade you. And I shall spare you the embarrassment of my presence during your ordeal, Settimo, partly, as I said, out of gentlemanly scruples, and partly out of affection for Chessie Deavors."

At the mention of Chessie's name Carlo's throat tightened. He tugged at the cords that bound him and cursed the sharp pain.

"I can assure you that Chessie bears no affection for you," Carlo blurted and immediately regretted his words.

"No, perhaps she doesn't. It doesn't matter, really. I wish Chessie no harm, but my patience with her, too, is quite at an end. Nevertheless, I am determined that we conclude our friendship in a manner that gives me pleasure . . . And her, also, I hope, despite herself . . ."

Carlo felt a jealous rage that left him so helpless he could barely see. He struggled to throw himself against the count's body.

"Is this your plan for coercion, then?" Carlo asked. "You make threats against Chessie Deavors to force me to talk? How vulgar and cowardly! You have damned little interest in any information. You've brought me here simply out of jealousy, because Chessie loves me! Do you have the courage to admit it? To untie me and give me a weapon? Arm yourself and face me, man to man. Or stand labeled a coward!"

Count Croce yawned. "Stand labeled a coward, indeed! Arm myself! How droll. How touchingly naive, Signore Settimo. You young rebels have such imagination, such distorted views of reality . . ."

"You arrogant bastard," Carlo said. He tensed on the balls of his feet. "I long to kill you!"

"Fortunately, you won't have the opportunity," the count said. He sipped his wine. "Very shortly, you'll be glad to tell me all you know, and as for Chessie, you could beg me to trade her for your secrets and I would refuse. She's no part of your ordeal. I shall take my pleasure with her at my leisure and convenience."

Carlo gave a howl of rage and tried to throw himself forward. The count shoved him back with a single thrust. He walked to the fireplace and pulled a bell cord.

Panting, Carlo waited and watched the count smile.

After a minute, the door opened. Carlo glanced around. An unnaturally enormous, hulking man and a grotesque dwarf stood there.

The count refilled his glass, sipped at his wine and walked back to Carlo. "Settimo, you're a handsome young man," he said. "A virile man, who likes women. You're an aristocrat, a man of taste and breeding, a man of sensitivity and culture. Look at these two again. A moron and a freak of nature. Your pain means nothing to them. Absolutely nothing. You, come here."

The dwarf waddled forward and stood beside Carlo's chair. His eyes bulged. The giant was blind in one eye and his hands were as large as shovels.

The count gestured toward the dwarf's groin. The dwarf grinned and slid off his pants. He had the largest penis Carlo had ever seen. Carlo was repulsed and frightened.

"Well, Signore Settimo?" the count asked.

"Go to hell!" Carlo muttered.

"In good time, sir," the count said. "Meanwhile, have you any last message for Chessie?"

Carlo lunged to his feet. "Damn you!" he shouted. "If you so much as touch Chessie . . . I'll survive this . . . And I'll kill you, I swear it!"

"When he's ready to talk, call me," the count said. "I'll be in my quarters."

The giant picked up Carlo and threw him onto the table face down. Carlo cursed and struggled but he was helpless in the giant's hands and when the dwarf climbed onto the table Carlo trembled with fear.

58.

Clayton fled into the Piazza della Rotunda and climbed up onto a fountain to see what was taking place beyond a huge, noisy crowd. He gasped with horror as he looked on a rough wooden scaffold and thought he saw Carlo's neck being forced down across the block.

The crowd hushed. The executioner, a hulking man in a red-and-orange marionette costume and black mask, raised his ax.

He paused. Clayton was sick with fear and disgust as the condemned man thrust up his distorted, tear-stained face in supplication. Was it Carlo . . . ?

The ax fell. The severed head wobbled across the scaffold, spurting blood onto the nearest spectators. The headless body convulsed twice, then lay still. The executioner seized the head by its bloody hair. He paraded it around the edges of the scaffold for the crowd's examination.

The dead man's eyes stared into Clayton's own. Clayton choked back a sob. It was a cry of relief, for the man wasn't Carlo, after all.

Clayton looked away—right into the eyes of a small man with a gnarled ear whom he knew to be one of Countess Corloni's men.

Clayton jumped off the fountain's edge and plunged into the crowd streaming out of the piazza. He paused a moment as he saw the dragoons, thought of asking them for protection, but decided against it. His first concern was Chessie's safety and he dared not delay and risk letting Rafaella's men reach her first.

Rafaella: Clayton brushed sweat from his forehead as he relived those sickening minutes when she had tried to seduce him, when she bared her scarred white breasts and the hideous stub of her thumb, when he realized who she was! Rafaella!

Clayton, fleeing through the crowded streets, trying desperately to reach Chessie, hadn't made sense of it all. But he did not doubt that Rafaella, or the Countess Corloni as she called herself, was truly dangerous, and truly mad.

Clayton looked apprehensively into the crowd, but no one seemed to notice him. Perhaps he had successfully evaded Rafaella's men.

Perhaps he would make it safely to Chessie. With more hope, he ran on. He neared the Via del Corso. Only a few more blocks, he thought. He prayed that Chessie was still safely at home.

Then he ran directly into the carnival parade, into dozens of painted, gaily decorated open carriages filled with shouting, laughing Romans in fancy dress, flowers and enormous sacks of confetti and sugarplums. It was gaiety gone mad—the carriages rattled and the merrymakers howled and hurled nosegays and sugarplums at Clayton.

He ducked under an overhanging stone balcony. Dragoons with drawn swords were directing the carriages into orderly lines for entry to the Corso. Clayton tried to fight his way to the front of the procession but he was stopped by two dragoons. He lurched back into a narrow, empty street and ran directly into the man with the gnarled ear. Both men gasped, startled, and Clayton took advantage of the other's surprise to shove the man to the ground before he turned to flee down the narrow street.

But the downed man's shouts to his fellows echoed after Clayton. All Clayton's instincts warned him that he was running into a trap. From the left, he saw a man coming down an alleyway, so he took an abrupt right, but from the right, another man jumped out, knife in hand, and forced Clayton back against the wall.

"Submit, give me your pistol or I'll take out your heart," the man said. He shoved the point of his dagger against Clayton's ribs.

I'm lost, Clayton thought, and believing himself as good as dead anyway, he ignored the threat and seized the man's wrist. They struggled an instant before Clayton shoved his knee violently into the man's groin. The man screamed and crumpled. Clayton ran on and turned into a street that led into the Corso.

In his misery and exhaustion Clayton thought he was dreaming. As far as he could see, banners of the brightest gold-and-silver, green-and-red, blue-and-yellow silk hung from every roof and every balcony. Billowing silken curtains and draperies of purple and pink and scarlet fluttered from every window and everywhere, in the windows, storefronts, on gas lamps and fountains and statues, were draped garlands of bright flowers intertwined with myriads of colored ribbons.

It was the Corso in full carnival regalia, a mile-long street of colors and of masked and costumed people, lining the streets, leaning from windows and balconies. A cannon boomed and set off a barrage of cannons and suddenly a blizzard of multi-colored confetti exploded into the air.

Clayton gasped. It was hard to believe that danger and death lurked in this mad celebration. He looked back down the narrow street that had brought him to the Corso, trying to decide what to do. There was a line of dragoons on each side of the Corso holding back the crowd. Then he saw two of his adversaries approaching. He forced his way into the crowd, receiving curses and elbows in his ribs, but in his desperation making some progress through the throng.

And then, in a little crevice, he saw a red-jacketed man lying face down, his fingers curled around a wine flask.

Clayton fought his way over to the drunk man and bent over him. The man was snoring. He reeked of wine. Clayton stripped off the man's jacket and red mask and put them on. He grabbed the empty wine flask and stepped away.

Ten feet farther he encountered the man with the gnarled ear again, but the man looked directly at Clayton and passed by. Clayton shuddered with relief and wiped his forehead with the back of his hand. But his relief was momentary. He had still to cross the Corso and reach Chessie, he had still to devise some plan to save her, and Gianna . . .

He turned at the thundering sound of hoofbeats. From his left, from the Piazza del Popolo, came dozens of racing horses adorned with brightly colored blankets, colored ribbons in their manes—and balls with cruel, needle-sharp spikes bouncing over their flanks. The spiked balls maddened the horses, forcing them faster and faster over the cobblestones, their approach a rising, deafening clatter that drowned out even the roar of the excited crowd.

The horses whinnied and their nostrils flared with excitement and pain. A trail of blood ran down the flanks of the lead horse as he began to stumble. He threw back his head and snorted. His legs buckled and as he fell forward he was hit broadside by the charge of another horse and knocked into the crowd.

"My child!" a woman screamed, seeing her son crushed beneath the horse, but her cry was lost as the rest of the crowd followed the progress of the race to its finish at the far end of the Corso. There the horses were stopped by carpets tied across the street.

Clayton fought his way through the crowd, away from the mass of injured, screaming people but the dragoons with their drawn swords would not let him cross the Corso. He panicked, battering the crowd near the curb, trying to find a weak spot in the line of dragoons. Everyone now looked hostile. He tensed at every touch and glanced fearfully about the crowd.

Then, finally, Clayton made it to the end of the Corso, where, in an opening in the mob, prizes were being given to the owners of the winning horses, prizes provided by Rome's Jews as payment for not being forced to run the race themselves as they had been in earlier centuries.

Suddenly it was over. The dragoons relaxed their lines and people surged into the street and at the same time carriages began to drive onto the Corso from the side streets. Once more the air was thick with confetti and there was a cross-fire of flowers and sugarplums from windows and balconies. Then, thousands of tiny candles began to appear. Everyone but Clayton was holding aloft a candle in the deepening dusk.

Clayton gasped in confusion. The candles were beautiful and astonishing. They cast an eerie and shimmering light—but what did they mean? What was going on?

He realized that everyone was trying to extinguish everyone else's candle. Washerwomen in rags held their candles high over their heads while they fought furiously to snuff out the candles held daintily but desperately by countesses and duchesses in extravagant silk gowns. Lackeys and priests jostled to save their candles and put out the others', and when someone lost his flame everyone around hooted: *"Senza moccolo, senza moccolo!"*
. . . Without light, without light!

Clayton became lost in the frenzy, spun around, knocked down, nearly crushed by carriage wheels as the excitement increased. The poor assaulted the carriages of the rich and the well-born squealed, protecting their candles with kicks and fists. Clayton saw a man climb up a pole to attack a ring of candles on a balcony. He saw candied fruit and sugarplums and bouquets of flowers hurled at the little flames. He lost his way in the mindless melee.

An apple struck his ear and he was knocked off his feet by a lurching horse. He fell against a carriage and his pistol dropped from his pocket. He bent to retrieve the pistol, but had to jerk his hand away before it was crushed by a carriage wheel.

For a quarter hour Clayton was propelled along willy-nilly, swept cursing and struggling along the Corso, dazzled, at times nearly blinded, by the wildly gyrating candles. And in the glare and the acrid gray smoke that stung his eyes, the bizarre masks and costumes took on unreal dimensions and he began to lose his inner balance, his sense of reality. Panicked, he twisted this way and that and realized with a sudden, chilling fright that he was completely and totally lost.

A handful of candles was thrust toward his face. He jerked up his hand to protect his eyes. His mask was gone!

A candle singed his aching ear. He gasped with pain. Tears streamed from his eyes. Another candle burned his hand. His ribs throbbed with a dull pain.

He was near-deafened by the roar of the crowd, the booming of the cannon, the loud, steady tattoo of horses' hoofs on the cobblestones.

His head throbbed . . . His vision was blurred. All the women's faces seemed to be the women in his mind . . . Gianna . . . Chessie . . . Rafaella . . . His mind was spinning . . . And then a black carriage appeared in the street directly before his eyes.

He stopped. He stared. It was a moment before he realized that it bore the black, double-eagled crest of the Corloni family.

Clayton gasped and fell backward, bounced off the edge of a fountain. He fell forward, fighting for balance, and in the next instant he was seized and thrown into the carriage. Three hulking men overpowered him and bound his hands.

Knowing the instant before he saw her, Clayton looked up into Rafaella's triumphant smile and rode down the Corso on the floor of her carriage with her feet resting securely on his chest.

59.

Torine stared from the parlor window at the dimly lit street that was deserted except for one man in the shadows and an ominous black carriage that rumbled slowly out of sight.

Chessie had been away for hours, and Torine was sick with worry. Chessie had gone out to some seaport, to find out if Clayton had sailed back to America. Torine was worried about Clayton, too. But he was a young man. He was far more capable of taking care of himself in a place like this Rome. Chessie was a naive, vulnerable girl, who had absolutely no business being out alone, not with that old count mad as a wet hen at her.

Torine hadn't told Chessie, but she had heard from

other maids that when the count fancied a girl who resisted him, he always took her to that castle of his and forced her to give him pleasure.

Torine left the window. She walked nervously about the apartment, trying to keep up her spirits so she wouldn't start imagining things again, as she had earlier. She forced herself into Chessie's bedroom and, slowly, she approached the tall French windows that led onto a balcony.

Cautiously, her body tense, she stuck her head out of the window. Earlier, she had suspected that there was someone out there, amid the shadows and the potted palms and orange trees. She had been certain she had heard something.

Now, there was no sound, no sign of movement. She pulled her head back inside. Yes, she had to stop imagining a haint, come from that bad count, ready to grab her Chessie at any moment. There was no danger here in the apartment. The danger was out there in the streets.

The man was gone from the shadows, she realized. But another man was walking slowly down Via Frattina, a man with his collar pulled up so that his face could not be seen.

As Torine turned to leave, she heard a carriage and looked over her shoulder. It was another black carriage but she couldn't be sure it was the same one.

Torine went into the parlor again, looked from the window, then crept to the front door. She listened. She was almost certain she heard someone walking in the outside hall. But she could not be sure. She hoped it was Chessie! Two minutes later there had been no further sound. Chessie was still out there in the night.

Torine went back to the parlor window. The street was deserted now. She resumed her vigil.

Chessie walked along the desolate Via del Corso as an army of convicts in leg-irons swept up piles of confetti, wilted flowers and crushed sugarplums. It was evening, the time of the *passeggiata,* but no one was out tonight. It was the first day of Lent, and all Rome was exhausted by the frantic carnival that had ended at midnight.

Chessie had just returned from Anzio, the seaport near Rome. There, the captain of the American ship in port had assured her that her brother had not booked passage for home. Chessie's journey to Anzio had been her last resort. She had not really believed that Clayton would desert her in such a way but she had searched for him everywhere and dared not overlook any possibility.

Chessie's carriage had been barred from the Via del Corso because of the convicts cleaning the debris and she had decided to dismiss the carriage and walk home. She hoped there might be news of Clayton there, and she had not finished packing. She must finish packing, for she and Torine and, she could only hope, Clayton and Gianna, were to leave for Paris early the next morning. If Clayton was still absent, Signora Nantes would accompany her to Paris.

Chessie saw six convicts sloshing water over bloodstained cobblestones. She stifled a sob at the thought of the carnival's violence.

Everything in Rome seemed ominous to Chessie, and she realized how naive and unrealistic she had been, particularly concerning Count Croce. She could only thank heaven that tomorrow she would be safely away from him.

Even the incessant clanging of bells calling people to vespers disturbed Chessie. She stopped abruptly. A convict had attempted to escape into a building and two guards were beating him with clubs.

Chessie ran to the next corner and turned into a narrow street to escape the sight of the beating and the man's screams. The vespers bells seemed even louder in the tiny street, unbearably loud, the sounds of a hundred bells cascading off the stone walls of the dark street. For, quite suddenly, the sky had grown dark and the only light came from the votive candles flickering under the statues of saints in the walls.

The sound of horses and carriage wheels startled Chessie. She glanced over her shoulder. In the light of a small candle she saw the carriage's driver, an ugly man with a gnarled ear.

The carriage was coming faster. Chessie felt mounting panic. She bolted across the street and into a small piazza. She had the sudden feeling that Count Croce had sent the carriage to abduct her!

The driver cracked his whip. There was the pounding of the horses' hoofs, the strident creaking of the iron-banded wheels on the cobblestones. Chessie nearly stumbled. She glanced around frantically and saw the crest on the doors of the black carriage. It was a black double-eagle.

Every door and every shutter was closed. There was no shelter. She was alone in the dark piazza.

She ran faster, though her legs began to fail her. She saw her own street just ahead. The carriage was overtaking her . . .

With a final burst of strength she reached Via Frattina, but the galloping horses could not turn the corner. She heard the frantic driver trying to slow them down before the carriage was thrown against a wall.

Chessie was gasping for breath as she entered her building. She paused an instant, to catch her breath, and realized that the porter wasn't on duty. She didn't pause to wonder why. She forced herself up the stairs, realizing slowly that the stairs were darker than usual, that only one small light burned.

She became apprehensive as she dragged herself through the shadows toward her apartment. She finally reached her floor. The hallway was dark. She lurched down it, paused, straining to hear sounds in the darkness. She did hear sounds, she was certain. Ahead of her . . .

And behind her, on the stairs! Creaking sounds, someone creeping behind her . . .

Panic propeled her toward her apartment and she ran blindly, expecting to be grabbed at any moment.

She lurched against the door and pounded with both fists.

"Torine!" she screamed, too frightened to look around.

She screamed again. Her fists were raw from beating. Where was Torine? She heard a sound so near she bit her lips and tasted blood.

The door opened. Chessie stumbled in and collapsed against the wall.

"Close it! Bolt it!" she gasped.

Torine slammed the door. She slid the heavy bolt into place, then ran over and took Chessie in her arms. She comforted Chessie, crooning that she was safe now, that the door was too heavy, the lock too strong, for anyone to break in.

Chessie brushed tears from her eyes. She tried to compose herself. She was safe now, she repeated to herself. She asked about Clayton and sighed miserably when told there had been no word of him.

"Then we must leave without him," she said. "Now, Torine. We dare not wait until morning. I was chased by a dreadful black coach . . ."

"Oh, Miss Chessie, I seen it down on the street, twice I seen it!" Torine said. "Yessum, let's leave now, don't worry none 'bout no luggage or nothin'! But how'll we get out?"

"That secret passageway in the back that Carlo used," Chessie said. "Yes, Torine, the count's men will be watching the front of the house, or coming up the stairs, maybe they're out there now. But they don't know about the passageway. We must escape, get to Signora Nantes. I only want to change into a dark traveling dress, so I won't be conspicuous in the street."

"Yessum," Torine said. "And I'll shove some of this here furniture 'gainst the door, just in case."

Chessie began unfastening her dress as she ran into her bedroom. She was debilitated with fear and anxiety. She remembered the count's ominous threats about getting what he wanted in Rome. How could she have been so stupid as to have thought he would let her leave Rome without taking his pleasure with her?

She stepped out of her dress. As she stood in her

petticoats she thought she heard a noise out on the balcony. She went rigid and peered into the dark shadows. She could see nothing among the potted plants. Only my imagination, she told herself. With trembling fingers she got herself out of her petticoats and her pantaloons and paused suddenly, quite naked, as she heard the sound again. She nearly screamed as she saw a movement in the shadows.

The scream was stillborn and born again as a nervous, relieved laugh when a cat leaped from the balcony.

"Thank God," she muttered as she took a traveling dress from her closet. She was all but safe now. Two minutes, three at the most, and she and Torine would be in the secret passageway.

There was a loud knock on the front door. Chessie gasped. The knocking came again and again, louder and louder. Then someone was trying to break the door down.

Torine came running into the room.

"They here, they here!" she screamed. "Lord, no time to dress, Miss Chessie! Get out of here, put that thing on in that secret passage, once we safe . . ."

"Yes," Chessie said. She scooped up her dress, Torine her slips and pantaloons and boots, and she started running from the room, relieved that the sounds from the front of the apartment indicated that the men in the hall were having little success in trying to break in.

As Chessie reached the door two men bolted from the balcony and seized her.

Chessie screamed and fought but her arms were twisted behind her back. Pain shot through her shoulders. Torine turned and tried to help but she was knocked backward and crumpled to the floor.

One of the men ran to the front door while the other immobilized Chessie by twisting her arm until she nearly fainted from the pain.

A minute later several people entered the bedroom and Chessie raised her head to face Count Croce.

But it was a woman's face she looked into. She screamed hysterically.

The face from the brooch was smiling at her, but it wasn't the smile of a beautiful young girl. This face was ugly and distorted and its black eyes held agony and death.

It was Rafaella! Rafaella had risen from the swamp grave and come to smother her again!

Chessie was too stunned to breathe. She could not find room in her lungs. She was choking. She fought for breath, swayed, and would have collapsed if the man had not held her up by her arms.

"No, no . . ." Chessie babbled as Rafaella stepped closer and removed the black glove from her right hand.

Chessie whimpered at the sight of the mutilated thumb. Rafaella smiled again and moved her thumb stub toward Chessie's face.

Chessie screeched as the hideous lump of flesh brushed the tears from her cheeks.

"Take her down to my carriage," Rafaella said. "The porter has been bribed. Don't bother to dress her. Chessie Deavors will never wear clothes again."

Chessie gagged and spasms swept her body as she was forced from the room, bobbing like a puppet in the man's grip.

Through her haze of agony and pain Chessie realized that someone else had entered the apartment. She raised her head.

Count Croce stood in the door.

"Stay out of this, Paolo," Rafaella hissed. "You can't stop me! Not even you . . ."

"I care nothing for your vendetta against the American family," he said. "I want Chessie."

"No!" Rafaella said. "The girl's worth nothing to you, Paolo. I won't give her up! I've waited so long! You can't take her. You're only one. I have four men."

Count Croce pulled his sword. "Four tavern rats," he said. He turned to the man who was holding Chessie. "You, release the girl! Or you'll rot in the dungeons of San Angelo for the rest of your life!"

"I take my orders from the countess," the man said. He released Chessie and pulled his sword.

"You'll soon take your orders from the devil," Count Croce said.

He parried twice, sidestepped an awkward thrust, then gracefully shoved his sword deep into the man's stomach. The man went white and screamed. Croce removed the blood-smeared sword and turned to the other men, but they backed away.

"You'll regret this, Paolo," Rafaella said. She was trembling as she pulled on her glove. "Despite our years of friendship, you'll pay dearly. And I'll get the girl, one way or another!"

Count Croce sheathed his sword. He wrapped his cloak around Chessie and threw her over his shoulder as if she were as helpless as a child, then walked out of the apartment. Fear and pain had left Chessie only half conscious.

"Oh, Paolo, darling," Rafaella called as she followed them into the hall, "why should we fight over the little bitch? We can both have her. When you've taken your pleasure with her, send her back to me."

60.

Chessie woke with a start. She glanced around the strange room, then climbed out of bed. The marble floor was cold. She shivered. Where was she?

The room was large, with elegant furnishings and wall hangings. She ran to the door. It was locked, as were the two shuttered windows. She looked around, still confused.

She realized she was barefoot, and the clothes she wore did not fit. They were too small, too tight, hugged her hips and breasts in too cheap and provocative a way.

On the floor by the bed she saw a large cloak. She began to remember . . .

She looked through a crack in the shutters. She could see stone walls, battlements. She seemed to be high up.

Below her she glimpsed a slice of the Tiber River and to her right, the dome of St. Peter's.

She was in the Castle of San Angelo! She stifled a scream.

Memory came in a rush; the men, Rafaella—she shuddered as she recalled that evil face, the touch of the thumb stub—then Count Croce . . .

The count had brought her here. He had saved her from Rafaella and imprisoned her in this elegant room.

She began to tremble. She did not doubt why she was here.

"No!" she said. No, dammit, she would never yield to the count. Somehow, she would outwit him. She would promise him anything, yes, she would pretend to show her gratitude by promising to yield to him later, in her apartment. She would convince him of this, would call him "Paolo," and once out of the castle, she would contact Signora Nantes and flee Rome.

Chessie saw a pair of boots across the room. She ran over and was trying to squeeze her feet into the tight boots when Count Croce entered the room.

Chessie jumped up.

"Oh, Paolo," she said, avoiding his eyes. "I must thank you for rescuing me. And to tell you that I intend . . . Oh, it was horrible . . . That woman . . . And all my life I thought she was dead . . ."

"Calm down, Chessie," Count Croce said. He crossed to a sideboard and poured a glass of brandy. "Here, drink this, it will soothe you."

"No, no, I want nothing," she said. "I only want to thank you, Paolo. And to let you know I intend to . . . to show you my gratitude . . . as you wish . . ." Suddenly Chessie thought of her brother. "Paolo, you know everything that happens in Rome. Where's Clayton? Does the countess have him?"

"I know nothing of your brother," the count said. "And I refuse to concern myself with him. He was well warned to end his unwelcome pursuit of Gianna Corloni. You and your brother are in mortal danger only because he was stubborn and stupid."

Chessie remembered the countess' last words: "When you've taken your pleasure with her, send her back to me . . ."

"You wouldn't . . . Surely you wouldn't let her have me . . . Paolo . . . Oh, please, no . . ."

"I'd be more receptive to your pleas if you'd heeded my warnings and not resisted me," he said. "I've grown weary of you, Chessie, in every way . . . except the one way I've not yet come to know you."

Chessie succumbed to her growing panic. She forgot her plan. She glanced toward the door.

"Locked," the count said. "And there's a guard outside. You're going nowhere."

"I demand to be released!" Chessie said. "You can't hold me here! Have you lost your reason? I'm an American citizen and . . . and no matter how grateful I am for your kindness in rescuing me I . . ."

"Silly little Chessie," he said. "Still the innocent, naive tourist. And I've tried so hard to educate you in the realities of life in Rome."

Chessie forced herself to recover her composure. She hoped her smile was provocative.

"Paolo, I have come to accept the realities of life in Rome," she said. "I . . . As I said, I intend to show my gratitude by . . . by giving you pleasure . . . Oh, and I look forward to it, just as I used to look forward to your kisses, to the feel of your hands on my body . . . But you must allow me to yield . . . without duress, Paolo, to receive you willingly at home . . ."

"At home? In Mississippi?" the count asked. He sipped the brandy he had poured for her. "No, Chessie, save your desperate lies. You won't leave this room until I've taken my pleasure. And given you pleasure, also, I hope."

"You'll get no pleasure from me, sir," Chessie said. "You'll get only my resistance and my hatred."

But Chessie's voice trembled. She felt far from brave and defiant. She was terrified and weakened by a growing sense of helplessness. Her desperation forced her to believe that the count was bluffing. After all, she was certain he was a gentleman. Surely he wouldn't actually force her.

Then Chessie remembered Myrtis, her suffering, the power of men over women . . . Fear clenched her stomach and her knees nearly buckled.

"Take some brandy," the count said. "You may need it, my dear, so wickedly provocative in the new clothes I've provided for you."

"I don't want your brandy!" Chessie shouted.

She bolted across the room but the count caught her wrists in his hands. He released her and stood in front of the door.

"Surely you wouldn't leave without your boots," he said. "No proper lady would walk around barefoot."

"How dare you mock me!" she said. Tears stood in her eyes but she was determined not to cry. "I hate you, sir! You might as well take your pleasure with the cold marble floor!"

"I've had enough of coldness, Chessie," the count said. "I've courted you warmly and you've whetted my appetite. I don't want to hurt you. But you must be realistic, damn it! You're here because I'm attracted to you and unless you yield now, willingly, I'll take you by force."

"Go to hell!" Chessie screamed. "You're repulsive, despicable! I'll yield to only one man . . ."

The count's smile was malicious and frightening. "Oh, you mean Carlo Settimo? Well, my dear, your beloved Carlo has also been my guest here in the castle tonight."

Chessie gasped. "Carlo . . . here? I don't . . . What have you done with Carlo?"

"Enough to ensure that your love affair with him is over," Count Croce said. "I promise you that. You may as well forget Carlo Settimo . . . and therefore find a new love . . . and a new lover."

He smiled again. Chessie's stomach knotted. She wouldn't let herself believe the count's words, yet looking into his arrogant, confident black eyes she could not doubt that what he said was true. A sob choked in her throat.

"My patience with you is ended," the count said abruptly. He advanced on Chessie.

The sudden realization of what she must endure swept thoughts of Carlo from Chessie's frenzied mind. She backed away, her lips trembling. She looked around frantically for some object with which to defend herself.

Chessie's hand found a brass candleholder but the count easily knocked it from her grasp. She scrambled away. Squealing, she tried to crawl across the bed to the other side of the room, but the count was too fast. He caught her in the middle of the bed and threw her onto her back.

Chessie kicked and clawed with her nails. She sank her teeth into his hand. He grimaced but held her wrists and spread her hands up over her head so she could not reach him with her teeth. He endured her kicks, then immobilized her legs by pressing his knees into her thighs.

Chessie struggled and cursed as he tied her wrists to the bed, then stood up. She thrashed and rolled over, scrambled up and chewed at the tight knot. Two minutes later her wrists ached terribly and she lay back down, exhausted.

The count stood by the bed. He sipped brandy.

"I hate you," Chessie said. "I loathe you. I'll never surrender to you. You'll take no pleasure from me . . ."

"Oh, but I will, Chessie," he said. "I would have preferred that you become my lover willingly. But there was never the slightest doubt that I would have you, one way or another."

Chessie tried to muster strength for a new resistance, but her wrists throbbed with pain and the dread, the stark reality of her helplessness, made her whimper.

Count Croce finished the brandy. Chessie tensed, prepared to defend herself with her legs. She kicked him once as he plunged onto the bed. But in a minute he had spread her legs and tied her ankles to the bed.

"Oh, God, no," Chessie whimpered as he took a knife from the table. "Don't hurt me . . ."

"Quiet, you fool," he said.

He slit her gown and petticoats up the front. Chessie twisted and thrashed and bit her lips as the count peeled away her lace bodice and petticoats.

"Ah, yes, you're remarkably beautiful, Chessie," he said. "I'm not disappointed. I've longed to see your breasts, your thighs, your vagina . . . And if you give me as much pleasure as I expect, perhaps . . . perhaps I won't deliver you to Countess Corloni . . ."

The count stroked her breasts and nipples. Chessie strained against her bonds at the first touch. She tried to twist from his hands. Then she sank to the bed, drained and trembling, and endured endless minutes of his caresses.

She jerked violently as he caressed her stomach, then her thighs. She lay board-stiff, her lips clamped between her teeth, as he tickled her upper thighs. His invading fingers slid into her vagina. A convulsion swept her body. Her thighs quivered. She shook with rage and helplessness and the humiliation of having her body touched and toyed with—spread open and vulnerable.

When the count started to undress, Chessie stared straight ahead and tried not to watch him, but from the corner of her eye she saw his penis. She looked around.

The penis was huge and fully erect.

Count Croce climbed back onto the bed. He approached her, and his penis touched her thigh . . .

"Oh, no, no, please," Chessie begged. "I can't bear it! I'll do anything, anything. Don't hurt me, don't do this to me, please . . ."

The count moved between her thighs. "Oh, you're far preferable to a cold marble floor, Chessie. You're warm, soft . . ."

Chessie closed her eyes and prayed that she would faint. At the first touch of his penis against her vagina she screamed and thrashed desperately. For a moment he was gentle, touching her with little probing, exploring thrusts that just barely penetrated.

Then he thrust forward with such force that Chessie screeched and bit her own shoulder. She was stunned, astonished. How could she take so much, so much flesh into her own body? It was overwhelming, intolerable, unbelievable.

She babbled and crooned and writhed against the pain she knew would split her open at any moment.

61.

Chessie woke with a start, panicked by the rolling, tumbling motion that had sickened her ever since Count Croce had escorted her aboard the ship and told her that the pleasure she had given him had saved her from the Countess Corloni. Then she smiled, although she could not quite laugh at her mistake. It was only the motion of the swing on the veranda of The Columns which had startled her from her nap. She swallowed hard then stepped away from the swing. It was a mild breezy evening and she took several deep breaths, inhaling the familiar, reassuring smells of freshly turned earth and summer roses, wet with early evening dew.

Near the veranda, two slaves were humming gently as they weeded in the rose garden and gathered red-and-pink blossoms into a basket. Chessie looked past them. On the far horizon was the familiar sight of field hands hoeing weeds from the rows of green cotton, and drivers on horseback holding their never-used whips as small girls strolled about with jugs of drinking water on their heads.

It was late July at The Columns and, for a moment, bathed in the warm, flower-and-earth-scented smells and lulled by the sounds of humming, Chessie forgot all her troubles and had the sense that nothing was changed, that she had never left the plantation, never been to Rome and suffered so much . . .

But she had been to Rome!

The realization brought on the feeling of panic again, and Chessie stepped off the veranda, walking aimlessly but quickly, seeking some activity to distract her from her increasing melancholy.

She wandered into the rose garden but barely nodded at the slaves who greeted her as she passed. This time of day, the dimming hours of twilight, were the most difficult for her. If she could, she would have slept through it each day. But sleep in general was a luxury her nerves often denied her, and sleep often brought with it nightmares, some of them so horrible she woke screaming.

At least arriving safely home had ended weeks of fears that Rafaella was still pursuing her, that she would be seized at any minute—on the ship, at the dock in New Orleans, on the trip up the Mississippi River.

With loving patience, her mother had finally convinced Chessie that she was safe on The Columns. Lucinda had notified the sheriff that Rafaella Blaine Ridgeway was still alive and, since there was no statute of limitations on a murder charge, she would be arrested at once if she appeared in Mississippi. In fact, the sheriff had taken steps to have Rafaella extradited from Italy, though Chessie knew very well that it would be next to impossible to extradite so powerful and wealthy a woman.

Since her talk with the sheriff, though, a talk kept private so that the slaves on The Columns would not know that Rafaella was still alive, Lucinda had been unwilling to discuss anything about Rafaella or her past in Mississippi. Lucinda insisted that any such discussion must wait until Chessie had fully recovered from her ordeal. Chessie accepted this but sensed that there was more. Her mother, she suspected, had other, more serious reasons for avoiding discussion and explanation of Rafaella's hatred for the Deavors family.

So, although she was determined some day to learn the truth, Chessie did not press Lucinda. For one thing, she had discovered on her return that her mother had been seriously ill for several months and had only recently begun to recover her health. Lucinda was still delicate, Doctor Telson had warned, and the news of Chessie's ordeal and Clayton's disappearance had nearly caused a serious relapse.

To spare her mother, Chessie had never told her about the horror of being raped. Only Torine knew, and she had sworn Torine to secrecy, but there was little she could do to ease the family's shock and suffering at Clayton's disappearance—or her own great loss.

Everyone missed Clayton, but at times Chessie thought she missed him most of all. Everything here at The Columns reminded her of her twin, and his loss, coupled with that of Carlo, was almost more than she could bear.

The Roccalinis had been helpful in contacting their family in Italy and using their influence to force an investigation into the possibility that Rafaella had abducted Clayton as she had tried to abduct Chessie. And Lucinda had hired the best agents in New Orleans and sent them to Rome to search for Clayton.

But nothing had come of this yet and Lucinda fretted so much over Clayton that Chessie tried her best to be optimistic in front of her mother.

"So much has changed here," Chessie mumbled as she reached the gazebo.

For one thing, she thought, something had changed drastically between her mother and Anthony Walker. Chessie didn't know why, but she saw that her mother was no longer at all infatuated with her husband, but at times seemed actually wary of him.

Perhaps it was only a result of her long illness or her reaction to what had happened in Italy, but Chessie suspected it was more. She had never forgotten seeing Anthony sneak out of her mother's bedroom on the night of their wedding, and a man who would do that . . . Well, Chessie would not be surprised to learn that Anthony had been unfaithful to her mother since.

Perhaps he had been indiscreet and had forced Lucinda to become aware of his infidelity. But, although she pondered the unhappiness she sensed her mother felt, Chessie had no proof of her suspicions, and dared not upset her mother even further by asking.

To her surprise, Chessie had returned to find that Jolette was still living at The Columns and was established in everyone's eyes as a member of the Deavors family. Chessie had been a bit jealous, at first, seeing how close Jolette was to her mother, seeing the intimacy and easy familiarity between them, but then her jealousy had turned to gratitude. She owed Jolette a lot, Chessie thought, for Jolette had spent months nursing Lucinda in her illness, and Jolette herself seemed to have changed. She had become much more Southern in her ways, warmer and softer-spoken and she seemed less conceited and less self-confident.

But the biggest change in everyone's life, of course, was also the saddest and most exciting. Chessie had come home to the same city and the same state, but she was now living in a new country: The Confederate States of America, for the day she had arrived home, in April, war had broken out between the North and the South, when Confederate troops opened fire on the Union's Fort Sumter, in South Carolina.

Now war was raging, and it seemed that people could talk of little else. Every family in Adams County had either sent up a man to enlist or knew someone else who had. Many of the young men Chessie had grown up with were already officers in the Army, officers with fine new uniforms and swords who were full of plans for battles and victories and glory.

But most of their talk disturbed Chessie, though she prayed every night for a Confederate victory. She had seen enough suffering in Italy, had heard enough talk of war and glory and death in the cause of justice. She could not bear to think that the young men she knew would soon ride off to battle, where some of them might be maimed, and some might well be killed.

Chessie's thoughts and reflections were interrupted by a horseman coming up the house road. It was her old friend Dunbar Polk, splendid in his gray captain's uniform, riding a prancing white horse.

Dunbar had recently told her that he was in love with her. His declaration had made Chessie a bit sad. She knew she would never love anyone again, not the way she had loved Carlo. But she was fond of Dunbar. He was handsome and charming and she appreciated his love in a way she would never have been able to before loving Carlo.

She sighed. After all, she had to be realistic. She had to try and make a good life for herself, even though it would have to be a life without Carlo. So she saw Dunbar often and she had begun to be able to respond to his eager kisses.

Dunbar waved. Chessie waved back. Slowly, she walked down the steps and waited for him, surprised and pleased that she was anxious for his company this evening.

62.

Anthony Walker limped across the parlor to greet some neighbors who had come to visit at The Columns on a hot July afternoon. The guests asked about the gout that had recently afflicted his foot and he said that it was about the same. Actually, the medicine prescribed by Dr. Telson had reduced the pain and swelling and as long as he took the medicine each day, his foot was nearly normal. But Anthony was determined not to go into the Army, and he had seized on the illness as a good excuse. His limp was affected.

So Anthony remained a civilian who seemed to be a devoted patriot, whose only concern was to further the Confederate victory. Anthony was sincere enough in his preference for a Southern victory, but it was not his primary concern. There was money to be made in this war, he had realized as soon as the shots were fired at Sumter, and he intended to make his share.

Anthony was a man obsessed with money—and its

lack. Although no one in the parlor at The Columns knew it, he was a poor man. In less than two months he had lost both of his ships, one devastated in an Atlantic storm, and the other seized by Union ships after Abraham Lincoln proclaimed a blockade of the Confederacy. His profits from smuggling African slaves had already gone to pay off the high-interest loans he had taken out to buy the ships. Before he lost the ships he had been out of debt for the first time in years.

To other people, Anthony pretended that his loss was slight and he had ready money to buy new ships. While courting Lucinda he had pretended to be wealthy and he had to maintain that pose. He had even turned down her offer of money. His pride wouldn't let him admit the truth and become dependent on his wife, especially a wife who now looked at him with cold and suspicious eyes.

The talk in the parlor was, as usual, of the war, the blockade and the brave and successful efforts of some Confederate ships to run the blockade and bring in munitions and medicine. Blockade-runners took great risks but their profits were high, and Anthony knew they would get higher as the Union blockade became more effective. And although the blockade-runners were actually mercenary, they were hailed as patriots, praised and admired.

Anthony intended to become this kind of patriot as soon as he could afford to buy another ship. He foresaw a long war. He did not feel the optimism for a quick Confederate victory shared by Dunbar Polk and the other men in the room, who talked of "a few more victories like Bull Run, to send the Yankees runnin' home with their tails between their legs . . ."

No, Anthony reasoned as he sipped a gin fizz, the Union was rich and strong. The North had a far larger population, a dozen times more factories than the South and a president determined to preserve the Union at any cost. The Union could lose another half dozen Bull Runs and still remain strong. The war would not be ended soon.

And that was fine with Anthony. A longer war meant time for him to get in on the profits. No matter how well the fighting went on land, and, so far, it had gone well for the South, the Confederacy had no navy and would not be able to match the output of the Union shipyards. The Confederacy would never be able to challenge the Union on the seas, and the blockade would slowly strangle the flow of goods to Southern ports.

In time, the South would pay even more dearly for guns and ammunition, supplies and medicine. Anthony could see the time when one shipload would be so profitable that a blockade-runner could afford to lose that ship the next time.

And just now, after several anxious, desperate weeks, Anthony had a scheme to get the money he needed to buy ships, a way to accumulate cash very quickly. He knew that certain types of medicine used to kill pain and treat wounds had always come from the Northern states or from Europe. These medicines were already becoming scarce.

With his last money Anthony had contacted an old business acquaintance, a shipper now a blockade-runner, and had purchased several cases of a vital painkiller that had been smuggled in from England. The medicine was valuable now, but Anthony's business sense told him that it would be ten times as valuable in a very short time. He intended to hold it back and wait to sell it at a very large profit. Yes, there was money to be made on war . . . And he might as well be the one to make it.

Anthony drank another gin fizz and listened to several young officers talk about a Tennessee skirmish in which they had sent a Yankee patrol into retreat with heavy losses. Anthony realized that Dunbar Polk was not interested in the conversation, although he had led the Confederate troops. Polk couldn't keep his eyes off Chessie, Anthony noticed. It was clear the young captain was in love with her.

With all his heart, Anthony hoped that Chessie would marry Dunbar Polk. Polk's family owned a large plantation just to the south of The Columns. If Chessie married him, there would be no danger of her choosing some fool without money and land and deciding to live on The Columns, which would by law become hers, if she chose to live there, since her brother Clayton was missing and almost certainly dead.

And Anthony still intended to gain control of The Columns, not only because of the money to be made raising cotton and the value of its land and slaves, but also because of the social standing, the sense of arriving, that being master of the plantation would give him. He had intended to own The Columns ever since he met Lucinda Deavors, and now only Chessie stood in his way. He was determined, but not desperate. He was confident and would wait a while, wait for Chessie to marry, wait for his own financial situation to improve.

Earlier, before Clayton had disappeared, his prospects had seemed much dimmer, and he had realized that there was no limit to what he would do to be master of The Columns. He would, he had admitted, kill, though killing some slave back in the swamp was a different thing than murdering Lucinda and her children.

But now, if he were patient, and if Chessie married Polk, nature might well solve his problem, and Lucinda might die from her illness, which was far more serious than she had admitted to Chessie.

Anthony glanced across the room. Lucinda, in a pale blue silk, and Jolette, in bright green, sat together near the window. For a time, he had thought he could manage to live happily with Lucinda. He had honestly tried, and she had been willing to do anything to please him. But in the past year, her illness had made her fretful and suspicious. She no longer appealed to him. And of course her suspicions of his infidelity were well founded. He frowned.

At least, thank the Lord, Lucinda had no idea that the other woman in his life was Jolette. No one knew. They had kept their affair totally secret. Anthony would be ruined if anyone knew, but he could not resist Jolette. He was obsessed with her, although when he had begun their affair, he had never expected it to last. In his life, he had had many women, but none of them had given him as much physical pleasure as Jolette.

Their involvement had been passionate but far from ideal, for Jolette had become willful and had begun to beg him to divorce Lucinda and marry her. That I would never do, Anthony thought, although he had promised Jolette many times that he would, and had seized upon Lucinda's illness as an excuse for postponement. Looking at the blond, willowy Jolette, Anthony felt a powerful stirring of lust. It was truly incredible, he thought, how much she could rouse him.

Jolette was talking to Lucinda now. It was bizarre, Anthony realized, but out of a mixture of guilt and real affection, Jolette had come to love Lucinda and had nursed her faithfully.

Far too bizarre to dwell on, Anthony decided. He drained his glass and took another from the tray offered by a slave.

"Anthony, what's happenin' with those runaway niggers in the swamp?" Dunbar Polk asked. "Anything new happen while we were in Tennessee?"

"Well, Dunbar, it's hard to separate the truth from what the niggers in the quarters imagine," Anthony said with a lightness that belied his true feelings. Probably emboldened by all the talk of free niggers up North, a gang of runaways had banded together, avoided all the sheriff's posses and patrols, and unfortunately captured the imagination of even the good slaves on Adams County plantations. Anthony had his own reasons for wanting them to be caught. Traces of the camp where he had hidden the Africans might still be found. He didn't like having slave patrols poking around in there.

"A couple of niggers said that they raided their chicken coops two days ago, but we don't put too much stock in that kind of talk. Niggers all lie," Anthony said.

"And that nigger girl of yours," a red-headed lieutenant asked, "the one who was raped? Myrtis, is that her name? Whatever happened to her?"

"Oh, she's settled down," Anthony said. "She's married now and doing good work, I believe."

Anthony was relieved when several ladies joined the men and the talk turned back to the war.

"Darling, I couldn't have stood it for much longer in there this afternoon," Jolette said. She lay, naked, full length along Anthony's body. He was still dressed except for having unbuttoned his trousers, but he had penetrated Jolette fully.

"Move! Oh, don't stop!" Anthony ordered. His hands stroked Jolette's full, fleshy breasts, hanging down over him. He passed his hands down her smooth sides, her sleek buttocks, and held her fiercely against him.

They lay, as they so often had, in the small wooden granary, unused since a newer one had been built closer to the big house. Jolette's bright green silk dress and petticoats were in a heap near the door, which was barred and allowed just a narrow strip of late-afternoon light to come into the dry, dusty room.

I'm tired today, Anthony thought. Let her do all the work. "Move, Jolette," he said firmly. Her long golden hair fell down over his face and he caught a strand of it in his teeth. You bitch, he thought, no good woman could be as sexy as you are.

Obediently, Jolette moved, undulating over her lover and feeling him deep inside her. She gasped, closed her eyes, and lost herself in the sensation of being fully possessed.

"Oh! Yes!" Anthony gasped. Whatever happens, he thought, I must always have her. He dug his fingernails into Jolette's buttocks until she screamed in pain and he felt his climax.

63.

The Countess Corloni held her gloved hand over her nose against the smell in the dungeon as she watched two men force Clayton Deavors into wrist irons. His struggles were feeble. Months of imprisonment in this dank cellar had left him emaciated and weak. The countess had persuaded an old lover who was a high judge to condemn Clayton to this secret prison and he had been brought here the last day of carnival.

And here she had let him waste away, slowly, in frightening isolation, and occasionally, as on this hot September afternoon, she had come by to watch him be whipped. She did not know what she would do with him, ultimately, for she dimly realized his death would end her revenge. Vaguely, she planned to keep him alive until she had brought his sister here, too.

At times, as he grew weaker and his strength ebbed, she felt some compassion for him.

But today, as Clayton swung around in his chains and his glazed eyes met hers, the countess' memories revived her hatred for all the Deavors family. A tall man with a whip began his work. Clayton screamed. The countess moved closer, lost in recollection of her lost father and her agony and humiliation in Mississippi.

The countess hugged her daughter possessively. "You look much better today, darling," she said. "I'm so happy to see color back in your cheeks."

"I feel better," Gianna said. "I hope I'll be strong enough to get out of bed in a few days."

"I'm sure you will, darling," the countess said. "Now you sleep. You need your rest. You're still weak."

"All right, Mama. Thank you for looking in."

"I'll come back when they bring you your dinner."

She kissed Gianna's cheek and left the room.

Once again she's my sweet, obedient, loving girl, Countess Corloni thought as she walked down the stairs. She had been badly frightened by Gianna's strange, recurring illness—an illness that had baffled the best doctors in Rome for months and postponed all marriage plans. Now that Gianna was recovering, she could again set a date for the wedding to Prince Vittori.

And it was high time. Each postponement had made the prince more fretful, petulant and evasive, and he had made no secret of the fact that more delay would force him to marry someone else.

His threat had caused the countess to shake with anger. After all she had been through to arrange this marriage, she could not fail now, and she had already forgotten all the cruelty and duplicity her success had involved.

How the countess had laughed when she had learned that someone—Lucinda Deavors, she imagined—had sent agents to Rome. They had paid huge bribes and learned nothing of Clayton Deavors. Just for her amusement, she had had one of the American agents poisoned and heard that the others sailed for New Orleans the next day.

If the Deavors family thought she had forgotten them, they were very wrong. As soon as Gianna was safely wed, she would set into motion her plans to destroy Chessie, whose visit to Rome had cost her her old and dear friend Paolo Croce. Poor Paolo. From the start he had been foolish over that girl, and it had been his ruin.

The countess sighed as she hurried through the labyrinthine corridors of her villa. She must find the steward and make sure he had the right wines for the prince's visit. Poor Paolo, she thought.

It seemed, she had learned from friends and the ever-efficient *pasquini,* that the handsome *Garibaldino* Chessie Deavors had always preferred to Count Croce had been imprisoned and tortured by the count. That surprised no one. But the young man had managed to escape from the Castle San Angelo, and later he had sought out Paolo in the park of his Frascati villa and confronted him.

And there, right in his own park, he had died. Some accounts said that the Sicilian had ambushed and murdered Paolo. Others said that they fought fairly, with swords, and that both were gravely injured. No one knew what had happened to the young man, but Paolo had died of his wounds.

I miss him, the countess thought. Even though he deprived me of Chessie Deavors, he was an old and trustworthy friend, and his death is one more grudge I'll always hold against the Deavorses.

Gianna forced herself to lie still for another minute after her mother left the room. Then she sat up in her bed and threw off the covers. She waited another minute, then crept to the door and listened. Satisfied that no one was outside, she locked the door and took Sister Teresa's herb preparation from its hiding place.

"This is a recipe every young girl should know," Sister Teresa had told Gianna when she showed her how to mix the herbs. It was a lesson that wasn't in the convent's curriculum, a private lesson the nun gave her favorite pupils.

"You must protect your virtue with your intelligence," Sister Teresa had said.

When she was a girl of sixteen, she recounted, a war had raged around her isolated southern village and several other village girls had been abducted by soldiers. But when Teresa had been carried away by a lustful soldier she managed to take with her the herb solution given her by her grandmother.

Left alone for a few minutes while the soldier foraged for food at a farmhouse, she had swallowed the potion. By the time the soldier returned, ready to take his pleasure with her, she was pale as death, her pupils were dilated and she was feverish and shivering.

"Nothing dampens a man's lust more than illness," Sister Teresa had told Gianna. "He would not touch me. The brute, who had slit another girl's throat for resisting him, threw me aside."

On the day that Clayton failed to keep their rendezvous, Gianna had become alarmed and frightened. By the next day she was desperate. She had slipped away from her chaperone for a few minutes, and visited Clayton's apartment building. But his *portiere* had told her that Clayton Deavors and his sister had sailed for America the day before.

Gianna had returned home shaken and trembling. Misery replaced disbelief and she despaired. Clayton's leaving changed everything. She had many things to decide. She had taken to her bed broken-hearted and feeling painfully alone, and finally cried herself to sleep.

That next day, Sister Teresa, who had come to Rome to visit her brother, called on Gianna. She found her former pupil drained and miserable. Gianna confessed her secret love affair and its miserable end to her beloved teacher.

Sister Teresa was sympathetic. She loved Gianna and hated her suffering. She stroked Gianna's hand and nodded, and when she left, she promised to help.

The next day Sister Teresa brought news that both angered Gianna and improved her spirits.

"As you know, dear, I've a brother who works in a hotel," Sister Teresa said. "He knows everything that happens in Rome. He had heard that your mother knows about Clayton Deavors, has known for months." In fact, the nun explained, the countess entertained Clayton in her villa during the pre-Lent carnival.

"Here?" Gianna asked. "Clayton here? . . . I remember I was sent to Frascati just then! I couldn't understand why. Of course! Mama knew about Clay and . . . Oh, I see it all! I know my mother forced Clayton to leave Rome. Oh, Sister Teresa, help me! I love him so. Please help me, Sister!"

Touched, Sister Teresa promised further help and Gianna conceived a desperate and dangerous plan to be reunited with Clayton. First of all, she must feign illness to delay her marriage. She would take Sister Teresa's herb preparation, secretly, so as not to raise her mother's suspicions.

As well as time, Gianna needed money. She would steal some jewelry from her mother, pretend some of her own was missing, then steal larger silver and gold household objects. Sister Teresa, through her brother, would sell all of them in the thieve's market.

And after that night, despite awful reactions to the herbal potion, despite guilt toward her mother and fear of being caught, Gianna never wavered in her plan. Her strength was in her belief that Clayton truly and deeply loved her—and she him.

Gianna knew she still loved her mother, too, but her mother had forced her to choose, and she loved Clayton far more.

The herbs left Gianna pale and thin, but she only dreaded meeting Clayton in this condition. Half a dozen of Rome's most prominent surgeons were unable to diagnose her illness, and all their bitter medicines, their nasty leeches, their sickening emetics, could not break her spirit.

But Gianna's ordeal was not yet over. When she thought of the courage she must muster to creep from the villa at night, to be a fugitive, to buy transatlantic passage, to sail alone to a strange country, and of her mother's anger and disappointment, she nearly lost hope.

But if she gave up, she would lose Clayton—and she would find herself married to Prince Vittori. She shuddered, then stirred Sister Teresa's herbs in a cup of water. As she drank, her courage returned, and she set her mind on the day she would see Clayton again.

64.

Chessie rode along the edge of the fields and saw scores of field hands stooped over rows of bursting cotton pods, working to fill the huge gunnysacks they dragged behind them. It was an autumn scene that had been familiar to her all her life. She lifted her gaze to admire the sweeping beauty of the cotton fields, stretching green and white to the edge of the sky.

Harvesting brought long hours and the tension of getting in all the cotton before it rotted in its pods. The custom was that all the cotton should be picked by Thanksgiving. And then there was an annual harvest ball, an affair attended by hundreds of family friends while the slaves drank beer and whiskey and made their own music in the quarters.

But this first autumn of the war was different in so many ways. Now the Deavors' cotton had to be sold within the Confederate States instead of being shipped to the East or to Europe, and it would be paid for in the new Confederate currency.

No one knew yet quite what that meant, but Chessie had overheard the men discussing it in the parlor of The Columns one recent afternoon. Most of them felt that their decreased profits would be only temporary, and were, like so many other things, the fault of the Yankees.

The cotton pickers looked tired, Chessie realized. Harvest was a strain on every one of the slaves, and this year, for the first time she could remember, their spirits in general were low. And, also for the first time, there had been several runaways from the plantation. The Columns had suffered an occasional runaway over the years—Chessie remembered Bernard—but nothing like the number that had disappeared since the war started.

The defections had particularly upset Lucinda. She still believed that her people were well-off and content, that they would be confused and unhappy if they were set free, especially if they fell into the hands of the Yankees. Chessie herself had been shocked and saddened to think that so many of her family's slaves were so desperate for freedom.

Yet, during the past year, she had entertained some

doubts about slavery, particularly after her trip abroad and her awareness of the suffering of Bernard and Myrtis. Thank goodness Myrtis had recovered from her ordeal and had even fallen in love and married. Myrtis, Chessie was sure, would never run away.

The war itself had changed everything. Not that there was any sense of imminent danger in Natchez, or at The Columns. For one thing, there was a Confederate camp down the road. The actual fighting was far away, and people felt it would never come to Natchez, which was protected by strong fortifications on the Mississippi River north of the city and, to the south, by New Orleans and its impregnable Forts Jackson and St. Philip.

But many everyday items were already becoming scarce, either stopped by the Union blockade or requisitioned by the Confederacy. This new conscription had completely changed civilian life. Women did work that men had always done in the past, running farms and families and businesses while their men were away. Everyone had pledged to sew Confederate uniforms and flags, and many young women Chessie knew had volunteered to work as nurses in the Natchez hospital.

But if Southern women were busier than they had ever been before, at least they were not in danger.

Already many men Chessie knew had gone off, either to fight in Tennessee or far away in Virginia. From one Adams County social gathering to the next Chessie never knew which young men would be gone. And now, Dunbar Polk was due to leave for Tennessee again within the week.

Chessie glanced at the darkening sky, then reined her horse into a trot and headed back to the house. Dunbar was calling for her that evening, to escort her to a ball at the nearby Sumrall plantation, a ball given in honor of the company he commanded.

Chessie was sad and apprehensive about Dunbar's leaving to face the dangers of battle. She was very fond of Dunbar, although she knew she could never love anyone but Carlo, and she was aware of his deep feelings for her.

Chessie enjoyed the Sumralls' ball. Everyone made an effort to be gay and the Sumralls' ballroom was candlelit and banked with autumn flowers. The musicians played polkas, waltzes and mazurkas, and Chessie danced every dance, but as midnight approached she became alarmed at the sight of her mother, who sat near a window fanning herself, and, Chessie noticed, looking quite pale.

"Are you feelin' all right, Mama?" Chessie asked. "Can I get you somethin'?"

"Oh, I'm fine, Chessie," Lucinda said, her hands fluttering nervously. "I guess I'm just not used to stayin' up late and dancin' so much. A woman my age . . ."

"What do you mean, your age?" Chessie asked, surprised. It was the first time she had ever heard her mother speak in such a way. "Why, you're still beautiful, Mama. I even got a little jealous, Dunbar stood talkin' to you so long after that last dance."

Lucinda smiled. It was a sad, sweet smile that seemed to take a great deal of effort. Chessie was touched and disturbed. She knew her mother wasn't really tired out from the exhaustion of dancing. Indeed, Doctor Telson had said that more exercise would be good for her, that she should get out of the house more often. Lucinda had suffered "miasma," a disease whose origin wasn't understood but was felt to be an adverse reaction of the internal organs to "bad air." All that could be done for it was to make sure the sufferer took heavy doses of medication each day and avoided undue worry and strain.

Doctor Telson had told Chessie that although her mother might never recover fully, she could lead a "fairly normal life for any number of years." Chessie had taken heart at the news, for a time, but then Cellus had hinted to her that the illness was far more serious. Telling her, his stoic composure had broken down and he had confided in Chessie that Lucinda "was not the same at all."

Chessie suspected, though, that her mother's worries had taken a greater toll on her health than the miasma.

She knew that Lucinda was desperately upset that despite all the efforts of the Roccalinis and the agents sent to Rome, there had been absolutely no word of Clayton. Months had passed, and now, as the war grew worse and the Union blockade became more effective, they were unlikely to have any news from Italy for a long while.

"Please, Mama, don't look so sad," Chessie whispered, taking her mother's hand.

"Oh, I'll be all right," Lucinda promised, but Chessie felt her stiffen as they both looked up to see Anthony approaching.

Chessie's concern changed to anger. She was absolutely sure that Anthony was to blame for part of her mother's unhappiness, though she wasn't at all certain exactly what had happened. At any rate, her mother didn't seem pleased to see her husband, and barely controlled a shiver as he bent to kiss her cheek.

"You two are as pretty as flowers sitting over here together," Anthony said, but his flattery rang false to Chessie's ear, and she made a hasty excuse to leave them.

As she walked toward the refreshment table she was overtaken by Jolette and Dunbar, who had been dancing the last mazurka together.

"Chessie, he's the best dancer in Adams County," Jolette said. "You better keep him under lock and key or some other lady will try to steal him from you."

"Oh, I know, Jolette," Chessie said. "I'd like to. But how can I possibly lock him up? He's about to rush off to Tennessee to fight the Yankees . . . and to do the Lord only knows what else."

"I'll only be fightin', Chessie," Dunbar said. "And then I'll be comin' right back here to you."

Chessie tried to think of something sincerely tender or even flirtatious to say, but she lacked the enthusiasm. She was truly fond of Dunbar and truly sad that he was leaving. She knew that he loved her, and she knew she could never find a better man . . . except

. . . Except that she was not in love and, once, she had been so much in love . . .

Stop it, Chessie, she told herself. Stop living in the past and spoiling the present.

"Dunbar, would you please fetch me . . . ? You, too, Jolette? . . . Would you please fetch us some punch?"

"Of course, I should have remembered to ask," he said.

As he walked away Chessie glanced back at her mother and Anthony. Lucinda looked even more nervous and even paler. Chessie longed to know the truth about her mother's marriage to Anthony. But who could she ask? Even if he knew, Cellus would never betray such a confidence of her mother's.

"I'm so happy for you and Dunbar," Jolette said.

"Happy . . . What?" Chessie turned back to her cousin. "Dunbar and I? What do you mean, Jolette? . . . We're just special friends . . ."

"Well, maybe you see it that way," Jolette said. "But not Dunbar. Why, he talks of nothing but you, Chessie. Before he goes off to war, I'd be surprised if he didn't ask you to marry him. Oh, Chessie, I'm so sorry! You looked so sad, just then. Have I upset you with my chatter? I know how much you've grieved for your Carlo, but I hoped, with Dunbar . . ."

"It's all right, Jolette," Chessie said. "I know you meant well. And I'm very fond of Dunbar. Maybe things will work out for us, sooner or later, but I'm not ready yet."

"Don't think I don't understand the kind of love you feel for Carlo," Jolette said. "I know what it's like . . . being hopelessly in love with one man, knowing you'll never love anyone else, no matter the consequences, no matter what people think . . ."

"When you're in love, I don't suppose what people think has much of anything to do with it," Chessie said. "And I'm glad for your love. I had no idea, Jolette. Tell me about him. Is it somebody you met recently? I won't tell a soul if you don't want me to."

The color drained from Jolette's face. "Oh, no, no, Chessie. I don't know what got into me, talking like that. I just . . . Sometimes I feel I have to talk to someone. I have to stop bottling up all my feelings inside."

"Then tell me . . ."

"I can't! Because . . . because it would . . . hurt too much. It's been some while back. I should have forgotten him by now."

"I understand," Chessie said.

Poor Jolette. She had never dreamed that her cousin was concealing a broken heart. Then she remembered how close Jolette had been to her mother. Perhaps her mother had confided in Jolette?

"I want to discuss somethin' that worries me about Mama with you," Chessie said.

"What do you mean?" Jolette's voice rose half an octave.

"I know that you and Mama became quite close while I was away," Chessie said. "Mama's mentioned more than once how good you were, sittin' up with her nights and all. She's real fond of you, Jolette, and I wondered if . . ."

"Oh, Chessie, I'm terribly fond of her, too!" Jolette said. "I couldn't bear to let anything hurt her. I really couldn't. I only want her to get well and be happy. I know she can't bear any serious worries . . ."

"Yes, that's what concerns me," Chessie said. "She seems very concerned. Tonight, particularly, she seems pale and far too nervous. May I ask . . . ? I wonder if you have any idea what might be upsettin' her so much. This is just between you and me. I'll never breathe a word of what you tell me . . ."

"I swear I don't know!" Jolette said. "I'd do anything to keep her from worrying. Clayton . . . I know she's worried sick about your brother Clayton. And of course the war and all. But nothing else I know of. Really, Chessie . . ."

"Jolette, calm down," Chessie said. She was startled and touched by Jolette's obvious feeling for her mother. "I didn't mean to upset you."

Jolette looked so miserable that Chessie was thankful when Dunbar returned with two other officers.

They were Rawley Collins and Davis Markson. They were both drunk and in high spirits about going off to fight the Yankees. Chessie had grown up with both of them.

Collins, a tall, red-headed man with a full red beard, held special memories for Chessie. He had been the first boy to kiss her, when she was just sixteen, at another party on this same Sumrall plantation. For a few weeks after that kiss she had thought she would some day marry Rawley but the feeling seemed long past. Now he was happily married to a Natchez woman and had three children.

The officers' drunken, witty, flirtatious talk picked up Chessie's spirits and she and Dunbar enjoyed another waltz together before he suggested they take a walk.

For nearly half an hour Chessie and Dunbar strolled, hand in hand, through the gardens and arbors behind the Sumralls' house. They pulled scuppernong grapes from the overhanging vines and ate them and when they kissed, the grape pulp was sweet and yellow-green on their lips.

Then, standing in front of the rose-covered gazebo as sudden lightning lit their faces, Dunbar took Chessie's hand and told her he was in love with her. If he came back safely from the war, he said, he wanted to ask her to marry him.

Chessie was touched by Dunbar's declaration, but replied honestly. She spoke of her deep affection for him, of her respect. She said that she did love him, but that she was not in love with him, which was much different.

"Perhaps . . . perhaps my feelin's will deepen by the time you return," Chessie said. "I do love you, Dunbar . . . in an affectionate way. Maybe . . . maybe later I'll feel that I can marry you, but I can't promise for sure . . ."

"Oh, Chessie!" Dunbar exclaimed, but thunder nearly drowned out his expressions of love and then rain chased them into the gazebo.

Inside, in the shadowy shelter of the garden house, their kisses became boldly passionate and Dunbar's hands found Chessie's breasts with a knowing hunger that brought an unexpected response from Chessie's tense body. She found herself eager and returned Dunbar's kisses with fervor.

Soon he had slipped her gown off her shoulders and she was naked from the waist up. She groaned softly. Her fingers dug into his hair as he sucked her taut nipples. The rain lashed the gazebo and sprays of splashing rain left them damp and shivering despite the heat of their passion.

A desperate sadness engulfed Chessie. She felt a staggering sense of loneliness, even of friends lost and leaving, of her life changed for all time.

In reaction she kissed Dunbar's ear and sought his lips with her own. She held him tighter. Dunbar was her only anchor. He truly loved her. She understood his urgent love. And understanding it, she felt a responsibility for it. She could not respond to his love the way he wanted. But she could respond to his need and give him some pleasure before the harsh reality of war. Her body begged her to respond, urged her . . .

Chessie began to surrender to his passion, and her own, began to drift into an ecstasy of excitement . . .

Dunbar lifted her skirts and slid his fingers along her upper thighs. She tensed. Her thighs stiffened. Sudden, unbidden memories of Count Croce's attack on her came flooding back, and her mind flashed images of his huge penis, her helplessness, pain, humiliation, her vulnerable body being opened and invaded . . .

"No, no, I can't," she gasped, twisting away from Dunbar's frantic hands. "Dunbar, please! No, dammit, get away from me!" she snapped.

"Please! What have I done?" he asked.

Lightning flashed and his face showed such love and pain that she regretted her harsh words. She could not be cruel to Dunbar. She could not deny him now that she had worked his passion to the exploding point. He was leaving, he loved her, he might be wounded, or worse . . .

"Nothin', it's all right, Dunbar," Chessie whispered as she caressed his feverish cheeks. "I . . . I can't do quite what you want. But I . . . I want to make you happy. Here, lie down between my thighs. Like that, with your pants on. Yes, now, can't you . . . That's right, darlin' . . ."

She felt little excitement but she wrapped her thighs around his heaving body and endured his passion until he thrust so hard he hurt her, thrust again, then gasped and collapsed on her rigid body.

Chessie lay wrapped around Dunbar, cradled him, spoke softly to him. She felt lonely and sad and tears formed in her eyes, and she thought of what she had lost and wondered what the future held for her.

65.

Chessie sat beside Dunbar's bed in the Natchez hospital and tried not to flinch as she held his withered hand. His gray flesh was flaky in some places, oddly sleek in others. He had no fingernails. She could not look at his face, which had lost its lashes and eyebrows. And he was bald.

Though he could speak only in a coarse whisper, Dunbar insisted on talking. He said that he still loved Chessie but that he could never expect her to return that love now, or expect her to marry him. He spoke without bitterness or self-pity. He spoke matter-of-factly, as though resigned to his hopeless condition.

Chessie held his hand tighter and promised him that his condition made no difference. Then, in a fit of despair and pity, she lied and insisted that while he had been off fighting in Tennessee she had decided that she did indeed love him and wanted to marry him.

Dunbar protested, and their visit ended in this argument when a pipe-smoking steward chased Chessie out, insisting that visiting hours had been over for a quarter-hour.

Chessie shuddered as she followed the steward through the crowded wards. It was a scene of horror she knew she would never forget. Dozens of men, many of whom she had known since childhood, were now grotesque cripples, ruined, withered, hairless, without fingernails, some blind. Some of them stared up at nothing with huge, colorless eyes, others cried out in their misery or moaned in drugged sleep.

Chessie was thankful that both Rawley Collins and Davis Markson were sleeping, so that she did not have to say good-bye to them. They, too, had been poisoned and deformed, and Rawley was so embittered and murderous that he had to be tied to his cot.

Most of these soldiers had been wounded while fighting with General Albert Sidney Johnston at Ft. Henry in Tennessee. Their wounds had caused them to be sent home to recuperate away from the battle zone, and they had expected to return to the fighting within a month.

"And most of them would have recovered, I'm certain," Dr. Telson had told Chessie. "We had all the right facilities and medicine. At least I thought we did. Oh, when I think that I prescribed that painkiller, Chessie! I helped create this horror. But how could I have known that some money-crazed devil had adulterated our medicine with a cheap poison to stretch his profits . . ."

Chessie swallowed a lump in her throat. Everyone said that only a monster could have been so greedy as to cause this suffering. It was hard to comprehend. With the Union blockade of Southern ports becoming more effective every day, all the blockade-runners who brought in munitions and medicine were making enormous profits—without having to resort to such hideous treachery as this.

As Chessie neared the door she thought of her argument with Dunbar. He knew she had lied. She had never fallen in love with him. And she did not know how she could live with him now. Yet she knew she must try. Dunbar loved her. He must have some reason to live. And so must she. Perhaps he would get better . . . though the doctor held out little hope.

Cellus was waiting with Dr. Telson in the corridor outside the ward. They talked of the deformed soldiers for a minute. All Natchez could talk of little else. Dr. Telson seemed to have aged years in the past few weeks. His voice broke as he spoke. Cellus was angry, as angry as Chessie had ever seen him.

"What kind of man would do such a thing?" Cellus asked. "He should be hanged twice for this. What is it, Doctor? What did he put into the medicine to cause such sufferin'?"

Patiently, the doctor explained that the medicine was derived from a plant called hellebore and that someone had substituted a poisonous form of hellebore, which was cheap and plentiful for the benign, healing hellebore, which was scarce and expensive.

"The poisonous kind grows everywhere in Adams County," the doctor said. "You've probably seen it. It has greenish flowers and large leaves . . ."

"What folks call Indian-poke?" Cellus asked.

"Indian-poke, that's right," Doctor Telson said.

"Old Aunt Froney, the healer out at The Columns, why, I've heard her talk of Indian-poke," Cellus said. "She keeps some in her cabin, says it'll cure you, if she likes, or kill you, if she chooses . . ."

"I hope she can tell the difference between the two kinds," the doctor said.

"Have they any idea who could have adulterated the medicine?" Chessie asked.

"No, not yet," Dr. Telson said. "With all these wounded boys comin' in here, we've had to purchase medicine in a hurry. There was a lot of confusion and with the increasin' shortages, we'd been takin' the medicine from anyone selling it, and often in huge lots. It will be difficult to find out who's to blame, I'm afraid."

Chessie and Cellus said good-bye and left. Chessie was so relieved to get out of the hospital that she felt ashamed. She took several deep breaths of fresh air as she climbed into the carriage, then she avoided Cellus' eyes and thoughts of Dunbar as the driver cracked the whip and the carriage lurched forward.

66.

Cellus and Chessie were a quarter of a mile from The Columns when they heard the first shot. It was followed by a steady barrage of gunfire, and Chessie shouted for the driver to whip the horses into a gallop.

As they drove onto the house road, a file of Confederate soldiers rode along the horizon in front of the swamp, firing their pistols. There were shouts, a scream.

"You shouldn't go any closer, Miss Chessie," Cellus said.

"No," she said. "I want to see what's happenin'. I'm worried about Mama. And the people."

Over Cellus' protests they drove on up to the house, where two gray-clad soldiers with rifles helped Chessie out of the carriage.

"What's wrong?" Chessie asked. "Where's my mother? . . ."

Lucinda hurried out the door. She was even paler than usual. "I'm right here, dear," she said. "I'm fine, though I did have something of a fright for a few minutes."

"They come right out of the swamp, Miss," one of the soldiers said. "Bunch of runaways, couple of 'em had guns, too. Took to raidin' you folks' storehouse, and in broad, open daylight, too. Lucky we was just down the road."

"Where are they now? Was anybody hurt?"

"Well, Miss, they done high-tailed it back into the swamp," the soldier said. "Captain Dickson and some of the boys chasin' 'em. He left me and Musgrove here to look after you folks. Captain's a good man. Got good nigger-dogs with him. Right as not, he'll catch the lot of 'em."

"Nobody's been able to catch them yet," Lucinda said. "I hope your captain is as good as you say. None of our people were hurt, Chessie. It would seem the swamp niggers weren't out to hurt anyone, just to steal food and, Lord knows, with what goes to the armies and all, we have precious little to spare."

"I'm so glad nobody was hurt!" Chessie said. "Where's Jolette? And Anthony?"

"Jolette's visitin' at the Sumralls'," Lucinda said. "And Anthony grabbed his gun and rode after the soldiers, before I could stop him. I wish he hadn't gone. But you know how he hates those niggers. He worries that they'll harm us one day."

"He'll be all right, Mama," Chessie said. "There seemed to be a lot of soldiers."

Chessie and her mother and Cellus all went inside to wait. Lucinda sent out refreshments for the soldiers. As Chessie sat in the parlor she worried about her mother's condition and decided to ask the doctor to come out the next day. I'll do that, Chessie resolved, but worrying won't help anything. She got up and went to see if she could help in the kitchen.

Anthony and the soldiers returned from the swamp three hours later, sweating and cut by thorn-vines and bruised by low-slung limbs that had ambushed them in the darkness. One soldier had been grazed by a bullet and he was sent back to camp. Captain Dickson and his other men accepted Lucinda's offer of a light supper and whiskey.

The captain had not been as efficient as his soldier had boasted, though the fleeing Negroes had been tracked to their camp in the swamp.

"We killed one of 'em," the captain said.

"Do you think they'll try to come back tonight?" Lucinda asked. "After all, they didn't get away with any food and they must have been desperately hungry to have attempted a raid in daylight."

"I doubt it," the captain said, "but just to be on the safe side, I'll leave a few men here overnight. I don't imagine the niggers are doin' all this on their own, by the way. I'd bet a bundle they got a Yankee agent hidin' out with 'em, tryin' to stir up trouble, tryin' to weaken the war effort here well behind the front lines."

"That may be true," Lucinda said.

"Well, we got to be gettin' back to camp," Captain Dickson said. "Lieutenant, form up the column and leave six men here. Ma'am, Miss, Sir, on behalf of my men I want to thank you for your hospitality . . ."

Good-byes were exchanged and the soldiers rode off, with six men deployed around the house and slave quarters.

Chessie was awakened by shots during the night. She huddled down in her bed, then sat with her arms wrapped around her knees. She waited a minute, two minutes, five minutes. Her heart pounded. She knew she should stay in her room, where she was safe. But her curiosity got the better of her, and her determination to save her mother from this emergency, whatever it was.

She dressed quietly and crept out of her room and down the stairs. Most of the lamps were out and the two that burned were so low that Chessie could barely make her way down the stairs and into the front hall.

After a few steps she stopped. She barely dared to breathe. She was certain that someone was nearby, in the shadows, or just inside the parlor door, which was partly ajar.

A board creaked. She thought of Yankees, of the raiding runaways. Where were the soldiers? She glanced around frantically, trying to decide whether to run back up the stairs or out onto the veranda where she might call to the soldiers. After all, there had been shooting. Perhaps the soldiers had chased someone away and were now gone. Perhaps some Negro had sneaked past them and now stood in the shadows, ready to grab her . . .

Another board creaked. A huge shadow filled the doorway. Chessie gasped and bolted back toward the stairs, her hands raised in front of her face.

A scream caught in her throat . . . And then she saw that the figure was Anthony, a pistol in his hand.

She sighed with relief but the sigh also caught in her throat. Anthony had leveled the pistol at her. And he had not turned it away, even though he was staring right at her. Chessie was shocked with fear. Was he going to shoot her?

"Anthony!" she shouted.

He lowered the pistol.

"Christ, it's only you, Chessie," he muttered. "What in hell are you doing down here? I damned near shot you."

"I heard gunfire," Chessie said. "I was worried. What happened? Did they come back?"

"No, they didn't," Anthony said. "We haven't seen hair nor hide of any niggers. But the soldiers did capture some Yankee bastard they think is the one stirrin' up the niggers."

"A Yankee? You mean, a white man?"

"Yes, a white man. He was on horseback coming along the house road. Now go on back to bed, where you belong."

"Oh, I couldn't sleep," she said. "And I want to . . ."

Chessie was interrupted by a man's figure looming in the front doorway. Anthony swung his pistol around. But it was only a soldier.

"Mr. Walker, sir, we got the Yankee out here, all trussed up, and we . . . Oh, mornin', Miss, I didn't see you there. Like I said, we got the Yankee tied up and two of the boys takin' him back to camp. He's a Yankee spy, for sure. Don't even know how to talk proper. He's speakin' some foreign language, but he can't fool us none. It's a hangin' for him, sure as shootin'..."

"Well, then, get him out of here," Anthony said. "I don't give a damn what you do with him."

Chessie stepped to the front door. In the faint moonlight she saw three figures, two soldiers with rifles slung over their shoulders and a tall, slim man between them with his hands tied behind his back.

Another poor man has to die, she thought, sadly. She resented his being a Yankee spy, resented his trespassing on The Columns, his stirring up the Negroes. The Lord only knew how much harm and suffering he had caused. But Chessie was beginning to hate the reality of war and suffering and death and her visits to the hospital had both saddened her and hardened her.

She started to walk away but a sudden movement caught her eyes. There was something familiar about the man who was struggling between the soldiers. He reminded her of . . . She looked again. He was muttering, cursing. Then, as the man turned in a desperate attempt to twist free, a soldier raised his rifle butt to club him into submission.

Chessie burst into tears as the man saw her and called out, "Chessie, Chessie."

"Stop! Oh, dear God, don't hurt him!" Chessie screamed as she ran out the door, but the rifle butt had already silenced Carlo and he crumpled to the ground.

67.

By the time Carlo awoke an hour later in the parlor at The Columns, Chessie had been transported into an ecstasy of love and excitement. She hugged and kissed Carlo and they talked rapidly in Italian and joked about the few English words that Carlo knew. Then she kissed him again and clung to him as if she would never let go.

Bit by bit, Carlo told her the story of his journey—how he had taken a ship to New Orleans and how there and in Natchez he had little difficulty because so many people spoke Italian and French. But outside of Natchez, riding toward The Columns, he hadn't been able to make himself understood to anyone—especially to the suspicious, illiterate soldiers who had captured him.

"My poor darlin'!" Chessie gasped. "They might have killed you!" Her eyes filled with tears, but then she forgot tears and began kissing him again.

A few minutes later, Chessie called in her mother, who had been waiting circumspectly outside the parlor door. Next she summoned Anthony and Jolette and Cellus and the house slaves and introduced them all to Carlo.

Fifteen minutes later Chessie wanted to be alone with Carlo again. She had never felt so happy or so excited. And she felt utterly changed. I can't believe it, I can't believe it, she thought, and then she said it aloud to Carlo.

"I believe it, Chessie," he whispered. "It's true, and only because we both wanted it to be. Nothing could stop me from coming to you. I hope you'll never know what I suffered to come here. I've vowed to myself never to tell you and never to think of it again. All that matters now is that we're together."

"Carlo," Chessie whispered, "I love you so much ... so much!" Taking his hand, she kissed it, and then led him out of the house. "I want to show you the plantation, and let the plantation see you."

As they walked, the sun rose bright red over the swamp. Chessie showed Carlo the barn and other outbuildings, the rose garden and the gazebo. Then they went into the quarters, where the people were getting ready for their day's work. They smelled cookfires, bacon frying, coffee boiling. Everywhere they walked the people looked at them with astonishment then joy, as they saw, unmistakably, that Miss Chessie's young man had come to her.

"It's a miracle!" Chessie cried out, her face lit with a smile.

"Love will find a way," one old woman muttered.

"Good morning, good morning," Carlo said, trying out his English on the slaves. Everyone smiled and laughed at his pronunciation and they were curious and awed when Chessie told them that he had come all the way from Italy.

Next, Chessie and Carlo walked through the dew-soaked cotton fields. They talked little during this walk, but they held hands and half a dozen times they stopped to kiss and hold each other.

Finally, when the sun was already high, they went inside the house to eat breakfast with the family. As they entered the dining room, Chessie left Carlo's side for a brief moment and ran to her mother.

"Mama," she whispered. "I'm so happy, and I want you to love him as much as I do!"

Breakfast was an ample meal of ham and beaten biscuits, hoecakes and grits, which Carlo had never tasted, and pronounced, very solemnly, to be delicious. Chessie translated all the conversation for Carlo, and translated his remarks to her family, but she found that she resented sharing him with her family, at least just yet, and before he had finished his second cup of coffee, she jumped up and announced that she and Carlo wanted to go out riding, though Carlo had not voiced such a desire.

So Ed saddled two horses and they set off, riding through the green fields just being plowed in preparation for the spring planting. Chessie was careful to avoid the swamp and hesitated about riding into the forest on the other side of the house road. But surely the soldiers had scared off the runaways, and with the troops so near the plantation she felt safe enough.

And any risk was worth it, she decided, just to be alone with Carlo all morning, to look into his eyes and caress his scar and kiss and talk.

Carlo knew that Clayton had disappeared, but they had not yet spoken about him. As they rode in the forest, Carlo questioned Chessie about her brother.

"I'm afraid, very afraid," Chessie told him, "that we'll never see him again, although Mother still hopes . . ." Her voice broke, and Carlo rode closer to her and leaned over to kiss her cheek.

He asked, then, how she had escaped Rome. Chessie hesitated. She lowered her eyes to avoid Carlo's. Whenever she allowed herself to think of it, the lasting shame and taint of being raped overwhelmed her. It had happened and could never be changed. She could never be pure for Carlo, he could never be her first lover, and she was afraid that he could not love her if he knew the truth.

Trembling, she told him that she and Torine had managed to get on board an American ship, believing that Clayton had already made it safely out of Rome.

Carlo seemed satisfied.

"And you, darlin'?" Chessie asked. "What happened with you . . . and Count Croce?"

"When I left the apartment in Rome," Carlo explained, "I was arrested almost at once. I was so glad that you weren't with me! Anyway, Croce captured me and imprisoned me. Yes, his men tortured me, but I didn't tell them what they wanted to hear. Afterwards, I was kept in prison and a few months later, I managed to escape. First, I traveled south to see Garibaldi. I began at once to make arrangements to come here to America, to you, Chessie. But before I left, I did what I had to do. I went up to Frascati and when the count was alone in the lower park of his villa, I confronted him, with swords, and challenged him to a duel."

"Oh, Carlo, how dangerous!" Chessie exclaimed. She was bewildered. "Did you hate him so much? Darlin', you could have been killed! We might never have seen each other again . . ."

"I had to, Chessie," he said. "I swore that I'd make him pay for what he did to . . . to me. Otherwise I couldn't have survived it. And I knew I'd win the duel.

My love was too strong to allow me to die at his hands."

"Still, when I think that you . . . So he's dead. Count Croce's dead . . ."

She realized she was trembling. She was not sorry that Carlo had killed the count. Yet, despite her bitterness, Count Croce had saved her from Rafaella. If not for him, she would not be standing here with Carlo. She would be dead, or worse, still in Rafaella's hands, as she feared her brother was, or had been.

"Chessie, what's wrong?" Carlo asked. "Darling, don't cry!"

"Am I cryin'?" she asked. "They're just tears of happiness, darlin'. I'm afraid I can't control my emotions this mornin'. But enough talk. We have plenty of time to talk about everything. And we've had so few kisses."

For the next hour there were many kisses, some soft and some passionate, and some gentle petting as they lay on a bed of pine needles in an isolated part of the wood. When they lay together Chessie could feel his blood pound and was aware of his erect penis. His touch, his body, thrilled and frightened her. More than anything, she wanted to surrender her body to Carlo, but she was cautious and hesitant. Her memory of being raped was still vivid and troubled her, mixing with her confusion about whether to tell Carlo that it had happened.

There's time, plenty of time, Chessie told herself, and as the days passed and became weeks, she became more and more relaxed with Carlo, and less anxious when he was out of her sight. No one was surprised when they announced their engagement and began to make plans for a wedding.

Carlo had begun to study English and was an apt pupil. By choice, he and Chessie spent most of their days alone together: walking and talking, riding in the cool mornings and evenings, planning for their future and delighting in their mutual happiness.

Still, both of them managed to keep their passions reined, although one lazy afternoon Chessie became so excited by Carlo's kisses that she became the aggressor and felt a wonderful trembling inside her body.

"Darlin'!" she gasped, clinging to Carlo, feeling the trembling build to a peak and overwhelm her before Carlo withdrew his hands from her thighs and his lips from her lips.

When it had subsided, Chessie gave into tears.

"What is it? What's wrong?" Carlo asked.

"Nothin's wrong, nothin'," she said.

"Chessie," Carlo said softly, "I think the time has come. I love you and I want to make love to you."

"And I want you to," Chessie whispered. "More than anythin' in the world."

And so, very gently, Carlo undressed her, removing her gown and long petticoats one by one, unfastening her camisole and admiring her.

"Bella, bellissima," he whispered, "you're so beautiful and I love you so much . . ."

I must tell him, I must, Chessie thought, and she opened her mouth to explain about Count Croce and what he had done, but Carlo closed her mouth with a kiss, and set about caressing her body so that she lost all powers of speech.

"Chessie, I loved you from the first moment I saw you in Palermo," Carlo confessed, "and I would've crossed the ocean ten times to be with you like this."

Trembling, he removed his own clothes and took Chessie into his arms. Very tenderly, he kissed her lips. She was so lovely, so fragile, so maddening. The soft light, shaded by the bougainvillaea and moon-flower vines that hung over them, played across her pale, naked body and bathed her face.

Then, as Carlo watched, Chessie's eyes opened and clouded with hesitation and an expression that was unmistakably fear.

"There's somethin' I must tell you," she said. "Somethin' happened to me . . . in Rome. Count Croce . . ." A sob caught in her throat and she looked down. Swallowing, she continued. "Against my will, he . . . violated me ...."

"Chessie, I knew it and I never want you to think of it again," Carlo said.

"You knew? I thought . . . I feared that you could never love me if you knew."

"Darling, why do you think I was determined to kill him? But we'll never speak of it or of him again. I know he must have hurt you terribly! It makes me furious to think of it. And I've tried, for your sake, to be very very gentle with you, not to force you ...."

"You could never force me to make love to you, Carlo, because it's what I want," Chessie said, and opened her arms to him.

Carlo held her so close she could feel him trembling, feel his stiff penis between her legs as he kissed her and stroked her ever so gently, running his hands over her reddish-gold hair, kissing her neck and shoulders and ears. Chessie sighed with pleasure.

Her skin tingled at his touch and she felt herself responding to his needs and her own with easy, instinctive confidence. Carlo had stirred her profoundly and she opened to him naturally, like a sensitive flower blooming in the moonlight.

His fingers aroused her and delighted her. Her skin was flushed but she shivered, then cried out with passion and felt the wonderful trembling beginning again as he entered her and filled her with his strength and his love.

Afterwards, they lay together and kissed until the afternoon light had begun to fade and they heard hoofbeats on the house road that signaled the return of the family from town.

68.

Chessie's happiness from the pleasure of frequent lovemaking with Carlo and the round of pre-wedding parties and showers was offset, during the next few weeks, by Lucinda's lingering illness and her own indecision and guilt about Dunbar Polk.

Lucinda had not improved and on Dr. Telson's recommendation she had traveled to New Orleans to visit specialists there, but they could not cure her. Lucinda was depressed as well as ill. She had accepted the fact that she would never see Clayton again and this had weakened her condition. She was under the constant supervision of her nurses and took increasingly large doses of the medicine which Dr. Telson prescribed.

But, to Chessie's relief and joy, Lucinda adored Carlo and she took it on herself to tutor him in English. They spent many hours together, and these were the only times Chessie saw her mother laugh.

As for Dunbar, Chessie had continued to visit him in the hospital regularly. Each time she saw him she intended to tell him about Carlo. But, each time, faced with his suffering and his debilitated condition, she continued to lie, despite his constant vows that he would never let her marry him.

Anthony was often away on business, which pleased Chessie, and Jolette was often in Natchez, visiting friends.

Chessie and Carlo were kept busy, with Chessie running the house, and helping nurse Lucinda, and Carlo giving himself an education in how to run a cotton plantation. Finally, however, Carlo could no longer conceal his aversion to slavery and he and Chessie had several serious arguments on the subject.

Still, their love and happiness were too great for

any of their arguments to last long or become bitter. One rainy night they settled an argument with kisses and Carlo promised that, as a wedding gift, he wouldn't bring up the matter again until after they were married.

Carlo was ambivalent about the war. He'd seen enough of fighting and killing in Italy and couldn't muster any enthusiasm for a war that might endanger him and Chessie, a war that defended the institution of slavery. Yet the longer he lived in Mississippi the better he came to understand the determination of Mississippians not to be "ruled" by the "foreign, alien" Yankees. They were the same sort of sentiments, after all, that had prevailed in Sicily when Garibaldi landed at Marsala.

In public, Carlo never revealed his true feelings about slavery and the war. He maintained a pose of mild enthusiasm, since his happiness and Chessie's were all that really mattered to him. Any position other than enthusiasm would have been dangerous, despite the Deavors family's prestige and influence, for a strong tide of patriotism had swept Adams County. There was little public dissent. Everyone felt that the South was the injured party, that God backed the South's cause, and that if the Union persisted in trying to use force then the Union would be taught a military lesson it would be a long time in forgetting.

This strong patriotism became a kind of xenophobia and the foreign-born in Natchez were watched closely and suspiciously for their sentiments and their actions. In reaction, many of the foreign-born became particularly fervent supporters of the war effort. When the first Confederate war bonds were offered in April, foreign-born were among the first subscribers in Natchez, as were three free Negroes who lived in the city.

Carlo also made the public gesture of buying these bonds.

As time passed, everyone's daily life became more and more closely involved with the war. At The Columns, the arrival of a newspaper or a friend with news was a major event. In Natchez, there was consternation every time a boat or wagon transport arrived, for they inevitably brought wounded men and news of others.

Feelings ran high and there was general compassion for the suffering and the dead, particularly for the wounded men who had been poisoned by the adulterated painkiller. Outrageously, those responsible for the bad medicine had not yet been caught.

But in general the war, and particularly any sense of danger, seemed far away, even though the Union army in the west, under a new general, U.S. Grant, had pushed Confederate troops out of Kentucky and taken two forts in Tennessee. Jeff Davis, the president of the Confederacy, had sent one of his best generals, Albert Sidney Johnston, to Tennessee, and people felt sure Johnston would take care of the Union army in short order.

In any case, that fighting on land was over four hundred miles away. No one expected the fighting to come much closer or last much longer, and with the Confederate forts on the Mississippi and the boat-blockading rams in the river, there seemed no way Union boats could come down the river, either.

David Farragut might patrol off the Gulf Coast with his armada but there was no way his Union ships could get past Forts Jackson and St. Philip and make the four-day run up the river to Natchez.

However, Farragut's blockade had made itself felt in other ways.

One evening early in April the Roccalinis gave a party in honor of a Natchez rifle company that was leaving at dawn the next day. It was not a party in the Roccalinis' usual style.

The four hundred people who attended found no imported wines or champagnes to drink, no oysters or caviar or delicacies from Europe. None of the ladies appeared in fine, high-fashion gowns from the east or the Continent. They all wore plain, serviceable home-spun, some of it rather roughly woven on their grand-mothers' looms that had been pulled out of storage in their attics. Instead of lavish bonnets from Paris or New York, the ladies wore hats of palmetto fronds, decorated with dogwood and other spring flowers.

Shortages were still so new that it all seemed almost like a game, a grand patriotic game that everyone was playing. If there was no wine or champagne there was plenty of "good Mississippi drinkin' whiskey" and plenty of turkey and ham and catfish and trout. Every-one was determined to be cheerful and the music and dancing were as lively as ever.

At the Roccalini party, the dancing went on until dawn, when it was time for the rifle company to leave for the depot. Some three thousand people had gath-ered there to send off the troops aboard a train hung with the bright stars-and-bars of the Confederacy. There were flags of every size and fabric, flags that had been made of scraps by poor women and flags stitched in elegant parlors of the finest linens and silks.

The people gathered sang the French revolutionary song, the "Marseillaise," and revolutionary songs com-posed for the Confederacy, such as "Adieu to the Star-Spangled Banner Forever." As the train carrying the drunken, cheering troops pulled out of the station a band played "The Grand Secession March."

More serious were the shortages of essentials such as soap and candles. But experimentation soon eased these shortages. It was found that an adequate soap could be made from the fruit of the chinaberry tree, dissolved in lye. And cottonseed oil, burning in lamps, took the place of candles.

Chessie and Carlo and the others at The Columns joked about the shortages and their "Confederate home-spun high fashion," but their life went on, rather more happily than not. Chessie and Carlo had set a date for their wedding and still took a ride into the forest each day to make love in secret bowers and to renew their vows to each other.

Time passed, and Chessie continued to fret about Dunbar. She continued to visit him in the hospital, but could not bring herself to tell him she was in love and engaged to be married. Finally, she resolved that she must go into Natchez the next day and tell him the truth about Carlo—a truth that even his family had spared him so far.

But that evening, when Dr. Telson came out to visit Lucinda, he brought word that Dunbar Polk had shot himself to death in his hospital bed that afternoon.

Two days later, Chessie and Carlo went into Natchez together to attend Dunbar's funeral. Jolette was visiting friends in Rodney and Chessie was reluctant to leave Lucinda alone, but Anthony insisted that Chessie had an obligation to attend the funeral. She need not worry, he assured her, for he would look after Lucinda himself, sit with her and make certain she took her medicine.

Dunbar's casket was closed and the service was mercifully short but Chessie was so weakened by her grief that Carlo had to take her back to the Roccalinis, where they were staying, and give her a brandy and put her to bed.

That night she had nightmares of choking, of being smothered, and she slept little. Finally, just before dawn, she fell asleep.

She was awakened an hour later by Cellus, who stood grim-faced and trembling by the bed.

"Your mama," he said, his voice breaking. "She passed away durin' the night."

69.

Lucinda Deavors' funeral was a simple affair. The Very Reverend John Kilbourne conducted the service and so many of the family's friends and neighbors made their way to The Columns to pay their respects that the house road was choked with carriages and there was not enough room in the house for all the sweet-smelling wreaths and bouquets. Chessie had cried so hard all the day of the funeral that at the service itself she was ashen-faced and dry-eyed.

When her mother's coffin was lowered into its grave in the small family cemetery, Chessie winced in pain, and Carlo, fearing for her, escorted her directly back to the house. For an hour after the service she sat speechlessly in the front parlor, barely able to acknowledge the expressions of grief and affection from her mother's friends.

Despite Carlo's love and support, Chessie felt terribly alone. She had lost Clayton, and now her mother. She was the only remaining Deavors. Now she was mistress of The Columns and responsible for all the operations of the vast plantation and the hundreds of slaves who lived there.

She doubted that she had the strength to run the plantation, even with Carlo's help, and she remembered all the times she had resented Clayton's inheriting The Columns. How glad she'd be, she thought, to have him here now. Thinking of Clayton was painful, all the more so because she still did not know for sure if he were alive or dead.

"Darling, it will all be better when we're married," Carlo said softly, and Chessie nodded, though she had no enthusiasm for weddings, or for anything else. She had never felt so exhausted or dispirited.

As Chessie brushed back tears and felt she would

smother in the cloying scent of the floral tributes, a delegation from the quarters arrived. Seeing them, Chessie sat up straighter, determined not to cry.

She might be allowed to seem indifferent to the gestures of friends and relatives, but she had a serious obligation to the people. She knew they would be worried and frightened by Lucinda's death. They might have known Chessie all her life but a new mistress always disturbed slaves, particularly one who was about to marry a foreigner they had known for only a short time.

All of the slaves had attended the funeral, standing in the background. Now, as was the custom at The Columns, their delegation was coming to acknowledge their new mistress for the first time.

The slaves were dressed in their best clothes, neatly washed and ironed. The men were freshly shaved. Some of them were red-eyed and had obviously been crying.

Chessie fought back her own tears as she stood to accept their condolences and their pledges of loyalty. She hugged each of them in turn, and promised that she would continue to treat them as the Deavors family had always treated them and promised that, as always, no Deavors slave would ever be sold out of the family.

After five minutes they left and Chessie turned to comfort Anna Roccalini, Lucinda's closest friend, who was sobbing uncontrollably. Grief-stricken as she was, Chessie knew that her mother would be sorely missed by all her friends—Jolette among them. Jolette had become hysterical when she heard of Lucinda's death and now sat in the opposite corner of the parlor, crying quietly and trembling as she talked with Anthony.

Chessie couldn't hear what they were saying but the tone of their voices indicated that they were arguing. She rather resented Jolette and Anthony arguing at such a time. It was disrespectful and would not help anyone.

"Bastard!" Chessie heard Jolette say as she jumped up and stumbled out of the room.

Anthony limped after her. There was an embarrassed silence in the parlor for a minute, then Cellus broke the tension by calling for the servants to serve supper to the guests.

The next day there did not appear to be any further dissension between Anthony and Jolette. They kept their distance from each other. But now it was Cellus whose behavior upset Chessie.

Characteristically, Cellus' face never showed any emotion, but Chessie noticed now that he wore an expression of pure menace whenever he went near Anthony. He seemed angry and was barely civil to Anthony. Even in allowing for his grief, Chessie found this behavior intolerable. She tried to ignore it, but the few remaining family members were thrown together too closely for this to work, and as Cellus' hostility continued to be obvious, she resolved that she must say something to him.

It's up to me, Chessie told herself, and realizing that for the first time in her life she was angry at Cellus she also realized, for the first time, that she was his mistress. She owned Cellus. The thought shocked her and did more to weaken her belief in slavery than a lifetime's stories of brutality or all of Carlo's arguments.

Chessie could not bear the thought that she might have to scold or discipline Cellus. The idea was preposterous. Cellus was so . . . old. He had been the mainstay of the Deavors family since long before she was born.

Yet what was she to do? His hostility was painful for all of them. She had never seen him behave in such a way and as the next day went on, endless rainy hour after hour, he did not alter his attitude toward Anthony.

Chessie told herself that she could not shirk her responsibility any longer. If she had to assert her authority as mistress, she might as well begin immediately. In time, she would come to depend on Carlo, she knew, but he was not yet a full-fledged family member, so she must handle Cellus herself.

Chessie summoned Cellus to the study and waited in the old, oaken swivel chair at the rolltop desk. Her heart began to pound.

When Cellus came into the study, she could not look into his face.

"Cellus, I asked you here," she began, "to . . . sit down, please."

She had no idea what to say. She remembered that her mother had told her that whenever three generations of Deavorses had summoned Cellus to the study to discuss plantation business, they always began with the gesture of offering him whiskey, which he accepted but seldom drank.

"Would you like some whiskey?" Chessie asked.

Cellus accepted her offer. He took one sip, then set the glass on the desk.

"Oh, Cellus, I'm goin' to depend on you so much," she said. "I can't take on all this responsibility without your help, even with Carlo. You're like a Deavors . . . You and I are the only real Deavorses left, Cellus . . ."

"Yes'm, I know, Miss Chessie," he said. "And you can depend on me. Just like your family always has, for all these years. Don't you worry. You'll make a fine mistress for The Columns. I've always thought you would, thought you'd be the best Deavors to run the place."

"Oh, Cellus, thank you. I . . . But since the funeral you've been, well . . . I know you've been grievin' and all, but, I don't know how to put it . . ."

He interrupted her. "I know I upset you with the way I acted," he said. "I'm sorry, Miss Chessie. The mood's gone now and I'll let the past be the past. What's done is done, I reckon."

"What do you mean?" Chessie asked.

"Nothin'. It's just that . . . Well, we got to go on livin', Miss Chessie. That's what your mama would have wanted. Take care of the family and the place and people. And you got yourself a fine young man, and soon there'll be children."

Cellus spoke without emotion. There was no expression at all on his dark, wrinkled face, but something about his voice and his manner disturbed Chessie. He wasn't being entirely honest with her, she sensed. But she had done her best, avoided a confrontation, and all she wanted now was to go to bed.

70.

The next day news of a terrible battle in Tennessee reached Natchez, and, like everyone else, Chessie was caught up in the news and temporarily forgot her grief.

General Johnston and General Beauregard had attacked Grant's Union Army, which had its back to the Tennessee River near Pittsburgh Landing, at a place called Shiloh Church. The surprise attack caught Grant's troops unprepared and for the first day they were nearly pushed into the river. But the Union Army held and then came disaster for the Confederates. A second Union Army arrived at dusk and General Johnston was killed in the attack.

The next day the Union counterattacked. Well armed and well organized, they turned the tide in the greatest battle ever fought in America and one of the bloodiest in the history of mankind. In the afternoon Beauregard ordered his battered troops to begin the retreat to Corinth, Mississippi.

As badly wounded survivors poured into Natchez they brought grim descriptions of the fighting that had killed 13,000 Union and 10,000 Confederate soldiers. Such casualty figures stunned the people of Natchez.

The xenophobia became rampant and there was a hint of panic. Some patriots demanded that every citizen be forced to swear an oath to the Confederacy and to wear a badge stating: "I'll fight to the death for Confederate rights." This measure wasn't adopted but the county grand jury was summoned to investigate any cases of disloyalty and indict anyone who spoke out against the Confederacy.

Much more ominously, a group of self-styled "prominent citizens" formed a vigilante group that operated secretly at night to hunt out spies or Union sympathizers.

Then the near-panic subsided and life returned to its pre-Shiloh pace. The fighting was still far away, with strong Confederate forces between Natchez and the enemy.

Chessie began to recover from her grief at her mother's death. She and Carlo set a new wedding date, the fifteenth of May, and both of them began to look forward to it. Together, they took charge of the plantation. The cotton was planted. Anthony was away most of the time, on business, and Jolette often visited out-of-town friends.

Chessie and Carlo resumed their rides and their lovemaking every day. Despite the war, life had a certain rhythm and certain satisfactions, although Chessie was still a bit worried about Cellus. He no longer displayed blatant hostility toward Anthony, but Chessie was certain that something serious was still on his mind.

Saturday, April 26, was a hot, sunny day. Chessie and Carlo went into Natchez to attend a party at night and shop during the day for whatever essential items they could find in the depleted showrooms and storerooms of Natchez merchants.

As usual, the streets of Natchez were busy and crowded. Women sipped tea in the Blue Bird Tearoom and men drank whiskey in a grayish haze of cigar smoke at the Parker House hotel. In dozens of less elegant places, less elegant men and women drank cheaper whiskey or beer. Under-the-Hill, on the Mississippi River, whores posed on the barges waiting for clients and the gambling halls and cockfight pits drew the usual crowds.

Then, in late afternoon, a church bell suddenly began to ring. Another followed. In a few minutes every bell in town was tolling. Cannons boomed. Everyone poured into the streets to hear the news, news that at first was greeted with disbelief: New Orleans had fallen to the Union!

Later reports confirmed it. Farragut's ships had launched a fierce mortar bombardment on the forts defending the city and during the night the ships had managed to withstand withering cannon fire and run upriver past the forts. New Orleans, which counted on the forts for defense, was helpless. The city had surrendered to General Butler and the forts surrendered soon after.

The people of Natchez heard the news with consternation. Natchez was only four days by steamboat from New Orleans. The Union army could be in Natchez in four days. Panic quickly became endemic. The war was suddenly so real that men were sick in the street and women fainted.

Everyone rushed about, shoring up their houses against attack and hiding any valuables they had not already hidden. People scurried to pack up their belongings and leave, if they could. Cotton was moved out of city warehouses into the country. Martial law was declared. The call went out for volunteers to defend Natchez.

Chessie and Carlo left Natchez for The Columns, so that they could prepare the slaves for the news and decide what to do.

They arrived at the plantation, weary and thirsty, to discover that the slaves had already gotten the word about the fall of New Orleans, "from some nigger over to the Sumrall place, and we hear he heard it from some nigger up the road . . ." Chessie wasn't surprised. It was common, she told Carlo, for slaves somehow to learn important news before the white people.

That night, Captain Dickson sent word to Chessie that he was fortifying the Deavors' landing and stationing a squad of men near The Columns immediately, in case any runaways taking Yankee orders tried to come out of the swamp to pillage and murder, or in case the Deavors' slaves got any of the same notions.

There was a strange mood in the quarters, Chessie had to admit, but she could not bring herself to believe that the family was in any danger from the slaves.

After supper, she and Carlo and Cellus made an inventory of all the family's fine paintings and furniture, the jewelry and silver and a few other valuables. Then, of course, there was the cotton stored in the barn. Anxiously, they made plans to take the cotton inland and to hide the valuables underground.

Chessie found Cellus to be even more morose than usual and she suspected that before the evening was over she would learn what was troubling him. When Carlo rode off with Theron Sumrall to discuss plans for the cotton with other planters in the area, Chessie was not surprised when Cellus asked if they could talk.

"Let's go into the study," Chessie said. "Would you like a whiskey?"

Cellus looked tired as he accepted the whiskey and slumped into a chair in the study. His face was impassive but Chessie was stunned to see how he had aged since her mother's death. Wrinkles that she had never seen before were now prominent around his deep-set eyes.

"I know somethin's wrong, Cellus," Chessie said. "What is it? Is it the Yankees comin'? The people? I've never seen you in such a state."

To Chessie, Cellus had always been indestructible, ageless, beyond normal human emotions, and in the midst of her growing apprehension, she had a sudden and poignant memory of being carried on his massive shoulders when she was a very small child.

"Well, Miss Chessie," he said, "the Yankees bein' so close and all, bound to arrive soon and change everything, maybe for all time, it's made me decide

332

to tell you somethin' I been keeping back . . . just in case anything happens to me . . ."

"Oh, Cellus! Nothin's goin' to happen to you! And what could be so terrible?"

"About the meanest thing I hope you ever have to hear," he said. "But you got to know, 'cause I'm afraid you might be in danger. That Anthony Walker! He wants this here plantation bad! I've known it all along, from the first time he set foot on this place . . ."

"Cellus, you're frightenin' me," Chessie said. "What do you have to tell me?"

"I've never killed a man," Cellus said, "but I almost decided to kill Anthony Walker. Miss Chessie, your mama didn't have to die that night. It was Anthony Walker's doin'. Your mama's maid, Drucille, she peeked while he went into her bedroom to take care of your mama. Truth is, he didn't give her no medicine and then, when she died, he poured out the bottle, so it'd look like she'd taken it all . . ."

Chessie gasped. What Cellus was saying was too awful to be true. Why, it was nearly murder!

Chessie's head began to spin and she couldn't breathe. She slid from the chair but Cellus lifted her up and held her as she cried hysterically.

71.

The Countess Corloni trembled with rage as she stared through the peephole into the tower cell and watched Clayton pace back and forth. He had gained weight and color in the two months since the countess had been warned that he was on the verge of death. To keep him alive, the countess had ended the torture, had him given adequate food and transferred him from the dank dungeon to this larger, sunlit cell in the tower.

The countess wanted Clayton to regain his strength

and looks, then force him to become her love-slave—just as Lawton had been. She intended to teach him that certain kinds of sexual torture and humiliation could be as painful as the lash.

But then, two days earlier Gianna had disappeared and just this morning the countess' agents had discovered that she had sailed to New Orleans. There was no doubt—she had run away to search for Clayton. The countess was devastated.

Bitterly she told herself that even in a prison cell one of the accursed Deavorses had been able to hurt her badly.

But the cost to Clayton Deavors would be far worse. She would deny him the privilege of being her love-slave. The countess had acted quickly for revenge. She booked passage on a ship leaving for New Orleans in two days and during her last forty-eight hours in Rome she intended to witness Clayton's being tortured to death, slowly, in a way that she found particularly horrible and satisfying.

The countess hurried down the dimly lit corridor and entered a room that usually served as quarters for the prison's captain-of-the-guard.

She ordered a flask of sherry and summoned the guard.

"Bring the prisoner here," she told him. "Do you have the razor-sharp . . . ? Oh, yes, there they are."

When the guard left she examined the instruments of torture displayed on a table beside a large wooden chair with broad arms and straps for ankles and wrists.

She was sipping a glass of sherry when two guards dragged Clayton into the room.

Clayton reluctantly met the countess' gaze: he was sullen, almost defiant again. Seeing her refueled his hatred. The countess was delighted.

Clayton cursed and struggled against the hands that held him.

"We're going to relive my night in the swamp, Clayton, dear," she said. "But you'll take my part this time, while I watch. I want scores of deep scars cut across your chest. Then I want your thumbs and fingers sliced off bit by bit . . ."

Clayton glanced at the collection of surgical-sharp instruments. His face turned white. His lips quivered. The countess saw the resistance and defiance drain from his body as his body slumped.

The countess sipped her sherry and nodded for the guards to strap Clayton in the chair.

Clayton screamed and struggled furiously as the men dragged him across the room, but as they reached the chair, his body sagged once more, as though all the marrow had suddenly run from his bones. He trembled and turned a pitiful, tear-stained face to the countess.

She smiled and drank her sherry.

One guard was thrown off balance as he tried to shove Clayton into the chair and the other guard took a hand from Clayton's arm to reach for a strap. Clayton came alive with surprising strength.

He wrenched free of one guard's hands. He shoved him away and kicked the other in the genitals.

Clayton dashed to the table and grabbed a long, thin-bladed knife.

The countess screamed as Clayton advanced on her, taunting her with the knife. Nausea flooded her body as she relived the agony and terror of being mutilated so long ago. At the memory, her breasts and thumb began to ache.

One of the guards drew his sword and rushed in front of the countess. The other man was climbing to his feet. Clayton ran from the room. The countess followed the guards as they chased him into the corridor.

Clayton ran toward the stairs but three guards blocked his way. They drew their swords. He turned back but stopped when he saw that he could not get past Rafaella's guards.

Frantically, he glanced around, then he dashed through an open door and slammed it. The guards rushed the door. It was bolted and far too heavy for them to break down with their shoulders.

"Find something to use as a battering ram," the countess ordered.

While two guards went off to find a ram the countess stood beside the door and raved about what Clayton would suffer when he was recaptured. It wouldn't be just his chest and fingers, she howled, but his toes, his genitals . . .

There was no sound from behind the door. The countess grew frantic as minutes passed and the men did not return. She ordered the remaining guards to try and break in again, but they failed, ramming the door helplessly with their shoulders.

Nearly half an hour had passed when the guards returned with a huge log. Three other guards joined them. Four men began to swing the log against the door while the others drew their swords.

"Take him alive!" the countess said. "At any cost!"

She stood back a few feet, her heart pounding, every nerve tense.

But the door proved even stronger than expected. The men had to swing the log again and again, rest, let other men take turns, until finally the hinges began to give.

With one final effort they smashed the hinges and the door fell open. The guards rushed in. The countess hesitated, then followed them.

"No!" the countess screamed. "No, I won't be cheated this way! He's not dead!" Clayton had slit his wrists and lay face-up in a pool of blood.

A guard bent to examine Clayton. "Dead, all right," he said.

Countess Corloni's face twisted into a grimace of hate. She stared down at Clayton. In death, he smiled and she nearly kicked at his smile, but she would not put her feet into his blood.

She pivoted and ran from the room.

72.

The Countess Corloni clung to the ship's railing as the *Dito Pollice* entered the busy harbor of New Orleans. The countess was ill, but not as a result of the rigors of crossing the Atlantic. Her illness was caused by fear and apprehension—fear at being in America again and apprehension about finding Gianna. *I was so glad to leave this wretched city,* the countess thought, recollecting her departure with Flora many years earlier. *Only my search for Gianna could ever bring me back to this damned country.*

The gunboats in the harbor, the Union flags and Navy, the war itself meant nothing to her. Without Gianna her life lacked focus or meaning.

With her usual efficiency, the countess established herself in a comfortable hotel and began to make inquiries. The supreme power in Union-occupied New Orleans was General Benjamin Franklin Butler, a Yankee from New Hampshire. The countess sent him a note inviting him to tea and when he came she explained her mission.

General Butler, in return for certain favors, promised her his cooperation. There was no possibility, he assured her, that Gianna could have traveled out of New Orleans up the Mississippi River, since the area was a war zone.

A short time after the countess' arrival, a colonel on General Butler's staff located Gianna in a small hotel near Canal Street. The countess rushed to the hotel, frantic to see her daughter. Sweeping past the hotel staff, she went directly to Gianna's room and knocked on the door.

Gianna was stunned to see her mother. At first, her only emotions were shock and fear. She backed up and cringed in a corner as the countess moved near her. The countess was both hurt and annoyed, for despite Gianna's retreat there was no mistaking the rebellion in Gianna's eyes and the set of her mouth.

"Mama, I had to run away," Gianna said. "I don't think I can ever forgive you for trying to separate Clayton and me. But don't think you'll have your way with me now. I'm still determined to reach Clayton and be with him!"

The countess was infuriated by Gianna's defiance but took pains to conceal her anger. She tried to line her voice with contrition and concern and lied expertly. Yes, she told Gianna, she had indeed sent Clayton home, but she had done it only because she thought it the best thing for the only person she loved in all the world.

"I was selfish, my darling Gianna," she added. "I'll never forgive myself, but I did it for you. Everything I do is for you. And now I'm here to make amends and to do everything in my power to help you find Clayton."

"Oh, Mama!" Gianna said. "Mama . . ."

Gianna burst into tears. The countess ran over and put her arms around her daughter. She held Gianna like a child and spoke softly and soothingly into her ear.

Gianna is mine again, she thought. Nothing, no one, will ever separate us again. Her hopes rose, and her determination. In a short time, she vowed, the old, dutiful, docile Gianna would return with her to Rome and marry the Prince Vittori, who had been bribed with a quarter of Gianna's dowry to be patient.

But for now, Countess Corloni knew she had to play out her lie about Clayton and convince Gianna of her support. She would arrange it so that Gianna would find out on her own that Clayton was dead.

She thought quickly. Yes, it would be advantageous if Gianna believed that Clayton had died here in America, perhaps in battle. Then she would be willing to go back to Rome. Arranging it would be an easy enough matter, the countess thought.

Gianna hugged her mother again and wiped her eyes

with a small lace handkerchief. "Oh, Mama," she whispered. "I've always loved you and could never really hate you. But you've caused me so much grief and suffering . . ."

"Don't speak of it. It's all in the past, my dear," the countess said. "Now we're together again. That's all that matters. That . . . and, of course, finding your Clayton."

"I've been so lonely and frightened here in New Orleans," Gianna said. "I don't know what to do. They won't let me leave the city, Mama. Because of the war, they won't let me go up to Natchez, where Clay lives . . ."

"Natchez, yes, that's up the Mississippi, isn't it?" the countess asked. Merely saying the word "Natchez" sickened her. She scratched her thumb. "Darling, I have influential friends. They'll let you go up to Natchez soon enough. I'll see to it, I promise you. But we must be patient for a short time. I'll do all I can, but there's a war on, you know."

"I'll try to be patient," Gianna said. "It will be easier, now that you're here and you're helping me. Oh, Mama, can't we three all live together? You and Clay and I. I know you two would get along, and you'd come to love Clay as much as I do."

"I'm sure I will, dear," the countess said. She grimaced and forced a smile. "But you're not being practical, Gianna. We must be realistic . . ."

"Be realistic? About what, Mama?" Gianna asked anxiously.

"For one thing, Gianna, Clayton is undoubtedly in the Army," the countess said. "He surely wouldn't be in Natchez and even when we find his family it may take time to locate him. And you must prepare yourself, dear, for if he's been fighting, well, he may have been wounded."

"Yes, I know, Mama," Gianna said softly. "I've thought about all that. But with all my heart and soul I believe that he's all right and that we'll be together again. His family will surely know where he is. Oh,

Mama, he has a twin sister. I met her once briefly. In Rome. It was in our park, where she was sketching. Wasn't that a great coincidence?"

"Yes, Gianna, that was indeed a coincidence," the countess said. The talk of Chessie Deavors and of seeking out the Deavors family disturbed and excited her. She struggled to hide her emotions from her daughter.

That afternoon the countess moved Gianna out of her hotel room and into an elegant house that General Butler had found for them in the Garden District.

73.

And there they remained, two foreign women in a war-torn city, both obsessed with desperate personal missions that had nothing to do with American politics or the war.

Gianna could think of nothing but finding Clayton, but her mother had more complicated and devious schemes. At first she thought briefly of indulging Gianna's wish to somehow get through the barriers and go north to Natchez. The idea of getting so close to the Deavorses again was tempting—with the advantage of surprise she might be able to destroy them all!

But the thought brought with it a paralyzing fear. She was terrified to return to Natchez and The Columns. She had barely escaped from them with her life, and when she thought of being there again she began to tremble with an unfocused, irrational fear.

It would be better, far better, she thought, to somehow lure Chessie Deavors down to New Orleans. It would be difficult, of course, but not impossible.

Long ago, the countess had decided that nothing

was impossible, and considering her popularity with
General Butler, she was sure she could do with Chessie
just as she liked, once she had tricked her into making
the journey.

In order to maintain a good relationship with Benjamin Butler, the countess entertained lavishly in her
home, both for certain high-ranking Union officers,
lonely and far from home, and for certain members
of New Orleans society, those who had harbored secret
Union sympathies and who now had come into the
open with their feelings, and those who accepted the
reality of the Union occupation and wanted to curry
favor with the conquerors.

However, most of the people of New Orleans were
sullen and defiant under the occupation by Union
troops. Some felt the very air was polluted and the
soil poisoned by the presence of the Yankees. The
lower classes greeted Yankees with rudeness, the upper
classes with haughtiness. Many New Orleanians wore
black crepe bows to mourn the death of their city,
and some prominent society women went so far as to
spit in the faces of Yankee soldiers and officers when
they saw them in the streets.

In contrast to this treatment, Countess Corloni's dinners and parties were all the more captivating and delightful to the Union officers. Her popularity grew and
she was well provided with all the spoils of war. She
enjoyed her triumph and hated the haughty society
women as much as General Butler did, for she well
remembered how they had snubbed her and treated
her with contempt in Natchez when suspicions had
been raised about her father's background.

She greeted with delight, then, General Butler's general order against the patriotic society women who ha-
rassed Union troops.

If they acted like whores, he told the countess, they
should be treated as such. His order read: "As the
officers and soldiers of the United States have been
subjected to repeated insults from the women (calling

themselves ladies) of New Orleans, in return for the most scrupulous non-interference and courtesy on our part, it is ordered that hereafter when any female shall, by word, gesture, or movement, insult, or show contempt for any officer or soldier of the United States, she shall be regarded and held liable to be treated as a woman of the town plying her avocation."

Butler's order was called harsh and barbaric throughout the South but the countess laughed to see New Orleans' society women treated like common prostitutes, and one day saw a haughty neighbor of hers who had insulted a Yankee colonel dragged from her own mansion and taken to the workhouse.

Watching the woman being carried off from the security of her parlor window, the countess was seized with an irresistible notion. How she would love to see Chessie Deavors treated as a prostitute, degraded, humiliated, taught pain and suffering, but not just by being thrown into a workhouse. No, Chessie Deavors should live the rest of her life forced to satisfy men's jaded sexual whims!

But even with her influence in New Orleans, the countess did not see how she could keep Chessie in such bondage for any considerable amount of time, and she became so furious that such delicious revenge was impossible that she paced about the parlor, shattered four vases against the marble fireplace and ranted aloud until she realized people in the street were stopping to stare in at her through the window.

One evening after a performance of Donizetti's opera, *Daughter of the Regiment,* one of the few cultural events in the city since the Union troops arrived, the countess gave an elegant party in her mansion. Nearly two hundred Yankee officers and a sprinkling of civilians danced to a twenty-piece orchestra under fourteen crystal chandeliers in the grand ballroom.

For the countess the evening was tedious, although she took pleasure in seeing Gianna had a partner for every dance. She welcomed anyone or anything to divert Gianna from her preoccupation with finding Clayton. Gianna had begun to grow restive and spoke every day of finding some way to travel upriver to Natchez. Soon, the countess thought, soon I'll get Chessie here and punish her . . . And then Gianna and I will return to Rome.

"A delightful evening, Countess Corloni," General Butler said, bowing low before the countess. Butler, a nervous, autocratic man with one cock eye, was now called "the Beast" by New Orleanians, but the countess was pleased at his compliment.

"Thank you, General," she said. "It's my pleasure, as always, to welcome you to my home."

"A home as warm and charming as its mistress," Butler said. "Dear Countess, may I introduce to you my friend Antonio Mano, the Italian consul? I believe you have once lived in Rome?"

The countess was delighted to meet the consul, all the more so as he was an excellent dancer and led her gracefully onto the floor. Then, just after midnight, Signore Mano introduced her to another foreign visitor. He was a Greek ship owner and captain named Dmitri Shavros, who had recently arrived in New Orleans.

"And how do you like this sullen, starving city?" the countess asked, to make conversation.

"I've been here when the city's mood was much better, Countess Corloni," Shavros said. "But then I'm accustomed to cities in various states of siege, occupation, and starvation. It's a hazard of my profession, Countess. I travel wherever cargo takes me. For instance, when I leave New Orleans I must sail to Alexandria, in Egypt, despite the danger there at the present time . . ."

A chill raced up the countess' spine. Her cheeks grew warm with excitement. Egypt! She couldn't bear to think of Egypt! Why, those wretched Deavorses had tried to convince people that her poor father had been born a Mamaluke, a white slave, in Egypt. Egypt had been the origin of all her troubles—of her father's death, of all her suffering and humiliation!

And now this Greek was sailing for Egypt, a country where white women were prized as slaves, living in harems, or so she understood, only to serve the sexual whims of decadent Egyptian masters. The countess smiled. Her lips quivered. She had difficulty controlling her emotions.

"Mr. Shavros," she said, lowering her voice as she stepped closer to him, "I've enjoyed our talk immensely. Could you possibly call on me in the morning, to discuss a matter of some importance to me?"

Shavros smiled. "I'm delighted to be of service to you, Countess Corloni," he said. "I'll certainly call on you the first thing in the morning."

The countess excused herself. She hurried upstairs. Her excitement and anticipation were so intense that she vomited. Then she ran into her drawing room and began to laugh hysterically. The laughter became high-pitched howls she couldn't control. Even in her hysteria she realized her guests must not hear her.

She stumbled blindly into a closet and slammed the door, and as she stood in the dark and howled she saw Chessie's face in front of her . . . And then the face was Clayton's, and she howled louder.

74.

On the eleventh of May Chessie and Cellus drove into Natchez to buy a white wedding veil. Chessie had found the dress her mother had worn when she married her father and planned to be married in it. Lucinda's dress for her marriage to Anthony Walker was no longer in existence. Chessie had taken particular pleasure in donating it to the Natchez Confederate Women's Club to be cut up for flags. The old wedding dress was lovely but it had no veil. The ceremony would be spartan enough and Chessie had set her heart on having a traditional white veil.

It was a last-minute trip, for Chessie and Carlo were to be married the next day. Union boats had been sighted only a few hours from Natchez and they were determined to be man and wife before they had to face hostile troops.

There seemed little doubt that shortly all of Adams County would be at the mercy of the Union Army. After all its displays of patriotism, all its boasting about standing off the Yankees, the city of Natchez, unlike many other Confederate cities, had discovered, in the two and half weeks since New Orleans fell, that it had no stomach for a heroic stand.

In truth, the city was not well fortified. The forts below New Orleans had been thought impregnable, so that only a few companies of regular troops had been stationed in and around Natchez. Now the battered Confederate Army could spare no support, no regular units. Holding Vicksburg, up the river, was considered far more vital than defending Natchez, and most of the troops in Natchez, including those near The Columns, had been dispatched to defend Vicksburg.

Confederate Brigadier General C. G. Dahlgren, a big man, bearded to cover scars from many duels, had been assigned to command the forces Natchez could raise for its own defense. Dahlgren soon had reason to despair. Despite the imminent danger, in over two weeks' time he had been able to raise only fourteen volunteers in the entire county. And the men who had been conscripted were a rebellious, sullen lot who threatened at every opportunity to slip away into the swamps and forests.

While Chessie went about her errands in the desperate, deserted streets of the city, Cellus went to visit a friend who worked as a waiter in the elegant private salons of the Parker House hotel. Cellus' friend had managed to accumulate some money and valuables during his many years of serving wealthy clients and he was worried that the Union soldiers would steal them from him. Cellus had promised to hide them on The Columns, with the Deavors family's own valuables, most of which had already been buried in huge leather-bound chests.

Chessie was appalled at the state of Natchez as she walked its streets on that hot afternoon. Others might flee the Union troops, but she and Carlo had to stay on The Columns. It was her home, although she knew that life there had already changed forever. She saw few familiar faces in Natchez, and all the news of old friends was depressing. So many were gone already—killed or lost—and it seemed likely that their suffering was not yet over.

Except for Carlo and their wedding tomorrow, her own prospects were uncertain and frightening. When she thought of the Yankees coming she felt fear and apprehension. When she thought of Anthony Walker she felt a loathing that made her cheeks go hot and her hands clench into fists.

Anthony had not returned to The Columns from his business trip since Cellus had told her about his complicity in her mother's death. Chessie did not know what she would do when she saw Anthony again.

She had prayed for the courage to harm him, but she feared she was incapable of physical violence. She suspected that there was no clear way to have him prosecuted and even if there were, all civil justice and the state's old laws would almost surely be suspended within a day or so.

To keep her sanity, Chessie tried to put aside her hatred of Anthony, tried to walk faster and faster to dissipate her melancholy. All her efforts at shopping had proved futile. None of the cloth merchants had any lace at all, and at Santini Brothers, where she and her mother had always shopped, she had been made to feel almost unpatriotic when she asked for it.

Chessie was depressed to the point of numbness when she met Cellus at their carriage. Even news that a Union flotilla of five warships and two troop ships was nearing Natchez had little impact on her, but she emerged from her lethargy long enough to realize how much she wanted to be back at The Columns with

Carlo before the Union troops came, and she told the driver to make all possible haste.

On the ride back to the plantation Cellus was even less talkative than usual, and Chessie was glad. There was nothing she wanted to talk about. Chessie sat quietly and watched the lush forest glide by the fast-moving carriage, taking pleasure in the beauty of the enormous, white magnolia blossoms, so vivid they could be seen a mile away.

Chessie had just decided she would wear a magnolia blossom in her hair when Cellus turned to her abruptly.

"Didn't mean to frighten you, Miss Chessie," he said. "I know you got a lot on your mind and this should be the happiest time for you, your wedding . . ."

"What's wrong, Cellus?" Chessie asked.

"All the way since town, I been thinkin' if I ought to burden you with this," he said. "But I'm afraid I have to. I can't do anything alone. Folks wouldn't take a slave's word, not against a white man . . ."

"Dammit, Cellus, what is it? Tell me!"

"Well, you know I visited with my old friend Buckson Tiler at the Parker House," Cellus said. "Buckson can't help but overhear a lot of private conversations. Lord, over the years, the things that Buckson's heard when men got drunk and talkative and thought no one would hear . . . Well, couple of weeks ago, two men were at the Parker House drinkin' all night. One was a man named Conrad Decauter. And the other man was Anthony Walker . . ."

Chessie was disturbed by Cellus' face. His skin looked slack and his wrinkles glistened in the late afternoon sunlight.

"What about Anthony?" she asked sharply. Her throat had tightened at the mention of his name. "What can you tell me about that man that's worse than what I already know?"

"Buckson overheard them talkin', drunk talk, for over three hours, heard every detail," Cellus said. "And he told me . . . and I don't doubt his word . . . that it was Anthony Walker who adulterated that medicine with Indian-poke and sold it to the hospitals . . ."

Desperation lightened Anthony's steps and brought back the night cunning he had developed when he had smuggled slaves into the swamp. He had waited while the last of Chessie's wedding guests left, then waited longer, until the house became dark and quiet.

Only then had he slowly, carefully, dragged his sacks of money from the horse hidden in a thicket and across the edge of the rose garden to a small patch of swamp behind the barn. A hundred yards into the swamp he paused, looked around at the darkness, then tore off his coat and began to dig into the soft ground, pausing only to brush sweat from his face with the back of his hand.

He finished digging and stood up and grimaced. His foot was troubling him again. He cursed. The gout had returned in the last few days. His foot was swollen and it ached when he forgot to take his medicine. He pulled out a vial and swallowed the medicine.

As he buried his money and covered the hole he thought with pleasure of the extent of his fortune. He had made nearly a hundred thousand dollars selling the adulterated medicine. And now he wouldn't have to share any of it with that fool, Conrad Decauter. After that drunken night at the Parker House Decauter had tried to blackmail him for more of the profit. The next night Anthony had killed Decauter and sunk his body in a swamp bog.

Now that his money was safely hidden, he would set out to ingratiate himself with the Union officials and soldiers in Natchez. He knew the time for this was ripe. It would be an easy thing to do. He would see what happened and whatever was best for him he would do.

Anthony scattered limbs and leaves over the fresh-turned earth, then put on his jacket and walked out of the swamp. As he limped back to his horse, he congratulated himself on how well everything was going. He had secured this tidy fortune, but this was only the beginning.

Perhaps he would move on to a port in a secure area of the Confederacy and increase his fortune by running the blockade. Or perhaps he would stay here. A clever man with money and friends in the Union Army would be in a good position to make a lot of money. The Yankees were likely to confiscate many Adams County plantations. A local man would be needed to run them, a man not too closely connected with the Confederacy.

Anthony was prepared to be very cooperative and could easily see himself as that man. After all, these people were nothing to him. He had never liked them or felt one of them, and now perhaps he could make money from their cotton and slaves. Of course, his main objective was to secure The Columns, an objective that now seemed excitingly close.

It would give him great pleasure, he reflected, finally to be the master of The Columns and to expel Chessie and her husband. He would be glad to see her destitute. And as for Cellus, that arrogant bastard who had plagued him from his first days in Mississippi, he would teach the old black man some real humility with the end of a lash.

And he could marry Jolette.

Yes, Anthony said as he led his mount to the house road and then trotted up to the house as though coming from town. He could have it all, his fortune, Jolette, the plantation. He could and he would, as he had always intended to. But he would bide his time, now, until he saw what the Yankees were up to and if they could be useful to him. Then he would make his decision.

In the meantime, he would pretend to have just returned from his trip, an honest but weary businessman shaken by the Union occupation of Natchez, full of concern for the plantation, happy for the newly married couple and still grieving for Lucinda.

Anthony had poured himself a whiskey and was sitting down to pull off his boots when he heard a noise and looked up to see Chessie come into the parlor.

He stood up and smiled. "You're up late on your wedding night . . ." he began. "Congratulations, Chessie. I'm sorry I didn't . . ."

Chessie's face stopped him cold. Her blue eyes were cold and narrowed. Her lips trembled and she was ashen-faced.

"My God," he mumbled. "What's . . . ?"

"You murderer!" Chessie cried. She flew across the room and dug her nails into his cheeks.

Anthony screamed in pain. Cursing, he grabbed Chessie's wrists and hurled her aside. She climbed to her feet and attacked him again, shouting and swinging at him. Anthony parried her fists and stumbled back.

He was stunned as she screamed that she knew he had withheld the medicine and murdered her mother, knew that he and Decauter had adulterated the medicine and maimed and killed the soldiers, that she would see him hanged . . .

Fear and rage overcame his surprise. Taking the defensive, he had only one thought: to shut up Chessie —to kill her if necessary to save himself. He slapped her face solidly with the back of his hand, stunning her, then shoved her against the wall, grabbed her throat and squeezed.

Suddenly, from the corner of his eye, he saw someone else across the parlor. Anthony released Chessie's throat and turned just as Carlo smashed a fist into his face. Anthony fell backward and crashed into a marble-top table. Carlo advanced on him. Anthony scrambled up and backed away. He heard voices, footsteps coming from other parts of the house.

Then he realized they must all know. He couldn't kill them all. He had to escape!

Carlo had trapped him in a corner. Anthony pulled out his pistol. Carlo stopped. Covering Carlo with the pistol, Anthony moved toward the door. Carlo tried to follow him.

"No, Carlo!" Chessie screamed. "No, he'll kill you!"

Anthony backed into the hall. He glanced over his shoulder.

Jolette stood on the stairs, trembling violently, her eyes wide, her mouth open. She, too, must have overheard what Chessie said, he realized.

But he couldn't worry about Jolette now. He inched to the front door, then out onto the porch. Carlo followed, at a distance. Cellus came down the hall. Other slaves appeared.

Anthony reached his horse. He made a menacing gesture with his pistol, fired once, then swung up into the saddle and galloped away.

75.

"You monster!" Jolette shouted as Anthony entered her room at the Mansion House hotel. "You filthy bastard! You let Aunt Lucinda die and you killed all those soldiers with your medicine! I found out while you were out of town . . ."

"Calm down and hold your goddamn tongue, Jolette," Anthony said. "Many soldiers die in war and I've made enough money for us to live in style and comfort. Lucinda was sick anyway and her death brings you what you most wanted. Now you can marry me. Isn't that what you wanted? We'll never again have to meet in the woods and in hotel rooms . . ."

"I didn't want Aunt Lucinda to die, Anthony," Jolette said. "I'd never have condoned such a despicable act, not for anything on earth. I loved her. Oh, my Lord, I'm so miserable! What am I doing here? I've been weak, selfish, blind . . ."

"Christ, stop your sniveling!" Anthony said. "Why should I want to marry a whining, self-righteous bitch? And you're hardly one to preach morality, after being my whore. Don't try my patience. I'm tired and I'm randy. Get undressed and get into bed . . ."

Anthony reached out for Jolette's arm but she stepped back.

"Don't you dare touch me," she said in a low, angry voice. "You're a murderer, many times over. I may be bad but I'm no murderer! How could I have loved you so blindly? You're a monster, Anthony Walker! Yes, I despise myself . . . almost as much as I despise you!"

Jolette was seized by a blind and violent rage. A convulsion shook her body. She rushed at Anthony and slapped at his face, shouting, scratching. "Murderer! Filthy murderer!"

Anthony ducked her attack and twisted her arm. He hit her with the back of his hand. Blood spurted from her nose. A shock of pain scalded her face. For a moment her vision was blurred.

She shook her head and her vision cleared and she saw Anthony advancing on her, his face twisted with pain and hatred.

"You bitch!" he muttered. "You've hurt me. I don't need you—you need me! You'll pay for what you've done!"

Jolette stumbled backward against the bed. She put up her hands in an attempt to protect herself. They were of no use as Anthony smashed his fist into her face. Her head snapped around. The pain made her gag. She tried to scream but the sounds that came from her throat were weak and hacking.

Anthony towered over her, his hands curled into tight fists. Jolette screamed in fear, but she was too weak and wracked with pain to defend herself.

"No, I don't believe I will marry you, Jolette," Anthony said. "I can easily buy myself a better whore than you. I'm wealthy now and I've just purchased an important post with the Union Army . . ."

"Don't hurt me anymore, please," Jolette begged through puffed lips that tasted of blood. "Please, Anthony . . ."

Anthony put his hand to his face. He winced as his finger touched the scratches she had made.

Anthony cursed and hit Jolette again. A screech died in her constricting throat. She crumpled to the floor and lost consciousness.

A few days later, Jolette looked at her swollen, discolored face in the mirror. Her head was feverish and ached terribly. At least I'm alive, she thought. He could have beaten me to death. And I loved him. I really loved him. The realization made her cry.

Weakly, she dragged herself back to the bed and collapsed for a few more minutes. I must not give up, she told herself. She dabbed at her face with cool water and flinched at every stinging touch.

She had never been so miserable, so alone. Everyone had abandoned her.

Yesterday, she had sent a note out to The Columns, humbly confessing her guilt to Chessie, begging forgiveness, and asking for money to leave Natchez. Chessie had replied that as far as she was concerned Jolette could rot in hell, and that if she tried to visit The Columns the dogs would be turned loose on her.

Without Chessie's protection, Jolette was on her own. All the Deavors friends would shun her. She would be out of money in a few days. All she wanted was to get out of Natchez and return to New York and her parents. Of course, Natchez was occupied by the Yankees, but she had heard that with enough money it was possible to buy passage through Union lines.

She had even asked Anthony for help. He could have easily helped her if he wished.

Anthony was well on his way to being the most despised man in the county. But he had ingratiated himself with Colonel Dirkley, who was chief Union engineer and officer in charge of fortifications, munitions and the confiscation of Confederate property in Natchez. The colonel had appointed Anthony "Provisional Liaison Officer for Confiscation of Enemy Property," and, flanked by the dozen Yankee soldiers needed to protect him from the relatives of the soldiers his medicine had maimed and killed, he traveled throughout the county and made plans to take over businesses and plantations that were essential to the Union war effort.

With obvious pleasure, Anthony had told Jolette he had convinced Colonel Dirkley that the location of The Columns was essential to the control of the river and that the house should be razed and a fort built on the land.

"I'll build myself a much finer house after the war when I'm master of The Columns," he had said. "Perhaps I'll hire Chessie Deavors and her wop husband as servants, get them to work alongside the niggers . . ."

Her anger spent, alone and frightened and in pain, Jolette had begged Anthony for help. Desperately, she offered to become his mistress once more.

"Look at yourself in the mirror," he had said. "You couldn't sell youself Under-the-Hill the way you look. Though, in time, if your face heals decently, I'll hire you myself—just for one night—and get you to do somethin' special."

Then Anthony told Jolette about some of the sexual duties he would expect of her. Jolette had shuddered and run from the room.

Remembering, Jolette choked back a sob. Then she eased herself out of bed and walked over and pulled the velvet bell cord for the Negro maid. She didn't know if the woman would come. A lot of the Negroes in Natchez had become surly and rebellious since the Union troops arrived.

Five minutes later the maid appeared. When Jolette asked the woman to bring food to her room the woman merely grunted and walked out. Jolette hoped the grunt meant, "Yes." She would rather starve than appear in public with her face in this condition.

She returned to the bed, sank onto the pillows, and tried to cry. But the sobs were dry heaves that caught in her throat.

She touched her face. Perhaps she would look better

in another week, at least enough for Anthony to find her attractive. There was no other way. When her money ran out she would go to Anthony and do whatever he demanded of her, if that were the only way to leave Natchez.

Chessie seethed with anger as she stood on the lawn and watched the Yankee colonel direct his men about The Columns. The men were an engineer brigade. They had arrived with plumb-lines and surveying equipment and they were measuring and marking with lime and pacing off the distance from the house to the river. Colonel Dirkley had informed Chessie that, as chief engineer for the Union forces in Adams County, he planned to confiscate The Columns and probably raze it, to build fortifications.

There was no logic in the colonel's plan. There were no Confederate troops within many miles. There was nothing in this area to defend. There were only the widely scattered plantations and the forests and swamps.

The only logic, as Chessie knew well, was that the colonel had become a "very special friend" of Anthony Walker and that Anthony had been appointed to a high position with the Yankees. Chessie suspected that Colonel Dirkley had been bribed by Anthony and was doing his bidding.

Chessie was glad that Carlo and Cellus had been away during Anthony's visit the evening before. She knew they would have tried to attack him, despite his bodyguards. She had restrained herself with difficulty as she looked into Anthony's smug face and tried not to think of what he had done to her mother and Dunbar Polk and the other men.

It was too painful and the anger she felt left her nearly speechless. She had never hated anyone as she hated Anthony, and her hatred increased when he bragged that he would never be arrested by the Union troops for having poisoned Confederate soldiers.

Chessie walked slowly around the house, toward the

barns and the quarters. Dirkley's blue-clad soldiers swarmed over the house and the back yard and explored all the outbuildings. She watched them helplessly, trying not to lose her temper, worried only that they would discover the trunks of silver and other valuables that had been buried behind the barn.

She heard a crash in the house. She knew the soldiers were making a shambles of the house but Colonel Dirkley had ignored her protests.

Other Union troops had come out to the plantation in the three weeks since Natchez surrendered. The other Yankee officers had been courteous and considerate, even when they searched the house and outbuildings and confiscated food and horses.

One of them, a short, swarthy major named Brunelli, had been overjoyed to encounter Carlo. Brunelli was a native of Naples, and he and Carlo had talked at length. When the major accepted Chessie's dinner invitation, he had provided a bottle of good whiskey and a ham for the occasion.

But Major Brunelli had not been able to help them with Colonel Dirkley. Nor had the other Union officers, though they had been sympathetic. As an engineer officer Dirkley was out of the normal chain of command. If he declared that a place was necessary for fortifications, it was almost impossible to overrule him.

It was obvious that Dirkley was not popular with his fellow officers. One captain had told Chessie that if General Grant knew of Dirkley's corruption he would probably be relieved of his command. But Grant wasn't in Natchez. He was busy with his siege of Vicksburg. The Deavorses and some influential Natchez families had sent a message to Grant complaining about Dirkley, but Chessie had little hope that it would do any good.

Chessie joined Carlo and a group of slaves, including Cellus and old Aunt Froney, the midwife and healer, standing at the edge of the quarters, watching the soldiers work. Carlo put his arm around Chessie but no one spoke.

Most of the slaves at The Columns had little work to do. Nearly all the cotton fields had been destroyed rather than let them fall into Union hands, and the status of the slaves was rather confused. They had all heard talk that Abe Lincoln might issue a proclamation freeing all slaves, but until he did, they were still bound men. They were also war contraband, the same as cotton and munitions, and the Union was determined that they not help the Confederate war effort.

Some of the Deavors' people had run off when the Yankees came. Some had gone to Natchez, where Chessie had seen them wandering aimlessly about the streets, but most of them had remained on The Columns and rather listlessly performed whatever little work they were given.

Chessie glanced past the assembled slaves to the barn. A platoon of Yankee soldiers was setting up their surveying equipment on the very spot where all the family valuables were buried. Chessie exchanged a look with Carlo, then sighed.

With all that had happened in the past months, the possible loss of the family jewelry and other valuables seemed a small matter. Compared to the loss of friends and family and the imminent destruction of The Columns, it hardly seemed to matter at all.

"All this is Anthony Walker's doin', Miss Chessie," Cellus said. "You know it. A man like that . . . Lettin' Miss Lucinda die, maimin' and killin' those boys . . . He's got to be punished, got to be stopped before he ruins The Columns . . ."

"I don't see how," Chessie said. "He seems immune from the law, and he has his own little army to protect him."

"All the same, he's got to pay," Cellus said. "Somehow, he'll suffer, won't he, Aunt Froney?"

The ancient, wrinkled black woman nodded. When she looked up at Cellus she smiled a toothless smile that sent a shiver down Chessie's back.

76.

A few days later, on the day before a meeting with Colonel Dirkley, concerning, as his summons said, "the confiscation of the plantation known as The Columns, for the site of fortifications to be constructed by the Union Army," Chessie was sitting in the parlor when an envelope arrived.

She took the envelope from a slave but did not open it immediately. She was too dispirited over the hearing and what seemed the inevitable seizure of the plantation and the destruction of this house, this lovely old house in which she had been born. She had been up all night, she and Carlo, and she had cried, and they had both vowed that somehow they would thwart Colonel Dirkley and Anthony and keep possession of The Columns.

But now, on this rainy June morning, their vows seemed futile. Chessie had retained Riley Wilkens, one of the best lawyers in the county, to argue against the confiscation. And people in Natchez were indignant and bitterly opposed and they had protested to Union officials. But Chessie knew a lawyer or the protests of prominent citizens were useless against ruthless, corrupt men, or against the guns of the Union troops.

A quarter hour later Chessie remembered the envelope in her lap. She looked at the envelope. It was addressed to her, in small, neat handwriting. There was no return address. But in one corner was written the word, "Urgent."

As she tore open the envelope Chessie let herself hope that it concerned the confiscation, that there would be some message that would be her salvation.

Chessie tensed as a ring fell out. When she picked up the ring she gasped. It was Clayton's ring!

Her heart pounded as she read the note. It said:

"Miss Deavors, I've just arrived in New Orleans from Italy and I'm desperately in need of money. If you wish to save your brother's life, it is imperative that you meet me at the foot of Pier 9, on the Mississippi River, in New Orleans, at 10 p.m., on the evening of 18 June. You must come alone. If you fail to appear, or do not come alone, you will forfeit all hope of aiding Clayton Deavors. Bring $10,000."

Chessie was so elated that she forgot Colonel Dirkley and the confiscation. She ran to tell Carlo and Cellus. They, too, were excited and hopeful. But Carlo insisted he go to New Orleans with her. And Cellus pointed out the difficulty of raising that much money and getting through Union lines to New Orleans.

Chessie agreed that Carlo should accompany her to New Orleans but was adamant that she follow the note's instructions and meet its author alone at the river. She would take no chances of jeopardizing Clayton's safety.

As for the problems of money and transportation she refused to consider that she could not work out everything. That night she went out and dug up a chest of valuable silver, so that she could sell it and raise the money, just as she had sold a much smaller amount of silver earlier when she relented and gave Jolette enough money to buy her way out of Natchez.

The next day, Chessie, Carlo and Cellus went into Natchez and sold the silver. They arranged passage to New Orleans with enormous bribes to half a dozen men who had influence with the Union Army. This all took hours and they were quite late for their session with Colonel Dirkley.

The colonel was livid with anger when they entered the office he had set up in the confiscated Roccalini mansion.

"This is a deliberate insult to the Union Army," he said. "An act of arrogance. In New Orleans, General Butler found a most effective way to deal with such insults, as you've perhaps heard. Don't ever try my patience again, or I might resort to similar tactics. I would have declared the plantation confiscated without a hearing but Mr. Walker interceded on your behalf."

Anthony smiled and nodded at Chessie. She bit her lips in anger. Of course, Anthony would have interceded. He would not miss the pleasure of this hearing. Now that passage to New Orleans was arranged the horror of losing The Columns hit Chessie so hard it seemed a physical blow and she felt nauseous.

A lieutenant read the regulation that allowed the Union Army to seize enemy property. Then Colonel Dirkley began a summation of the military reasons why he must confiscate and raze The Columns. But he glanced at Cellus and stopped in the middle of a sentence.

"What's that nigger doing here?" he asked. "Lieutenant, get him out of here!"

"No, wait, let the nigger stay," Anthony said. "He practically runs The Columns and he'll soon be my nigger. And that's a day I'm looking forward to."

Cellus stared at Anthony with an expressionless face. But Chessie saw that his lips quivered and his hands trembled. She had never seen Cellus in this kind of nervous state but he'd been like this since he came from Aunt Froney's cabin just before they left the plantation for town.

The colonel resumed his summation, which dragged on and on in sophistic military terms.

The afternoon was almost unbearably hot and humid. Sweat lined Chessie's forehead and matted her clothes to her body. Anthony finally took off his coat.

"Here, nigger," he said to Cellus. "Hang my coat on that rack by the door."

Chessie feared Cellus' reaction to such an insult and order. But, still trembling, he took Anthony's coat, smoothed out the wrinkles and hung the coat up, then took his seat again.

"Well, nigger, I guess you're finally learning how to be a useful nigger," Anthony said. "But not as useful as you'll be when I've finished with you. Proceed, Colonel."

The colonel finished his summary and turned to Riley Wilkins, the Natchez lawyer that Chessie had hired to argue against the confiscation. Wilkins quickly demolished the colonel's excuses for the confiscation. But Colonel Dirkley brushed aside the lawyer's arguments.

"Under the military authority invested in me," the colonel said, "I hereby declare the Adams County plantation known as The Columns, and all its contraband niggers, confiscated and owned by the United States, as of eight a.m. on the morning of seventeen June, 1862. All members of the Deavors family are to have vacated the plantation by that hour or they will be forced off the property and arrested by Union troops who will occupy the plantation, along with Mr. Anthony Walker . . ."

Chessie whimpered. A shudder passed over her body. Carlo kissed her cheek and put his arm around her. She looked at Anthony, who was standing up. How she loathed him! The Columns had been the Deavors' home for generations, since the last century. She had grown up there, it was her only home, and now she was its mistress, responsible for protecting it.

But she had been unable to save it from Anthony. He had won everything. She looked at him with cold hatred. She wanted to run across the room and hit him, choke him, but her grief stopped her.

Cellus walked over to Chessie. She stood up and looked into his face, an old face, displaying all its wrinkles.

"Cellus, what'll we do?" she asked. Tears streamed down her cheeks. She hugged Cellus. "What will happen to you? Anthony will destroy you. Oh, we're lost, Cellus . . ."

"We'll do what we have to," he whispered. "Anthony Walker will never be master of The Columns, as God is my witness, Miss Chessie."

His voice chilled Chessie. It sounded barely human.

Anthony had started over to Chessie and Cellus. He

was limping. He stopped and returned to his chair and sat down.

"Nigger," he called to Cellus, "get my medicine out of my coat and bring it to me."

"Yessir, Mist' Anthony," Cellus said mockingly in the same inhuman voice. "Right away, Mist' Anthony . . ."

Chessie watched as Cellus walked over to the coat-rack. She saw him take something from his pocket. She glanced around. No one else was watching Cellus.

Chessie started to speak out, to stop Cellus. She began to shiver. She clutched her hands across her arms against the chills. She realized that she had known what Cellus was going to do, had known, without admitting it, since Cellus left Aunt Froney's cabin this morning.

And now Cellus was putting Indian-poke, the lethal hellebore that had poisoned the soldiers, into Anthony's medicine. This was too horrible, no matter what Anthony had done. She could not condone inflicting such suffering on any human being. She must speak out . . .

Chessie's eyes met Cellus' as the old man carried the medicine to Anthony. But her mind was filled with images of other eyes: Lucinda's gentle, suffering eyes, Dunbar's bulging, pain-filled eyes and those of the other bald, crippled soldiers in the Natchez ward.

Chessie said nothing. Silently, she watched while Cellus handed Anthony the vial, watched while Anthony gulped down the measure of medicine.

Anthony brushed his mouth with the back of his hand and frowned at the bitter taste. Seeing that Chessie was watching him, he smiled mockingly, then rose and turned toward Colonel Dirkley.

Suddenly Anthony grasped his throat. He gasped, then screamed. His face twisted into a hideous grimace of pain and suffering.

He looked at Cellus, then Chessie, and Chessie stared without blinking at the accusing, unbelieving look in his bulging eyes.

Chessie did not look away, not even when Anthony howled like an animal and clawed at his face in agony.

77.

At twenty-five minutes past seven on a warm evening Chessie and Carlo stood on Canal Street in New Orleans and argued about the ten o'clock rendezvous on the river. They had arrived in the city half an hour earlier, after traveling down the Mississippi with forged documents they had bought in Natchez.

Their argument had started as they left the steamboat and took a room in a hotel. And now it continued here on a street crowded with soldiers in blue, Negroes in rags, and sullen, slow-moving white people who seemed hungry and without any purpose in their walking.

"I won't hear another word about it, Carlo," Chessie said. "I'm goin' alone, just as the note instructed. I won't jeopardize Clayton's safety. I'll be all right, darlin'. I'll take a pistol in my purse . . ."

"You wouldn't even know which end of the pistol to point, Chessie," Carlo said. "The more I think of this venture, the less I think you should go alone."

"Dammit, Carlo, I must go alone! If the note's author sees you with me he may never show himself."

"You shouldn't use such language, Chessie . . ."

"I'll use whatever damn language I want!" Chessie said. "And I won't be scolded! You sound just like Clayton . . ."

Chessie shuddered as she remembered her argument about profanity with her brother in Rome. She saw Clayton's face . . . the mirror of her face. A longing to know he was safe, to see him again, overwhelmed her. She sniffled.

"Chessie, are you all right?" Carlo asked. "Are you going to cry? Here, take my handkerchief."

Chessie shook her head. "No, no, I won't cry," she said. "But I must do whatever is necessary, if there's the slightest chance I can find out something about Clayton. Perhaps this is just . . . just some thief from Rome with a scheme to get my money. But I'll gladly risk the money. Oh, Carlo, I'm so desperate and this may be my last chance, ever, to save Clayton. Please don't oppose me, or jeopardize my chances. I could never forgive you."

Carlo sighed. "All right, Chessie," he said. "It's against my better judgment. But I'll let you go alone tonight."

"Oh, darlin', thank you," she said.

She leaned up and kissed his cheek.

Countess Corloni forced herself to endure Dmitri Shavros for a few more minutes as she offered him a brandy in the study of her mansion and listened to his boastful accounts of adventures in North African ports. She had come to loathe the fat, swarthy man whose pig-like black eyes stared openly at her breasts.

She suspected that the captain was a volatile man, a man who was easily insulted and easily angered. She would endure his stupid talk a while, rather than offend him, because she wanted his full and enthusiastic co-operation two hours later when he abducted Chessie Deavors.

After five minutes the countess interrupted Shavros' monologue as politely as she could.

"My word, the time," she said, glancing at a porcelain clock on the mantel. "Your accounts are fascinating, Captain Shavros. But I'm sure you have much to do, to prepare for a prompt sailing. I hope . . . You're certain nothing can go wrong?"

"Quite certain, Countess," he said. "My crew and I are very efficient in such matters. And, of course, I have my own interests at stake. Not only the ten thousand dollars the girl will be carrying. But, as you've suggested, the pleasure of initiating her into . . . certain sexual practices. You may be certain that not only her youth and beauty will please her Arab masters, but also her sexual knowledge. But Countess, are you quite certain that the girl will be at the pier alone at ten this evening?"

"Without a doubt," the countess said. "She arrived here in the city an hour or so ago, I've been informed. Have no fear. She'll be on time. And alone. She'll do anything to find her twin brother."

"Very well," he said.

"And you'll sail immediately? Some alarm could be sounded . . ."

"Countess, within minutes after the girl is taken, my ship will slip down the river," Shavros said.

"Good," the countess said. "Then, sir, I assume we've concluded our business. Be sure you remember to give Chessie Deavors my message."

"Yes, I'll remember, Countess," Shavros said. "However . . . I must satisfy my curiosity. Would you please tell me why you hate this girl so much?"

"What affair is it of yours?" the countess asked angrily. "No, I won't tell you. Now, good evening, sir . . ."

The captain stood up. He walked to the door, opened it slightly, then turned back to the countess.

"I fear I must insist," he said. "Knowing will increase my pleasure with the girl. Why jeopardize our arrangement by refusing to tell me?"

The countess was incensed at the man's arrogance and at his threat. She looked into his small, malevolent eyes. The hint of a smile on his heavy lips angered her further.

The fool must have a score of things to do before sailing, she was sure. And she would never be ready in time for the lavish midnight ball she was giving to celebrate a triumph only she and Chessie would know about.

She tried to swallow down her resentment and her anger. A few minutes more could hardly matter. Gianna wouldn't be back from the tea for an hour. She dare not antagonize Shavros. Indeed, she might find satis-

faction in sharing her revenge and triumph with someone.

"Sit down, Captain," the countess said. "I'm fortunate to have chosen a man who understands the thirst
for revenge . . . and justice, the kind of justice the
courts don't recognize."

Then, briefly, she told him what had happened to
her and her father in Natchez because the Deavors
spread rumors that her father had been a white slave
in Egypt.

Shavros smiled and nodded. "Yes, now I understand," he said. "I'd do the same in your situation.
What a poetic, almost biblical sense of revenge you
have, Countess! To send the girl into slavery in Egypt!
And what of her brother?"

"Clayton Deavors . . ." the countess began. She
hesitated. She feared she had told Shavros too much.
She lowered her voice. "Clayton Deavors is of no concern to either of us. My revenge now concerns only
his sister, and I've waited many years to conclude this
Deavors affair." Impatiently, she raised her voice.
"And if you're as efficient as you say, Captain, the
Deavors affair will finally be settled in less than two
hours. Now, surely, we've concluded our business."

The captain stood up and bowed slightly. "You may
rest assured, Countess, that the matter will be settled
this evening at Pier Nine."

Shavros left and the countess stood up. She scratched
her thumb and tightened each finger of her black
gloves. She was pleased and excited and decided to
send a servant down to the pier so the abduction could
be described to her.

Tomorrow she would begin the final part of her
scheme, to present perjured testimony and forged documents to prove to Gianna that Clayton had been
killed in battle. She and Gianna would sail for Italy
in less than a week.

Gianna, her beloved daughter, her only reason for
living now that her revenge was complete, would become a princess. And Chessie Deavors would spend her

life as a slave to the sexual whims of her Arab masters.

I'll drink champagne and dance all night, dance until dawn, she told herself, and she picked up her skirts and began to swirl around the study.

Gianna strolled down the path to the house, glad that she had left the boring tea an hour early. She was told that her mother was in the study and she walked down the hall slowly.

The study door was cracked open. Gianna had raised her hand to knock when she heard her mother say, "Clayton Deavors . . ."

At the sound of his name Gianna sucked in her breath. She stepped closer to the door. The next words were muffled. Then her mother's voice was a bit louder: ". . . And if you're as efficient as you say, Captain, the Deavors affair will finally be settled in less than two hours. Now, surely, we've concluded our business."

"You may rest assured, Countess, that the matter will be settled this evening at Pier Nine," a man said.

Gianna bolted back from the door as though it had grown hot. She feared her legs would not support her as she ran down the hall and out into the front yard. She sucked in her breath, then stepped behind a huge palm tree. The man came out and climbed into a carriage and drove off.

Gianna felt hot, then cold. She trembled. She tried to clear her frenzied thoughts and remember exactly what she had overheard.

Apparently, Clayton was in New Orleans and would be on the river this evening at Pier Nine for some kind of business with the captain.

For a moment Gianna was elated.

Then she was terribly frightened. What could her mother have arranged with this captain? Surely, it meant harm to Clayton!

Gianna became angry, furiously angry. Once again, her mother had deceived her about Clayton and seemed determined to keep them apart! Gianna vowed that this time her mother's scheme would not work because she would go to the river tonight and be reunited with her beloved Clayton!

78.

Carlo watched Chessie walk down the shadowed street lined with warehouses. The tall masts of ships were silhouetted against the dark sky. He watched until she disappeared, then turned to walk back to the tavern a block away where he was to wait for her.

After a few steps Carlo paused. He turned and stared into the darkness. How could he have let her go alone, no matter how much she insisted? How could he know what waited for her along the dark river?

Carlo knew that if he interfered now, and jeopardized Chessie's chances of finding Clayton, he would never forgive himself. And Chessie would not forgive him, either.

No, it's too dangerous for her alone, he muttered. He ran down the street, but stopped abruptly.

He had given her his word. The worst that could go wrong was that she would lose the money.

Carlo pivoted and walked away from the river. He paused at the corner, almost changed his mind, then moved slowly toward the tavern.

Chessie was nearly paralyzed with apprehension and dread as she moved along the dark, shadowed street. Her bravery in front of Carlo had only been a pose.

The dread was not exactly fear, she knew, though she constantly glanced at the shadows. She didn't doubt that there was enough to fear down here at the river. But worry about some drunken sailor or petty criminal was not the cause of her feelings.

They came from deep within her. They came from

an endemic horror that had become part of her life
and that she feared would always gnaw inside her.

The horrors in Rome had only been the beginning.
They had continued in Natchez, right up until the half
hour she watched in agony, watched the futile attempts
of the doctors to save a man whose hair fell out and
whose nails grew loose and whose flesh became inhuman, a man whose screeches of supplication for
death were finally granted . . .

And there was still the horror that when she returned
to Natchez she would no longer be mistress of The
Columns, and might find the house razed . . .

Now she felt the embryo of a new horror in her
stomach, and she feared she was about to give birth
to something so dreadful she could not name it, but its
birth pains were the smothering feelings from which
she had suffered all her life.

Chessie paused at the foot of the first pier. She was
debilitated by her dread. Blood pounded at her temples. She glanced over her shoulder. She longed to
turn and run back to Carlo.

But she walked on down the river. She had an obligation to Clayton, an obligation that came from the
cradle . . . No, she realized, from the womb: For the
special, nearly incestuous love that had almost ruined
them both carried an obligation of love now, sacrificial,
if necessary, and if there was any chance she could
save her twin, she would swallow down her dread and
do what was necessary.

She tried to cheer herself up. What if the note's
author had accurate information about Clayton? He did
have Clayton's ring. What if, in a few minutes, she
learned that Clayton was alive, learned how she might
help him?

Chessie had passed several piers. She glanced up
and, in the moonlight, she saw a weathered sign: PIER
8. There was no ship at this pier.

But there was a ship at the next pier, a ghostly black
ship with filthy sails all furled to leave, with drunken,
cursing sailors scurrying about its decks.

As Chessie reached Pier 9 she was startled by a short, dark-complexioned man who stepped from behind a stack of banana crates.

"Miss Deavors?" the man asked.

"Yes, I'm Chessie Deavors," she said. "What about Clayton? What can you tell me? What further proof do you have?"

"Did you bring the money?" the man asked. His dark eyes frightened Chessie.

"Yes, I brought it. But I'm not giving it to you until I'm convinced . . ."

The man made a gesture and Chessie broke off the sentence. She glanced around as a sailor ran from the shadows. She opened her mouth to scream but a greasy hand choked the scream. Her arms were pinned behind her back.

"Miss Deavors, I bring compliments from an old friend," the man said. "From Rafaella . . . who promises that your death will be much slower than Clayton's . . ."

Chessie gagged at the sound of the name. All the way along the river she had suspected what gnawed inside her, had suspected what waited here! And now she was lost . . .

"Take her to my cabin," the man said. "Strip her and tie her spread-eagle. And prepare to sail immediately!"

Chessie struggled furiously as she was dragged onto the pier. She fought for breath. She was choking! She couldn't breathe . . .

A sudden sound of fighting halted her captor. She strained her head around.

Carlo was fighting with the short man!

The man had pulled a knife. Carlo twisted it around in the man's grasp, then forced it into his arm. The man screamed. Carlo smashed his fist into the man's face. He crumpled to the ground.

The sailor released Chessie and turned to face Carlo. But a blow from the butt of Carlo's pistol knocked him down.

"Quick, Chessie!" Carlo said. "Before the others are off the ship!"

He grabbed her hand and they ran from the pier.

Shavros cursed as he staggered to his feet. He squeezed his hand over his bleeding arm and grimaced against the pain as he watched Chessie Deavors disappear into the shadows.

Several men ran down the gangway from the ship.

"Captain, what happened?" a sailor shouted. "Where's the girl? Shall we go after her?"

"No, dammit!" Shavros said. "You'll never find them in the dark. And the man is armed. That bitch countess! May she roast in hell for this! I've been betrayed! She lied to me . . ."

"Your arm, Captain," the sailor said. "The bleeding. Here, let me . . ."

He made a tourniquet from a handkerchief and tied it around the captain's arm.

"Look, over there," another sailor said. He pointed to the other side of the pier. "Isn't that . . . ? That's a girl! Is that the one? Shall we take her?"

Shavros stared at the girl who was peering from behind a stack of crates. For a moment, he couldn't believe that he was looking at Countess Corloni's daughter. Then he smiled maliciously.

"That's not the same one," he muttered. "But she'll bring a high price in North Africa. And do just as well for me on the long voyage. Yes, take her aboard. Quickly! Before she flees!"

The girl had backed away from the crates as two sailors moved toward her. She turned and ran. But she stumbled and the sailors caught her and dragged her toward the ship.

Shavros, holding his arm and cursing the pain, staggered behind them, staring into the terrified eyes of Gianna Corloni as she struggled and twisted her head around.

"I'll teach that arrogant, lying countess something

about revenge," Shavros said, then shouted out the order to sail.

The twenty-piece orchestra played another waltz and the fourteen chandeliers blazed in the first pink light of dawn as the Countess Corloni swirled around and around the huge, empty drawing room.

The countess danced alone and the orchestra was frightened of the grinning woman who had been babbling to herself since she locked the doors to keep out the guests.

"Yes, Daddy," the countess crooned as she closed her eyes and enjoyed another waltz with Roger Blaine. "Yes, isn't Gianna lovely this evening and doesn't everyone here admire her and won't we all be happy together now that we're reunited? . . ."

The countess opened her eyes and danced faster, her brain scalded by grief and disbelief.

"Oh, there you are, Gianna," she said to the frightened black girl who hovered beside a table of caviar and champagne. "Come here, come and dance with Daddy . . . Come on, Gianna . . ."

Reluctantly, the girl went onto the floor and, as she had done earlier when her mistress took a whip to her, she swirled around and pretended she was dancing with a man.

"Oh, what a handsome couple," the countess whispered. "And to think I was told by that wicked servant that something had happened to you down at the docks, Gianna. Why, I'm glad I whipped that nigger senseless! Nothing could ever happen to you, Gianna darling, Gianna dearest, Gianna of my heart, my beloved Gianna, the purpose of my life, my only love, my only hope . . . The dance is finished now, Gianna, come here and let me hug you . . ."

The black girl walked slowly to the countess. The countess hugged her, then a spasm swept the countess' body. She blinked, glanced around, then shoved the girl away.

"Why, you're a nigger girl," she mumbled.

The girl's mouth flew open and she stepped backward as she stared into the countess' face: she had never seen such a hideous, wrinkled face, the eyes wide and all white, the nostrils flared, the flesh deathpale, with large red blotches.

The countess tore off her black gloves and scratched the stub of her thumb as she howled and swirled around the room . . .

Epilogue

Chessie shifted in her chair on the veranda of The Columns and savored the stirring in her stomach. Both she and Carlo hoped for a boy, and agreed that he would be named Clayton.

Knowing that she would never see her brother again was Chessie's only painful thought on this mild autumn afternoon and it was a memory that Chessie knew would slowly fade.

As the other painful memories had faded, including that of Rafaella and of the threat to the plantation. When complaints of Natchez citizens against Colonel Dirkley had reached General Grant's headquarters, Dirkley had been relieved of his command. The new chief engineer had ruled that there was no need to occupy or raze The Columns.

As for Rafaella, the loss of her daughter had so unhinged her mind that she was a threat to no one, Chessie had learned.

These were hard times . . . for Chessie and Carlo, as for the rest of the South. The Union would confiscate this year's cotton harvest. Food was scarce. Everything seemed uncertain, including the war.

But Chessie and Carlo were secure in their happiness and confident, now, that they would always live on The Columns.

They had survived too much not to appreciate what

they had—not to feel that despite the war, the occupation, and the scarcity of food, they would live to see the plantation prosper and regain its former glory—and they both knew it would be a prosperity without slaves, since Lincoln had issued a proclamation freeing the slaves at the beginning of the year.

"We'll find a way," Cellus told Chessie and Carlo that afternoon, as he poured them each a half-glass of homemade beer. "Here at The Columns, we always have . . ."

On the same evening, in New Orleans, schoolchildren hurried past the Corloni mansion, scared by odd, mournful sounds and the cloying smell of funereal lilies, afraid to see the ugly old haint who lived there and who might rush out, as their parents threatened them when they were naughty, to beat them with her hideous, deformed hand.

Behind the thick draperies, amid the smell of festering lilies and decaying food, the Countess Corloni lived. She gave no thought to the children.

As she did every evening, the countess danced in her empty ballroom, crooning to the specter of her beloved lost daughter, then finally, late at night, she took to her bed and her lover, well paid to lie between her thighs and to hear out her litany of madness . . .

ABOUT THE AUTHOR

A Mississippian by birth, GEORGE MCNEILL graduated from the University of Mississippi and worked as a journalist on various Southern newspapers. As a free-lance writer he has written magazine articles as well as a number of paperback originals (under a pseudonym). He is the author of the very successful novels *The Plantation* and *Rafaella*.

The Turbulent Saga of the Deavors Family

THE PLANTATION

The first book in the original series that traces the stormy lives of many generations of the Deavors family. Set amid the glorious and terrible days before the Civil War, *THE PLANTATION* shows the family torn by all the lustful sins and hidden guilts of a world half-white and half-black. It is the tale of brother against brother—Lavor and Athel Deavors—as they fight to control a plantation upriver from Natchez.

RAFAELLA

The world of the Deavors is dramatically changed with the arrival of Rafaella Blaine. At seventeen she was a treacherous temptress, a ripe sensual beauty who used her body to conquer and destroy men. Her main target —Lawton Deavors, son of Athel. But no man was safe from her scheming—including her own father.

THE HELLIONS

Cynthia Deavors and her twin brother become heirs to the richest plantation in the South. However she could not control her lustful brother or her own raging love that swept her into the perilous path of the one woman who haunted the family—Rafaella. Rafaella, who must pursue the brother and sister to revenge the sins of their father.

Read this series written by George McNeill. They are Bantam Books, available wherever paperbacks are sold.

THE LATEST BOOKS
IN THE BANTAM
BESTSELLING TRADITION

Bantam Book Catalog

Here's your up-to-the-minute listing of over 1,400 titles by your favorite authors.

This illustrated, large format catalog gives a description of each title. For your convenience, it is divided into categories in fiction and non-fiction—gothics, science fiction, westerns, mysteries, cookbooks, mysticism and occult, biographies, history, family living, health, psychology, art.

So don't delay—take advantage of this special opportunity to increase your reading pleasure.

Just send us your name and address and 50¢ (to help defray postage and handling costs).